FREE SOFTWARE

TONY BOVE,
CHERYL RHODES,
AND
KELLY SMITH

With Dan Dugan and Bob Wolff

FREE SOFTWARE

A Baen Book

Baen Enterprises
8-10 W. 36th Street
New York, NY 10018

First Printing, March 1985

ISBN: 0-671-55948-6

Cover art by Robert Tinney

Printed in the United States of America

Distributed by
SIMON & SCHUSTER
MASS MERCHANDISE
SALES COMPANY
1230 Avenue of the Americas
New York, NY 10020

ACKNOWLEDGEMENTS:

We gratefully acknowledge the support of Jerry Pournelle, Elizabeth Mitchell, Jim Baen, Lon Shoemaker, David Jung, Bob Scott, Joel L. Seber, Gale Rhoades, Bill Shoemaker, and the staff of *User's Guide* magazine. Dedicated to the volunteer "sysops" who make it happen.

FREE SOFTWARE

The personal computer is only the first thing you buy. You need a full pocketbook in order to start with even the general software: word processors and spreadsheet programs are $100 to $500 each; communications programs are $100 to $300; data base managers are $300 to $1000. Wouldn't it be nice if all this stuff was free?

We have gone through these libraries and found some gems as well as many turkeys. We are now using about four disk volumes worth of free software on a regular basis, which is about 2% of what is actually available. There are one-of-a-kind programs that do things no commercial program has ever done. We may be using only 2%, but our 2% would be worth thousands of dollars if you *could* buy it.

Communicating with a bulletin board is not necessary, nor is joining a user group, but either or both could be more cost-effective than sending away for disks. It helps to know what to look for. Scan the public domain digest in Appendix D before ordering disks or calling bulletin boards. Bring this book with you to a user group meeting and let someone help you.

Typesetting Conventions

We use This Typeface to show commands and expressions you type at your keyboard, and this typeface to show displayed messages.

We also use the symbol ⊃ to represent the standard Return key (CR or ENTER on some keyboards), and the caret symbol ^ to represent the Control key (CNTL, CTRL or ALT on some keyboards).

TABLE OF CONTENTS

PREFACE

You are reading this book because like everybody else you know a bargain when you see one. What could be a better bargain than something for free, without a catch? Free software is there for the asking, if you know who to ask and what to ask for. This book prepares you for your search. If you're new to this, you will want to know the following things:

What is out there?

Thousands of free programs. Unless you are a programmer, you will probably only want from 1% to 10% of what you find. To narrow your search to the programs that appeal most to you, scan the disk volumes in Appendix D.

What is a user group?

See Chapter 1, the section on user groups. For addresses of user groups, see Appendix C.

What is a bulletin board system?

Chapter 1 explains bulletin board systems.

Where do you start looking?

Chapter 1 tells you what to expect when you start looking for software. Chapter 2 explains what equipment and software you need to order and use free programs. Appendix D contains brief descriptions of each volume in the public domain.

How do you order the software on disk?

Read Chapter 1 about user groups, and Chapter 2 about disk formats and operating systems. When you're ready, use the catalog information and addresses in Appendix C.

How do you find software on a bulletin board?

Read Chapter 2 to get the right equipment for calling a bulletin board system, and Chapter 3 for the actual procedures for calling a BBS, reading and leaving messages, and downloading software. For a list of BBS phone numbers, see Appendix B.

How do you "unlock" the software you receive?

Almost all of the software in the public domain is "locked" in "library files" and compressed into a "squeezed format." Chapters 5 and 6 cover the details about squeezed files and library files.

As of this writing no other book goes into such detail in describing how to obtain and use the public domain software. It is not easy to write because the techniques change very quickly as new access software is developed. For example, six months ago you needed two separate programs to extract and un-squeeze a squeezed file in a library; now you need only one program. The instructions on how to use it have also changed as new versions appeared.

We decided to freeze the information at this time because many of the access techniques have stabilized enough for us to explain them and for you to use them. It is sometimes better to use an older version of a program that has been debugged rather than use a newer version that has only been used by a few people. We hope you find this book useful in your search for gems in the public domain.

Tony Bove & Cheryl Rhodes
Woodside, CA
December, 1984

CHAPTER 1:
WHAT IS
PUBLIC DOMAIN
SOFTWARE?

The personal computer age is upon us, and everybody now knows that the personal computer is only the first thing you buy. You can't stop after spending $500 to $2500 for your first personal computer — you have to spend at least $1000 to $5000 for the *software* you need to make it work.

You need a word processor, a spreadsheet program, a data base manager, a communications program, and *then* you need whatever application programs you wanted in the first place — the stuff that actually runs your business or profession. You may have to *develop your own* spreadsheet models for complicated financial or scientific calculations. This could take several hours or even cost thousands of dollars!

You need a full pocketbook in order to start with even the general software: word processors and spreadsheet programs are $100 to $500 each; communications programs are $100 to $300; data base managers are $300 to $1000. If you want more specific software solutions, the specialized application programs can vary from $50 to $3000 *each*, depending on the application.

Wouldn't it be nice if all this stuff was free?

You may have already heard about "free software" in *public domain libraries* — communication and word processing programs, spreadsheets, entire data base management systems, and so on. You can imagine a software "gold mine" hidden behind a smokescreen of poor documentation, the province of hobbyists and esoteric programmers, not very easy for ordinary people to get.

We have gone through these libraries and found some gems as well as many turkeys. We are now using about four disk volumes worth of public domain software on a regular basis, and another four disk volumes on an irregular basis, with our CP/M and MS-DOS personal computers. This represents about two percent of what is actually available.

There are simple word processors, but we prefer to use more sophisticated ones. There are no spreadsheet programs that compare to the ones on the commercial market; however, there are *templates* for those commercial spreadsheet programs so that you don't have to learn spreadsheet programming.

There is also a good data base manager that compares favorably against $500 packages (DIMS, described in Chapter 9). Two of the best communications programs in use on personal computers are free programs in the public domain. There are several complete accounting packages for business — BIZMASTER, BusinessMaster II, and the Osborne/McGraw-Hill Accounting Series, to name a few. But there's more.

There are programs in these libraries that are one-of-a-kind programs that do things no commercial program has ever done. Disk Utility, for example, can perform delicate "data surgery" on disks, even damaged ones (Chapter 8). There are librarian and cataloguing programs to help you keep track of your data files. There are hundreds of spreadsheet templates and thousands of programs for every conceivable application.

We may be using only two percent, but our two percent would be worth thousands of dollars if you *could* buy it.

Where did it come from?

In the spirit of cooperation that was the hallmark of the early personal computer industry, hobbyists and professional programmers wrote the programs for their friends and for anyone who showed up at the early user group meetings. That feeling of community spirit inspired many more to enhance these programs and make new ones for the general public. Everyone shared in the effort and in the rewards of recognition and self-motivation.

Most of the software donated today is written by programmers and hobbyists who use the network of electronic bulletin board systems to freely exchange information and programming techniques. They are motivated to write programs to solve their problems, and they are generous enough to give their solutions to the general public.

The majority of the software is for professional and amateur programmers — languages, utilities and programming aids. There is also a fair amount of general-purpose software, spreadsheets for popular spreadsheet programs, mini-programs for dBASE II® and WordStar®/MailMerge® users, communications programs, educational software and games.

Did we say games? How about Monstrous Startrek? Othello, Chess, Dungeon, Castle, Hobbit, Lander, Rubic, Biorythm, or the Original Adventure? Playing a game is a good way to reduce fear and anxiety about using a computer for the first time. Some of these games will have you up all night typing mysterious magic words and searching for keys in the Hall of the Mountain King.

On the educational side, you can learn about macro-economics using a program called The FED®, an Econometric Model by Decision Sciences and Software, Irvine, CA, used by the St. Louis Federal Reserve District to test alternate money supply policies. And the Yale Catalog of Bright Stars, compiled by the National Space Science Data Center, contains information about every star in the sky.

What's the catch?

None. For material in the public domain, there are usually no legal restrictions to using it.

In legal terms, *public domain* refers to materials that all members of the public can freely copy, distribute, or otherwise use without a restriction. Under this definition, anyone can copy and use public domain software. A legal question arises when someone sells the software for commercial gain.

This question has come up and was unofficially resolved between the two parties. A software publisher was selling a disk with "some of the best programs" of the public domain, but one program's author balked at the disk's high price. His program was removed from this disk.

Rumors circulated in the network of public domain contributors that a version of the free Modem7 program, a very useful communications program, had been copied and sold under another name with a $395 price tag. Another rumor was that the US Postal Service had bought hundreds of copies of a $200 program that was "pirated" from the public domain.

Whether these stories are true or not, they made everyone aware of how easy it was to exploit the contributors. As a result, a new definition of "public domain software" has emerged: software is free for non-commercial use only. Today there are several software publishers who provide disks of public domain software for a nominal fee covering expenses (listed in Appendix C). These companies consider their public domain activities to be for the public good and not for profit.

Some public domain enthusiasts saw the libraries as a new distribution medium for *commercial* software they called "user-supported" software. The distribution method was unique: no copyright restrictions, and placement in the public domain libraries with a request for a $35 donation to the author "if you found the program useful." Users who donate the $35 would get additional helpful information and even extended documentation.

User-supported software is mixed freely with public domain software, but there is copyright ownership involved — user-supported software is not legally public domain. You can't "borrow" from it to make commercial products, nor can you sell the program to anyone; it must be copied freely, and contributions are encouraged.

Something for everybody

Our first experience with the public domain came when we first bought a modem to go with our personal computer. As we describe in Chapter 2, you can equip your computer to communicate over telephone lines with a modem and with communications software. We used a Hayes Smartmodem and a program called Modem7, running on a computer with the CP/M operating system.

At roughly 30 characters per second (300 baud), it took about 45 minutes to receive an "electronic catalog" of free software in our computer (through a telephone-modem hookup). At that time the catalog listed "disk volumes" 1 through 60. Today that same catalog lists over 250 volumes of software for CP/M computers. There are also 200 volumes of software for IBM PC and PC-compatible computers.

In terms of number of programs, there are more free programs available for CP/M computers than for IBM PCs as of this writing. The PC disk volumes hold roughly 180,000 characters each, whereas the CP/M disk volumes hold 250,000 characters each. There are also volumes for specific CP/M computers maintained by the local user groups and FOG (First Osborne Group) Affiliates.

We showed our first catalog of 60 volumes to a computer hobbyist, a computer service technician, and a business computer user, to see their reactions and determine whether this software could be useful.

When we dumped a list of thousands of miscellaneous programs into the business person's lap, it was nearly enough to scare her away from personal computing. However, she eventually crossed an invisible threshold that every personal computer user must cross, and became more interested in productivity. She wanted easy-to-use copying utilities, a program to recover data from a bad disk, and a program to make her office computer act as "home base" while she used a portable computer "on the road." She found public domain programs to do all these things.

The computer service technician scanned the list and found programs that he found useful in testing computer components and disks, including Disk Utility (Chapter 8). He also found programs that would be useful to his customers — such as utilities for managing disk space, recovering data files from damaged disks, and preparing archival copies of disks.

For the computer hobbyist, the public domain library was a dream come true, and he is now an avid collector of the latest programs and program revisions and a true bulletin board system (BBS) addict.

The bulk of the software donated to the public domain is for computers that run the CP/M operating system. There is also a large amount of software for IBM PC and PC-compatible computers.

The software described in this book runs on nearly every CP/M system. The PC software runs on the IBM PC and on most PC-compatible computers. We can't be certain that the software will run in your system, because there could be differences (such as terminal display characteristics, or internal memory requirements) that could require modifications to the software.

Some of the CP/M public domain software has been modified to run on the IBM PC under the PC-DOS and MS-DOS operating systems. PC-DOS is supplied with the IBM PC; MS-DOS (Microsoft, Inc.) is supplied with PC-lookalike computers.

Most of the programs catalogued for CP/M computers and PCs work and are somewhat documented. There is no guarantee, and programs frequently have "bugs" (flaws that hamper performance or make certain functions unusable), but you can usually work around them. Programs that find there way into customized disks or bulletin boards may not be the catalogued versions, and may not work properly and may not be adequately documented.

Descriptions of catalogued programs fill up several catalogs, and new public domain software accumulates faster than anyone can measure. For IBM PCs there is one catalog, but if you are a CP/M computer user, you have more choices, depending on the type of computer you have (complete catalog access information appears in Appendix C).

Scanning the catalogs you will find useful programs for specific applications, and general purpose programs that are useful in any system, especially system utilities for managing disk space, recovering data files from damaged disks, preparing backup copies of disks, and such operations.

It is the nature of public domain software to have *new versions* of programs appear several months later. Brand new programs tend to have more bugs than new versions of older programs, because the author had a chance to fix them. However, the reverse is sometimes true: old programs are revised to have new features, which introduce new bugs. Sometimes the only reliable version is the one everybody is still using.

You may not be able to find enough information to tell if a program is useful or not. You can spend a lot of time and money ordering "free" software that may be of little value because you didn't know what you were getting, or you didn't get the right version. The best way to know is to read descriptions of the most useful programs (you'll find them in this book), and to ask around at user group meetings.

How to get free software

It used to be that free software was available only to members of user groups or clubs. These groups have grown very large, and many are expanding their distribution efforts to non-members.

The two methods of exchanging free software are by disk and by computer-to-computer connection, usually over telephone lines. Libraries of public domain programs are organized for both types of exchange.

Although public domain software was first exchanged on eight-inch floppy disks in a standard format for CP/M systems, today there is no one disk standard (although the $5^1/4$" disk for the IBM PC is becoming the most widely used disk format for other computers).

A *disk format* is a recording technique used by the disk controller electronics to put information on a disk. The disk controller is actually "controlled" by software that in most cases is proprietary to the computer manufacturer; hence, all computers tend to use different proprietary formats.

However, software distribution was hampered by so many proprietary formats, and computer and software manufacturers introduced programs that let your computer imitate another's format. For example, you can get MediaMaster for an Osborne computer that will read Kaypro, Morrow and even IBM PC disks.

IBM PC users have no trouble getting disks from the public domain libraries, and neither do users of CP/M computers employing the Osborne, Kaypro, Morrow, TeleVideo or Sanyo disk formats, or the eight-inch CP/M standard disk format.

Of course, Apple, Radio Shack and Commodore computer users have no trouble getting free software from *their* user groups.

If you have some other computer that is not one of the above, nor IBM PC-compatible, nor Apple- or Commodore- or Radio Shack-compatible, nor running CP/M with eight-inch disk drives, you have very limited choices of mail-order public domain libraries.

Whether or not you have one of the popular disk formats, you will find that "free" software volumes are usually at least $5 to $10 per disk and sometimes more. You may want to try getting it by calling a bulletin board system, which may cost less if you want many programs, especially if the phone call is a local one, because you can get more programs at once with one call.

Bulletin board systems

The multiple disk format problem motivated hobbyists to develop other ways to transfer programs and data to each other. The most successful method was established using the fastest, most widely used communications network: the phone network operated by AT&T. Personal computers equipped with devices called *modems* could use the telephone line to transfer programs and data.

The *electronic bulletin board systems* were formed, at first, to make it easy for hobbyists to exchange programs and information. Now there are BBSs, RBBSs (remote bulletin board systems), RCP/M (remote CP/M) systems, and software exchanges throughout the world. There are several directories of known BBSs in the world. Appendix B is a list of well-known RCP/M BBSs that have complete public domain libraries available to general callers.

The network of bulletin board systems allow callers to download public domain software stored on the bulletin board systems' disks. We describe what equipment you need to call a BBS in Chapter 2, and how to call one in Chapter 3.

The drawback of receiving software over your phone line is that it ties up your phone for a while, and you may run up long distance charges for the phone call. If you don't already know what you want, you will have to search large catalogs for the names of the programs.

It takes a long time to browse electronically through any of the catalogs. Refer to our digest of public domain volumes in Appendix D, so that you know what to look for. You can download a summary catalog over the phone, directly from the BBS. Other alternatives are to send away for catalogs in the mail, or join a local user group.

User groups

If you're lucky to have one nearby, your local user group is the best place to look for copies of public domain software volumes. Other users of the same computer are your best sources of information.

Personal computer enthusiasts usually congregate in computer clubs and user groups, where meetings are held once a month, much public domain software is copied, and new members get acquainted. The atmosphere of free exchange of public domain software, application tips, methods and guidance helps sustain the enthusiasm for beginners.

User group members usually provide the best information about public domain software, such as whether a particular program is useful in a particular computer configuration (configuration details are the hardest details to get). Some user groups can point you to excellent consultants for setting up complex operations, or to professional programmers who can be contracted to solve problems.

You can also get public domain programs through these user

group associated distribution routes:

- Direct from a large group called SIG/M (described below, addresses in Appendix C) for $6 per eight-inch single-sided disk, or direct from another group called CP/MUG for $13 per eight-inch disk, and $18 for Apple or Kaypro disks. You do not have to join the groups to purchase disks.

- Volunteer non-profit organizations such as local area computer clubs, national computer societies (such as FOG, described below) and mail-order distribution points (associated with SIG/M or FOG) that usually have a complete set of public domain disk volumes available for a nominal charge per disk. After joining a club or group (and paying a membership fee), copies of volumes are often free if you bring your own disks.

- Commercial software publishers that are associated with user groups and provide public domain software on various disk formats, usually for a charge that is more than that charged by non-profit organizations.

The best way for you depends on where you live, and how much time you want to spend browsing through catalogs or directories on the bulletin board systems, or waiting for such catalogs in the mail.

There are thousands of user groups worldwide. Some are more organized than others and specialize in specific computers, and others are general computer clubs. Most provide public domain software in some form, and the largest provide complete libraries of public domain software.

One of the largest groups offering CP/M public domain software is SIG/M (Special Interest Group/Microcomputers), part of the Amateur Computer Group of New Jersey (ACGNJ, a non-profit organization). SIG/M tests public domain programs and organizes them into disk volumes. The New York Amateur Computer Club prints catalogs of these volumes, and sells the catalogs for $10 each volume ($15 overseas), to fund their user group activities.

Volunteers send copies of disk volumes to various distribution points (designated bulletin board systems and user groups). SIG/M offers one disk format — the eight-inch CP/M standard single-density format — to the distributors for $6 per disk. Distributors offer a variety of disk formats, adding membership fees or overhead to the price per disk.

In many cases the distributors operate bulletin board systems from which the software can be copied for free (although you may have to "join a club" by paying a BBS membership fee). Some bulletin board systems are operated by user groups who favor particular disk formats. Such user groups often have a computer and the library of software available to members to copy during group meetings.

CP/MUG (CP/M User's Group) is supported by Lifeboat Associates in New York (a commercial software publisher). CP/MUG provides several disk formats for a higher price — $13 per eight-inch single-density disk, and up to $18 for Apple and Kaypro formats. CP/MUG feels justified in charging a higher price because the organization promotes the public domain library world-wide, maintains libraries in several disk formats, and provides steady distribution using paid staff.

With two main distribution points across the Hudson River from each other, bulletin board systems on the West Coast accumulated software from both places. Some of the bulletin board systems on the West Coast have the largest public domain software libraries, and most are connected with local user groups.

The largest organized user group distributing free software (over 15,000 members worldwide) is the West Coast FOG (First Osborne Group), which supports many CP/M computers as well as the Osborne 1 (a CP/M computer). This group is the umbrella organization for over 300 affiliate FOGs across the country.

FOG assembles and tests thousands of public domain programs and offers versions for a variety of CP/M systems including the Osborne, Kaypro, Morrow, CompuPro, PMC Micromate and Zorba computers. FOG ships 2000-4000 disks a month to FOG affiliate chapters requesting public domain software.

Sending away for volumes of disks can be time-consuming and a waste of money if you don't already know what's in those volumes. One way to find out what the volumes contain is to send a self-addressed stamped envelope to SIG/M for the list of available catalogs. You can then order the catalogs you want ($10 each) from the New York Amateur Computer Club.

Another way is to join FOG ($24/year), receive the FOG newsletter (which provides access information for public domain software, reviews of programs and helpful hints for Osborne computer owners), and use your telephone to dial into the FOG BBS. FOG disks and a $5 catalog are available by mail to members, or free if you send an article to the FOG monthly publication *FOGHORN*. FOG is also listed in Appendix C.

These may not be the least expensive ways, but they are the easiest for beginners. This book shows you how to do all of these things and more.

What can you expect to find?

The public domain libraries are brimming with tools for programmers and users. If you're interested in programming, you will undoubtedly find useful things.

If you're not interested in programming, you may want to skip programming tools and focus on *utility programs* (also called *system utilities*). Hiding among the programming goodies are excellent utility programs that perform routine or general functions that everyone can relate to — functions like recovering data from damaged disks, or copying multiple files to another disk.

It makes sense that utilities are the most popular programs in the public domain because utility programs perform file and disk "housekeeping" chores which are common to nearly every computer application.

The most common system utility programs are ones that make it easier to manage files, fix disk problems, and set up automatic application disks. If you're using floppy disks for all your operations, these utilities are good "housekeeping" tools.

For example, if you're using limited-capacity floppy disks, you need to pay attention to disk space when running application programs. Some application programs will stop abruptly ("crash") and cause errors if you run out of disk space while running them. On the other hand, if you're using a hard disk, you may need a "backup" utility to make multiple copies of files (called "backups"). You may also need a library utility to store common files under one library name.

Some manufacturers and computer dealers provide an enhanced DIR (directory display) utility with the operating system software, which displays the names of files *and* their sizes. In most cases the utility supplied came from the public domain — many are derivatives of the original SD (Sorted Directory) utility written by Ward Christensen. This utility displays filenames in alphabetical order with file sizes, the total amount of disk space used, and the amount still available for file expansion or new files.

If a program does crash and cause important data to disappear from your disk, you may need one of the disk fixup utilities. We present the grandfather of disk utilities in Chapter 8: Disk Utility (DU), also written by Ward Christensen. This program lets you change the information on your disk. Using it you may be able to recover a file you accidentally erased, or recover data from a disk with bad sectors.

Nearly every computer user can make use of disk fixup and disk management utilities, so it is not surprising to find that they are at the top of the list. However, the majority of the free programs are games that run under MBASIC or IBM PC BASIC, and tools to enhance programming. There are entire languages available in the public domain — RATFOR, XLISP, Pascal, C and Forth to name a few. Only in the public domain will you find languages not in common use, or languages that are very appealing to a specialized group of professional programmers.

Somewhere between the most common utilities and the ones that are extremely specific are ones that enhance your ability to manage your system. Examples are programs that convert data to other file formats, and the famous "squeezer" utilities that lets you "squeeze" files to make them smaller and "unsqueeze" them to use the data. Still others control data transfer from your computer to the world and back again.

The most popular programs

The most popular software in the CP/M public domain is a telecommunications program called Modem7 (described in detail in Chapter 4). After Modem7, the most popular CP/M system utilities (according to an unofficial survey) are:

SD (Sorted Directory)
> This program displays an alphabetically-sorted list of files on your disk, with the size of each file and the space still available on disk. (Original author is Ward Christensen; this program has been extensively revised by others). Described in Chapter 7.

SQ, USQ, and TYPESQ (The Squeezer Utilities)
> This set of programs let you "squeeze" files to make them smaller, and "unsqueeze" them to bring them back to normal. Squeezed text files are considerably smaller and take up less disk space and transmission time, thereby saving you money when you are transmitting. (Author is Dick Greenlaw). Described in Chapter 5. Other programs (notably NSWP, below) perform squeezing and unsqueezing as well as other operations.

DU (Disk Utility)
> This utility lets you perform "electronic surgery" on a disk to recover erased files, isolate bad sectors from use, and make data transplants. (Author is Ward Christensen). Described in chapter 8.

ZCPR2 (Z-80 Command Processor Replacement)
> As an experienced CP/M user, you may want more flexible commands than CP/M provides. ZCPR2 replaces the CP/M "butler" (known as the CCP module of CP/M, the part that waits for your command) and adds new

commands and functions to the familiar CP/M commands. It also performs them with rare gusto for a typical CP/M system. (Author is Rick Conn). Extensive documentation is available with the ZCPR2 volumes. Unless you are skilled in assembly language programming, you should look for a version of ZCPR2 that is already installed for your computer.

FindBad and UNERA+ (disk utilities)

FindBad finds bad sectors on your disk (ones not currently used by other files) and isolates them from future use. This lets you use disks that you would otherwise have to discard. FindBad is described in Chapter 7. UNERA helps you recover erased files from a disk (described in Chapter 7), and UNERA+ is a new menu-style version of UNERA. DU also performs these operations, but FindBad and UNERA are easy for beginners to use.

LU and NULU (library utilities)

LU lets you organize many similar files into one library file, and is very useful for managing archives and hard disks. LU is described in Chapter 6. NULU is a new program that extracts files from libraries quickly and easily.

NSWP, WASH

NSWP, WASH and other file copying/renaming/deleting utilities are usually much easier to use than the CP/M commands for these operations. These are described in Chapter 7.

The most popular programs in the public domain libraries for the IBM PC are not actually public domain. They are called "user-supported" programs, and one is trademarked as Freeware® (Headlands Press). The programs can be copied freely as public domain programs, but the authors ask for a donation from the user ranging from $10 to $35. Typically they expect a donation "only if you find the program useful."

They are:

- PC-Talk III, a communication program for the IBM PC that incorporates the Modem7 protocol (Freeware, published by Headlands Press; author is Andy Fluegelman).

- PC-File, a complete data base management system for the IBM PC (author is Jim Button).

- GUMUPs, or Garber's Unsupported Moderately Useful Programs, are system utilities for checking the status of devices (SYSTAT), logging in disks (CD), handling function keys (FK) and other system operations (author is Jeff Garber).

User-supported software (Freeware)

While searching for public domain software on The Source and CompuServe, we came upon this announcement of the availability of PC-Talk, a communications program for the IBM PC, free to anyone who could send a disk to the address. Recipients were asked to make a *voluntary contribution* if they used the program and liked it. This was the message which also accompanied copies of the program:

"If you have used this program and found it of value your contribution ($25 suggested) will be appreciated. Regardless of whether you make a contribution, you are encouraged to copy and share this program."

The result of this simple experiment was the founding of a new type of software distribution originally called Freeware (which is now a trademark of Headlands Press), but is now referred to as *User-Supported Software*.

This is not public domain software. The experiment is to distribute *commercial* software for a profit. So far the experiment has been a success, with contributions pouring in, and the program is widely used on IBM Personal Computers.

Andrew Fluegelman, the publisher of Headlands Press, wrote PC-Talk (and the enhanced PC-Talk III) in an effort to make his

into the *serial port* of the other computer over a cable. A serial port is a physical connection point on your computer where you can attach a cable. Data can usually flow either way through this cable.

The problem with transferring programs using this method was that errors could occur in the transmission. An error in a text file was no big deal — perhaps a character in a word is missing or wrong, or at most an entire paragraph is missing or garbled. However, if one character of a program instruction is wrong, the entire program could be useless.

Kelly Smith made it easy for us to get a copy of the Modem7 program, which let you transfer programs *without errors* from one computer to another using the serial ports (with or without modems). Kelly showed us how to modify the program to work with our computer, and we were able to start receiving public domain programs from his bulletin board RCP/M system.

As early as 1980, Kelly and friends in the Valley Computer Club in southern California established one of the first public RCP/M systems. Kelly was comparing methods of sending and receiving data using communications programs available at that time, and stumbled upon an early volume of public domain software from CP/MUG that included Ward Christensen's MODEM.ASM program, a forerunner to Modem7 and the first implementation of the "Xmodem/Modem7 protocol" as we know it today.

Kelly and Mike Karas (president of the Valley Computer Club) used MODEM.ASM to transfer CP/M programs to and from their computers. Ron Lisberg (also of the Valley Computer Club) was maintaining the VCC Computer Bulletin Board System, which could be used for messages but not for software downloading. In January of 1980, Kelly and friends started giving real consideration to a VCC "file exchange system" that would allow the club members to call and use an unattended CP/M system.

In a flash of hacker's insight at 3 a.m. one morning, Kelly decided to write modem input/output routines within the CP/M module called the BIOS which handled console input/output among other things. The design would allow a caller to activate the keyboard of Kelly's system at the same time Kelly typed on the keyboard. A quick test proved that the design worked.

Within a few weeks the Valley Computer Club had set up a password-controlled bulletin board system with file send/receive capability. They called it an RCP/M (remote CP/M) system. The passwords were necessary to keep non-members and pranksters out of the system, because anyone could theoretically call the system and use destructive CP/M commands like ERA or REN, or send to the system destructive programs.

Kelly soon improved the system so that passwords were no longer needed. Kelly took out the CP/M commands ERA, REN and SAVE (so that no one could erase files, rename files or save destructive memory images), and modified the action caused by typing Control-C, so that the RCP/M system would be almost prankster-proof.

Eventually a second system was set up in the San Fernando Valley, and Kelly heard from Eddie Curry of Lifeboat Associates (a software distributor in New York that sponsors CP/MUG) that *another* RCP/M system had been set up in Milwaukee — the Calamity Cliffs Computer Center. After calling that system, Kelly found two more RCP/Ms operating on the East coast (Keith Petersen and Bruce Ratoff of SIG/M).

These first "sysops" (system operators) collaborated on RCP/M design and implementation techniques, and within a few months several programs were designed for running bulletin board RCP/M systems: Ward Christensen introduced the original $50 CBBS program for messages; Keith Petersen wrote MINICBBS and Bruce Ratoff wrote RBBS and put them in the public domain.

As these programs developed, more RCP/M systems came on line during 1980, including the Technical CBBS (Dave Hardy), the Pasadena CBBS (Dick Mead) and many others. The RCP/M systems became collection points for new public domain CP/M software and information, and more people learned about programming for CP/M computers by accessing these RCP/Ms than from any other source of information.

We learned a lot about general CP/M software by calling these systems and reading the bulletin board messages. We are not assembly language programmers, yet we learned a great deal about running system software and utility programs, about recovering data from bad disks and program crashes, and about care and maintenance of computers and floppy disk drives. The bulletin boards were entertaining as well, and an excellent source of conventional computer wisdom.

To many users, the RCP/M network was like having a large group of problem solvers and CP/M experts visit your home with the answers to all your computer questions. They would come on any night you chose, bearing software gifts from the public domain libraries, and not wanting anything in return.

Jumping off point

Historically, what is known as "the public domain" is the repository of the best of human endeavors — the literature classics, old songs, old plays, treatises on philosophy, holy texts of alchemy, experimental data.

The classics, old songs and plays are readily accessible, but to use the rest of the public domain knowledge, one must be skilled in the specific science or aware of the art form.

Not true with public domain software. Software requires nothing more than a minimal investment in computer hardware, and anyone can use the free programs. Anyone can become aware of this new art form and find ways to derive use and benefit from it.

What you have to know to use public domain software is the same knowledge you need to use sophisticated commercial programs. You must know how to use your operating system. We recommend that you first get used to using your computer for word processing and other general applications. Communicating with a bulletin board is not necessary, nor is joining a user group, but either or both could be more cost-effective than sending away for multiple disk volumes.

It helps to know what to look for. Scan the public domain digest in Appendix D before ordering volumes or calling bulletin boards. Bring this book with you to a user group meeting and let someone help you.

CHAPTER 2:
WHAT YOU NEED
TO START

You need a personal or small business computer to take advantage of public domain software.

If the computer you choose is an Apple, Atari, or Commodore, you need either a CP/M or an MS-DOS add-on module for that computer, in order to run either CP/M or MS-DOS, and thereby run the free software described in this book.

If the computer is a DEC Rainbow, a Zenith Z100, a Seequa Chameleon, or any other computer that is supplied with both an eight-bit CP/M and sixteen-bit MS-DOS processor, you can run nearly all of the software presented here, because these computers can run *both* CP/M and MS-DOS.

Other computers can have a processor added to them to run CP/M or MS-DOS. You would do this to make the computer more flexible and enable it to run more software. For example, you can add something to an IBM PC to make it able to run eight-bit CP/M: the Baby Blue Z80 board from Microlog (Microlog Inc., 222 Route 59, Suffern, NY 10901), or the Z80 software emulator from Lifeboat (Lifeboat Associates, 1651 Third Ave., New York, NY 10128). The IBM PC would then be able to run CP/M software as well as MS-DOS. Some add-on boards are available for PC-compatible computers like the Corona PC and the Compaq which enable them to run CP/M.

Another way to make an IBM PC or PC-compatible able to run CP/M software is to get the Concurrent-DOS operating system from Digital Research, Inc. (P.O. Box 579, Pacific Grove, CA 93950). This system enables a PC or PC-compatible to run both MS-DOS and CP/M software *at the same time*.

On the other hand, if you own a Kaypro or Osborne computer

(which runs CP/M), you may want to add the CO-POWER-88 co-processor board (SWP Microcomputer Products, 2500 E. Randol Mill Rd. #125, Arlington TX 76011). This board makes a CP/M computer able to run sixteen-bit MS-DOS software. This board is also available for the Osborne Executive and other CP/M computers.

If you want to communicate with bulletin board systems and with other computers, you need a device called a *modem* (which is usually supplied with a cable connecting the modem to the computer), a telephone line jack and cord to connect it to the modem, and a working telephone line. We used the Hayes Smartmodem 1200, which works with almost any computer. More modems are described in this chapter.

In addition, you need a *communications program* (also called a "modem program") to set up communication. This is essential because the computer and its operating software cannot perform some of the necessary functions you need to communicate with a bulletin board system.

If your computer is one that runs CP/M-80, we recommend you find a version of the public domain Modem7 program for your computer and modem; if you can't find one, we recommend in this chapter several commercial programs that should be available for your computer and modem.

If you have an IBM PC or PC-compatible computer running MS-DOS, we recommend PC-Talk III (a $35 donation requested but not required) as one of the best communications programs; we also describe others in this chapter.

Operating Systems

As with commercial programs, public domain programs cannot run on your computer unless an operating system is running also. Generally speaking, all programs run *under* the *operating system* that is installed for your computer. For the software described in this book, there are two major "families" of operating systems: CP/M (Digital Research, Inc.) and MS-DOS (Microsoft, Inc.).

The CP/M family started first and is the most firmly established, with more public domain programs available for it than any other system. The original CP/M (also known as CP/M-80 version 2.2) is the "flagship" of the many different eight-bit computers that have been in use since 1976. Most were designed around the Intel 8080, Intel 8085 or Zilog Z80 processors. CP/M Plus is an enhanced version of CP/M-80 (version 3.1) that can run most of the software written for version 2.2, but not all. That leaves version 2.2 the "most vanilla version" of CP/M and the most widely used version.

CP/M-86 resembles CP/M version 2.2 in many ways, but is not as widely used. It is designed for sixteen-bit systems (such as the IBM PC) that use the Intel 8086 and 8088 processors. Software written to run with CP/M-80 (such as the public domain software described in this book) will not run with CP/M-86 without modification.

As of this writing, Digital Research produced a new operating system that combines CP/M-86, CP/M version 2.2 and MS-DOS into one system called Concurrent DOS. This system lets you run MS-DOS, CP/M or CP/M-86 programs at the same time. It is available for the IBM PC and some PC-compatible computers.

MS-DOS is the "flagship" of the IBM PC-compatible computers. PC-DOS (IBM DOS), supplied with the IBM PC, is a customized version of MS-DOS. However, some programs available for the IBM PC will not work with some PC-compatible computers. One major reason is because MS-DOS does not have all the IBM-specific features of PC-DOS.

Why is this so? PC-DOS was created to take advantage of IBM hardware, and some programs drive this hardware by using the IBM-supplied software coded in a special memory chip called the BIOS ROM (Basic Input Output System in Read-Only Memory). This ROM software is copyrighted by IBM and is not available to the other manufacturers; therefore, programs written to take advantage of the IBM BIOS ROM may not run properly in another computer.

Of course some manufacturers found a way to emulate the BIOS ROM without infringing on IBM's copyright. This is the reason why some manufacturers claim 99% compatibility with the IBM PC. If you have a "99%-compatible computer" you might be able to run all of the software designed for the IBM PC.

Another reason for incompatibilities in the MS-DOS world is that newer versions of MS-DOS and PC-DOS are not completely compatible with previous versions. Some programs developed to run with MS-DOS version 1.1 (PC-DOS version 1.1) may not work with MS-DOS 2.0 (PC-DOS 2.0) or newer versions. The problems can be solved in most cases by editing the programs. This is easy to do if the programs are written in BASIC, or, if written in another language, "source code" for the program is provided.

It certainly doesn't hurt to keep older versions of MS-DOS or PC-DOS on your shelf, to be used if needed to run some of the older programs. With CP/M systems you might want to keep version 2.2 available if you run CP/M Plus; however, different versions of CP/M, if greater than version 2.0, are more compatible than different versions of MS-DOS.

In order to know what public domain software you can use, you must start with the operating system available for your computer. You can run only the software that runs under your operating system. If you have a computer that can run more than one operating system, then you have the flexibility to use much more free software than if you have only one operating system.

For that reason we suggest that if you're considering free software as a major reason for getting a computer, we recommend you look at the computers that can run *both* CP/M version 2.2 *and* MS-DOS. An IBM PC or PC-compatible computer can run both software if it is properly equipped with Concurrent DOS or with the Baby Blue board from Microlog or the software emulator from Lifeboat. Other computers that run both systems are the DEC Rainbow, the Zenith Z-100, the Seequa Chameleon. Kaypro, Osborne and some other CP/M computers can be modified to run both systems by adding the CO-POWER-88 board.

If you already have (or want to buy) an Apple II or IIe, we recommend any of one of the following CP/M add-on boards: the SoftCard II/IIe from Microsoft (Microsoft Corp, 10700

Northrup Way, P.O. Box C-97200, Bellevue, WA 98004), the z-Card II or CP/M Card from ALS (Advanced Logic Systems, 1195 Arques Ave., Sunnyvale, CA 94086), the Appli-Card from MicroPro (MicroPro International, 33 San Pablo Ave., San Rafael, CA 94903), or the Z80 Plus card from Applied Engineering (P.O. Box 47031, Dallas, TX 75247). To run MS-DOS on your Apple II or IIe, get the add-on disk drive from Rana Systems called the Rana 8086/2 (Rana Systems, 21300 Superior St., Chatsworth, CA 91311).

If you want the best of the CP/M world (without MS-DOS), we recommend CompuPro (any model), Kaypro (II, IV or 10), Morrow (MD-2 or MD-11), Osborne (1, Executive or Vixen), Epson, Ampro, PMC MicroMate, Lobo MAX-80, or any "S-100 type" CP/M computer. There is more public domain software for CP/M (especially S-100 type) computers than for any other computers.

If you want the best of the MS-DOS world (without CP/M), there is an obvious choice: the IBM PC. All other computers in this category are measured by the degree of compatibility with the IBM PC (Columbia, Compaq, Corona, Eagle, Zenith and many others).

There are many other factors to consider before buying a computer. If you choose solely on the basis of public domain software, you may miss out on a lot of excellent commercial software. Decide by choosing the software you need, then find the right computer to run this software.

Catalogs For Finding Software

To do business with mail order software distributors or user groups, be prepared to spend eight to twelve dollars per disk volume. Catalogs of the disk libraries range from $4.95 to $24.95 (see Appendix C for a list of catalogs).

Disks are expensive, but so are phone calls unless you are making a local call. There are bulletin board systems in almost every major city (see list in Appendix B). You may be able to make a local call to a free bulletin board system and browse through an electronic catalog without spending any money. Or you might have pay for a long-distance call and also for membership in a fee-only bulletin board, but the combined cost might still be less than it costs to obtain several disks of software.

You have to use a catalog to find what you want. We present a brief summary of disk volumes in Appendix D, but the list increases daily. The most up-to-date catalogs are ones on electronic bulletin board systems and available from user groups. The New York Amateur Computer Group publishes eight catalogs of public domain software descriptions and documentation. The catalogs are $10 each (see Appendix C).

Disk Formats

When you order disks from user groups, you must be sure to order the correct disk *size* and *format*. As of this writing, your computer must use one of the following disk sizes to be able to obtain disk volumes by mail:

8"   Eight-inch disks are formatted to be in the single-density standard format, known as the IBM 3270 format, or in a variety of non-standard double-density formats.

$5^1/4$" There are a variety of formats for five-and-a-quarter inch disks, including the IBM PC and DEC Rainbow formats in the sixteen-bit world, and Kaypro, Osborne, Morrow and Radio Shack formats in the eight-bit world.

There are currently no groups providing public domain software on $3^1/2$" or other size disks.

SIG/M in New Jersey provides eight-inch disks by mail order for $8 a disk. SIG/M also exports its library to clubs and groups that serve as distribution points (listed in Appendix C). The distribution points carry a variety of sizes and formats depending on the specific interest of each club or group. SIG/M also has a bulletin board system that distributes software to other bulletin board systems.

Nearly all clubs and groups have membership fees. Some bulletin board systems are free, others are free for messages but not for software exchanging (such as the FOG BBS, where the $24/year membership fee is not required for bulletin board messages, but is required for accessing the public domain libraries). Other bulletin boards require fees before logging on. Prices vary from one group to the next.

If you have to pay a membership fee, you should first check to make sure that your local FOG affiliate or similar local group has software for your computer and on your disk format. Most user groups are well organized, but some are not.

Like FOG, PicoNet is another well-organized group sponsoring a bulletin board with free messaging. You must join the group to gain access to its public domain libraries. The PicoNet group is for technically-oriented hobbyists and programmers.

CP/MUG (CP/M User's Group) in New York offers other $5^1/4$" disk formats (the $5^1/4$" disks are higher in price than 8" disks, and they sometimes carry less programs on them.) However, CP/MUG requires no membership fee — it is mostly a clearinghouse for public domain software, not an active user group that meets every month.

Other software publishers have "best of public domain" disks, some with added documentation, for prices ranging from $8 to $35 each disk.

The best value for the dollar is membership in a local user group. You get all the benefits of joining a user group — free advice, unrestricted copying (bring your own disks and the software is completely free), and a helpful newsletter (such as FOG's *FOGHORN*, an outstanding source of tips and techniques on using your computer and summaries of public domain volumes).

All of these organizations are listed in Appendix C. If you're going to get all your free software from a user group that supplies disks, you don't need a modem or any special equipment. You are then limited to the software you can find on your disk format. This is no problem for IBM PC, Osborne, Kaypro, and other popular systems for which disks are available from user groups, nor is it a problem if you have a program like MediaMaster or Uniform for your computer (they let you read and write disks in other formats).

Modems

We just said you don't need a modem if you get your software on disk; however, a personal computer without a modem is like an office without a telephone. You can get a lot of work done (which is fine for many applications), but you may be missing out on a lot of information, free software, and the convenience of electronic mail.

To communicate by computer with another computer over a telephone line (this is basically what you're doing when you call a bulletin board system), you must have a modem connected to each computer. There are basically two kinds of modems:

- *Direct-connect* modems (a board within your computer, or an external unit) connect directly to phone lines without the use of a telephone.

- *Acoustic couplers* (an external unit, or built-in as on the Actrix computer) connect through the telephone handsets. These can be used with pay telephones or lines that do not have modular phone jacks.

Modems are connected to your computer through the *serial data port* (usually an "RS232" connector) on the back of your computer. Most if not *all* personal and small business computers have an RS232 connector or something similar, for plugging in a modem.

The newest personal computers have "standard" connectors, but you can never be too sure that the modem will work. The best approach is to first have it demonstrated in a computer store that a particular modem and cable will work with your brand of computer. Then go ahead and buy the modem and cable from the store, with the knowledge that if you get it home and it doesn't work, the store personnel will help. This is one area where mail order isn't always the best buy — you may get stuck with a cable that doesn't work with your computer.

Don't be shy about asking whether or not a cable will work with your system. Some of the best minds in personal computing have trouble with RS232 connectors. Steve Ciarcia of *BYTE* once confessed to having spent two hours trying to get an RS232 connection to work.

The rule to follow when buying a modem and cable is to see a demonstration of the modem and cable working with your brand of computer, then buy the equipment.

The most popular modem is the Hayes Smartmodem 1200, a direct-connect modem which retails for $699 and is available at most computer stores. This modem operates at both 300 baud and 1200 baud. *Baud* refers to the speed of data flow: 300 baud is roughly 30 characters per second, which is slow enough to read (sometime too slow); 1200 baud is four times faster (120 characters per second), which may be too fast to read, but is slow enough to scan paragraphs. The regular Smartmodem is less than $300 and operates only at 300 baud.

Should you go ahead and spend more for a modem that can transmit at 1200 as well as 300 baud? We think so, because at 1200 baud you will save money on phone bills if you intend to use the modem for downloading software from bulletin boards, or communicating via modem with fellow computerists or with the office computer. You should get a modem that operates at both speeds because some bulletin boards operate only at 300 baud.

Operating at 1200 baud does not save you money when you are using information services like The Source or CompuServe. This is because these services charge more when you "log on" in 1200 baud. This situation may change because users are demanding that the special rates associated with 1200 baud be dropped to be equal to the rates for 300 baud. When this happens, you will save money if you use 1200 baud.

Modems that operate faster than 1200 baud (e.g., 2400 baud, 4800 baud, 9600 baud, etc.) are mostly used between large computer systems. There are differences in these modems that may make them incompatible with personal computers or with

AT&T's telephone network. Although AT&T has standards designed to "protect" its network, the specific modems mentioned in this chapter meet these standards, as do most modems designed for use with personal computers. The only standards to check are that the modem complies with the "Bell 212A" standard for 1200 baud, and the "Bell 103" standard for 300 baud.

"S-100 type" CP/M computers can be outfitted with the PMMI modem board, which contains all the modem electronics inside the computer itself. The PMMI is the favorite of S-100 computer enthusiasts, and all versions of Modem7 work with it (Modem7 is described later). However the PMMI only goes to 600 baud, and is no longer manufactured (Potomac Micro-Magic went out of business). You can still get it at computer flea markets and swap meets.

Most other modems emulate the Hayes Smartmodem. The Anchor Volksmodem is one of the least expensive 300-baud modems; the Anchor Signalman MK XII is one of the least expensive 300/1200-baud modems.

For the IBM PC there are several modem boards packaged with communication software. For example, the Novation PC1200B modem board (the ACCESS 1-2-3) comes with Crosstalk XVI ($595), the Hayes Smartmodem 1200B board comes with Smartcom II ($539), and the Qubie PC212A/1200 board ($299) comes with PC-Talk III.

Before you choose a modem based on the communication software supplied with it, keep in mind that these communication programs (described below) work for a variety of modems, not just the ones they are packaged with. Choose the modem that best suits your pocketbook and your computer.

ACCESS 1-2-3

Novation
20409 Prairie St.
Chatsworth, CA 91311

Anchor Volksmodem and Signalman MK XII
Anchor Automation
3913 Valjean Ave.
Van Nuys, CA 91406

Smartmodem and
Smartmodem 1200
Hayes Microcomputer
Products
5923 Peachtree Industrial Blvd.
Norcross, GA 30092

PMMI
Potomac Micro-Magic Inc.

(out of business — try
computer flea markets)

Qubie
4809 Calle Alto
Camarillo, CA 93010

Smart-Cat and Auto-Cat
Novation
20409 Prairie Street
Chatsworth, CA 91311

Communications Programs

If you want to communicate with bulletin board systems, any program that performs simple computer-to-computer communications will do. There are hundreds of such programs for CP/M and MS-DOS computers that can dial a bulletin board phone number and connect with the system.

If, however, you want to receive public domain software from these bulletin boards, or send to them your own software creations for the public domain, you *must* use a communications program that employs an *error-checking protocol.*

An example of a protocol in social gatherings is the shaking of hands; with computers, a *protocol* is a shared understanding of the starts and stops of words. Sometimes the computers have protocols built-into the hardware, but it is more often with personal computers to use protocols defined by software programs.

Either way, a protocol is required for any computer communication. When you send data from one computer to another, some protocol must be in place so that the receiving computer can synchronize itself and recognize each data word. Usually there is a very limited protocol in place that allows the computers to recognize each data byte.

In most communication programs you can set a limited

protocol that governs the size of each byte. You usually have these choices:

• Seven bits per byte, with one bit acting as a "stop" bit (a pause between bytes). A "bit" is one electronic pulse that is either "on" (1) or "off" (0); seven such bits make up one character (byte) of data. Some host computers require this setting. With this protocol you can only transmit and receive regular text, not programs.

• Eight bits per byte, with one bit acting as the stop bit. This is the usual setting for bulletin board systems and personal computers. Note that the eight bit setting is required for transferring software, but not for transferring text.

• Eight bits per byte, with two stop bits; same as the above setting, but some host computers require two stop bits.

• Parity: odd, even or none. Parity is a simple protocol for determining whether or not one of the bits in a byte is wrong. Bulletin board systems usually want "no parity" or "none," but some computer services may require odd or even parity. Consult any information you have about logging onto the system, or assume "no parity" for communicating with a BBS.

These settings do not provide the *error-checking* protocol necessary for sending and receiving programs, but are sufficient for sending and receiving text.

Xmodem Protocol

There are levels of protocols, from the simplest "parity check" (not used often in personal computing) to the more sophisticated error-checking protocols used in large computer systems. For CP/M and MS-DOS computers there are several "error-checking" protocols used in different communications programs, but only one has become a "standard" because it is used in free programs: the "Modem7/Xmodem" protocol.

With an error-checking protocol (also called "high level" protocol) you can receive a file and know that you are receiving an *exact* duplicate. The file can contain anything including ASCII text or executable program code. It is essential when transferring an executable program that you receive an exact duplicate, otherwise the program will not work.

What causes inaccuracies in transmissions? Telephone wire static and "noise" is common in data transfer, especially at speeds higher than 300 baud (more than 30 characters per second). Computers connected to each other directly may not have as much line noise, but fluctuations in current can cause minor errors.

You may be able to transfer text from one computer to another with minor errors that do not cause major problems — the text may have one or two misspelled words, or a strange graphic symbol embedded in a word. However, when transferring a data base or an executable program (such as a ".COM" or ".HEX" file), you need to be absolutely sure of accuracy. One erring bit of one byte could cause a system crash when you try to run the program, or could cause loss of data in a data base.

The need for an error-checking protocol was evident in the early years of bulletin board systems. Ward Christensen, a prolific writer of public domain software and one of the first bulletin board operators, wrote a communications program with such a protocol built-in, and he called it Modem. The protocol made it possible to send a file, block by block, to and from any two CP/M computers of any make or model, without regard to disk formats.

The Christensen Modem program has been modified and enhanced over the years to become Modem7, now the most popular program in the public domain. Modem7 is widely known as the key to getting public domain software from bulletin board systems, because it has this error-checking protocol that goes by a number of names: the Christensen Protocol, the Modem7 Protocol, or the Xmodem Protocol (it is not trademarked). We devote Chapter 4 to explaining how to obtain and use Modem7.

The term *downloading a program* came to mean receiving a functional program from a BBS using an error-checking protocol. *Uploading* means sending a program to the BBS using this type of protocol. In the world of CP/M and MS-DOS computers, this capability provides a medium for software exchange between different types of computers using different disk formats.

Although many communications programs have error-checking protocols, they only work if the other computer is using the same program. For example, Crosstalk® (from Microstuff) employed its own proprietary protocol, useful only if both computers are using Crosstalk. COMMX (from Hawkeye Grafix) has both its own protocol, which communicates with computers running COMMX, and it also has the "Xmodem Protocol" as an option ("Xmodem" refers to a Modem7 derivative program used on bulletin board systems to transfer files to your computer). Crosstalk also now offers the Modem7/Xmodem protocol starting with version 3.4.

The "Modem7/Xmodem/Christensen" Protocol appears as an option on many communications programs including Apple MacTerminal for the Macintosh, PC-Talk III and Crosstalk XVI for the IBM PC and MS-DOS computers, COMMX, MITE, RCPMLINK and AMCALL for both MS-DOS and CP/M, and many others.

It is notable that the computer industry's public domain spawned a standard that is being adopted by many computer, modem and software manufacturers. We appreciate the effort that has gone into making the "Xmodem" protocol a standard for sending and receiving information. We use it for a lot more than just receiving public domain software. We use it more often to transfer manuscripts and articles to editors, writers and typesetters. The error-checking protocol is the first step toward "smart" communications.

Communications Software

In the free category for IBM PCs and MS-DOS computers, PC-Talk III is the best choice even at the $35 donation "price."

PC-Talk III comes in two versions: the interpreted BASIC version, which requires 64K of internal memory (RAM), and the faster compiled version, which requires 128K of RAM. Note that PC-Talk II and earlier versions do not provide the Xmodem/Modem7 protocol.

To get PC-Talk III for free, order it from the PC Library (address in Appendix C), or get if from your local IBM PC user's group. To get an IBM PC disk directly from Headlands Press (publisher of PC-Talk III), send $35 to: Headlands Press, P.O. Box 862, Tiburon, CA 94920. (Do not send your own blank disk because they have no time to copy the software to fill such orders. They will send you a disk.)

PC-Talk III can communicate from 75 baud up to 9600 baud, and it provides the Xmodem/Modem7 protocol as well as other methods of downloading (but not "batch mode" as described in Chapter 4). You can turn on your printer to get a hard copy of your communications, and a "snapshot" of your display can be printed. Like most commercial communications programs, PC-Talk III can act like a "dumb" terminal or one that sends data at regular, timed intervals paced to the "host" computer. The program uses the IBM PC function keys and lets you assign text to special keys (for example, your password or sign-on information).

For IBM PCs and MS-DOS computers there are many commercial communications programs using the Xmodem protocol, including Crosstalk XVI, Hayes Smartcom, MITE, COMMX and AMCALL. The vendors of a $40 commercial program called SYSCOMM/ABSCOMM, from Microlife, claim it does everything PC-Talk III does, plus offers "batch mode" downloading (specifying more than one file at a time), which is a Modem7 feature (described in Chapter 4).

In the free category for CP/M systems, it is hard to beat Modem7 (described in Chapter 4), but some programs claim to. MEX is a new program in the public domain that supports the Xmodem/Modem7 protocol and provides many other functions for calling BBSs — like alternate dialing. There is also YAM (Yet Another Modem program), and derivatives of Modem7 that work with specific modems, such as SMODEM for the Hayes Smartmodem. SMODEM works much like Modem7.

OTERM4 (in the public domain) is a communications program for the Osborne 1 computer that offers several protocols including Xmodem/Modem7 and CompuServe's CIS protocol. It does many things Modem7 cannot do, including the ability to review text already received while also receiving more text.

For CP/M computers there are also many communications programs with the Xmodem protocol including COMMX, MITE, AMCALL, SUPRTERM (for Kaypro computers) and Z-Term (for Apple II and IIe computers with CP/M add-on boards).

PC-Talk III
Headlands Press
P.O. Box 862
Tiburon, CA 94920
Send $35 donation for disk.

SYSCOMM/ABSCOMM
Microlife, Inc.
P.O. Box 340
Jessup, MD 20794
(301) 799-5509

Crosstalk 3.4
Microstuff, Inc.
1845 The Exchange, Suite 140
Atlanta, GA 30339
(404) 952-0267

Hayes Smartcom
Hayes Microcomputer Products
5923 Peachtree Industrial Blvd.
Norcross, GA 30092

MITE, MITE/86
Mycroft Labs, Inc.
P.O. Box 6045
Tallahassee, FL 32314
(904) 385-1141

COMMX
Hawkeye Grafix
23914 Mobile
Canoga Park, CA 91307
818-348-7909

AMCALL
Micro-Call Services
P.O. Box 650
Laurel, MD 20707
(301) 776-5253

RCPMLINK
Wizard of OsZ
P.O. Box 964
Chatsworth, CA 91311
(213) 709-6969

How To Use What You Get

The most popular programs mentioned in Chapter 1 and described in detail in this book are programs you can use without further ado, as long as you have the operating system and the computer.

These and many other public domain programs are available as files with the filename extension ".COM", and are ready to be used as a program on a CP/M or MS-DOS system. Many others are available in "object file format" with the extension ".OBJ" (e.g., DU.OBJ). Sometimes they have associated files with the extensions ".TXT", ".DOC", etc. These and other extensions are shown in Table 2-1.

When you receive ".OBJ" files, you can rename them on your computer to have the extension ".COM" (e.g., DU.COM) using this command:

```
A>REN DU.COM=DU.OBJ ⏎                      (CP/M)

A>RENAME DU.OBJ DU.COM ⏎                   (MS-DOS)
```

You can then run the program by typing its name as a CP/M or MS-DOS command:

```
A>DU ⏎
```

This command runs the DU program (Disk Utility).

If you can get DU.COM on disk, you don't have to rename it as shown above. Some libraries have files with ".COM" extensions. For example, PC-SIG disks have ".COM" files ready to use with MS-DOS.

FOG and other user groups keep their libraries available to bulletin board systems, where ".OBJ" is used to differentiate public domain programs available to callers from other programs used to manage the bulletin board system. Otherwise, ".OBJ" is synonymous with ".COM", but ".OBJ" files must be renamed to ".COM" before you use them.

Files with other extensions (".EXE", ".BAT", ".SUB", etc.) are shown in Table 2-1.

Assembly Language Programs

Programs supplied as files with the ".ASM" or ".A86" exten-

.ABS   Abstracts (brief program descriptions).
.ASC   ASCII text files — usually MBASIC source files.
.ASM   Assembly language source files (CP/M-80 and MS-DOS).
.A86   Assembly language source files (CP/M-86).
.BAS   CBASIC source files, BASICA (PC BASIC) programs, or MBASIC programs.
.BAT   MS-DOS "batch" file, can be typed as a command.
.BAK   Backup file created by ED, WordStar or other word processing program or spreadsheet program.
.C   "C" language source file.
.CAL   SuperCalc spreadsheet.
.COM   CP/M-80 or MS-DOS program, can be typed as a command.
.CMD   CP/M-86 program, can be typed as a command.
.CMD   dBASE II command file (CP/M-80 only).
.DAT   Data file used with a program or system.
.DOC   File containing text explaining how a program works — called a "document" file.
.EWF   Easywriter test file format.
.EXE   MS-DOS executable program, can be typed as a command.
.FOR   Fortran language source file.
.HEX   File produced by using LOAD to prepare a program for memory and usage in a CP/M-80 system.
.H86   File produced by using GENCMD to prepare a program for memory and usage in a CP/M-86 system.
.INT   "Intermediate" (semi-compiled) CBASIC program.
.JRT   JRT Pascal source file.
.LBR   Library file containing regular files.
.LIB   "Library routines" for use with a computer language.
.LST   Printable listing of a program.
.MAC   Assembly language source file for use with the MAC macroassembler from Digital Research, Inc.
.MSG   File containing important messages.
.PAS   Pascal language source file.
.PIC   IBM PC color graphic screen images.
.PRG   dBASE II command file (CP/M-86 and MS-DOS only).
.PRN   Printable listing of a program.

.REL "Relocatable" module of a program, for use with another
      program.
.SUB Submit file for use with SUBMIT utility (CP/M-80 or
      CP/M-86).
.TXT General text file, may contain explanations of how to use
      programs.
.VC   VisiCalc spreadsheet.
.WS   WordStar text file.

NOTE:

There are many other filename extensions in use in the public domain, but their usage is not standardized. The best way to tell the
type of a file is to read the ".DOC" or ".TXT" or other text file
associated with the file in question. Also, any extension that has
the letter "Q" as the middle letter (second letter of the three-letter extension) is a *squeezed* version of a file. You must use USQ,
NSWP or similar utility to un-squeeze a squeezed file (squeezed
files are described in Chapter 5).

Table 2-1. *Filename extensions you may find in the public domain, with their meanings.*

---

sions have to be *assembled* before you can use them. You need to
learn how to use the ASM program (CP/M-80) to assemble
".ASM" files, or the ASM-86 program (CP/M-86) to assemble
".A86" files, or the Macro Assembler program (IBM or
Microsoft) to assemble MS-DOS ".ASM" files. (There are not
nearly as many ".ASM" source files for IBM PC and MS-DOS
computers as there are for CP/M computers; most of the IBM
PC and MS-DOS public domain programs are written in BASIC
or available as ".COM" files.)

    First you should understand how an assembly language pro-
gram is created. A programmer starts by writing the program's
text and storing it in a "source file." This file has the extension
".ASM" or ".MAC" for CP/M-80 programs, ".A86" for
CP/M-86 programs, and ".ASM" for MS-DOS programs.

In order to test the program, the programmer must first prepare the program to be loaded properly into the computer's memory. In CP/M-80 systems, the programmer uses the LOAD utility; in CP/M-86 systems, the programmer uses the GENCMD utility. Both are described briefly here. In MS-DOS, the programmer uses the macro assembler from IBM or Microsoft.

After preparing the program for memory (it now has the ".COM" or ".CMD" extension), the programmer can run the program and test it. If the program needs modification, the programmer must return to the source file (".ASM", ".A86" or ".MAC" extension) and make the changes in that file, then assemble the program again and prepare it for memory.

For more information about programming in assembly language, we recommend *Inside CP/M* or *Inside CP/M-86* by Dave Cortesi (Holt, Rinehart and Winston). There are also many other books about programming CP/M systems.

Assembly language source files are text files created by a text editing program like ED, or a word processing program like WordStar® (MicroPro). Someone with minimal training can open a text file with ED or WordStar and change its contents. You may not understand the text in the file, because it is written in assembly language, not English. But given the appropriate instructions for what to change, you can perform the change as you would edit any text file.

The procedures differ for CP/M-80 (eight-bit), CP/M-86 (sixteen-bit) and MS-DOS, so we separate the instructions.

CP/M-80: Assemble & Load

Assembly language source files can be turned into working programs by *assembling* them with the ASM utility and preparing them for memory (*loading* them) with the LOAD utility. The two operations produce a program that can run on almost any computer using the 8080, 8085 or Z80 processors.

Assuming you've made the changes you need to make to the source file and you're ready to assemble it, and assuming your source file is named SAMPLE.ASM and located in drive A, the command you type to assemble it is:

```
A)ASM SAMPLE ⊃
```

The ASM utility produces two new files on the drive A disk: SAMPLE.HEX and SAMPLE.PRN. The first one (".HEX" file) is the important one for creating a program — it is called the *object file* for the program. It contains the program in hexadecimal code for use with the LOAD utility. The second is a printable listing of the program, which takes up more disk space than the first one.

If you run out of space on disk, or run out of directory entries, you will get one of these error messages: OUTPUT FILE WRITE ERROR (no space left) or NO DIRECTORY SPACE (no room for new filenames).

You can use other drives for these files by adding a special extension to the filename on the ASM command line to control where to find the ".ASM" source file and where to put the ".HEX" and ".PRN" files. The extension has three letters:

```
A)ASM SAMPLE.ABX ⊃
```

The first character (A) tells ASM to look in drive A for the source file (".ASM" file). The second (B) tells ASM to put in drive B the object file (".HEX" file). The third character (X) tells ASM to display the listing rather than create a listing file (".PRN" file). This saves space on the disk, and you can print the listing if you type Control-P before typing the ASM command line (Control-P turns on printer "echo" of the screen).

To summarize, here's the generic form of the ASM command line:

```
ASM filename.ahp ⊃
```

Substitute your own filename without the ".ASM" extension (ASM assumes all source files have ".ASM" as the extension), and use the extension to tell ASM which drive to look into for the ".ASM" file (a), which drive to store the ".HEX" file (h), and which drive to store the ".PRN" file (p). You can substitute a Z for p to cancel the ".PRN" file, or X to display it first on the screen and then cancel it.

After assembling the ".ASM" file to produce the ".HEX" file, your final step is to produce the ".COM" file using the LOAD utility (LOAD.COM). Assuming your ".HEX" file was produced from SAMPLE.ASM (and has the name SAMPLE.HEX), you would type this command (assuming also that SAMPLE.HEX and LOAD.COM are on drive A):

    A)LOAD SAMPLE ⊃

This produces SAMPLE.COM, which can then be executed by typing SAMPLE and pressing Return (⊃). The ".COM" file is a directly-executable CP/M program, which means you can run the program by typing its name as a command. The ".HEX" file is not directly executable, but it can be loaded into memory and run using the DDT utility, which is shown later.

CP/M-86: Assemble & Generate

Assembly language source files can be turned into working programs by *assembling* them with the ASM-86 utility, and producing executable programs (preparing them for memory) with the GENCMD utility. The two operations produce a program that can run on almost any computer using the 8086, 8088, iAPX 186/286 or iAPX 188/288 processors.

Assuming you've made the changes you need to make to the source file and you're ready to assemble it, and assuming your source file is named SAMPLE.A86 and located in drive A, the command you type to assemble it is:

    A)ASM86 SAMPLE ⊃

The ASM-86 utility produces three new files on the drive A disk: SAMPLE.H86, SAMPLE.LST and SAMPLE.SYM.

SAMPLE.H86 is the important one for creating an executable

program — it is called the *object file* for the program. It contains the program in hexadecimal code for use with the GENCMD utility.

SAMPLE.LST is a printable listing of the program, which takes up more disk space than the first one and may not be needed.

SAMPLE.SYM is a *symbol file* used when "debugging" a program (something you are not likely to do without first reading about assembly language).

If you run out of space on disk, or run out of directory entries, you will get one of these error messages: Disk Full (no space left) or Directory Full (no room for new filenames).

You can use other drives for these files by adding *parameters* to the ASM-86 command line following a dollar sign:

A>ASM86 SAMPLE $AA HB PX ⊃

The first parameter (AA) tells ASM-86 to look in drive A for the source file (".A86" file). The second parameter (HB) stores the object (".H86") file in drive B. The third parameter (PX) displays the listing rather than create a listing (".LST") file. This saves space on the disk, and you can print the listing if you type Control-P before typing the ASM-86 command line (Control-P turns on printer "echo" of the screen).

To summarize, here's the generic form of the ASM-86 command line:

ASM86 filename *$ Ad Hd Pd Sd FI* ⊃

Substitute your own filename with any extension, or an ".A86" file's name without an extension (ASM-86 assumes the ".A86" extension). Type optional parameters following a dollar ($) sign to control the files as follows:

Ad   Look for source (".A86") file on drive d.

Hd   Store the hexadecimal object (".H86") file on drive d.

Pd   Store the listing (".LST") file on drive d. Type X for d to display the listing rather than store it in a disk file; or type Y to print the listing rather than store it; or type Z to skip it altogether.

Sd   Store the symbol (".SYM") file on drive d. Type X for d to display the symbol file rather than store it in a disk file; or type Y to print the symbol file rather than store it; or type Z to skip it altogether.

FI   Produce a hexadecimal object file using the Intel format; otherwise, ASM-86 uses the default Digital Research format.

After assembling the ".A86" file to produce the ".H86" file, your final step is to produce the ".CMD" file using the GENCMD utility (GENCMD.CMD). Assuming your ".H86" file was produced from SAMPLE.A86 (SAMPLE.H86), you would type this command (assuming also that SAMPLE.H86 and GENCMD.CMD are on drive A):

```
A>GENCMD SAMPLE ⊃
```

This produces SAMPLE.CMD, which can then be executed by typing SAMPLE and pressing Return (⊃). The ".CMD" file is a directly-executable CP/M-86 program, which means you can run the program by typing its name as a command. The ".H86" file is not directly executable, but it can be loaded into memory and run using the DDT-86 utility, which is shown later.

GENCMD has optional parameters you can use in the command line to produce programs that are similar in nature to CP/M-80 programs, or that have certain memory requirements. The optional parameters follow the filename in the command line. Here's a quick summary of the parameters:

8080

    The keyword 8080 tells GENCMD to generate a program (".CMD" file) that closely resembles an eight-bit CP/M-

80 program that fits within a 64K memory space. This type of program has overlapping code and data areas and starts at memory address 0100H within the 64K memory space. This parameter is often used to generate a program that was converted from a CP/M-80 version to run with CP/M-86.

```
CODE[An,Bn,Mn,Xn]
DATA[An,Bn,Mn,Xn]
STACK[An,Bn,Mn,Xn]
EXTRA[An,Bn,Mn,Xn]
```

The keywords define *segment groups* (areas of memory associated by a relationship) that have specific memory requirements, which you can spell out within the brackets using the parameters with n, which in all cases is a paragraph boundary (paragraphs are 16 bytes long).

Within the brackets associated with any or all of the above keywords, use the following where needed:

An   Load a group at an absolute location in memory (paragraph boundary n).

Bn   Begin a group at address n in the hexadecimal file. Usually this parameter is not needed if you used ASM-86 to produce the hexadecimal (".H86") file and chose the default Digital Research format. If you used the Intel format, you will need this.

Mn   The group requires a minimum of n paragraphs (n times 16 bytes). Use this when you include a data segment that has an uninitialized data area at the end of the segment.

Xn   The group can use up to n paragraphs (n times 16 bytes) more than the minimum defined by Mn. Use this if your program can use a larger data area.

Here are two examples of GENCMD command lines — the

first generates a CP/M-86 program that is similar in organization to a CP/M-80 program, and the second generates a CP/M-86 program with specific instructions for the CODE and DATA groups:

```
A)GENCMD FIRSTPRG 8080 ↵

A)GENCMD SECONDPR CODE[A50] DATA[M40,XFFF] ↵
```

Variations of GENCMD command lines are possible, but not likely to be used unless you are doing special programming. If you are given a source file to generate into a program, you would normally use the least complicated versions of ASM-86 and GENCMD, unless you are given specific instructions on using the parameters.

For more information about using ASM, ASM-86, LOAD or GENCMD, we recommend *Inside CP/M* or *Inside CP/M-86* by Dave Cortesi (Holt, Rinehart and Winston). There are also many other books about programming CP/M systems.

BASIC Programs

Many public domain programs were written in a version of the BASIC language for CP/M-80 called MBASIC (Microsoft BASIC). The MBASIC programs usually have filenames that end with the ".BAS" extension. These programs cannot be run in your computer unless you have a program called the MBASIC Interpreter.

The MBASIC Interpreter is a commercial program you need to write and run MBASIC programs. Fortunately it is provided free with many CP/M-80 computers including Osborne, Kaypro and Morrow computers, and is available for every CP/M-80 computer from dealers who carry CP/M software.

Microsoft, which created both MBASIC for CP/M and BASIC for the IBM PC, also created CP/M's rival MS-DOS. MS-DOS is very similar to CP/M, and the IBM PC BASIC (also supplied with MS-DOS for PC-compatible computers) resembled MBASIC in many ways. It is not surprising that many MBASIC programs written for CP/M systems have now been rewritten for MS-DOS and PC-DOS. These programs can be run in your IBM PC or PC-compatible computer if you have the IBM PC BASIC Interpreter or Compiler, or the Microsoft generic versions of the Interpreter or Compiler. Usually the Interpreter is supplied with the computer.

Other BASIC languages are also used in the CP/M and MS-DOS world, most notably CBASIC (Digital Research, Inc.). CBASIC programs that were compiled by the CB-80 or CB-86 compilers have ".COM" in CP/M-80 systems (".CMD" in CP/M-86, ".EXE" in MS-DOS) as the filename extension and can be run without your purchasing the CBASIC Compiler. Programs that were compiled by early versions of the CBASIC Compiler have the extension ".INT" and cannot be run unless you have the CBASIC "run-time" program called CRUN or CRUN2. Both are available from dealers who carry CP/M software.

Some programs in the public domain were written in Radio Shack's version of BASIC and can run only on Radio Shack TRS-80 computers. Others are available for Apple's, Atari's and Commodore's BASIC languages, and are not mentioned in this book.

MBASIC, PC BASIC and BASICA

You get two BASIC language "interpreters" with the IBM PC: regular BASIC and Advanced BASIC (BASICA). The differences between the two versions are primarily in the way each handles graphics. The BASIC programs you get from the public domain should work with either BASIC or BASICA.

Both versions of the IBM PC BASIC were developed by Microsoft, whose MBASIC interpreter (also called BASIC-80) is already widely used on CP/M computers, and whose Applesoft BASIC, used on many Apple computers, is remarkably similar. All of these BASICs work in much the same way: you type the name of the BASIC interpreter to start BASIC, then you use the RUN command with the name of the program in quotes (or use

LOAD with the program name in quotes, then RUN by itself).

Here's an example of running the program SAMPLE.BAS, using MBASIC (for the IBM PC BASICs, substitute BASIC or BASICA for MBASIC in this example):

```
A>MBASIC ↵
Microsoft BASIC
Version xx.yy
nnnn Bytes Free

OK
RUN ''SAMPLE'' ↵
```

This should work if SAMPLE.BAS is a proper BASIC program. You can also use this method:

```
OK
LOAD ''SAMPLE'' ↵


OK
RUN ↵
```

By using LOAD first before RUN, you are able to load the program into memory and perhaps make changes to it before using RUN. If you make changes to it, be sure to use the SAVE command to save a new copy of it:

```
OK
SAVE ''NEWPROG.BAS'' ↵
```

Programs supplied in ".BAS" files can be run directly from the operating system if you supply the name of the file along with the command to start the BASIC interpreter. For example, to run NEWPROG.BAS using MBASIC from the CP/M command line, type this:

```
A>MBASIC NEWPROG ↵
```

This MBASIC command performs the RUN command automatically, and assumes NEWPROG has the extension ".BAS" (NEWPROG.BAS). For IBM PC BASIC and BASICA, substitute the command (`BASIC` or `BASICA`) for `MBASIC` in the above example — it works the same way.

Some BASIC programs are supplied as ASCII text files with the extension ".ASC". To run these programs, you *must* use the MERGE command in place of the LOAD command, then use the SAVE command to save the file as a BASIC file (with the ".BAS" extension), then LOAD and RUN the ".BAS" file you created.

Note that the MERGE command simply takes the ".ASC" file contents and merges them with anything that is already *in* memory. Therefore, if you are using MERGE to bring a new program into memory (i.e., you're not trying to merge pieces of a program together, just make an ".ASC" file useful), use the NEW command first, then the MERGE command.

For example, if you downloaded or otherwise received a copy of the public domain program SAMPLE.ASC, you would do the following to create and run SAMPLE.BAS:

```
Ok
NEW ↵

Ok
MERGE ''SAMPLE.ASC'' ↵

Ok
SAVE ''SAMPLE.BAS'' ↵

Ok
LOAD ''SAMPLE'' ↵

Ok
RUN ↵
```

You should keep an archive copy of the ".ASC" file in case you destroy the ".BAS" file.

After using MERGE to load an ".ASC" file, or LOAD to load a ".BAS" file, you can use the LIST command to display the lines of the program, or the LLIST command to print the program:

```
Ok
LIST ⊃
        (This command displays all of the program lines.)
Ok
LIST 10-100 ⊃

        (This command displays only lines 10 through 100.)
Ok
LLIST ⊃

        (This command prints the entire program.)
```

Here's a summary of what to do in order to use an ".ASC" file in the public domain, whether you have IBM PC BASIC or BASICA, or Microsoft BASIC for MS-DOS, or MBASIC (BASIC-80) for CP/M systems:

1. Start the BASIC interpreter by typing its name (e.g., BASIC, BASICA, MBASIC, etc.).

2. Use the MERGE command to bring the ".ASC" file (which contains BASIC statements as regular ASCII text) into the BASIC interpreter's memory.

3. Use the SAVE command to save the contents of memory as a regular BASIC program with the filename extension ".BAS".

4. Use the RUN command to run the ".BAS" file, or use LOAD and then RUN.

For more information on using IBM PC BASIC and BASICA, we recommend the IBM manuals for the most accurate information.

CBASIC and Other Compiled BASICs

Compiling a program usually means making the program faster and more compact. Most compiled programs can be run from the operating system and are available as ".COM" or ".CMD" files; you need no further information to use them. For the IBM PC the most popular compiled BASIC is Microsoft's BASIC Compiler, also available from IBM. For CP/M computers, the most popular compiled BASIC is CBASIC from Digital Research (supplied with some CP/M computers).

The CBASIC language produces programs that are faster and more compact than those produced with MBASIC and most other BASIC languages. CBASIC programs can be *semi-compiled* (using the CBASIC or CBASIC-86 compiler) or *fully compiled* (using CB-80 or CB-86 compilers). All compilers are available from Digital Research, Inc. (DRI).

Some of the ".COM" or ".CMD" files in the public domain are actually programs written in CBASIC that were fully compiled. The CB-80 compiler produces a ".COM" file which you can run in a CP/M-80 system by typing its name as a command. The CB-86 compiler produces a ".CMD" file which you can run in a CP/M-86 system also by typing its name as a command. You need no further instructions to do this, nor do you need copies of the CBASIC, CBASIC-86, CB-80 or CB-86 compilers.

However, some of the CBASIC programs available in the public domain are *semi-compiled* or in source file form. Semi-compiled programs have the extension ".INT" (such as LEDGER1.INT). To run such a program, you need a version of the CBASIC *run-time* utility, called CRUN or CRUN2 (CRUN2 runs both CBASIC and CBASIC2 programs). This utility is available from DRI by itself, or with the CBASIC compiler. Here's an example of running CRUN2:

```
A>CRUN2 LEDGER1 ⏎
```

You don't have to include the ".INT" extension because CRUN2 assumes the file has that extension.

Many CBASIC programs are available in the *source file* form

so that you can modify the programs (you cannot edit ".INT" or
".COM" or ".CMD" files). The source file has the extension
".BAS" (as in LEDGER1.BAS). To run such a program, you
must first *compile* the program using the CB-80 or CB-86 com-
pilers, or you must *semi-compile* the program using the
CBASIC-80 or CBASIC-86 compilers. Here's an example of the
CBASIC compiler (CBAS2 is the name of the CBASIC-80 ver-
sion 2.0 compiler):

```
A>CBAS2 LEDGER1 ↵
```

This command produces the semi-compiled program
LEDGER1.INT, which can then be run as shown above in the
CRUN2 example (CRUN2 is version 2.0 of the CBASIC run-
time utility).

Here's an example of using the CB-80 compiler to fully compile a program (CB is the name of the CB-80 compiler):

```
A>CB MYPROG ↵
```

This command compiles the program MYPROG.BAS to create MYPROG.COM, which you can then run by typing the name
MYPROG by itself on the CP/M command line.

Many public domain CBASIC programs are supplied as both
".BAS" and ".INT" files (such as the complete
Osborne/McGraw Hill accounting system, found in CP/MUG
volume 43 through 45). You can choose which type of file to use
— either the ready-to-run ".INT" file or the ready-to-edit
".BAS" file.

If you choose the ".INT" file you must use the CRUN or
CRUN2 utility to run the program. If you choose the ".BAS" file
you have two more choices: either the CBASIC-80 or CBASIC-
86 compiler to create the ".INT" file to use with the CRUN or
CRUN2 utility, or the CB-80 or CB-86 compilers which produce
".COM" or ".CMD" files to run directly from the operating system.

For a detailed guide to CBASIC, try the *CBASIC User's
Guide* by Adam Osborne, Gordon Eubanks and Martin McNiff

(Osborne/McGraw-Hill). Gordon Eubanks is the author of CBASIC, which evolved from a public domain BASIC he also wrote, called EBASIC.

To get the CBASIC-80, CBASIC-86, CB-80 or CB-86 compilers and associated utilities, contact a software supplier for CP/M computers, or DRI itself (Digital Research, P.O. Box 579, Pacific Grove, CA 93950).

Programs In Other Languages

The public domain libraries contain programs written in a variety of commercial languages such as the ones mentioned above plus Pascal, Fortran, "C," Forth and others. Some public domain programs are written in languages that are also in the public domain and not available commercially, such as EBASIC (a forerunner to CBASIC), PILOT (very popular among computer-using educators), FIG-Forth (from the Forth Interest Group), PISTOL (evolved from Forth), Tarbell BASIC, Tiny BASIC, Lawrence Livermore BASIC and SAM76 to name a few.

The SIG/M library contains several volumes of programs written in the Pascal/Z language for CP/M-80 systems. To run these programs, you need the Pascal/Z compiler from Ithaca Intersystems (Ithaca Intersystems, 1650 Hanshaw Rd., Ithaca, NY 14850). The Pascal/Z users' group may be of some help: Pascal/Z Users Group, 7962 Center Parkway, Sacramento, CA 95823.

There are also a large number of programs written in the "C" language from BD Software called BDS-C. The source files (with the ".C" extension) can be edited using any text editing or word processing program, then compiled with the BDS-C compiler, which is very popular among programmers. The BDS-C compiler is available for $150 (contact Leor Zolman, BD Software, P.O. Box 9, Brighton, MA 02135, phone 617-782-0836).

The IBM PC public domain libraries contain many programs written in PC BASIC (which is supplied with the IBM PC), and some others written in Pascal and Fortran (available from IBM or Microsoft). MVP Forth (Mt. View Press Forth) is available in the public domain. Ladybug, a user-supported program (contribution asked), is a graphics programming language for the IBM PC (PC-DOS) that resembles the Turtle Graphics of the LOGO language, which is a very easy-to-learn language now gaining popularity (it was first used by educators, then by game designers).

To learn how to run programs written in any of these languages, you have to consult the manuals or ".DOC" files associated with the language. There is not enough space in this book to describe each language in detail. Generally, a program that is not supplied as a ".COM" (or ".CMD" or ".EXE" or ".BAT") file has to be "prepared for execution" by either *compiling* it or *interpreting* it. Therefore, you need a compiler, interpreter or similar utility, which is either available in a public domain volume or is sold by a commercial dealer.

Now You're Ready

You now have almost everything you need to go out into the public domain and dig for gems. You should first browse through the public domain "digest" in Appendix D. You can order disks for an IBM PC, or for eight-inch disk systems running CP/M, or for Osborne, Kaypro, Morrow or other computers, using the ordering information and catalogs in Appendix C.

If you want to try calling bulletin board systems, read on. Otherwise, skip to Chapters 5 and 6 to read about *un-squeezing* the public domain files and extracting them from library files. One or both steps are necessary if you want to use many of the programs found in the public domain.

CHAPTER 3:
CALLING RCP/M
BULLETIN BOARDS

Across the world, day and night, computer systems with blinking modems are listening to telephone lines and answering phone calls.

The systems are called *bulletin board* systems (BBS) or RCP/M (Remote CP/M) bulletin board systems (RCP/M BBS). They serve as electronic bulletin boards for people reading and leaving messages.

RCP/M bulletin boards offer more than the typical BBS that offers only bulletin board messaging. You can use a computer and modem to call an RCP/M BBS and *download* free programs to your computer.

The term "downloading" refers to the direction of the data: from the system "down" to you. "Uploading" is also possible with these systems — you can send programs you've written "up" to the RCP/M BBS for general distribution.

The systems are owned and operated by volunteers who call themselves *sysops* (short for "system operators"). They provide a valuable public service, cataloguing public domain software and maintaining expensive equipment that lets you call in and receive software without any charges or hassles.

If you have a communications program and you're ready to use it, this chapter explains everything you need to know. You can use the information presented here to call most RCP/M bulletin board systems including the SIG/M and FOG RCP/M networks.

The RCP/M systems usually offer the entire CP/MUG and SIG/M volumes of public domain software (a digest of these volumes appears in Appendix D). FOG RCP/M systems have the

FOG libraries that have computer-specific versions of SIG/M and CP/MUG programs (FOG libraries are also summarized in Appendix D).

Calling an RCP/M BBS

You must have a modem connected to your computer, and a communications program as described in Chapter 2. Look up in the phone list in Appendix B for the RCP/M BBS nearest you. If the phone listing describes the system as a "CALL BACK" system, call the number and let the phone ring only once, and then hang up and call again. If no mention is made of "CALL BACK," simply call the number with your computer and modem.

You can call an RCP/M system with almost any communications program, and use the bulletin board system as well as browse through the catalog of software. But in order to download programs, you must be using a program that has the "Xmodem Protocol" (also known as "Modem7 Protocol" or "Christensen Protocol").

Communications programs for personal computers offer the same basic functions. If you have fancy auto-dial functions, you may be able to call a bulletin board system quickly and easily.

Before placing a call, make sure your modem is properly connected to the computer and the phone line, and set your modem to *originate* mode. This means that your modem will originate the call. The bulletin board system has a modem that will answer the call in *answer* mode. However, your modem must be in *originate* mode to talk to a modem that is in answer mode.

Most communications programs start operation at 300 baud, which on your display is about twenty to thirty characters (300 bits) per second. If you are familiar with data communications, go ahead and change it to 1200 baud; otherwise, try 300 baud until you get used to it. Once you set your baud rate, you will probably stay at that speed.

If you're using an inexpensive modem or acoustic coupler, you may be restricted to 300 baud or lower. If you're using a teletype machine or "hard-copy" terminal (one that uses paper rather than a display screen), you must select 110 baud.

The communication program must be set properly for communication. Most bulletin board systems require you to set the program to transmit and receive *eight bit* data with *one stop bit* and *no parity*. Some systems require that at speeds of 1200 baud you set it to use *two stop bits*. These settings were explained in the previous chapter.

Calling With Modem7

If you have Modem7 (for example, MDM720, which is a version of Modem7 described in Chapter 4, or Smodem) and a Hayes Smartmodem or PMMI modem, you can type the following command to get started:

```
A>MODEM7 ⏎
MDM720 - (type M for Menu)
Version for (your computer here)
Initial baud rate set for 300

AO>>COMMAND:
```

If you want to set the baud rate to 1200 baud, type this command:

```
AO>>COMMAND: SET ⏎
Input Baud Rate (300, 450, 600, 1200, 9600): 1200 ⏎
AO>>COMMAND:
```

Now type the CAL command to make a call from the list of phone numbers already stored in MDM720:

```
AO>>COMMAND: CAL ⏎
```

This command displays a list of phone numbers. You can select a phone number by typing the "library letter" for the name; however, you should first check the number to see if it will work from your area (for example, in some areas you don't start long-distance numbers with "1" and in some areas the numbers are not long-distance).

The easiest way to make sure the number works is to type the phone number as you would dial it, using the displayed library as a reference. Here's an example:

```
Enter library letter or phone number,
Hit RET to abort this function now or
CTL-X quits while dialing or ringing: 408-258-8128
```

This example shows MDM720, which is a version of Modem7 that can dial the number and try to establish a connection automatically. When connection is established, you get this message:

```
CONNECT
```

Quickly press your Return key two or more times, and the bulletin board system should display a message similar to this:

```
How many nulls (0-9)?
```

This mysterious message is actually a good sign — it means you're "on" the system. Skip to the next section on "Logging On."

Using an Acoustic Coupler

Most communications programs support auto-dialing for direct-connect modems, but this function is impossible with acoustic couplers. With acoustic couplers you have to dial the number first. Also, most acoustic couplers operate only at 300 baud.

Communications programs usually start with a menu, but early versions of Modem7 do not. If your program starts with a menu, select the "terminal mode" option. *Terminal mode* means that your computer will act as a terminal on the computer you are calling (the "host" computer).

If you're using Modem7, select the T option (for terminal mode) from the menu. Modem7 starts with a default baud rate (usually 300 baud), but if it doesn't, you may want to first use the SET command as shown above to set the baud rate to 300 baud for your acoustic coupler. For older versions of Modem7, type the T option with a period and a baud rate:

```
AO>>COMMAND:T.300 ⏎
```

Since some older versions do not start with a menu, we present the most common way to execute Modem7 and bring it up in terminal mode — specifying the T option on the CP/M command line:

```
A>MODEM7 T ⏎                        (Default baud rate.)
A>MODEM7 T.300 ⏎                    (300 baud.)
```

If you're using an acoustic coupler, turn it on and dial the phone number of your nearest RCP/M system (see list in Appendix B). If the phone listing describes the system as a "CALL BACK" system, let the phone ring only once, and then hang up and call again. If no mention is made of "CALL BACK," simply call the number.

Wait until the system answers with a high-pitched tone. Place your telephone handset in the coupler, and press your Return key several times, until a message similar to the following appears:

```
How many nulls (0-9)?
```

That's it! You're ready to use the RCP/M system (skip to the next section on "Logging On").

Using the Hayes Smartmodem

The Hayes Smartmodem lets you dial numbers from terminal

mode of any communications program. Some communications programs are configured to work with the Smartmodem, but if yours does not, you can still use the Smartmodem's commands from your program's terminal mode.

Communications programs usually start with a menu, but early versions of Modem7 do not. If your program starts with a menu, select the "terminal mode" option. *Terminal mode* means that your computer will act as a terminal on the computer you are calling (the "host" computer).

If you're using Modem7, select the T option (for terminal mode) from the menu. Modem7 starts with a default baud rate (usually 300 baud), but if you want to change it (if you're using the Hayes Smartmodem 1200), you may be able to do it from Modem7 using the SET command as shown above to set the baud rate to 1200 baud. For older versions of Modem7, type the T option with a period and a baud rate:

    AO>>COMMAND: T. 1200 ↩

Since some older versions do not start with a menu, we present the most common way to execute Modem7 and bring it up in terminal mode — specifying the T option on the CP/M command line:

    A>MODEM7 T ↩   (Default baud rate.)
    A>MODEM7 T. 1200 ↩   (1200 baud.)

In terminal mode you can type commands that the Smartmodem understands. Start by "waking up" the Smartmodem with the AT command:

    AT ↩

The Smartmodem should respond with:

    OK

If you get the OK from the Smartmodem, you can control your

modem and dial the RCP/M number using the Smartmodem commands. The following commands set the modem to touch-tone dialing, and dials the number for the FOG RCP/M system in Daly City, CA (area code 415):

```
OK
ATT ⊃                                    (set to touch-tone)
OK
ATD755-2030 ⊃                            (dial number)
```

The number may be busy, or there may be no answer. If so, the Smartmodem hangs up and displays a message saying NO CARRIER. Some communications programs configured for the Smartmodem make use of the special "try again" function and call the number again and again until you press a key to stop it.

If the other end answers the phone with a receiving signal (the BBS modem is always in "answer mode" and you are in "originate mode"), the Smartmodem will establish connection and display CONNECT.

When CONNECT appears, press your Return key twice, and you should see a message similar to the following:

```
How many nulls (0-9)?
```

That's it! You're ready to use the RCP/M system (skip to the next section).

If the other end is busy, and you return to terminal mode (you were using Smartmodem commands directly), you can re-dial the same number over and over again by typing the Smartmodem A/ command without typing a Return. The Smartmodem will abort the phone call if you type a Return while it is waiting for a connection.

Logging On

The How many nulls? question is easy to answer if you're using a modern personal computer or display terminal: type a zero and press Return.

If you're using a slow "hard-copy" (printing) terminal such as a teletype, you need nulls to be transmitted after each line, so that your "hard-copy" printing terminal or teletype can move its carriage back to the left margin in time to receive the next line. The number of nulls you need depends on the speed of your terminal or teletype — try nine for the slowest speed, and decrease it each time you call until your terminal can't keep up with the lines sent by the RCP/M system.

After typing a zero (or other number) for the "nulls" question, the RCP/M system may ask another question, such as:

```
CAN YOUR TERMINAL DISPLAY LOWER CASE? Y
```

This second question is simple enough: if you can type lower case characters on your keyboard, type Y for yes. If you type N for no, everything you type will be in UPPER case. Most bulletin board systems assume you can type in both cases and don't bother to ask this question.

In nearly every BBS we've tried, the system "logged" you in by name and password. If you're new to the system, it asks you for your name, your address, and a unique word for you to use as a password. Type the answer to each question and press Return to send each answer to the BBS.

```
           FIRST OSBORNE GROUP (FOG) RBBS RCP/M #1

     Welcome to the brand new version of this system. We are now
running the Heavy Metal software written by Tim Gary and Byron McKay. If
you are interested in obtaining a copy to Heavy Metal, you may contact
Byron by modem at (415) 965-4097.

     This system supports both 300 and 1200 baud. If you want to
download from this system, you must also use the MODEM protocol. This is
8 bit, no parity.

     As always, this system will operate 24 hours per day, except for
```

maintenance time which we try to restrict to daylight hours, Monday to Friday.

Because FOG membership funds support this system, a portion of it will be restricted to FOG members. Non members will be allowed to use the message system and user levels 0 thru 3. Members have access up to user level 8.

Xmodem (for downloading files) has a 30 minute maximum on it. This is because we do not yet have a clock installed on the system and some users were abusing the system by downloading very large libraries.

All of the FOG library disks are on this system. All library disks will be consolidated into .LBR files. For more information, use the command:

HELP XMODEM

If you are using 1200 baud, you will be able to download the entire ''disk'' (actually a .LBR file). If you are using 300 baud, this option will not be available to you.

For assistance with the use of this system, type the word: HELP ⏎ at any prompt.

This system has been completely reworked over the last several days. Non members have access to more areas and there are now subject sections such as UTILITY.PUB (for handy utility programs), GAMES.PUB (for games which should work on most systems), LOBOMAX.PUB (for programs which only work on the LoboMax), and so on. Use the SECTION command to get a list of available sections.

You should use this command to move around any of the FOG systems since not all systems are set up quite the same way. Type SECTION ⏎ for more info.

Another good command for moving around is the LOG command. Type LOG ⏎ for more information.

THIS SYSTEM IS FOR SERIOUS CP/M USERS!!

PLEASE use your real name and not a ''handle''
Thanks.... Gale Rhoades, sysop

AUGUST 10, 1984:   Using the philosophy of ''Them that don't use it, lose it'', I have deleted those callers who have not been using the system. This means FOG members who have not called in four months and non-members who have not called in three months. This was done to speed access to the system for those who do use it.

A reminder to non-members who have not sent in the required written application with a SASE (that's Self Addressed Stamped Envelope folks), without the written application, you will not be able to enter messages or the RCP/M system. There will be no exceptions for this.

JULY 30, 1984:   In response to the many requests, I will no longer do maintenance on the WEEKENDS. I will very quickly check the messages just to be sure that no one has posted a message that is inappropriate for this system. Other than that, no maintenance will be done between 2:00pm Friday and 12:00 noon Monday each week.

For those interested in knowing why, when they first called into this system several days (weeks) ago, I urge you to remember that use of this system is restricted to those who are properly registered with this system.

To be properly registered with this system, you must meet one of the following:

1. Leave a comment as you leave this system, including your name, address, and phone numbers.

AND

2. Be a FOG member and include that information in the comment you leave requesting access.

OR

3. Send a Self Addressed Stamped Envelope (SASE) with a note which you have signed which duplicates this information to the address below.

    I remind non FOG members that you have until August 30th to send in your SASE as per #3 above.

JUNE 25, 1984:   Several incidences of inappropriate use of this type of system requires a change in the registration procedure.
    Since we cannot verify the contact information for non FOG members, we have decided to institute a written registration procedure for these users. If you are not a FOG member, you must send a note with your name, address, home phone, work phone, and what equipment you use together with a stamped, self addressed envelop to the following address:

                    FOG RCP/M System #1
                    P. O. Box 3051
                    Daly City, CA 94015-0051

    You will be immediately sent a written notice of your status. Current users who are not listed on this system as FOG members will have until Aug. 31st to send in their registration. If the registration is not sent in, access will be reduced.

What's your name (or user ID)? **Tony Bove** ⤶
[Checking for previous logon]
....
Enter password? 123456

Is today 08/27/84 (y/n)?Y
[Updating logs]
[Loading the bbs]

Figure 3-1.   *Logging on to the FOG RCP/M BBS, with access controlled by the Heavy Metal Message System, used on many RCP/M systems. Dated bulletins from the system operator (sysop) appear in order with the most recent one first.*

Figure 3-1 shows the log-on session, including the welcome message and special bulletins, displayed when you log into the FOG RCP/M. The bulletins from the system operator (the "sysop") appear in order with the most recent one first. All of the bulletins are displayed, but the next time you log on, only the bulletins you *haven't* read would be displayed.

The software that runs the bulletin board system is used by the other FOG RCP/M systems and by many other clubs and groups including PicoNet. The software running the BBS is not public domain — it is the Heavy Metal Message System written by Tim Gary and Byron McKay, members of FOG and PicoNet. There is also bulletin board software in the public domain (see Appendix D for a "digest" of public domain volumes).

The Bulletin Board

We arrive at the program that helped start this computerized bulletin board phenomenon: the original CBBS program written by Ward Christensen (who also wrote MODEM.ASM, which MODEM7 is based on). The remarkable CBBS program was originally written for CP/M systems and was made available from Ward Christensen and Randy Seuss for $50.

There are versions of the original CBBS written in other programming languages; most notably, RBBS (written in C, another version in BASIC, another in Pascal). However the bulletin board system now used by the large groups (FOG, PicoNet and others) is Heavy Metal.

When you log into most RCP/M systems, you are put into the bulletin board messaging program. You may see something like the following:

```
Metal Message System..(A Heavy BBS)
Version 3.0b

You are caller 3435 (User #699).
High message is 749.
There are 142 active messages.
```

```
        Last message read was 735.

        [Checking for msgs]
        Sorry, no mail.

        (? or HELP for help) Command:
```

This may seem confusing at first, but after a while you will understand it. In this example we are the 3,435th caller since it started, and we are registered as user #699. Messages are numbered, with the highest numbered message the most recent. There are plenty of private messages (from 1 to 749), but there are only 142 active messages at this time, and the last message we read was message number 735.

We can read messages starting with number 735 by typing this command:

```
        (? or HELP for help) Command:RP ⊃
```

This command starts displaying the message with a number higher than the last message we read (735). A summary of the message is displayed, with the following prompt:

```
        [Read/y/n/r/q]
```

```
Functions supported:

B or BULLETIN   - )  Read the Bulletin file.
BYE             - )  Log-off without comment option.
C or CPM        - )  Go to RCP/M (Remote CP/M).
CH or CHAT      - )  Ring the bell to talk to the sysop (SYStem
                     OPerator).
E or ENTER      - )  Leave a message for another user (or all users).
EX or EXPERT    - )  Changes status from novice to expert user.
G or GOODBYE    - )  Log-off with option to return or leave comment (new
                     users should use this).
```

H or **HELP**   –) Display this listing of system commands.

J or **JUMP**   –) Jump to RCP/M (Remote CP/M).

K or **KILL**   –) Kill (remove) a message addressed to you.

K or Control-K –) Skip the remaining text display.

M or **MESSAGES** –) Gets list of messages addressed to you.

O or **OTHERSYS** –) Gets a listing of the other RBBS or RCP/M systems
which are part of the FOG network.

Q or **QUICKSUM** –) Gives a listing of message subjects. You are
prompted for the starting number.

R or **READ**   –) Read message(s). You are prompted for a message
number.

REP or **REPLY**   –) Reply to the message you just read.

RP   –) Scan all new non-private messages starting with
the highest message number you last read (from your
last call). THIS IS BEST COMMAND TO USE FOR READING
NEW MESSAGES!!!

RS   –) Read messages in ascending order starting with the
message number you specify.

RR   –) Read messages in reverse order, starting with the
latest message on the system.

S or **SUMMARY**   –) Summary of messages, including date and author.
You will be prompted for starting number.

U or **USERPARAMS** –) Allows you to change your password. You should do
this if your password has been in anyway
compromised.

W or **WELCOME**   –) Display the initial sign-on message. This is great
if you want to save a copy to disk so you can print
it out after logging off.

Y or **YELL**   –) Just like CHAT, this allows you to ask for assistance from the sysop.

X or **XPERT**   –) Changes status from novice to expert user. Save for
next call with U.

\#   –) List message status. This repeats information
about the number of callers and messages.

?   –) Help. Displays this list.

Figure 3-2. *The Metal Bulletin Board System commands.*

RBBS Functions Supported:

S —〉 Scan messages	R —〉 Retrieve messages
E —〉 Enter messages	K —〉 Kill messages
B —〉 Retype Bulletins	W —〉 Retype Information
C —〉 Enter CP/M	U —〉 List Users
T —〉 Toggle Bell	X —〉 Expert User tgl
P —〉 Change Password	G —〉 Goodbye (Exit)

Commands may be strung together, separated by semicolons. For example 'R;123' would retrieve message number 123.

Figure 3-3. *The command summary from the public domain RBBS program.*

Type y (or Y) to read the message, n (or N) to skip to the next message, r (or R) to reply to a message, or q (or Q) to quit this function. Eventually if you read every message, or quit, you come back to this command line:

(? or HELP for help) Command:

For a summary of the bulletin board system commands, type a question mark (?) or the word HELP followed by Return. Figure 3-2 shows a summary of Metal BBS commands, and Figure 3-3 shows a summary of the older BBS commands.

Reading Messages

When you log into an RCP/M BBS, you can go directly into CP/M and download software. However, you should take the time to first scan the messages left on the electronic bulletin board. Often the messages are the best source of information about public domain software.

There are many ways to read messages in the Metal BBS, as shown in the summary of Metal BBS commands. To see what the messages are about, the quickest method is to use the Q (QUICKSUM) command. Type Q and the BBS asks for the starting message number. Type the number and press Return, and the BBS should list the message subjects on the screen.

To see more than just the subjects, use the S (SUMMARY) command. This displays the date and author as well as the subject of each message. Figure 3-4 shows a sample summary listing of messages on the FOG BBS.

Enter the Message number of the first message you wish to start scanning at. You will be given a list of msgs from that number to the last message.

Msg # to start at (146-1309) ?**1142** ⤶

```
1142 08/02/84 From: DAVID WRIGHT To: ALL USERS : (12) TURBO PASCAL BBS
1144 08/02/84 From: BOND SHANDS To: ALL USERS : (18) A NEW FOG BOARD
1148 08/03/84 From: MICHAEL STIGALL To: ALL USERS : (11) DIAL.COM for COM
1156 08/04/84 From: THOMAS J. LATHE To: ALL USERS : (4) BBS in the Southe
1159 08/04/84 From: DAVID GIUNTI To: STEVE ASHLEY : (16) DEC MODEM PROGRAM
1165 08/04/84 From: ROY ROBINSON To: ALL USERS : (30) New RCP/M Command
1167 08/05/84 From: BOB HERRIN To: ALL USERS : (5) Southeast BBS
1180 08/06/84 From: GALE RHOADES To: THOMAS J. LATHE : (6) Comm-Pac 1200
1186 08/07/84 From: GALE RHOADES To: ALL USERS : (24) Osborne Moving Sale
1188 08/07/84 From: GALE RHOADES To: T. J. LATHE : (4) Uploading
1194 08/08/84 From: NEAL SCHINSKE To: ALL USERS : (5) IBM FILE TRANSFER
1197 08/09/84 From: JONATHAN OWENS To: ALL USERS : (7) rbbs in utah
1229 08/15/84 From: JOEL SEBER To: ALL USERS : (10) Cookeville RIBBS
[more] ⤶
1231 08/15/84 From: DAVID KEMP To: ALL USERS : (9) Osborne External Monit
1232 08/16/84 From: GENE KITAMATA To: ALL USERS : (6) COMPUTER GAME
  .
  .
  .
1299 08/24/84 From: GALE RHOADES To: ALL USERS : (10) Diablo 630 for sale
1309 08/25/84 From: JOHAN MOKHTAR To: ALL USERS : (14) disk drives
[End Msgs]

(? or HELP for help) Command:
```

Figure 3-4. *A summary of the current messages on the FOG bulletin board system. The messages are the best source of information about public domain software.*

The public domain RBBS program does not have the Q command, but it does have the S command. To read a message in either Metal or the public domain RBBS, use the R command. In both systems you have to remember the message number of the message you want to read, and supply the message number after typing the R command.

In both systems you can also type the message number in the command following a semicolon. For example, to read message #281, you can type R;231⊃.

The Metal BBS provides other reading commands to make it easier for callers to read only the messages they haven't read before. The RP command starts with the first message you haven't yet read, presenting each message summary with a prompt:

```
Msg #1341 posted 08/28/84 by GENE KITAMATA
To: TONY BOVE ‹Priv› About: MESSAGE #1324 NEW BOOK (9 lines)


[Read y/n/r/q]
```

This prompt asks if you want to read the message (type Y or y), skip over it to the next message (type N or n), reply to this message (type R or r), or quit this command (type Q or q).

The RS command starts with any message you select, presenting each message summary in the same fashion as RP. The R command bypasses the prompt and presents the entire text of the message.

Replying To Messages

After reading the message, you have the option to reply. Here is a partial message and reply:

```
DEAR TONY, THE NEW BOOK SOUNDS VERY GOOD!
THE INFORMATION WILL BE VERY HELPFUL TO
MANY OF US! I WOULD VERY MUCH LIKE TO
HELP IN ANY WAY AS FAR AS REVIEWING INFO.
I AM A NEW FOG MEMBER BUT A LONG TIME
```

```
USER OF THE OSBORNE... LET ME KNOW
IF YOU CAN USE MY HELP.


.......GENE KITAMATA...................

[Reply to this msg?]y
Message # will be 1354
To: GENE KITAMATA
About: MESSAGE #1324 NEW BOOK
(Private/Normal) ?p ⊃
Enter text following each line number.
To edit or end, hit RETURN alone on a line.
Up to 80 chars on a line, and 100 lines

1: Thanks for helping out! We'll message you on this FOG network ⊃
2: when we have the m.s. ready for reviewing. ⊃
3: Thanks again — Tony Bove. ⊃
4: ⊃


(A)bort, (C)ontinue, (D)elete, (E)dit,
(I)nsert, (L)ist, (S)ave :: Select ?s
```

We selected a "private" reply to the message, so that only the author of the original message (the one receiving the reply) can read and delete the message. A "normal" message is one anyone can read, even if the message is to someone else; however, only the receiver or author of a message can "kill" (delete) the message.

We typed a reply as shown above, then pressed Return on a line by itself to stop the reply. The BBS then asks us to do one of the following: abort the reply, continue typing a reply, delete what was typed, edit what was typed, insert something into the reply, list the entire reply on the screen for easy reading, or save the reply. We want to save the reply, which posts it on the bulletin board, so we type s (or S), and the following appears on our screen:

```
[Saving]
[Kill Message you've just replied to?]
```

The Metal BBS lets you delete the message you are replying to, in order to save space on the BBS disks. Type y or Y to delete the message:

```
[Kill Message you've just replied to?]y
Msg #1341 Entered 08/28/84
From GENE KITAMATA
To TONY BOVE (Priv)
About: MESSAGE #1324 NEW BOOK (9)
Confirm?y
[Deleting]
```

As you can see in the example, Metal BBS asks you to confirm first before actually deleting the message.

Sending Messages

In addition to replying to messages, you can send messages using the E (Enter message) command, which displays the following:

```
Message # will be 1354
To:Gale Rhoades ⊃
About:Free Software Book ⊃
(Private/Normal) ?p ⊃
Enter text following each line number.
To edit or end, hit RETURN alone on a line.
Up to 80 chars on a line, and 100 lines


1: Dear Gale, ⊃
2: The manuscript is ready for reviewing. We would like to ⊃
3: put sections of it on the FOG BBS for reviewers to retrieve ⊃
4: copies. Let us know which drive/user area. Thanks – Tony ⊃
5: ⊃


(A)bort, (C)ontinue, (D)elete, (E)dit,
(I)nsert, (L)ist, (S)ave :: Select ?s
```

We selected a "private" message, so that only the receiver can read the message. A "normal" message is one anyone can read, even if the message is to someone else; however, only the receiver or author of a message can "kill" (delete) the message.

We typed a message as shown above, then pressed Return on a line by itself to stop the reply. The BBS then asks us to do one of the following: abort the message, continue typing a message, delete what was typed, edit what was typed, insert something into the message, list the entire message on the screen for easy reading, or save the message. We want to save the message, which posts it on the bulletin board, so we type s (or S), and the following appears on our screen:

```
[Saving]
```

The message will stay on the bulletin board for a period of time controlled by the sysop, or until you or the recipient deletes the message. "Normal" (i.e., not private) messages can be deleted by anyone reading them.

Jumping Into CP/M

Some RCP/M bulletin board systems will not let you past the bulletin board unless you "join the club." Sometimes this means membership dues. FOG systems let non-members enter CP/M without paying any dues, but you first have to mail a registration card to FOG headquarters — see Appendix C for the FOG address.

If you have permission to jump into CP/M, you can do so with two commands in Heavy Metal, or one command in RBBS. This is the one command common to both:

```
(? or HELP for help) Command: CPM ⏎
```

In both bulletin board systems, you are then allowed to leave a special comment for the sysop:

Wish to leave comments (y/n/r/?) ?

If you answer with a **Y** or **y**, you can leave the message as you would leave a bulletin board message, and when you finish the welcome message appears. If you answer with an **N** or **n**, the welcome message appears immediately.

The Welcome Message

Read the welcome message carefully. It should tell you exactly how to find files in the various directories and libraries of the BBS disks. If you are using a communications program that can "capture" (or "log") the data on the screen to a disk file on your system, use that function to capture the welcome message so that you can refer to it again.

The following welcome message is from the FOG RCP/M BBS in Daly City, CA (thanks to Gale Rhoades, sysop):

Welcome to the First Osborne Group RCP/M #1

This is system operates almost like the computer your are sitting at. The largest difference is that this system is much larger than most Osborne systems. It is made possible by the addition of a TRANTOR 33 megabyte hard disk subsystem.

This system operates 24 hours a day, except for maintenance. It accepts both 300 and 1200 baud calls. All callers MUST use 8 bit, no parity in order to use this system.

There are also some minor changes to stop deliberate system crashing. You will not notice most of these changes.

If at anytime you are in need of assistance, you may either type:

HELP ⊃
(the ⊃ stands for your Return key.)

This will give you several listing for assistance.

If the sysop (SYStem OPerator) is available, you may ask for personal assistance by typing:

CHAT ⏎

To see what programs are on this system, type:

DIR *.* $UOADL ⏎

To disconnect from this system, type:

BYE ⏎

To move around this system, use the SECTION command. Type:

SECTION ? ⏎

for a list of available areas. Type:

SECTION name.typ ⏎

to move to a specific area. For example, if you wish to move to the public area with the utility files, type:

SECTION UTILITY.PUB ⏎

Please remember that access time on this system is one hour (60 minutes). Repeated abusers will have their access restricted.

– Gale Rhoades, sysop
First Osborne Group, System #1

[Entering CP/M]
A0⟩

You are now using the far-away CP/M system as if it were

your own. You are accessing the directories of the BBS disks, not your own disks (unless you are switching back and forth from your system to the RCP/M system using your communications program).

Disks, User Areas, Sections

The A0⟩ prompt (other RCP/M systems may use A⟩ or 0A⟩) is a variation of the CP/M prompt that shows the *user area* as well as the disk drive. You are automatically "logged in" to the disk in drive A, in user area 0 of the disk drive. There are sixteen possible user areas in one disk drive, with up to 16 disks available on some systems.

You can type the DIR command to see what files are on drive A in user area zero, or you can move to other user areas and other drives. However, if this is your first time, you can be easily overwhelmed by the sheer number of files, many with similar names. Some systems allow access to 2000+ files!

The FOG system is organized into sections, and you can display the various sections with the SECTION command:

```
A0⟩section ⤶
```

This command displays the following in the FOG system:

```
Available sections are:
        HELP.PUB        NOTICES.PUB        NOTICES.MFG
        NOTICES.FOG     NOTICES.AMO        NOTICES.LIB
        NOTICES.SYS     APPLIC.PUB         EXEC.PUB
        GAMES.PUB       HACKER.PUB         KAYPRO.PUB
        LANG.PUB        LIBRARY.FOG        LOBOMAX.PUB
        MICROMA.PUB     MISC.PUB           MORROW.PUB
        NOVICES.PUB     OSBORN1.PUB        UTILITY.PUB
        ZORBA.PUB       APPLIC.FOG         EXEC.FOG
        GAMES.FOG       HACKER.FOG         KAYPRO.FOG
        LANG.FOG        LOBOMAX.FOG        MICROMA.FOG
        MISC.FOG        MORROW.FOG         NOVICES.FOG
```

OSBORN1.FOG   UTILITY.FOG   ZORBA.FOG

To log into a specific section, you type the following command:

AO>SECTION sectname.ext ⊃

This command changes the prompt to another drive and user area — the drive and user area named by the section name (sectname.ext). For example, to log into section called NOVICES.PUB, you would type this command:

AO>SECTION NOVICES.PUB ⊃

To see an explanation of each section, type this version of the SECTION command:

AO>SECTION ? ⊃

Available sections are:

```
HELP.PUB......System HELP files
NOTICES.PUB...TEXT files - User sharing
NOTICES.MFG...TEXT files - About manufacturers
NOTICES.FOG...TEXT files - FOG members only
NOTICES.AMO...TEXT files - AMO officers only
NOTICES.LIB...TEXT files - FOG librarians only
NOTICES.SYS...TEXT files - FOG SYSOPs only
APPLIC.PUB....Open to all users
EXEC.PUB......Open to all users
GAMES.PUB.....Open to all users
HACKER.PUB....Open to all users
KAYPRO.PUB....Open to all users
LANG.PUB......Open to all users
LIBRARY.FOG...-FOG library listings - open to all
LOBOMAX.PUB...Open to all users
MICROMA.PUB...Open to all users
MISC.PUB......Open to all users
MORROW.PUB....Open to all users
```

```
NOVICES.PUB...FOR NEW USERS - Open to all users
OSBORN1.PUB...Open to all users
UTILITY.PUB...Open to all users
ZORBA.PUB.....Open to all users
APPLIC.FOG....-FOG/APP library disks
EXEC.FOG.......-FOG/EX1 library disks
GAMES.FOG.....-FOG/GAM library disks
HACKER.FOG....-FOG/HAK library disks
KAYPRO.FOG....-FOG/KAY library disks
LANG.FOG......-FOG/LNG library disks
LOBOMAX.FOG...-FOG/MAX library disks
MICROMA.FOG...-FOG/PMC library disks
MISC.FOG......-FOG/MIS library disks
MORROW.FOG....-FOG/MMD library disks
NOVICES.FOG...Special for new FOG users
OSBORN1.FOG...-FOG/OS1 library disks
UTILITY.FOG...-FOG/UTL library disks
ZORBA.FOG.....-FOG/ZOR library disks

A0>
```

You can use the DIR command (type DIR ⊃) to see a directory listing of the disk drive and user area you are currently accessing. The built-in CP/M commands ERA, SAVE and REN are not provided in RCP/M systems (to prevent someone from accidentally or purposely "crashing" the system).

You can see the directories of other drives and user areas by typing the DIR command followed by the name of another drive. For example, to see the directory of user area 0 of drive B, type:

```
A0>DIR B: ⊃
```

There are usually four to eight logical disk drives (A:, B:, C:, D:, E:, F:, G: and H:), with sixteen possible user areas in use on each disk drive: user areas 0 to 15 (only a few user areas are supported in some bulletin board systems).

Some RCP/M systems let you move from one drive to another *and* from one user area to another in the same step by typing the drive letter, followed by a space, followed by the user number:

```
AO)B: 2 ↵
B2)
```

This command moves you to drive B, user area 2. If the BBS you are calling does not allow this, try the reliable two-step method. First change the drive:

```
AO)B: ↵
BO)
```

Then type the USER command to change to a different user area:

```
BO)USER 2 ↵
B2)
```

If you're new to this, it is much easier to use the SECTION command described above to go to a drive/user area. The sections make it easier to find files of interest.

Finding Files of Interest

Perhaps the hardest part of getting public domain software is knowing the names of the files you want. Systems that are organized into sections make it easier because they help you narrow down your search. However, there are many RCP/M systems that are not organized into sections.

So how do you find the programs you want? If you know the approximate name of the file, you can use the FILE command (called FILEFIND or FIND on some systems). The following FILE command looks for all files whose names start with "MDM":

```
AO)FILE MDM*.* ↵
FILE version 21a - ^X to abort
```

```
searching...

D7:MDM730    .DOC  FO:MDM720    .LBR  FO:MDMNUM     .OBJ
FO:MDM712    .DQC  FO:MDM712    .IQF  FO:MDM712     .OBJ
FO:MDM712    .AQM
```

The FILE command (a public domain program written by R. Rodman and Dave Hardy) will look *throughout the entire system* (all drives and all user areas) for the filename or filename match (as we used above). These searches may take some time, so be patient! You can abort a search using Control-C or Control-X — some bulletin boards accept Control-C only, Control-X only, or both.

What's New

As you become familiar with the programs on the system, you may only be interested in new stuff — but the system is a blur of filenames! Depending on the RCP/M you call, you may find all new files in one section (drive/user area), or you may find that new files have been added to many different sections.

In those RCP/M systems where new stuff is added to the old stuff in different sections, you can usually find out what is new in a section by moving to that section (as shown above with the SECTION command, or by specifying the drive letter and user area number, or by using the LOG command as shown above), then typing the following command:

```
AO>WHATSNEW ⤶
WHATSNEW — First Osborne Group (FOG) RCP/M
CTL-S pauses, CTL-C aborts

—>New files:
D: -NOVICES.FOG ¦ WHATSNEW.COM ¦ DE-LBR    .DOC
D: DE-LBR    .OBJ ¦ DU-V86    .DOC ¦ DU-V86    .OBJ
D: LSWEEP    .DOC ¦ LSWEEP    .OBJ ¦ LU300     .DOC
```

```
D: LU300    .OBJ | LUHELP  .DOC | MDM730  .DOC
D: NSWP205 .OBJ | TYPEL    .OBJ | UNERA   .DOC
D: UNERA .OBJ | NSWP205 .DOC | DSKLABL2.AQM
D:

-)Deleted files:
D: ++NONE++
```

The WHATSNEW command is another public domain program, this one written by Dave Hardy (Technical CBBS). It displays all new files (with the date each was added to the system), as well as old files that were deleted.

Library Files and Disk Libraries

Some RCP/M systems (such as the FOG RCP/M) organize the public domain software into *disk libraries*. A disk library is simply a section (drive/user area) that contains a lot of public domain software of the same "type" (for example, the most useful utility programs are in the UTILITY.PUB section).

Do not confuse these "library disks" (which are arbitrarily called "libraries") with *library files*, which are stored on these library disks and other disks.

A *library file* is a file with the extension ".LBR". It is a file that contains files. To see what files are contained in a library file, you can use the LDIR command specifying the name of the library (you can omit the ".LBR" extension of the library name MDM720.LBR):

```
B2)LDIR MDM720 ⊃

Library DIRectory Ver:2.20 83-10-13
Press CTRL-S to pause; CTRL-C to cancel

Library: MDM720.LBR has 8 entries, 3 free:
MDM720.AQM   104k    MDM720.COM    18k
MDM720.MQG     5k    M7NM-5.AQM     4k
```

```
Active entries: 5, Deleted: 0, Free: 3, Total: 8.
```

This command displays the filenames of the files located inside
the MDM720.LBR library file (this is the library file holding the
version of Modem7 described in Chapter 4).

LDIR (version 2.0, written by Sigi Kleuger, ESKAY) is one of
many library file utilities described in the chapter on using LU,
the Library Utility. LU is the program you would use to create a
library file as well as extract files from libraries. LU and related
programs are shown in detail in Chapter 6.

If LDIR is not available, it is probably replaced by a souped-up
version of the DIR command that displays all filenames including
the names in library files. You can use this variation of the DIR
command:

```
B2>DIR $L ⏎
```

This command displays the filenames of all files in all libraries
on the current disk and in the current user area.

Another way to see the files inside a specific library file is to
use the TYPEL command:

```
B2>TYPEL MDM720.LBR ⏎
```

The TYPEL command may be renamed to TYPE on the BBS
you are using.

DIR Options

RCP/M systems have a souped-up version of the DIR command that displays the filenames of files on all drives and all user
areas to which you have permission to access:

```
A0>DIR *.* $UOADL ⏎
```

The $UOADL options tell DIR to display all user areas of all disk
drives, starting with drive A, user area 0, showing also the files

residing within library files.

To find a specific file or set of files, substitute the filename or filename match for *.* in the above DIR command.

Displaying The Contents of Files

Sometimes you will have no idea what a file contains, and you'll want to display its contents. The best way to find out about a program is to find a ".DOC" or ".DQC" file with the same primary name; for example, MDM720.DOC describes the MDM720 program, which is in the file MDM720.OBJ. On most bulletin board systems you can use the TYPE command to display MDM720.DOC as shown:

```
B2)TYPE MDM720.DOC ⤸
```

In some sections of a well-organized BBS you may find a file with the name READ-ME.DOC or READ.ME or HOWTO.USE or similar name. The file usually contains information about the programs on the disk. You can display this file by typing:

```
A0)TYPE HOWTO.USE ⤸
```

The HOWTO.USE or READ.ME file should explain what is in that particular section, or what to download from a particular section.

There are a variety of TYPE programs on RCP/M systems. The one you are using may scroll the text fast on the screen; if so, type Control-S as a "toggle-switch" to start and stop the scrolling on your screen. Other TYPE programs require that you press Return after each screenful of text.

If you want to look at the contents of a file, check its filename extension (the last three characters after the period, if any) before using the TYPE command. If the filename extension is one of the following, you can probably use the TYPE command to see its contents:

name.ASM (source prg.)
name.AQM (squeezed source prg.)
name.BAS (BASIC source program)
name.BQS (squeezed BASIC source program)
name.C (source program written in C)
name.CQ (squeezed C source program)
name.DOC (documentation)
name.DQC (squeezed documentation)
name.FOR (source program written in Fortran)
name.FQR (squeezed Fortran source program)
name.INF (information file)
name.IQF (squeezed information file)
name.LST (lists or listings)
name.LQT (squeezed list or listing)
name.MAC (source macroassembler file)
name.MQC (squeezed macroassembler file)
name.MSG (message file)
name.MQG (squeezed message file)
name.PAS (Pascal source program)
name.PQS (squeezed Pascal source program)
name.TXT (text file)
name.TQT (squeezed text file)
name.USE (user's guide)
name.UQE (squeezed user's guide)

Many files on RCP/M systems are *squeezed* into a special format that takes up less space on the disk. This is particularly true of long text files and program "source" files. If the file is squeezed, you won't be able to view its contents with your own CP/M or MS-DOS TYPE command, although you will be able to use the souped-up TYPE program on the BBS to display it. If the BBS you called does not display squeezed files using TYPE, substitute TYPESQ or TYPEL for the command TYPE and try it again. Chapter 5 explains squeezed files in detail and shows you how to unsqueeze them for use with your computer.

How do you tell if a file is squeezed? *All* squeezed files should have a "Q" in the middle of the filename extension. The extensions shown above are not the only extensions for squeezed files, but they are the usual ones for squeezed files that can be displayed with the TYPE, TYPEL or TYPESQ programs. Any file can be squeezed, including files that do not contain text (ASCII data); however, only textual (ASCII) files can be displayed with TYPE, TYPESQ or TYPEL.

Receiving Files From a BBS

There are two ways to receive data over the telephone using a modem program:

1.   Use the Xmodem/Modem7 protocol. This protocol (known also as the Christensen protocol and described in Chapter 4) is available with most communications programs including Modem7. The protocol detects any errors in transmission, and re-transmits data when it finds errors. The result is that you receive an exact duplicate of the file. You can transfer *any* CP/M or MS-DOS file using this protocol.

2.   Capture data as it appears on your screen and store it in a disk file. This method works only with text (ASCII) files (documents, program "source" files, etc.) and cannot be used to receive public domain programs that are ready to use (you cannot receive ".COM" or ".OBJ" files or any non-text files in this manner). The result may not be an exact duplicate.

The second method above does not provide any error detection in the transmission. Random "glitches" in the telephone connection (which are quite common in both long distance and local calls involving data communications) can cause mistakes in the transmission that can actually change characters of data.

NOTE
One way to test for errors is to perform a CRC check on the original file and the copy you received. The CRCK program is described in detail in Chapter 7.

To receive a program or file and be sure of its accuracy, you need to use the first method described above. Unfortunately, modem programs available for CP/M systems do not adhere to one standard, and their protocols for error detection and re-transmission are not compatible. This means that you must use the same modem program on both ends, or at least versions that use the same protocols.

Most (if not all) RCP/M systems can use the Xmodem/Modem7 protocol. Some have additional programs using other protocols, such as the Crosstalk and COMMX protocols.

The version of Modem7 used by the BBS is called Xmodem ("external modem"). This special version is used only to handle outside callers — you should use Modem7 or an equivalent communications program (as described in Chapter 2) to call the BBS.

Using Xmodem To Download

Once you are connected to the RCP/M and you've found the files you want to download, you can use Xmodem and your communications program to start receiving the files. You should first move to the section (drive/user area) that contains the programs to be downloaded. You should probably type the DIR command first to be sure of the spelling of the filename.

Before typing the Xmodem command and the rest of the examples here, read this entire subsection on using Xmodem to download. The commands you type have to be typed rapidly, because the Xmodem program waits only thirty seconds for you to prepare your communication program for downloading.

The two steps for downloading a program are (1) use Xmodem to tell the BBS to send the file, and (2) set up your communications program to receive the file. Xmodem will not work in "batch mode", which means you can transfer only one file at a time.

Step one is using Xmodem to send the file to your system:

```
B2>XMODEM S MDM720.DQC ⌐
```

```
XMODEM v9.0
File open: 309 records
Send time: 6 mins, 26 secs at 1200 bps
To cancel: use CTRL-X
```

The Xmodem program starts up by displaying some vital information. First it tells you what version of Xmodem you are using, then it tells you the size of the file in "blocks" in both decimal and hexadecimal numbers (one block is approximately 128 characters). Finally it tells you how many hours, minutes, and seconds the file will take to send at your currently logged in baud rate. It will then wait for you to accomplish step 2, or it will "time out" and stop in thirty seconds.

The Xmodem command sends the entire file. You can send an entire library file to your computer, then use LU or similar utility on your computer to extract files from the library. This is the most efficient way of downloading public domain software.

It is possible, however, to download a file from within a library file without downloading the entire library. For example, we use this version of the Xmodem command with the library file MDM720.LBR (you can omit the ".LBR" extension as shown), and the specific filename MDM720.DQC which resides in the MDM720 library:

```
B2>XMODEM L MDM720 MDM720.DQC ⊃
```

Step two is to prepare your communication program to receive the file. This step will vary from communication program to another, but in most programs, you have to leave terminal mode and request an Xmodem file transfer.

For example, in COMMX you type a Control-E to leave terminal mode, and then select C from its menu of operations (Copy from Xmodem). Then you type N to the question about batch mode (Xmodem does not work with Modem7's or COMMX's batch mode), and supply a filename for the file you will receive (the filename will be used to store the file on your computer's disk).

If you're using a version of Modem7 (such as MDM741), type

a Control-E to leave terminal mode (Control-O in Smodem7, or the Escape key in some versions). When you leave terminal mode, you should have a menu on your screen. You can then type a command like this to receive the file MDM740.DQC and store it on drive B:

COMMAND? RT B:MDM720.DQC ⤸

In this command, R specifies receive mode, and T tells Modem7 to return to terminal mode when the transfer is done. You can leave out the disk drive to specify a file to be stored on the current disk.

If you did everything correctly, you should see something like this on your screen:

AWAITING #1
AWAITING #2
.
.
.

This tells you that your communication program is waiting for the next "block" or "record" of data. Your program receives the file one block or *record* at a time (a record is 128 characters).

When the transfer is complete, Modem7 returns to terminal mode. Press a Return to "wake up" the BBS, and you can use Xmodem again to download another file.

Some versions of Modem7 do not allow the T in the RT command. In that case, use the R command as shown in this example in which the copy received is to be named MDM720.DQC and stored on drive B:

COMMAND? R B:MDM720.DQC ⤸
AWAITING #01
AWAITING #02

If your version of Modem7 does not have a menu, leave terminal mode with a Control-E and type the following command from

CP/M:

```
A>MODEM7 R B:MDM720.DQC ⏎
AWAITING #01
AWAITING #02
```

The R command sets up your Modem7 program to receive the file that Xmodem is waiting to send to your system. It may take up to 15 seconds, during which time your Modem7 program may display messages like AWAITING 01 and TIMEOUT. Once communication is firmly established, Xmodem sends blocks of the file to Modem7.

When you see the message TRANSFER COMPLETE (this may take a long time depending on the size of the file), you can return to the Modem7 start-up menu with a Control-E command.

You must get back to the RCP/M system A0> prompt before the RCP/M system detects no one on the other end and automatically disconnects the call. To do this, return to terminal mode by selecting T in menu version of Modem7:

```
A0>>COMMAND: T ⏎
```

In the non-menu version, you must type the Modem7 command with the T option:

```
A>MODEM7 T ⏎
```

Immediately after entering terminal mode, type at least one Return to get the RCP/M system A0> prompt. This tells the RCP/M system that you are still connected.

Receiving With Xon/Xoff

Modem7, COMMX, RCPMLINK, PLINK and other modem programs let you "capture" (or "log") data as it appears on your screen. This includes your keystrokes as well as what is displayed by the BBS or host computer.

The communication programs hold the data in memory and then stores it in a file on a disk in your computer. Before storing the data on disk, however, the communication program must send the ASCII Xoff character (Control-S) to stop the BBS from sending more data; otherwise, new data would be lost while the communication program is busy storing earlier data on disk. As soon as the communication program is ready to receive more, it must send the Xon character (Control-Q).

The Xon/Xoff is a simple protocol that does no error checking — it is *not* a substitute for the Modem7/Xmodem (Christensen) protocol. It is simply there to prevent loss of data during transmission.

You can send the Xoff character from your keyboard by typing Control-S. This is how you can stop the scrolling of lengthy displays.

Most communication programs have Xon/Xoff built into their "send a file" and "receive a file" options — you don't have to type them. You select the option to receive a file or to capture the data, and the program performs the Xon/Xoff when it needs to store to disk.

For example, if you are using COMMX in terminal mode, and you want to start capturing the stuff that will appear on the screen, you would type a Control-E to leave terminal mode, and select the Create a LOG file option (option 8). Then you return to terminal mode and continue using the BBS. Everything typed or displayed from this point on is captured in memory until you type another Control-E.

You can then select another file for another "logging" operation. This allows you to copy only selected portions of your dialog with the BBS, or portions of a file.

Other communication programs work in a similar fashion. MITE has a Capture option from its main menu which works the same way.

Using Modem7 you type the T command for terminal mode and, at the same time, type the filename for the file to receive the data. If you are now in terminal mode talking to a BBS, use Control-E (Control-O or Escape key in some versions) to leave terminal mode and return to the Modem7 menu (or back to your

CP/M or MS-DOS command line in stripped-down versions without menus).

If your version of Modem7 has menus, the Control-E command will put you back in the start-up menu. From there type the following:

```
AO>>COMMAND: T B:SAMPLE.LOG ⏎
```

This command sets up the file SAMPLE.LOG on drive B to receive the data, then it puts you in terminal mode. If your version does not have menus, the Control-E command will put you back at your CP/M or MS-DOS command line. Type the following command:

```
A>MODEM7 T B:SAMPLE.LOG ⏎
```

Once in terminal mode, you have to cause the display of the data in order to capture it. You must be able to see it on your screen (using the TYPE or TYPESQ command, or program that displays data on the screen).

The "capturing" of the data does not start until you type Control-Y. Control-Y turns on the capturing of all displayed or typed characters. With some versions of Modem7 you see a colon (:) at the start of each line when "capture mode" is turned on. Type another Control-Y to turn *off* the capture operation. This allows you to copy only selected portions of your dialog with the BBS, or portions of a file.

There is one caveat: in most of the early versions of Modem7 you must explicitly type the WRT command from the menu after leaving terminal mode. This command performs the actual save to the disk file.

If you forget to type the WRT command, some versions of Modem7 will tell you to do it, and some versions will do it automatically. However, if you see no message telling you the data was written automatically, you will lose the audited data if you leave Modem7. We suggest that you experiment first before trying to save anything important; otherwise, do a WRT to save the data in the file before you leave Modem7.

You can alternatively select the RET option to return to terminal mode and capture more data, and *then* use WRT to write the data to the file.

The capturing or "logging" method of receiving data only works with text (ASCII) files whose contents can be seen on your screen or typed on your keyboard.

If your terminal is a slow printing terminal (or is slow for some other reason), you may encounter "over-run" errors if your terminal and computer cannot keep up with the data rate. If so, do not use the V (video) sub-option with Modem7, and you may have to use the Q (Quiet) sub-option. Read about Modem7 in Chapter 4.

Baud Rate and Calling Mode

The NEWBAUD program (written by Keith Petersen and Dave Hardy) is on some bulletin board systems to let you change your baud rate (the speed the data travels) during communication with the BBS.

You can't change your baud rate to a higher speed than your modem allows. Some inexpensive modems and acoustic couplers operate at a maximum speed of 300 baud, and so can only be changed to lower speeds of 200, 110, or 100 baud. Some more expensive models allow baud rates of 600, 1200, etc.

Most bulletin board systems can handle any baud rate from 60 to 1200. When you call a BBS and press your Return key a few times, the BBS automatically acquires your baud rate. If the BBS supports changing the baud rate (many don't), you can change the baud rate by typing the NEWBAUD command:

    AO>NEWBAUD ⏎

Now: change your modem's baud rate switch setting, return to terminal mode, press your Return key a few times, and the BBS should acquire the new baud rate. (NEWBAUD proved very helpful when we were trying to transfer files in a bad rainstorm using an acoustic coupler easily affected by line noise. We had very poor transmission at 300 baud, but were able to successfully transmit our files after lowering our baud rate to 100.)

You can also change your *calling mode* with some bulletin board systems to improve transmission. When you call a BBS, you are in *originate* mode and the BBS is in *answer* mode (you originated the call, and the RCP/M system answered to allow you to use the system).

On those few bulletin boards that support this, you can improve the transmission by flipping these modes so that you are in *answer* mode and the BBS is in *originate* mode. To flip the modes, type the FLIP command (the FLIP program was written by Bruce Ratoff):

    AO)FLIP ↵

After flipping the modes, start your transfer operation within 15 seconds or the BBS will decide that you have hung up.

NEWBAUD and FLIP are supported mostly on bulletin boards that use the PMMI modem connected to an S-100 computer system.

Logging Off

To leave a BBS, simply type this command from any drive or user area:

    AO)BYE ↵

You can also leave the BBS by selecting the G option (for "goodbye"). You don't have to do this, but it helps make the BBS ready for the next caller. If you somehow lose communication with the BBS, either through equipment failure, carrier failure on the line, or other reason, the BBS waits for about fifteen seconds for you to respond, then it hangs up and waits for the next caller.

This operation is controlled by the BYE program, of which there are several versions (one original version written by Ward Christensen, another original version by Kelly Smith). BYE is available in the public domain for anyone who wants to set up a system that can answer the phone and provide access to CP/M.

The Most Up-to-date Libraries

RCP/M bulletin board systems like the FOG RCP/M, PicoNet and many others can provide most if not all and more of the collected works in the public domain, including the CPMUG (CP/M User's Group) as well as the SIG/M user's group volumes of public domain CP/M programs.

The programs contributed directly to RCP/M systems are eventually submitted to SIG/M, FOG and other groups through the group's librarians who operate "clearing house" bulletin boards for receiving new public domain software. The sysops access the clearinghouses on a regular basis for the newest programs and updates. This is why the RCP/M bulletin boards have the most up-to-date information and the newest public domain programs.

Why do sysops create and maintain such systems at their own expense of time and money? Many have the conviction that public domain software should be as free to users as possible. Most feel that telecomputing (using telephone lines or other computerized communications media to distribute software) has evolved to the point where all home computerists can and should participate. Sysops probably do it for their own enjoyment and education.

Anyone interested in public domain software, CP/M systems and computerized bulletin board systems will find RCP/M bulletin board systems fun and rewarding. Those interested in helping to form new de-centralized computer-user communities will see them as a giant step forward in the evolution of the information age.

CHAPTER 4:
USING MODEM7

Modem7 is one of the most popular programs in the public domain, and with hundreds of versions, it may be the most revised program in the history of software.

Modem7 controls the serial port of your computer (port to which you can attach a cable to a modem or to another computer) so that you can send data from one computer to another. The most recent versions of Modem7 can also control a modem and originate calls, answer calls, and change baud rates and other settings.

Modem7 is widely known as the key to getting public domain software from bulletin board systems. Modem7 lets you transfer programs and data files from the bulletin board to your computer with accuracy checking. It also lets you connect two computers directly by cable (without modems) and transfer data between them with accuracy checking.

All versions of Modem7 were derived from the original MODEM.ASM program written by Ward Christensen, founder of the Chicago area CACHE user's group, and an organizer of the CP/MUG libraries. Ward revised it into Modem4, and others revised it into Modem7. Soon there were thousands of versions of Modem4 and Modem7 on the bulletin board systems. Some were designed specifically for modems such as the Hayes Smartmodem (Smodem4, Smodem7), others were designed for other modems. The "vanilla" version of Modem7 was designed to run on any S-100 computer with the PMMI modem board. (PMMI, or Potomac Micro-Magic, is now out of business, but you can get working PMMI modems at flea markets). Every hobbyist with a knack for modem control tried to revise the program and add new functions.

Some of the unsung heroes of personal computing were involved in the evolution of Modem7. Ward Christensen, a prolific donor to the public domain (CBBS, BYE, DU, SD and many others), wrote the first versions. Kelly Smith, Dave Hardy, Keith Petersen, Ben Bronson and Bruce Ratoff were all involved in its evolution. The later versions were put together by Mark Zeiger and Jim Mills. The most recent versions (the MDM series) were written by Irv Hoff.

Revisions and modifications (mostly to accommodate new features, different computers and different modems) soon caused a nomenclature problem. As versions proliferated among the bulletin boards and libraries, Modem701 evolved into Modem798 (available in SIG/M volume 94 — see Appendix D). For a while different versions were made for specific computers and modems, causing a lot of confusion and occupying a lot of space on disks and bulletin boards.

Irv Hoff changed Modem7 so that the specific information for each computer and modem was isolated in separate files called "overlays". You pick the overlays you need for your particular configuration, and merge it with the main part of Modem7 to make a customized version.

To differentiate the re-organized Modem7 from the Modem798 series, he called it MDM700. Although the MDM series has of this writing advanced to MDM740 (version 7.4), the SIG/M library has caught up only to MDM712 (version 7.12, available in SIG/M volume 139), and the FOG library has MDM720. Also, customized versions are available from FOG and other sources. By the time you read this, MDM740 should be available in all libraries.

During the evolution of Modem7, Xmodem was created. Xmodem runs on the bulletin board system and controls downloading and uploading so that no one can upload a dangerous program to the BBS and "crash" it. Xmodem is limited to single-file transfers (no "batch mode"), but it can download a file residing within a library file (something Modem7 cannot do). Xmodem is designed to be used from a remote system.

There are many versions of Modem7, but unless you have an S-100 computer that uses the PMMI circuit-board modem, you have to find a customized version, or customize one yourself, to run on your computer with your modem. We describe how to do that in this chapter.

How To Get Modem7

You don't have to get the actual Modem7 program to have the Xmodem/Modem7 protocol. Some communications programs implement this protocol because it is a recognized standard. For example, If you have an IBM PC, you can get PC-Talk III directly from Headlands Press (Chapter 2). This program uses the same protocol as Modem7. COMMX, MITE, SUPRTERM, ENVOY and even the latest version of Crosstalk all support the Xmodem/Modem7 protocol and run on a variety of computers.

If you want Modem7 for your IBM PC, you can write to PC-SIG for a copy on an IBM PC disk (address in Appendix C). A program called MODEM.COM for the IBM PC is described briefly in this chapter, and another communications program called 1RD.COM is described briefly in Chapter 7. All are for the IBM PC.

If you have any Z80-based CP/M computer with the PMMI modem, you can use the "plain vanilla" version of Modem7. We suggest you try MDM720 or whatever newer version of this series you can find on your local BBS or user group.

If you have an Osborne, Kaypro, Morrow, PMC MicroMate, Televideo, Sanyo, Epson QX-10, Lobo MAX-80 or Zorba, you can write to FOG requesting the latest version of Modem7 on a disk for your computer (FOG address in Appendix C).

If you have any other type of CP/M system, you may need to customize a version of Modem7. There are many ways to do this, but you need at least a copy of the "plain vanilla" version, plus information about your computer and modem.

Since the program must be customized to work with your computer and modem, the best way to get a copy is to contact a local users group and find someone who at least has the same computer and possibly also has the same modem. No matter how many features are available in other versions of Modem7, you are ahead of the game if you can find a copy *that works for your computer.*

Of course you must get a version on disk, or use a communications program that uses the Xmodem/Modem7 protocol and download from a BBS a version of Modem7 and an appropriate overlay file. Some commercial programs mentioned in Chapter 2 could be used for downloading Modem7.

If you are nowhere near a user group, you may have no other choice but to scan the catalogs for the latest versions of Modem7. We provide in this chapter the names of all the overlays currently available — pick the overlay file for your computer, then find the disk volume containing the overlay library file and version of Modem7 that corresponds to it. You can order the appropriate disk volume from FOG, SIG/M or CP/MUG (Appendix C).

Customizing MDM712 and Newer Versions

Perhaps the easiest way to get a working version of Modem7 is to get one from a friend, associate, user group member or consultant. However, if you have to put one together yourself, you'll have an easier time with one of the most recent versions (MDM712 up to MDM740). With a little probing at user groups you can probably get a version that has all the "bells and whistles" as well as the Xmodem/Modem7 protocol.

What are some of the "bells and whistles?" MDM712 can automatically dial phone numbers from a directory, and can switch from one protocol style (CRC checking) to another (checksum). MDM712 also lets you transfer more than one file at a time ("batch mode").

The "MDM" series of Modem7 is much easier to customize than the earlier versions. We put together our version of MDM720 for the Ampro computer, and we use MDM720 on the Osborne 1 and Kaypro II. We also have an untested version of MDM740 running on our CompuPro. In all cases (except the Osborne) we customized them ourselves.

The problem with the older versions of Modem7 is that the program needs specific information about your computer and modem. You have to supply that information by putting the instructions directly into the program, using a programming tool such as DDT. Of course, it takes some learning about assembly language to change Modem7 for your computer and modem. Putting instructions directly into a program using DDT can cause errors in the program if you're not careful.

Irv Hoff's "MDM" series helps solve this problem. He changed most of Modem7 to be independent of the computer and modem hardware specifics, leaving only a small portion of the program dependent on these specifics. He isolated this portion in one area of the program, and wrote many versions of this portion of the program — one for each popular computer and modem combination. These portions are kept in separate files called "overlay" files. You merge the one you want with the main body of the program using the DDT utility supplied with CP/M.

The overlay files are shown in table 4-1. The main file, MDM720.OBJ, should first be renamed to MDM720.COM before using it with DDT.

To start the customization process, get the overlay file (one of the ".ASM" files in table 4-1) for your computer. Using a text editing or word processing program, edit the overlay file, paying close attention to the comments. You can set the initial baud rate, the "toggle" switches such as Xon/Xoff control, and many other secondary options described later in this chapter.

MDM7xx Overlay List

Rev. 1.6 by Dennis Recla

Locate your computer system in the list to find the proper overlay to use with the various versions of MDM7xx.

MDM7xx Overlay Name

Newest vers. Older	versions	Overlay description
MDM7ABC.ASM		Archives
		Business
		Computer
MDM7ADDS.ASM		
		ADDS
		Multivision

M7AC+3.ASM	M7AC-1.ASM	MDM711AC.ASM	AppleCat II
M7AJ-1.ASM	M7JC-2.ASM		Apple J-Cat
M7AL5-1.ASM	M7AL-1.ASM		Altos Series 5
M7AL8-1.ASM			Altos Series 8000
M7AM-1.ASM			Apple with Mtn. Comp. CPS
M7AP+3.ASM	M7AP-1.ASM	MDM711AP.ASM	Apple II
M7AQ-3.ASM	M714A3.ASM		Apple with MicroModem
M7AMPRO.ASM			Ampro Little Board
MDM712BB.ASM			Big Board I
M7C3-1.ASM			CP/M 3.0 AUX device
M7CD-1.ASM	MDM7CROT.ASM		Cromemco TUART @50H
M7-2710.ASM	MDM711CC.ASM		Calif. Comp. 2710 board
M7-2719.ASM	M7CC2719.ASM		Calif. Comp. 2719 board
M7-2830.ASM	M7CCS.ASM	M712CS.ASM	Calif. Comp. 2830 DART board
MDM7DB.ASM			Dynabyte serial port 1
M7DP-1.ASM	MDM711DP.ASM		DataPoint 1560
MDM7DUR.ASM			Durango
M7EP-2.ASM	M7EP-1.ASM	M712EP.ASM	Epson QX-10
M7EGL-1.ASM	M7EG-1.ASM		Eagle II and III
M7GP-1.ASM	MDM711GP.ASM		general purpose
M7H8-4A.ASM	M7H8-1.ASM		Heath/Zenith 89
M7HP-1.ASM	MDM712HP.ASM	MDM711HP.ASM	Hewlett Packard 125
M7HZ-1.ASM	MDM711HZ.ASM		Heath/Zenith 100 (2661)
M7IB7102.ASM			Ibex Model 7102
M7IM-2.ASM	MDM7IMS.ASM		IMS 5000 series
M7IN-2.ASM	M7IN-1.ASM		CompuPro Interfacer 3/4
MDM711I3.ASM			CompuPro Interfacer 3
M7ISB-1.ASM			Intertec Super Brain
M7KP-2.ASM	M7KP-1.ASM	MDM711KP.ASM	Kaypro
M7LO-1.ASM	M712LO.ASM		Lobo Max-80

M7MD-1.ASM	MDM711MD.ASM		Morrow MD I & II
M7MFIO-2.ASM	M7MF.ASM	MDM712MF.ASM	Electrologics MFIO Board
MDM7MIO.ASM			Intersystems MIO board @80H
M7MM+4.ASM	M7MM-1.ASM	MDM711MM.ASM	
			Morrow Multi-I/O board
M7MOL-2.ASM	M7MOL.ASM	M713MOL.ASM	Molecular Super Micro
M7NA-1.ASM	M712NA.ASM		North Star Advantage
M7NE-1.ASM	MDM711NE.ASM		NEC PC-8001
M7NH-2.ASM	M7NH-1.ASM		North Star Horizon w/HSIO-4
MDM7NS.ASM	M712NS.ASM		North Star Horizon port B
M7NSP-1.ASM	MDM711SP.ASM		National Semi. Starplex
M7NM-6.ASM	M7NM-1.ASM		PHONE NUMBER OVERLAY
MDM7NT.ASM			Northern Telecom system
M7-SCAT.ASM			Novation SMART CAT
M7OA-1.ASM	MDM712OT.ASM		Otrona Attache
M7OS-1.ASM	MDM711OS.ASM		Osborne with ext. modem
M7OS-1NE.ASM			Osborne with Nuevo Eq. 80-col. card
M7-OSCP.ASM			Osborne with DATACOMM modem
M7OD-4.ASM			Osborne with COMM-PAC modem
M7OX-1.ASM	MDM711OX.ASM		Osborne Executive
M7P1-1.ASM			PMC Micromate 101

M7PC-1.ASM	M712PC.ASM		IBM with Baby Blue Z-80
M7PM-1.ASM	M712PM.ASM		S-100 with PMMI modem
MDM7QUAY.ASM			Quay Series
M7R1-3.ASM	MDM7TRS1.ASM	M7R1-1.ASM	TRS-80 Model I
M7R2-1.ASM	MDM7TRS2.ASM		TRS-80 Model II
M7R3-1.ASM			TRS-80 Model III
M7R4-4.ASM	M7TR4-1.ASM		TRS-80 Model IV
M7RSCP+.ASM			TRS-80 Model IV CP/M+
M730RV.ASM	M724RV.ASM	M7RV-1.ASM	Racal Vadic VA212PA
M7303451.ASM	M7RV3451.ASM		Racal Vadic 3451
M7SBC-1.ASM	MDM7SBC.ASM		Superbrain Compustar
M7SD-1.ASM			SD Systems SD200
MDM7SOL.ASM			Processor Tech. SOL
M7SSM-2.ASM	M7SSM-1.ASM	M7UA-1.ASM	SSM I/O Board
M7SY-3.ASM	M7SY-1.ASM	MDM711SY.ASM	Sanyo MBC-1000
M7S1-1.ASM			Sanyo MBC-1100
M7TT-2.ASM	M7TT.ASM	M712TT.ASM	Teletek Systemaster S.B.C.
M7TV-1.ASM	MDM711TV.ASM		Televideo TS-802
MDM711TV3.ASM			Televideo TS-803
M7US-2.ASM	M7US-1.ASM		U.S. Robotics S-100 board
M7VG-1.ASM	MDM7VG3.ASM		Vector Graphics 3 & 4
M7VIO-1.ASM	MDM7VIO.ASM		Ithaca VIO board w/2651
M7VT-2.ASM	M7VT-1.ASM	MDM712VT.ASM	DEC VT-180/Rainbow
M7XE-1.ASM	MDM711XE.ASM		Xerox 820
M7XSMB-1.ASM	MDM711XI.ASM		Xitan SMB board w/6850

M7ZB-1.ASM   MDM712ZB.ASM   Telcon Zorba

The overlay file on the left is the preferred version for the various MDM7 overlays. Be sure that when you use DDT to overlay the proper ".HEX" file on the various MDM7xx.COM programs that you SAVE the proper amount of Memory to the ".COM" file. With each new version of MDM7xx the SAVE size increased. The size mentioned in the overlay file may not be correct. The best way to be sure is to calculate the number of SAVE pages yourself, following instructions in this chapter.

Table 4-1. *List of overlay files compiled by Dennis Recla. Pick the one you need for your computer equipment, assemble it with ASM, and merge it with the main Modem7 program using DDT.*

Your next step (after editing the ".ASM" overlay file) is to save the edited overlay file, and *assemble* it (convert it to a ".HEX" file) with the ASM utility supplied with every CP/M system:

```
A>ASM M7S1-1
```

This command converts M7S1-1.ASM, for the Sanyo MBC-1100, to M7S1-1.HEX (you don't specify the ".ASM" extension in the command, but ASM expects all assembly language source files to have the extension ".ASM"). Pick the ".ASM" overlay file for your computer.

Now use DDT to bring the main program into memory:

```
A>DDT MDM720.COM
DDT vers. 2.2
NEXT  PC
4600 0100
-
```

Jot down the hexadecimal number under the NEXT heading (4600H — we always put "H" after any hexadecimal number, to indicate it is not a decimal number).

Subtract 1H from the hexadecimal number under NEXT (e.g., 4600H minus 1H equals 45FFH). Using only the two leftmost digits of the result (45H), change it to a decimal number. You do this by multiplying the leftmost digit by sixteen (4 times 16 equals 64), and then adding the other digit (64 plus 5 equals 69). Remember, hexadecimal digits are 0H through 9H, then AH, BH, CH, DH, EH and FH, before you get to 10H.

The final result (69 in our example) is the number of *pages* of memory occupied by the program. You will use this number in a SAVE command; but first, we merge the overlay ".HEX" file with the contents of memory with these two DDT commands:

```
-IM7S1-1.HEX ↵
```

(Set up M7S1-1.HEX for merge.)

```
-R ↵  (Merge the overlay.)
```

```
NEXT  PC
4600  0100
```

You now have both the MDM720 program and the overlay file merged into one program in memory. You should now save the image in memory in a new ".COM" file, using the number you calculated above (the number of memory pages). To do this, type Control-C to leave DDT, then type this SAVE command:

-Control-C

```
A>SAVE 69 MYMODEM.COM ↵
```

The file MYMODEM.COM now contains the merged program. It should work without any trouble.

You can create as many versions of Modem7 as you like, by editing each ".ASM" overlay file, assembling each overlay file using ASM to convert it to a ".HEX" file, then using DDT to merge the main ".COM" file with the ".HEX" file, and finally using SAVE and a new filename to save the newly-created version.

Customizing Older Versions

To customize Modem789 (Modem7 version 7.89, from SIG/M volume 93), follow the instructions in MODEM789.SET, which tells you step by step how to use DDT to directly customize the file MODEM789.COM (renamed from MODEM789.OBJ). This might be the quickest method. There is a corresponding ".SET" file for each different version of Modem7, which tells you the actual memory addresses to use with DDT to make the necessary changes.

The other method, which lets you customize many more things in Modem7, requires use of the MAC macro assembler from Digital Research, Inc. Although ASM is supplied free with CP/M, MAC is more powerful and handles assembly language macros which are used in this version (and most of the older versions) of Modem7. MAC is free with CP/M Plus; otherwise it is extra.

With MAC you can directly edit the MODEM789 ".ASM" file, then assemble the file with MAC to produce a ".HEX" file (as described above, only substitute the command MAC for ASM). Or, you can edit the general purpose overlay ".ASM" files using MAC (SIG/M vol. 93), and use DDT to merge the resulting ".HEX" file with MODEM789.COM as we described above.

Just as there are many versions of Modem7, there are probably just as many ways to customize one for your use. Check the public domain libraries for one that is already customized for your computer, and you may be able to skip this entire step. But if you do this customization, you'll learn how to use ASM or MAC and DDT, which are very useful utilities.

How to use DDT to patch a program is beyond the scope of this book. Try the *User's Guide to CP/M Systems* (Baen Books, #4 in the Pournelle Series) for a complete description of DDT and ASM.

Features of Modem7

With thousands of versions of Modem7, some of them more different than others, it is not easy to choose which one to describe. When we started using Modem7, we used ModemH89 for

Heath/Zenith computers. We eventually got an Osborne 1 computer and used OSBMODEM, then upgraded to MDM720. We have also tried an early version for the Kaypro (KayModem), one for the Apple II with the Microsoft CP/M Softcard (APMODEM), and Modem789 on an Alspa computer.

The version we use most often is MDM720, one of the recent versions. If you don't have Modem7, we suggest you get one of the versions in Irv Hoff's MDM series (MDM712 or newer, up to MDM740 as of this writing).

However, if you are fortunate enough to have a working version of Modem7 for your computer, you must ask yourself this question before spending time and effort upgrading to another version: if the version you have works, why customize a new one?

Here are the general features of Modem7, with some mention of the MDM720 and MDM740 enhancements. If you have no need of the enhancements, we suggest you use the working version you already have.

Terminal Mode
> Every communications program has the ability to talk with another computer by acting like an external terminal (keyboard/display unit).

Upload and Download
> Modem7 lets you upload (send) or download (receive) programs from other computers using the Modem7/Xmodem protocol. The newest versions employ both "checksum" and "CRC" (cyclic redundancy check) error checking — you can choose which method to use (the other computer must be using the same method). Older versions of Modem7 employ only "checksum" error checking.

Copy To Printer
> Some versions let you copy incoming information on your printer. If the printer is too slow to copy the data directly, the extra characters stay in a large storage buffer until they can be printed.

Copy To Disk File
> This feature is sometimes called "logging" or capturing data
> on the screen. In terminal or "conversational" (echo) mode,
> you can copy all incoming and outgoing messages to a disk
> file.

Function Keys
> The newest versions of Modem7 let you pre-program your
> function keys to perform operations at the touch of a single
> function key. This is useful for signing on to call-up systems.

Automatic Disconnect
> The newest versions automatically disconnect from the
> telephone line when you type Control-N, or when you type X as
> an option during uploading or downloading. Two other
> disconnect commands are available in the version for the
> PMMI modem. Note: MDM712 and MDM720 use Control-
> D rather than Control-N for this function.

Automatic Dialing and Re-dialing
> Versions tailored for specific modems (such as SMODEM,
> and all versions in the MDM series) let you dial numbers
> from a list of phone numbers using a command. Some let you
> re-dial numbers after you get a busy signal. The modems
> supported include the PMMI 103 S-100 plug-in modem, the
> U. S. Robotics 300/1200, the Anchor Signalman Mark XII,
> the Hayes Smartmodem 300 or 1200 or other "Hayes-
> compatible" modems.

Using Modem7

When you run Modem7 it should display something like the
following message (this is from MDM720 configured for the
Ampro Bookshelf computer and the Hayes Smartmodem 1200):

```
MDM720 - (type M for Menu)
Version for Ampro With Hayes Smartmodem 1200
```

```
A))COMMAND:
```

If you type M⏎ after the A))COMMAND prompt, you should see a complete menu of commands for your version of Modem7. Figure 4-1 shows the menu for MDM740 (same as MDM720, but with more auto-dialing features).

You may recognize some of the commands because they have counterparts in CP/M: ERA, DIR and the ability to change disk drives and user areas as in these examples:

```
A))COMMAND:B: ⏎
```

This puts you in the same user area on drive B, and changes the prompt to show the change:

```
B))COMMAND:C: 12 ⏎
```

This command changes both the drive and the user area (include a space between the drive letter (C:) and the user area number (12).

The prompt changes to show both the drive and user area. To return to CP/M, type this command:

```
C12))COMMAND:CPM ⏎
```

This puts you back in CP/M, logged into the original drive and user area from where you executed Modem7.

One important command to remember is the one that changes the speed, or *baud rate*, of the transmission. If, for example, your modem can operate at 300 baud (30 characters per second) or 1200 baud (120 characters per second), you might want to switch from one speed to the other for calling different computers. Type the command SET (if your version of Modem7 supports baud rate changes):

```
AO))COMMAND: SET ⏎
Input Baud Rate (300, 450, 600, 1200, 9600):1200 ⏎
AO))COMMAND:
```

In this example we change the baud rate to 1200 baud. Your modem and communications port in your system must be operating at the same speed you choose.

(If you're using the PMMI modem, the SET command does not appear in the menu because you change the speed in a different manner — as a suffix to any primary single-letter command; e.g., T. 1200 ⊃ sets terminal mode at 1200 baud using the PMMI modem.)

Another important command is the one that lets you disconnect your modem from the phone line:

```
AO>>COMMAND:BYE ⊃
```

This command disconnects the line (hanging up the call), closes any file that may have been opened during the session, and returns you to CP/M.

MDM740 Help Message

```
Single Letter Commands
? - Display current settings
^ - Function key intercept character, then (0-9)
M - Display the menu
E - Terminal mode with echo
L - Terminal mode with local echo
T - Terminal mode
        For copying text to disk use T (or E or L) FILENAME.TYP
        Start or Stop toggles described on subsequent screen.
R - Receive CP/M file using Christensen Protocol
S - Send CP/M file using Christensen Protocol
        COMMAND: R (or S) FILENAME.TYP
        R and S can use the following subcommands:
            B - Bulk transfer using wildcards (e.g., *.*)
            D - Disconnect when done, return to command mode
            Q - Quiet mode (no messages to console)
            V - View (R) or (S) bytes on console
```

X – When done, disconnect, go to CP/M

The single letter commands may also be used on the
command line when the program is initially executed.

Three Letter Commands

CPM – Exit from this program to CP/M
DIR – List directory and space free (may specify drive)
ERA – Erase file (may specify drive)
LOG – Change default drive/user no. (specify drive/user)
     and reset disks.-e.g. LOG AO: or LOG B: (user # unchanged)
SPD – Set speed of file output in terminal mode
TIM – Select Baud rate for ''time-to-send'' message
TCC – Toggle CRC/Checksum mode on receive
TLC – Toggle local command immediate or after CTL-
TLF – Toggle LF after CR in ''L'' or ''T'' mode for a disk file
TRB – Toggle rubout to backspace conversion
TXO – Toggle XOFF testing in terminal mode file output
NUM – List remote systems
SET – Set modem baud rate
BYE – Disconnect, then return to CP/M
CAL – Dial number
DSC – Disconnect from the phone line

The following are terminal text buffer commands:

DEL – Delete memory buffer and file
WRT – Write memory buffer to disk file

Local Commands while in Terminal Mode

CTL-@ – Send a break tone for 300 ms.
CTL-B – Change Baud rate (PMMI only)
CTL-E – Exit to command mode
CTL-L – Send log-on message
CTL-N – Disconnect from the phone line
CTL-P – Toggle printer

```
CTL-Y – Start copy into buffer
CTL-R – Stop copy into buffer

          Start & Stop may be toggled as often as desired.
          A ''';''' at start of line indicates buffer is copying.
          XOFF automatically used to stop input when writing
          full buffer to disk, XON sent to resume.

CTL-T – Transfer ASCII file to remote

CTL-^ – Send local control character to remote
```

Figure 4-1. *Menu for MDM740, displayed when you type* M.

Automatic Dialing

Modem7 can dial a phone number for you, and continuously re-dial the number if the line is busy. Continuous re-dialing comes in handy when calling busy bulletin boards, because it increases your chances of getting connected as soon as the current caller hangs up. You don't have to implement this feature of Modem7 — you can dial the number yourself and use terminal mode to establish connection.

If you have one of the following modems, you can customize MDM720 to do automatic phone number dialing and continuous re-dialing:

- Signalman Anchor Mark XII modem
- Hayes Smartmodem 300 and 1200 modems
- U.S. Robotics 300/1200 modem
- PMMI 103 S-100 board modem

If you have a "Hayes-compatible" modem, it may work without any problem in place of a real Hayes. If you have some other kind of modem, you can try customizing an overlay for one of the above modems to make it work for your modem (at worst you may have to add new routines to the overlay, or you might only have to change the actual dialing commands and modem initialization).

The command to dial a number is NUM for other modems, and CAL for the PMMI, U.S. Robotics, Anchor and Hayes modems. In newer versions of Modem7, only one of these commands appears in the menu depending on which configuration overlay you use. Both commands display a "phone number library" from which you can choose a number.

You can change the phone numbers in the MDM720 library by using the M7LIB program, or by changing the phone number overlay while customizing MDM720 or earlier versions.

To disconnect the modem from the line use this command:

```
AO>>COMMAND:DSC ⊃
```

This command sends the proper instructions to the modem to disconnect the line.

Terminal Mode Controls

When you are calling another computer with your computer, most of the time your computer must act like a terminal to the other (called "host") computer. This assumes the other computer (the "host") is expecting to accommodate you.

To make your computer act like a terminal, choose *terminal mode* with the T command:

```
AO>>COMMAND:T ⊃
```

The T command puts Modem7 directly into terminal mode, in which the program sends everything you type at your keyboard to the other computer, and displays on your screen anything coming from the other computer (except during file transfers).

To make your computer act as a "host" computer, you must first establish the connection (your modem might be in "answer mode" to answer the call), then use the E command instead of the T command (the calling computer would use T to act as a terminal).

The E command puts Modem7 into "terminal mode with echo." When communicating with another computer that is in terminal mode, one of the two computers must send an "echo-back" to the other so that both computers can display what each person types. This can be accomplished with one computer using E and the other computer using T in "full-duplex" (two-way at the same time) transmissions.

Usually the caller types T and the person answering the call on the "host" computer types E, but you could switch roles while connected. However, if both use E, both will get a string of characters displayed on the screen since both computers are sending the same character over and over in a feedback loop. You can stop this by returning to command mode (Control-E in most versions, or Control-O in some versions of Smodem), then typing the appropriate command (T or E).

We have been describing *full duplex* communication, where what you see on the screen is actually the result of the other computer seeing it first (this is called "echoing"). In such communication, you know the other side saw what you typed because the other side sent it back to your screen. If the other side doesn't get it, you don't see it.

In *half-duplex* (one-way) communication, transmission only works in one direction rather than both directions. You are never sure that the other computer received what you typed, unless it responds with something you can see on your screen.

Some large computer systems operate this way — when you sign on using ordinary T terminal mode and start typing, you can't see what you typed, but the "host" computer responds. In these cases you can use the L command for "local echo" terminal mode instead of T, and see what you type as you type it.

The L command is also useful when one of the two communicating computers is using a modem that supports only half-duplex transmission. In these cases you can't use E to play "host" to the other computer. You can, however, use the L "local echo" mode. This mode can be used at both ends where ordinary terminal mode (T) doesn't display what you are typing because the other side isn't "echoing" (half-duplex mode).

A modem program that provides the T, L and E modes is sufficient for calling almost any BBS or "host" computer.

Capturing Text While In Terminal Mode

There are two ways to capture or "log" what you see on the
screen and what you type while in terminal mode (T or E modes).
One method, Control-Y, lets you capture everything that follows
into a text file on disk until you type Control-R (in versions older
than MDM712 you type another Control-Y to stop capturing). The
other method, Control-P, copies everything that follows on your
printer (if you have a printer connected and running) until you type
another Control-P

To capture text in a disk file, you must specify a filename when
starting your terminal mode session with the T (or E) command.
You separate the filename from the T (or E) command with a space
(the filename can have a drive prefix to specify another disk):

```
A0))COMMAND:T SESSION.LOG ⊃
```

The file SESSION.LOG is opened in the current drive/user
area, ready to receive data from the session. However, Modem7
does not start capturing data until you type a Control-Y When you
do type Control-Y, a colon (:) appears at the beginning of each line,
indicating that Modem7 is capturing the data in memory for storing in the file SESSION.LOG.

To stop capturing data, type Control-R or Control-Y depending
on your version of Modem7 (or Control-E to return to the Modem7
menu). The colons stop appearing, and you can resume your terminal mode session without saving the data in memory.

When you eventually leave terminal mode with Control-E and
return to the Modem7 menu, the newest versions of Modem7 warn
you to be sure to save captured data in a file by typing the WRT command. Most versions of Modem7 require that you type this command to save the data:

```
AO))COMMAND:WRT ⤺
```

If you forget to type the WRT command, you will lose the data in memory. This "feature" is in Modem7 so that you can throw away the data if it is irrelevant.

The Control-P feature of MDM720 is similar to the CP/M Control-P feature, except that MDM720 holds the characters in a buffer if the modem is working faster than the printer. You can turn on this feature by typing Control-P at any time during terminal mode (T or E modes). You can even turn it on while capturing data for disk storage, thereby getting both a hard copy and a disk copy at the same time.

Receiving Files With Accuracy

You can receive files from RCP/M bulletin board systems or from any computer that can send files using the Xmodem/Modem7 protocol for communications.

First you establish connection in terminal mode (T ⤺ with a BBS, E ⤺ or T ⤺ with another computer). If you are communicating with another person, type messages to synchronize your efforts. The other person must be prepared to send the file when you are ready to receive it.

If you are downloading from a bulletin board system, you have to prepare the BBS's Xmodem program to send a file. You should first move to the drive/user area containing the file you want to download. Remember the filename of the file, because when you use Xmodem to download, you have to specify the complete filename.

Downloading From a BBS

There are two steps for downloading a program from a BBS: (1) use Xmodem to tell the BBS to send the file, and then (2) use the R command to receive the file with Modem7. Xmodem will not work in batch mode, so you can transfer only one file at a time.

Step one is using Xmodem to send the file to your system:

```
B2>XMODEM S SAMPLE.OBJ ↵

XMODEM v9.0
File open: 309 records
Send time: 6 mins, 26 secs at 1200 bps
To cancel: use CTRL-X
```

The Xmodem program starts up by displaying some vital information. First it tells you what version of Xmodem you are using, then it tells you the size of the file in "records" in both decimal and hexadecimal numbers (one record is 128 characters). Finally it tells you how many hours, minutes, and seconds the file will take to send at your currently logged in baud rate. It will then wait for you to accomplish step 2, or it will "time out" and stop in thirty seconds.

The Xmodem command sends an entire file. You can send an entire library file to your computer, then use NULU or LU or similar utility on your computer to extract files from the library (see Chapter 6). This is the most efficient way of downloading public domain software.

It is possible, however, to download a file from within a library file without downloading the entire library. Type this version of the Xmodem command, with the library file's filename as library (you can omit the ".LBR" extension), and the specific filename as filename.ext, as shown in this example:

```
B2>XMODEM L library filename.ext ↵
```

Step two is to prepare Modem7 to receive the file. To do this you have to leave terminal mode by typing a Control-E (Control-0 in Smodem7, or the Escape key in some versions). When you leave terminal mode, you should have a menu on your screen. You can then type this command:

```
AO>>COMMAND:RT d:filename.ext ↵
```

In this command, R specifies receive mode, and T tells Modem7
to return to terminal mode when the transfer is done. The
d:filename.ext is the disk drive and filename to use to store the received file on your computer's disk.

If you did everything correctly, you should see something like
this on your screen:

```
AWAITING #1
AWAITING #2
```

This tells you that your communication program is waiting for
the next record of data. Your program receives the file one record
at a time (a record is 128 characters).

When the transfer is complete, Modem7 returns to terminal
mode. Press a Return to "wake up" the BBS, and you can use
Xmodem again to download another file.

Some versions of Modem7 do not allow the T in the RT command.
In that case, use the R command as shown in this example in which
the copy received is to be named SAMPLE.COM and stored on
drive B:

```
A0>>COMMAND:R B:SAMPLE.COM ↵
AWAITING #01
AWAITING #02
```

If your version of Modem7 does not have a menu, leave terminal
mode with a Control-E and type the following command from
CP/M   (substitute   your   filename   and   drive   for
B:SAMPLE.COM):

```
A>MODEM7 R B:SAMPLE.COM ↵
AWAITING #01
AWAITING #02
```

The R command sets up your Modem7 program to receive the

file that Xmodem is waiting to send to your system. It may take up to 15 seconds, during which time your Modem7 program may display messages like AWAITING 01 and TIMEOUT. Once communication is firmly established, Xmodem sends blocks of the file to Modem7.

When you see the message TRANSFER COMPLETE (this may take a long time depending on the size of the file), you can return to the Modem7 start-up menu with a Control-E command.

You must get back to the bulletin board system's A0⟩ prompt before the BBS detects no one on the other end and automatically disconnects the call. To do this, return to terminal mode by selecting T in the menu version of Modem7:

    A0⟩⟩COMMAND: T ⤾

In the non-menu version, you must type the Modem7 command with the T option:

    A⟩MODEM7 T ⤾

Immediately after entering terminal mode, type at least one Return to get the bulletin board system's A0⟩ prompt. This tells the BBS that you are still connected.

NOTE:

If Modem7 does not receive the appropriate signal, there must be transmission problems. Modem7 will "hang" for awhile and not receive the file. Our version of Modem7 eventually cancels the routine and returns control to the Modem7 menu and the command line. However, other versions may "hang" forever unless you restart your system. If you have to re-start the system or re-start Modem7, you should activate terminal mode immediately so that you don't lose your connection with the other system.

Receiving From Other Computers

Bulletin board systems usually do not let you receive more than

one file at a time, unless you download an entire library file that
contains files. However, two computers running Modem7 or similar program using the Modem7/Xmodem protocol can transfer
several files at once in *batch mode.*

The Modem7 R command receives one or more files. To receive
files from another computer, you type either R and the name of the
file you are receiving, or RB (batch mode) to receive several files,
and press Return.

To start a batch mode receiving operation, type the R command
with the B option:

    A0>>COMMAND:RB ⊃

The B option specifies "batch mode" and tells Modem7 to get
the names of the files from the sending program. Modem7 receives
the files in the order they are sent; you don't have to do anything
during the operation.

The program sending the file from the other computer could be
Modem7 or another program that does "batch mode"
Xmodem/Modem7 protocol transfers. The sending program must
also be sending in batch mode as described below, so that the receiving program receives the filenames as well as the data.

Sending Files With Accuracy

Modem7 can send as well as receive with accuracy. Modem7
can send one file at a time to another computer that is running a
communications program employing the Xmodem/Modem7 protocol (such as Modem7, COMMX, MITE, PC-Talk III and many
others). If the other program supports "batch mode" transfer,
Modem7 can send several files in a single transfer operation.

You can also send files to an RCP/M bulletin board system that
uses Xmodem or similar program. The BBS can receive files accurately if you send them using Modem7, and set the BBS's Xmodem
program to receive. You must have already established connection
in terminal mode.

To send a file that normally has the ".COM" extension (repre-

senting a binary program file or CP/M command), you must
rename it to have an ".OBJ" extension (e.g., SAMPLE.COM
must be renamed to SAMPLE.OBJ). Once renamed and transferred, you will not be able to rename the RCP/M system's version
of your file. RCP/M systems offer no rename commands for good
reason: pranksters have been known to send dangerous programs to
RCP/M systems and then use the programs to wreak havoc. Programmers with good intentions have also destroyed systems accidentally by sending programs that do not work.

When sending a file to another computer, the other computer
must be prepared to receive. When sending a file to an RCP/M
BBS, you have to prepare the BBS's Xmodem program. Type this
version of the XMODEM command (substitute your file's name
for SAMPLE.OBJ):

```
AO>XMODEM R SAMPLE.OBJ ⊃
```

This command sets up the RCP/M bulletin board system to receive a file from your system. You should now leave your Modem7
terminal mode by typing a Control-E. If your Modem7 has no
menu, type the following command:

```
A>MODEM7 S B:SAMPLE.OBJ ⊃
```

If your version of Modem7 has a start-up menu, select the
"send" option:

```
AO>>COMMAND:S B:SAMPLE.OBJ ⊃
```

Modem7 displays the following message before sending a file:

```
FILE OPEN - EXTENT LENGTH xxH
AWAITING INITIAL NAK
```

If Modem7 does not receive a NAK signal (a Negative Acknowledge), there must be transmission problems. Modem7 will
"hang" for awhile and not send the file. Our version of Modem7
eventually cancels the routine and returns control to the Modem7

menu and the command line. However, other versions may "hang" forever unless you re-start your system. If you have to re-start the system or re-start Modem7, you should activate terminal mode immediately so that you don't lose your connection with the other system.

When a successful transmission has finished, you should return to terminal mode quickly, to keep your connection with the RCP/M system. Return to terminal mode and press your Return key a few times.

Commands and Options

The following Modem7 commands immediately affect the operation of the program. You use the three-letter commands by themselves or with parameter settings or filenames. The single-letter commands can be paired with secondary options shown after this section.

Three-letter Commands

These commands do not have secondary options, but some require filenames or disk drive letters.

BYE   Disconnect the modem from the phone line. This command also closes any file that may be open and returns you to CP/M.

CAL   This command is only in versions for the PMMI and some other modems, taking the place of NUM to show the phone number library for automatic dialing. You can change the phone numbers with a program called M7LIB.

CPM   Leave Modem7 and return to CP/M. Some versions actually re-start CP/M; others merely terminate Modem7. Either way, this command does not disconnect the modem from the phone line; it lets you leave Modem7 to perform a CP/M operation, and then start Modem7 to go on-line again.

DEL If you are capturing incoming information in memory for disk storage, and you decide you do not want to bother saving it to disk after all, use this command to close and also delete the file you had opened.

DIR Display the directory of any disk, with the amount of disk space left. Use the LOG command to "log in" a new disk.

DSC Disconnect the modem from the phone line, but stay in Modem7.

ERA Erase one or more files from any disk. You can use the CP/M filename match "wild cards" (* and ?) to erase several files at once.

LOG "Log-in" a new disk so that CP/M can allow you to put new information on it. When you first insert a new disk, although you can see a directory of files and read files, you can't change or add any new information to the disk without getting a BDOS ERR. The LOG command performs the CP/M Control-C function that "logs-in" a new disk. You can type a user area number also with the drive letter:

```
A>>COMMAND:LOG B: ⏎
B>>COMMAND:LOG A5: ⏎
5A>>COMMAND:
```

NUM Display the phone number library so that you can dial a number. You dial the number by typing it and pressing Return. This is not shown in versions for the PMMI modem. Some versions let you pick a number to call from the library by typing a single letter; others require that you type the number, or manually dial the number.

SET Set the baud rate for the communication session. This command does not appear in versions for the PMMI modem, or in versions that cannot change the speed. Your modem and communications port in your system must be operating at the same speed you choose.

SPD Set the delay between characters and/or delay between lines for sending files from terminal mode (using Control-T). This command makes it possible to control the speed at which you send characters from a file while in terminal mode. Some computers cannot receive all the characters sent to it; many need at least a delay between lines. The preset delays are usually 50 milliseconds between each character and 500 milliseconds between each line. You can check your current values with the ? command.

TCC Change the type of error-checking from the default mode (CRC) to the mode used in older versions (checksum), or back to the default mode (CRC). CRC stands for cyclic redundancy checking, and it is used on all new versions of Modem7. Checksum checking is available on older versions that do not have CRC. MDM720 automatically switches to checksum if it cannot receive or send data using CRC.

TIM Set the file transfer timing calculation for the speed you are actually using. You can preset it (when installing the program) to the speed you normally use, but this command lets you change the time calculation to whatever speed you choose (110 to 9600 baud). This command does not change the baud rate you are using to communicate; in fact, it does not exist on versions that offer the SET command to change baud rates.

TLC   Normally you send a Control-key command to the remote computer by first typing Control-^ before typing the Control-key command. This command *reverses* the meaning of Control-^ so that you need Control-^ before any Modem7 Control-key command, otherwise the command is sent to the remote computer.

For example, normally you type a Control-E to return to the Modem7 menu, and if you want to send a Control-E to the remote computer, you first type Control-^, then Control-E. If you reverse this by typing TLC, then when you type Control-E it goes directly to the remote computer and does not put you in Modem7's menu. To go to Modem7's menu in such cases, you must type Control-^, then Control-E.

TLF   If you are sending the contents of a file to the remote computer from terminal mode (using Control-T), most remote computers require that you *not* send a Line Feed code at the end of each line (after the Carriage Return code — both are ASCII codes, defined in Appendix A). This command lets you turn on or off the sending of a Line Feed; initially it is off. You can always type a Line Feed by typing Control-J. Note that while in the E or L version of terminal mode, Line Feeds are automatically sent after each line.

TRB   This lets you change the Rubout (move backward and delete the character) function to your Backspace key.

TXO   You use this when you are sending text files while in terminal mode (using Control-T) to a remote computer and you want

your computer to stop after each line when it receives the
Xoff character, and start again when it receives the Xon
character.

WRT   Save what you have been capturing in memory to the disk file
      already opened when you specified a file with either the T, E or
      L command. When you return from terminal mode to the
      Modem7 menu, the program displays a warning that you
      may lose what has been captured unless you use the WRT com-
      mand.

Single-letter Commands

   Some of these commands can be paired with secondary options
shown in the next section. Each command performs some immediate action or displays information, and most of them return you to
Modem7's menu (command mode); T, E and L leave you in terminal
mode.

?   Show the current settings. The settings are governed by pri-
      mary commands and secondary options. We show an exam-
      ple in the next section with the secondary options.

^   Show the "function key intercept" character. This is usually
      a caret (^), used with the Control key. Its function is to allow
      you to send another Control-key command to the remote
      computer without affecting your Modem7 program. For ex-
      ample, if you want to send a Control-E to the remote comput-
      er without leaving terminal mode of Modem7 (because
      Control-E by itself makes you leave terminal mode), first type
      Control-^, then type Control-E.

M   Show the menu one page at a time. To stop the display at any
      point, type Control-C.

E   Switch to "terminal mode with echo," also known as "conversational mode" as described previously. When one computer chooses this mode, the other must choose terminal mode (T); otherwise you'll see a string of characters "echoing" indefinitely (type Control-E to get back to the Modem7 menu).

L Switch to "terminal mode with local echo." This mode shows what you are typing, but does not "echo back" to the other person what she/he is typing. You can use this at both ends if the T and E combination is not possible. Both E and L come in handy with certain modems that do not transmit in full-duplex mode, and with some remote computers that allow only half-duplex transmission.

T Switch to terminal mode. In this mode everything you type reaches the other computer and is "echoed" back to you before you see it. The other computer must be able to handle echoing — if the other computer is a personal computer, it probably has to be in "conversational" mode ("terminal mode with echo" — E command). Most "host" computers like The Source and CompuServe operate with echoing — you choose terminal mode to act as a terminal on the remote system.

R Receive one or more files using the Xmodem/Modem7 error-checking protocol. Modem7 will use CRC checking unless you switch to the older checksum mode with the TCC command. The messages you see do not mean errors are corrupting the data — if any such corruption occurs Modem7 cancels the operation. You either get a "99%-guaranteed" accurate file, or you get nothing.

S Send one or more files using the Xmodem/Modem7 error-checking protocol. Modem7 will use CRC checking unless you switch to the older checksum mode with the TCC command. The messages you see do not mean errors are corrupting the data — if any such corruption occurs Modem7 cancels the operation. The receiver either gets a "99%-guaranteed" accurate file, or gets nothing.

Secondary Options

MDM712 through MDM740 offer many options to select, some
of which appear also in older versions of Modem7. We cannot list
all the options of all the versions; therefore, we are listing the options of MDM720 with some commentary about whether they exist in other versions. You can display the options for your version by
typing the M command, which displays the entire menu. You can
display the actual settings of some of these options by typing a
question mark (?). Here's an example:

```
A))COMMAND:?⏎

Mode: CRC
Rub is backspace
Printer buffer is OFF
Modem speed is 300 baud
Terminal mode file buffer is inactive
Unused portion of buffer is 16384 bytes
Use CTL-^ to send local command to remote
LF NOT sent after CR in ''L'' or ''T'' for a disk file
XOFF testing NOT used in terminal mode file output
XON NOT automatically tested after CR in terminal mode file output

Char. delay (terminal file mode) is: 50 ms. per character
Line delay (terminal file mode) is: 500 ms. per character
```

What does all this mean? The options presented below explain
some of these things, but here's a general description:
Modem7 is set for the CRC mode of checking (as opposed to the
Checksum mode, used with older versions). The Rubout key performs like a Backspace key. The printer is not copying everything
at this moment (the "buffer is off"). The speed of transmission is
300 baud (approximately 300 bits, or 30 characters, per second).
You are not currently capturing data for storage in a disk file, and

you have 16384 bytes of memory for such capturing (it is not necessary to know this).

Other settings are: if you want to send a Control-key command to the "host" computer, first type Control-^ then type the Control-key command; Modem7 is not sending a Line Feed code after every line, which is the usual setting; Modem7 is not checking for the Xoff character from the "host" computer when sending data, nor is it checking for Xon after every line it sends; and the character and line delay factors are set to 50 milliseconds and 500 milliseconds, respectively.

You can change all of these options, but there are a lot! In fact, Modem7 has more options than many commercial communications programs. Read through this summary of the options, some of which are only available in the newest versions of the MDM series of Modem7, and some of which are available in versions of Smodem. These options, called "secondary" options, are single letters that appear immediately following the primary single-letter commands summarized above.

A   Switch to answer mode (used only with PMMI modems, and in some new versions of Smodem for the Hayes Smartmodem).

B   Send or receive in batch mode. This lets you transfer more than one file in one operation. Most bulletin board systems do not allow batch transfers, but computer-to-computer transfers are more efficient this way.

D   Disconnect from the line when finished with the transfer operation, but stay in Modem7. This lets you disconnect from one line, and use Modem7 to call another, without actually leaving Modem7.

J   Switch to Modem7 command mode when finished with a transfer operation.

O   Switch to originate mode (used only by PMMI modems, and in some new versions of Smodem for the Hayes

Smartmodem).

Q   Use "quiet" mode, which means that messages normally sent to the screen by Modem7 are suppressed. This is a special purpose feature rarely used except when you are operating Modem7 on a remote system, and you don't want the remote Modem7 messages interfering with the program you are using to communicate with that remote system.

R   Show the data received on your screen during a file receive operation.

S   Show the data you are sending on your screen during a file send operation.

V   Turn on visual inspection of a text file being transferred. This option should not be used with squeezed files, because the data is not character data that displays well unless it is "un-squeezed" with one of the un-squeezing utilities (USQ or NSWP, described in Chapter 5).

X   Exit to CP/M when finished with the operation. This option also disconnects the modem from the phone line.

0   Use odd parity during the transfer (used with PMMI modem only).

1   Use even parity during the transfer (used with PMMI modem only).

Control-key Commands

These commands affect operation while you're in Modem7's terminal mode (after using the T, E or L commands).

Control-@
Send the "break" character to the other computer. The

"break" character interrupts an activity on some remote "host" computers.

Control-B

Change the baud rate to any speed between 110 to 710 (PMMI modems only).

Control-D

Disconnect the modem from the phone line. Newer versions of Modem7 use Control-N for this purpose.

Control-E

Return to Modem7's command mode menu. This also cancels data capturing.

Control-L

Send the log-on message, if you set TRANLOGON to YES and included a log-on message in the version of Modem7 you put together. You can use this as a sign-on message to your remote computers, if you don't mind using the same password on all these systems. You have to modify your version of Modem7 to add a log-on message.

Control-N

Disconnect the modem from the phone line. Older versions of Modem7 use Control-D for this purpose.

Control-P

Turn on the printer buffer to begin copying everything displayed or typed to the printer. This is similar to the CP/M Control-P command, except that Modem7 maintains a print buffer so that if the printer is slower than the modem, the computer buffers the characters and doesn't lose them.

Control-Y

Turn on memory capturing of everything typed and displayed, for storage in a disk file. You must first open a file when you use the T, E or L command to go into terminal mode.

A semicolon appears at the beginning of each line while capturing is occurring. To cancel capturing, type Control-R and resume terminal mode, or Control-E and return to the Modem7 menu.

Control-R
Turn off memory capturing of everything typed or displayed. This stops the appearance of semicolons at the beginnings of lines, and stops the capturing of data. You can, at any time, leave terminal mode and save the data you captured by typing WRT from Modem7's command mode.

MODEM For MS-DOS/PC-DOS

The program MODEM.COM (version 3.2) for the IBM PC and MS-DOS computers is a rewritten version of Modem7 for CP/M computers. MODEM works with any version of PC-DOS or MS-DOS as long as your computer has 64K of RAM (random-access internal memory), one disk drive, and one serial RS-232 port.

New, enhanced versions of MODEM are created regularly. Electronic bulletin boards and user groups around the country have copies of MODEM.COM and similar versions like MODEM7.COM and XMODEM.COM. Often, the same source will have documentation for the program on the same disk or can tell where to get some. Usually, the documentation is very brief, or a variation of the menus or "quick reference" provided in the program. If you are into programming (especially assembler programming), the source for MODEM.COM is available and will give many hours of joy.

Version 3.2 of MODEM.COM was written by John Chapman (844 S. Madison Street, Hinsdale, IL 60521) for the IBM Personal Computer running under PC-DOS (and MS-DOS). The program is converted from a copy of Ward Christensen's MODEM.COM, version 3.0, found on CP/MUG disk #25.

MODEM is a simple program, designed to let two computers communicate with each other through their RS-232 serial ports.

The program sends or receives files through a serial port following standard setup features or parameters. Most commonly, modems are connected to each computer's serial ports so that they can communicate over telephone lines. MODEM works with almost any type of modem.

MODEM has three primary commands. You can use it to send a file to another computer running the same program (or a version that is compatible), or receive a file from another computer. You can also use MODEM to make your computer act like a terminal connected to another computer, such as when you call an information service like Dow Jones, CompuServe, or The Source.

Like most versions of Modem7, MODEM breaks its commands into two groups — primary commands and secondary options (see lists below). When starting up MODEM at least a Primary Option must be chosen. For example, to send a file to another computer you type:

```
MODEM S filename.ext ↵
```

You can combine a secondary option with a primary command. For example, assume you want to receive a file from another computer, but at the faster speed of 450 baud rather than the default speed of 300 baud. Also, assume you want to disconnect the telephone when the transfer is completed. You'd enter the following command and options with MODEM:

```
MODEM RD.450 filename.ext ↵
```

The primary command R tells MODEM to receive the file through its serial port. The secondary option D tells MODEM to disconnect automatically after the transfer is complete. The .450 option sets the baud rate for the transfer to 450 baud.

You can make your computer into a terminal by using the T primary command:

```
MODEM T ↵
```

Type a Control-D to disconnect from terminal mode.

Here's a summary of MODEM primary commands:

S   Send a file.
R   Receive a file.
T   Act like a terminal (terminal mode).
E   Act like a host computer — also called "conversational mode."
D   Disconnect the phone (S-100 modems only).
H   Print "help" information.

The secondary options can be used with the primary commands they would logically work with, but not with a command that contradicts the option. Here's a summary of secondary options:

A   Answer mode (modem answers the call).
0   Originate mode (modem originates the call).
D   Disconnect after executing the command.
I   Initializes the serial port UART chip to its default settings (300 baud, no parity, eight bits per byte with one stop bit).
T   Go into terminal mode after transferring a file.
E   Go into conversational mode after transferring a file.
Q   Quiet mode — no status messages are displayed.
R   Show the characters received during the transfer.
S   Show the characters sent during the transfer.
V   Show the file sent or received during transfer.
2   Switch to COM2:- the second serial port.
3   Switch to COM3:- the third serial port.

Roll Your Own With The Modem7/Xmodem Protocol

Some of you may like the challenge of writing your own program to perform like Modem7, using the Modem7/Xmodem protocol. The first MODEM program was written in assembly language, but others have written BASIC versions, and there may also be a Pascal version out there, somewhere. If you like the challenge of writing your own program to communicate, you'll appreciate this brief description.

For those of you who are merely curious techno-freaks, you may also appreciate this brief description of Christensen's protocol used by Modem7, Xmodem, PC-Talk III and many others.

Data is transferred in 128-byte blocks that are sequentially numbered. Each block has an extra *checksum* number (a calculation that differs with the specific data in the block) appended to its end. As the receiving computer receives each block of data, it performs its own checksum calculation and compares its number to the checksum number sent with the block.

If the numbers are the same, then "all is well" and the receiving computer sends an ACK acknowledgement signal (the ASCII code for ACK is 06 in hexadecimal, or Control-F). The sending computer waits for this ACK before sending another block. If the receiving computer detects an error (the checksums are not the same), it sends a NAK ("negative acknowledge") signal (ASCII code for NAK is 15 in hexadecimal, or Control-U).

How does this transmission start? When you start Xmodem to send a file from the BBS to your system, it waits for an *initial* NAK to get synchronized with your computer. Figure 4-2 shows what happens after you start Xmodem to send and your Modem7 program to receive.

After the initial NAK the sending computer sends a "start of header" (ASCII SOH), a block number in two bytes, the data in the block, and the checksum number. The receiving computer responds with an ACK if the checksums match.

What happens if the block is NAK'ed? The sending computer, remembering the block number, re-transmits the block. Aha, but what happens if the receiving computer received the block and sent an ACK, but the sending computer didn't "hear" the ACK? You might think that the sending computer would transmit the same

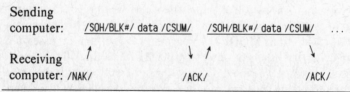

Figure 4-2. *After starting Xmodem to send a file, and your Modem7 program to receive a file, the two programs synchronize.*

block again, and the receiving computer would end up with two identical blocks (when it should only have one); however, this protocol takes care of the problem. The receiving computer, remembering the previous block's number, checks the number of the incoming block and, if it's the same as the previous block, it throws out the extra block.

The transmission ends when the receiving computer receives an EOT ("end of transmission" — ASCII code 04 in hexadecimal, or Control-D) from the sending computer, usually at the end of the file. If, for some reason, the receiving computer does not "hear" the EOT signal, it will eventually "time out" and return you to normal operation.

Most recent versions (version 4.3 and higher) of Xmodem support the SDLC (Synchronous Data Link Control) two-byte CRC checking on data blocks, and is provided as a sub-option C in newer releases of derivative Modem7 programs. SDLC is used in some large minicomputer networks. See *Computer Networks* by Andrew Tannenbaum (Prentice-Hall) for more information on CRC checking and SDLC.

Which Version?

Modem7 probably has more "authorized" versions than any other program in personal computing. Nearly every new version was added to the public domain without enough commentary to distinguish it from previous versions. Some enhancers departed from tradition and offered versions that used commands with different names, or even substituted different functions for some of the commands.

With this proliferation it is nearly impossible to describe the typical version of Modem7. We recommend that you use the version described in this chapter (MDM720), or an earlier version (such as Modem798), but we know that it may not be possible for you to get it. It doesn't matter which version you use as long as you find one that works. You can use a working version of Modem7 to hunt the bulletin boards for another version if you wish. But you must start with a working version for your computer and modem.

CHAPTER 5:
SQUEEZING AND
UN-SQUEEZING FILES

In your search for public domain software you will encounter "squeezed" files in almost every volume. You won't be able to use these files until you "un-squeeze" them. The files are "squeezed" into a smaller size so that they occupy less disk space and take less time to transmit.

The squeezed files prepared by public domain librarians always have a "Q" as the middle letter of the filename extension; for example, the squeezed version of PROGRAM.DOC is PROGRAM.DQC.

Any file can be squeezed (except a file that is already squeezed); however, squeezed text files cannot be displayed with the regular TYPE command. Most bulletin board systems have an enhanced TYPE command that can display a squeezed file; or there might be a program called TYPESQ, TYPE21 or TYPEL that will do it.

You can download a squeezed file, and copy it from disk to disk, but you can't do much else with it until you "un-squeeze" it. There are many utility programs that can un-squeeze files including USQ and NSWEEP (NSWP205).

Un-squeezing may not be the only thing you have to do to get public domain programs. Many programs reside in library files — files with the ".LBR" extension. In these cases you have to *extract* the file from the library, and *also* un-squeeze it if it is a squeezed file. The LSWEEP13 and NULU utilities, both described in detail in Chapter 6, extract and also un-squeeze files for you.

What do you do when you encounter squeezed files, in or out of libraries?

1.   Copy or download the entire library or the specific file to your disk. Make a copy of the file or library and store it in your disk archive.

2. Check your disk for enough space, or move the squeezed file or library of squeezed files to a new disk for un-squeezing. You must have enough disk space to hold a new un-squeezed file for every squeezed file; an un-squeezed file could be one-and-a-half times as big as the squeezed file. If you have a library of squeezed files, multiply the library size by two to get an idea of how much space you need.

3. Use a utility like USQ or NSWEEP (NSWP205 or newer version) to un-squeeze the files. If the files are in a library, use LSWEEP (LSWEEP13 is the best as of this writing) or NULU.

The latest version of USQ can un-squeeze many files at once. NSWEEP is a larger program that can un-squeeze many files and perform other file maintenance. LSWEEP and NULU are designed to extract squeezed or regular files from a library file (Chapter 6).

You have to know how to un-squeeze files and extract files from libraries in order to use anything in the public domain. The first two utilities you should get from a user group or download from a BBS should be NULU, LSWEEP13 or LU300 (described in Chapter 6) to extract files from libraries, and USQ or NSWP205, so that you can un-squeeze files not in libraries.

Always un-squeeze files on your own disks. Never un-squeeze files on the BBS disk because you will be wasting valuable time and using up the BBS's disk space.

Squeezed versions of files take up less space depending on the content of the original file. For example, ".CQM" or ".OQJ" files are not significantly smaller than their original ".COM" and ".OBJ" counterparts. However, text files and program source code files (which are usually text) can be squeezed to between 65% and 52% of their original sizes.

You don't have to squeeze files unless you intend to squeeze your own data files or text files. You may want to squeeze files before copying them to archive disks or transmitting them to other computers. This chapter not only covers un-squeezing in detail; it also explains how to squeeze files and use all the utilities that deal with squeezed files.

Un-squeezing Utilities

NSWP205 (NSWEEP version 2.05, written by Dave Rand) is designed to "sweep" through a directory of files and perform operations to a set of "tagged" files. NSWEEP is described in detail in Chapter 7. The program can replace most of the functions of PIP, STAT, ERA and REN, as well as perform squeezing and un-squeezing. However, the program cannot (as of this writing) extract files from ".LBR" files or display the filenames of member files in ".LBR" files (see Chapter 6 for ".LBR" files).

LSWEEP13 (LSWEEP version 1.3, written by Joe Volger) is designed to extract squeezed or un-squeezed files from library files, which are described in Chapter 6). LSWEEP un-squeezes as it extracts squeezed files, so by itself LSWEEP is sufficient for obtaining programs from public domain ".LBR" files. However, LSWEEP does not check the extractions to see if they're exactly the same as the versions originally stored in the ".LBR" file. It is possible to have errors in transmission "corrupt" a member of an ".LBR" file; in such cases you need NULU or LU (Chapter 6) to extract the member.

NULU is preferable to LSWEEP because it gives you a choice whether or not to un-squeeze a file while extracting it from a library. If you have limited space on your disk, you might not want to un-squeeze everything you extract. NULU is described in Chapter 6.

There may be other un-squeezing utilities now available, but the original "squeezer" utilities, and USQ, the granddaddy of un-squeezers, is the smallest and most trustworthy utility for un-squeezing.

The SQ/TYPESQ/USQ Utilities

The "squeezer" utility, SQ version 1.3, was designed by Dick

Greenlaw to compress CP/M files so that they take up less disk space and less time to transfer. However, the files cannot be used for their intended purpose while in squeezed format — you must un-squeeze them first. USQ (also written by Dick Greenlaw) was the first utility designed to un-squeeze files.

TYPESQ, written by Bob Mathias, lets you display the contents of a squeezed text file. This utility was incorporated into other utilities like TYPE21, which lets you display squeezed or un-squeezed files. (These utilities cannot be renamed to TYPE in normal CP/M systems because CP/M has a built-in TYPE command that does not display squeezed files. However, some bulletin board systems replaced the built-in TYPE command with TYPE21 or similar utility.)

The original SQ and USQ utilities were written in the C language (BDS-C Compiler, available from Leor Zolman, BD Software, P.O. Box 9, Brighton, MA 02135). The "source code" files (containing text in the C language) can be obtained if you want to customize your versions of SQ and USQ. The newest versions of SQ and USQ are faster because they are written in assembly language (by Jim Lopushinsky).

FLS (version 1.1), also written by Dick Greenlaw, is a program that works on the same command line with the original SQ or USQ program to let you expand an ambiguous filename (a match for several filenames using the CP/M * and ? "wildcard" symbols) into a list of filenames. With FLS you can squeeze or un-squeeze a list of files rather than one file at a time. The newest versions of SQ and USQ can handle a wildcard filename on the same command line without FLS.

Un-squeezing With USQ

The original USQ program (we describe version 1.4 here) expands squeezed files into exact duplicates of their originals. USQ can also provide a quick, un-squeezed display of the beginning of a squeezed file.

You can provide filenames, drive letters and options for USQ on the same command line with USQ, or in response to USQ prompts.

You can also provide them from a file you already saved with the information.

Before un-squeezing, be sure you have enough space on disk to fit another file nearly twice the size of the squeezed file. If you don't have enough space, see the second example below.

Here's an example of the USQ utility un-squeezing one file on the same drive:

```
A)USQ MDM740.DQC ⊃
```

USQ creates an un-squeezed file using the name the original file had when it was squeezed. All squeezed files carry their original names with them, so that un-squeezing utilities can re-create the same file using that name.

To put the un-squeezed file on a disk other than the one holding the squeezed file, specify the "destination disk drive" first (the one to hold the new un-squeezed file), then the filename of the squeezed file:

```
A)USQ B: MDM740.DQC ⊃
```

The space between B: and the filename tells USQ that B: is the destination drive, not the drive holding MDM740.DQC. If the first parameter of USQ is a drive letter without a filename, USQ assumes it is the destination drive.

You can un-squeeze more than one file, and on more than one disk drive, by naming more than one on the command line:

```
A)USQ MDM740.DQC B:M7LIB.DQC ⊃
```

This command un-squeezes MDM740.DQC on drive A and M7LIB.DQC on drive B. The resulting new file MDM740.DOC is put on drive A, and M7LIB.DOC on drive B.

The original squeezed files are not disturbed. If you have already copied them to archive disks, you can erase them from your work disks and use the un-squeezed versions. However, if you un-squeezed a ".CQM" or ".OQJ" (".COM" or ".OBJ") file, test it first before erasing the squeezed versions.

You can't specify the name of the un-squeezed file, so make sure there isn't a file with the same filename on the same disk. When USQ creates the new un-squeezed file, it overwrites any file by the same name. The name is stored in the original squeezed file.

When you type more than one filename with USQ, each file is processed in order. You can type as many filenames as you can fit on a command line (use Control-E to extend a command line to the next line). However, the filenames you give to the original version of USQ must be *specific* names, not ambiguous filename matches. You must use FLS with the original USQ to make use of filename matches.

More recent versions of USQ will accept filename matches using the * and ? symbols. For example:

```
A)USQ *.DQC ⊃
```

This example un-squeezes all ".DQC" files on drive A.

```
A)USQ B:MDM????.?Q? ⊃
```

This example un-squeezes all files on drive B that match the pattern MDM????.?Q?, where every ? is any single character or space.

There are many ways to display the contents of a squeezed text file. USQ lets you do this by specifying the number of lines of the file to display:

```
A)USQ -10 MDM740.DQC B:M7LIB.DQC ⊃
```

This command does not create new un-squeezed files from the squeezed ones; it simply un-squeezes in memory, then displays the first ten lines of both files. You can use this form of USQ to see the contents of files on a disk where there is no room to create un-squeezed versions.

If you don't know how many lines you need to see, try this version of the command:

```
A)USQ - B:M7LIB.DQC ⊃
```

This command displays the first 65,535 lines of the file in un-squeezed form. Most files have less than this number of lines, so the entire file is displayed until you type a Control-C.

The USQ display routine strips the "high bit" from each character (the "high bit", "high-order bit" or "parity bit" as it is known, is used by programs like WordStar to mark characters for printing features like underline, boldface, variable spacing, etc.); therefore, WordStar text files appear with normal spacing and underlining/boldfacing commands as text. Other "control characters" appear as periods, including the "empty" part of the file following the last word.

If you have a lot of files to un-squeeze, type the command USQ followed by Return to get the USQ asterisk prompt (*). You can then type USQ expressions to be executed immediately. To exit USQ, type Control-C in the assembly language version (1.20), or Return on a line by itself in older versions (similar to using PIP in CP/M). The following example shows the assembly language version (USQ120):

```
A>USQ120 ⤶
USQ v1.20 1/07/84
Use: USQ afn [afn afn ...] [destination drive:]

*B: NSWP205.DQC ⤶

Output drive = B:
NSWP205.DQC -> NSWP205.DOC

*OTHER11.TQT C: ⤶

Output drive = C:
OTHER11.TQT -> OTHER11.TXT

*^C
A>
```

With USQ version 1.20, you can put the destination disk drive either before the filename to un-squeeze, as in the first example above:

      *B: NSWP205.DQC ⊃

Or you can put the destination drive after the filename, as in the second example:

      *OTHER11.TQT C: ⊃

You exit this version of USQ by typing a Control-C.

Squeezing Files With SQ

You can squeeze any file, but squeezing executable ".COM" or ".OBJ" files does not shrink them significantly. An ASCII text file or program source code file (which is usually text) may reduce to between 65% and 52% of its original size.

When SQ squeezes a file, the data in the original file is looked at byte by byte. These bytes can contain anything. The squeezing operation first compresses repeated byte values into a code, then it generates a "Huffman code" to match the characteristics of the file. A "decoding table" is stored in the squeezed version of the file; therefore, squeezing very short files can actually lengthen them.

You can provide filenames, drive letters and options for SQ on the command line (as with USQ shown above), or in response to SQ prompts. You can also provide them from a file you already saved with the information.

Before squeezing, be sure you have enough space on disk to fit another file that will be at least two-thirds of the size of the original file. Here's an example of SQ:

      A)SQ CHAP1.TXT ⊃

SQ creates a squeezed file using the name the original file had when it was squeezed, but substituting a "Q" for the middle character of the three-character extension, thereby creating the file CHAP1.TQT.

To put the squeezed file on a disk other than the one holding the original file, specify the "destination disk drive" first (the one to hold the new squeezed file), then the filename of the original file:

```
A)SQ B: CHAP1.TXT ⊃
```

The space between B: and the filename tells SQ that B: is the destination drive, not the drive holding CHAP1.TXT. If the first parameter of SQ is a drive letter without a filename, SQ assumes it is the destination drive.

You can squeeze more than one file, and on more than one disk drive, by naming more than one on the command line:

```
A)SQ CHAP1.TXT B:CHAP2.TXT ⊃
```

This command creates the squeezed file CHAP1.TQT on drive A, and creates CHAP2.TQT on drive B.

The original files are not disturbed. You should keep at least one copy of the original file in case you mislaid your USQ or other un-squeezing utility. Squeezed files are excellent for archiving because they take up less space; however, you must remember to keep copies of USQ or another un-squeezing utility handy.

When you type more than one filename with SQ, each file is processed in order. You can type as many filenames as you can fit on a command line. However, the filenames you give to the original versions of SQ must be *specific* names, not ambiguous filename matches.

More recent versions of SQ will accept filename matches using the * and ? symbols:

```
A)SQ *.TXT ⊃
```

This example squeezes all ".TXT" files on drive A.

To squeeze many files with SQ, type the command SQ followed by Return to get the SQ prompt. You can then type SQ expressions that are executed immediately, and stop SQ by typing a Control-C in the assembly language version (1.11), or Return on a line by itself in older versions (similar to using PIP in CP/M). The following example shows the assembly language version (SQ111):

```
A)SQ111 ⊃
SQ v1.11
Use: SQ afn [afn afn ...] [destination drive:]

*B: NEWCHAP1.TXT ⊃

Output drive = B:
NEWCHAP1.TXT -) NEWCHAP1.TQT

*PROG101.DOC C: ⊃

Output drive = C:
PROG101.DOC -) PROG101.DQC

*^C
A)
```

With SQ version 1.11, you can put the destination disk drive either before the filename to un-squeeze, as in the first example above (NEWCHAP1.TXT), or after the filename, as in the second example (PROG101.DOC). You exit this version of SQ by typing a Control-C.

Directed Input/Output With SQ/USQ

If you frequently squeeze or un-squeeze the same files and you want to perform the operation without having to type the list of filenames again and again, you can create a *parameter list* of SQ or USQ parameters for the operation, and supply the parameter list to SQ or USQ as a file.

For example, you could create (using a text editor) a file named CHAPTERS.PAR to hold the filenames of each chapter of your book:

```
CHAP1.TXT ⊃
```

```
B:CHAP2.TXT ⊃
C:CHAP3.TXT ⊃
C:CHAP4.TXT ⊃
           ⊃
```

You would end this list with a blank line as shown (a line with a Return (⊃).

You can then use the following SQ command to squeeze all of these files at once:

```
A)SQ <CHAPTERS.PAR ⊃
```

SQ takes its parameters from the file following the ‹ symbol. Each file is squeezed as if you typed the SQ command by itself, then typed each filename to the SQ prompt. The final blank line (line with a Return only) sends a Return to SQ to stop the SQ program.

This is called *re-directed console input* in computer jargon. We call it *directed input*. The input is directed to the program from a file.

SQ and USQ both display comments and error messages if any errors occur during the squeezing or un-squeezing process. In a long operation these comments and messages can scroll off the screen (it is assumed you are watching for them and reading them).

If you wanted to start such an operation but didn't want to watch for messages, you can direct the output of the program to a file that you can look at later.

For example:

```
A)SQ <CHAPTERS.PAR >OUTFILE ⊃
```

This command sends any progress reports, comments or error messages resulting from the squeezing operation (whose parameters are in CHAPTERS.PAR) to the file OUTFILE. You can display OUTFILE later with the TYPE command.

This is called, predictably, *re-directed console output* in the jargon. We called it *directed output* to the file following the › symbol.

What if you want the console output directed to *both* the console where you can see it, and a file where you can view it later? Use a plus sign (+) in place of the ⟩ symbol:

```
A>SQ <CHAPTERS.PAR +OUTFILE ⏎
```

The FLS Pipeline to SQ/USQ

Richard Greenlaw invented the FLS program to put together a parameter list for SQ or USQ on the same command line. FLS lets you use * and ? as filename match symbols to refer to several files at once. You can also use directed input and directed output on an FLS command line.

To show how FLS can simplify operations, here's an example that un-squeezes all ".DQC" files on drive B and sends the results to drive C, and also un-squeezes all ".TQT" files on drive A and sends the results to drive D:

Example #1.

```
A>FLS C: B:*.DQC D: *.TQT |USQ ⏎
```

In this example, the first drive (C:) is the destination for the next un-squeeze operation (on B:*.DQC, all ".DQC" on drive B). The next drive (D:) is the destination for the subsequent un-squeeze operation (on *.TQT, all ".TQT" files on drive A).

This example simulates what is called a "pipe" in some sophisticated operating systems. The vertical bar symbol (|) indicates that the parameter list built by FLS should be "piped" or fed into the program USQ.

How does FLS work? Here are examples designed to show how FLS prepares parameters for SQ or USQ:

Example #2.

```
A>FLS C: B:*.DQC D: *.TQT ⟩TEMP.$$$ ⏎
```

This FLS command passes the parameters to the console output file TEMP.$$$. FLS knows that a letter followed by a colon and nothing else is a destination drive name intended for SQ or USQ.

With TEMP.$$$ containing the parameters from the above example, you could use the following commands to direct the parameters from the TEMP.$$$ file to USQ, and erase the temporary file TEMP.$$$:

Example #3.

```
A>USQ <TEMP.$$$ ⏎
A>ERA TEMP.$$$ ⏎
```

The commands in examples #2 and #3 can be shortened into the one FLS command we used in example #1. In example #1 we used the FLS command with a "pipe" (the symbol "¦"), which has the same effect as creating a temporary file (like TEMP.$$$), and then using it as input to the USQ program, and finally deleting it.

Here are more examples of using SQ, USQ and FLS:

```
A>FLS *.?Q? ¦USQ ⏎
```

This example un-squeezes all squeezed files on the current drive and puts the resulting un-squeezed files on the same drive.

```
A>FLS D: B:*.ASM C:*.ASM ¦SQ ⏎
```

This example squeezes all ".ASM" files on drives B and C, and puts the squeezed files on drive D. Note that without the D: drive parameter first in the parameter list, the squeezed files would have been put on drive A.

```
A>FLS C:*.TXT +NEW.PAR ⏎
```

This example builds a parameter list of all ".TXT" files on drive C and stores the list in NEW.PAR; the output is also displayed.

```
A>SQ <NEW.PAR ⏎
```

This example shows the parameter list file NEW.PAR, built in the previous example, used as input to SQ.

```
A>FLS B: *.TXT *.DOC |SQ >OUT ⊃
```

This example squeezes all ".TXT" and ".DOC" files on drive A and puts the squeezed files on drive B. The progress report and any error messages are directed to the file OUT.

SQ, USQ and FLS are available as source code files for you to modify if you wish. More detailed comments about the squeezing and un-squeezing operations are included in these source files.

Squeeze & Un-squeeze For MS-DOS/PC-DOS

Like the Squeezer utilities for CP/M systems, there are squeezing and un-squeezing utilities for the IBM PC running PC-DOS and PC-compatible computers running MS-DOS.

SQUEEZE.COM (version 1.8) compresses programs, text files and data. It searches for continuous character patterns like blanks. These characters are saved once with an indicator of how many times they appear consecutively in the file.

Compiled programs compress only a little (often to no more than 94% of the original size). Text files and hexadecimal files compress to as little as 50% of the original size, depending on the nature of the data in the file.

To compress a file type:

```
SQUEEZE filename.ext ⊃
```

SQUEEZE creates a new file with compressed data from the file you specified (filename.ext), changing the name only by substituting a "Q" for whatever is the middle letter of the extension (.ext). For example, if you squeeze the file SAMPLE.TXT, the newly-created file is called SAMPLE.TQT. If no extension is given for the file being compressed, SQUEEZE.COM adds the extension ".QQQ" to the new file.

SQUEEZE.COM is fast. A file over 100,000 bytes can be

squeezed in just minutes. You also have the option to show the compression on your monitor while it is being done. You do this by placing a dash (-) between the program's name and the name of the file being squeezed:

```
SQUEEZE - filename.ext ⊃
```

You decompress a squeezed file with UNSQUEEZ.COM. It reads the special information placed in the squeezed file, then expands the file back to its original size and contents.

To un-squeeze a file, the file's extension must have a "Q" as the middle letter (e.g., ".TQT" and ".QQQ"). Type the following command to un-squeeze a file:

```
UNSQUEEZ filename.eQt ⊃
```

The Squeezer utilities are useful in a variety of applications because they can squeeze any type of file. In the long run the utilities will save you money in disks and in transmission costs.

CHAPTER 6:
LIBRARY UTILITIES

Most public domain programs for CP/M systems are organized into *library files*. A library file is a file containing other files, usually of a similar nature. For example, all the files associated with the MDM740 program are in the MDM740.LBR library file. The MDM740.LBR file appears in the directory as one file, and although it has several *member files* contained within it (MDM740.DQC, MDM740.OBJ, MDM740.INF and others), it takes up the directory space of one CP/M file. A library file usually has the extension ".LBR".

Similar public domain program files are organized into a library file for three reasons:

- A library file takes up less disk space than the file's individual member files.

- It is easier to find all the files you need for running and modifying a particular program such as Modem7. Simply find the library file containing all the files you need.

- It is easier and faster to download a library file containing member files than it is to download each member file separately.

For these reasons you are encouraged to copy or download an entire library file rather than copying or downloading individual member files of the library file. You must, however, obtain a *file extracting* utility for your system, so that you can extract the member files from the library file on your system.

The easiest file extracting utilities to use are LSWEEP13 and NULU. Both programs let you open a library file and extract member files; if the member files are in squeezed format (as described in Chapter 5), LSWEEP13 automatically un-squeezes them, whereas NULU gives you a choice to un-squeeze or not un-squeeze.

If you want to be able to create library files for use with your computer, get either NULU or the full-blown LU300 utility. Library Utility version 3.00 (LU300), written by Gary P. Novosielski, is described in detail in this chapter, as are NULU and LSWEEP.

Looking At Library Files

When you call a bulletin board system such as the FOG BBS, you can display all files in a disk/user area using the enhanced DIR utility (type DIR and press Return). However, this command does not show the member files inside the library files.

To see each library file's member files in a DIR display, use these options that are available with the DIR utility:

    A0>DIR $L ⊃

If this command does not work on the BBS you are using, try this command, substituting the actual name of the library file for library below (you can leave off the ".LBR" extension):

    A0>LDIR library ⊃

The display should include the name of the library file and the filenames of all the member files. Some versions also display the sizes of these member files, and a special CRC (cyclic redundancy check) number for comparing versions of files. (CRC numbers are described with the CRCK utility in Chapter 7.)

LDIR (written by Gary P. Novosielski) accepts the "wildcard" symbols * and ? in filename matches; therefore you can use this command to see all member files for all libraries in the current drive/user area:

    A0>LDIR *.LBR ⊃

You can also use the LU or NULU utilities to display a directory of the member files in a library, or use LSWEEP13 or NULU to see each file.

Extracting With LSWEEP13

LSWEEP13 (Library SWEEPer version 1.3) was written in the BDS C language by Joe Volger with pieces borrowed from LDIR and LTYPE (Gary P. Novosielski), USQ (Dick Greenlaw) and TYPESQ (Bob Mathias).

LSWEEP was designed to make it easy to extract member files from library files using a "sweep" mode. You can step through the file's names picking files for extraction. LSWEEP looks a lot like DISK and NSWEEP (described in Chapter 7) and combines library extraction and un-squeezing into one easy step. However, LSWEEP does little else; you may still need LU or NULU for other library operations if you intend to use libraries on your disks. You may also need LSWEEP's "cousins" DISK or NSWEEP.

LSWEEP can extract or display a squeezed or un-squeezed member file of a library file. However, if a file to be extracted is squeezed, LSWEEP version 1.3 will un-squeeze it whether you want it to or not. (NULU gives you a choice.)

To start LSWEEP, type the command LSWEEP followed by one or more library names (unless the extension is ".LBR", which is assumed, you must specify the library name's extension):

```
A>LSWEEP MDM740
```

This command opens the library MDM740.LBR. You see the following on your screen:

```
                    LSWEEP
                Ver:1.03 84-22-01
                   Joe Volger

              Derived from: LDIR & LTYPE
```

```
COMMANDS:

  ? - Displays this menu.
  E - Extracts (and unsqueezes) a member.
  V - Views a (viewable) file.
  X - Exits this program.
     Any other input skips to the next member.

  Library: MDM740.LBR has 12 entries, 3 free:
  MDM740.LBR * 1. M7FNK    .COM  3k >
```

The "current member" is M7FNK.COM, and its size is 3k. You can extract this file by typing E, or you can display it by typing V. If you type ? you display the above menu again; if you type X, you leave LSWEEP and return to the operating system. Any other key advances you to the next member. You can skip easily from one member to the next by pressing Return or any key other than ?, E, V, or X. You can't move backwards, but when you reach the last member, another Return moves you to the first member.

```
MDM740.LBR * 1. M7FNK    .COM  3k >  ⊃
MDM740.LBR * 2. M7FNK    .DQC  2k >  ⊃
MDM740.LBR * 3. M7LIB    .COM  2k >  ⊃
MDM740.LBR * 4. M7LIB    .DQC  2k >  ⊃
MDM740.LBR * 5. M7NM-6   .AQM  5k >  ⊃
MDM740.LBR * 5. MDM740   .COM 19k >  ⊃
MDM740.LBR * 6. MDM740   .DQC 26k >  ⊃
MDM740.LBR * 7. MDM740   .IQF  8k >  ⊃


MDM740.LBR * 1. M7FNK    .COM  3k >  ⊃
MDM740.LBR * 2. M7FNK    .DQC  2k >  ⊃
MDM740.LBR * 3. M7LIB    .COM  2k >  ⊃
MDM740.LBR * 4. M7LIB    .DQC  2k >
```

To extract a member, type E. LSWEEP asks for the drive to store the extracted copy. Type a drive letter and colon, or press Return for the current drive:

```
MDM740.LBR * 4. M7LIB    .DQC  2k ) E
To Drive? (CR for default) ⊃
Extracting file -) M7LIB.DOC Done.


MDM740.LBR * 4. M7LIB    .DQC  2k )
```

LSWEEP extracts the file from the library file, and *un-squeezes* it if the file member was squeezed. If the file member was not squeezed, it is extracted as an exact copy. Either way, if a file with the same name exists on the same disk, it is deleted as the extracted copy is created.

LSWEEP version 1.3 (LSWEEP13) does *not* verify the accuracy of the file as LU300 does (Library Utility 3.00). Perhaps a future version will.

You can line up several libraries to sweep through by typing their names on the LSWEEP command line:

```
A)LSWEEP MDM740 NSWP205 UNERA15 ⊃
```

This command sets up three libraries: MDM740.LBR, NSWP205.LBR and UNERA15.LBR. As you extract or view or simply step through the member files of MDM740.LBR, you can use the X command to move on to the next library, NSWP205.LBR, and extract, view or step through the members of that library. Another X at this point moves you on to the final library, UNERA15.LBR.

If you want to sweep through all the ".LBR" files on a disk, try this version:

```
A)LSWEEP *.LBR ⊃
```

Try to specify a proper filename match (using * and ? symbols) that selects only library files. Non-library files are ignored by LSWEEP.

LSWEEP version 1.3 does not try to take the place of LU (Library Utility), which is essential for managing your own libraries. On the other hand, NULU is designed to replace both LSWEEP and LU.

Extracting With NULU

NULU (version 1.0 written by Martin Murray, System Solutions, P.O. Box 35972, Dallas, TX 75235) is a new program that replaces LSWEEP and LU that combines all the functions of LU with the easy file-by-file sweep operation of LSWEEP.

Before NULU, LSWEEP was one of the first programs to be downloaded from bulletin board systems, because it was the easiest to use for extracting files from libraries downloaded intact from bulletin boards. Now NULU is a candidate to be the first program to download, because it combines un-squeezing, extracting, and library management into one utility.

Start NULU by typing its name on the CP/M command line. This puts you into NULU's command mode, which lets you organize a library, extract member files, and do many other things. To learn how to use NULU quickly, we recommend using the "file sweep" mode of NULU.

To start "file sweep" mode, type the -F command and press Return (↩). NULU presents the file sweep mode commands you can use:

```
-AWAITING COMMAND AO:)-F ↩


                    NULU Filesweep Menu


     A Next member          B Previous member
     C Close the library    D Delete member
     E Extract member       L Log new library
     P Print member         Q Unsqueeze member
     R Rename member        U Drive/User change
     V View member          W Wildcard rename
     X Exit NULU            Y Disk directory
     Z NULU command mode    ? Menu


     Drive A: Total 600k, Used 552k, Free 48k


     No library open. Z
     -AWAITING COMMAND AO:)
```

We used the Z command from file sweep mode to return to NULU's command mode. To return to file sweep mode, type -F ⊃. To leave file sweep mode and return to command mode, type Z . To leave file sweep mode and return to CP/M, type X.

To extract members from a library, you must first "open" the library. Type L   (for "log" a new library). NULU then asks for the library file name. Provide the name and the drive letter or user area number if the library file is not in the same drive and user area as NULU.COM:

```
No library open. Library name:NSWP205.LBR ⊃
Library AO:NSWP205.LBR open.
(Buffer size: 302 sectors)
Active entries: 3, Deleted: 0, Free: 1, Total: 4.
1. NSWP205 .COM  12k : ⊃
2. NSWP205 .DQC   2k :
```

As soon as you "log" or open a library, the first member file appears. You can press Return (⊃) or type an A to move down the list of member files. NULU displays each member file's name along with the file's size in kilobytes (1K, or one kilobyte, is equal to 1024 bytes or characters) — this is the amount of disk space the file would occupy if it was extracted from the library to become a separate file on the current drive.

You can extract any member file you wish by pressing Return until the cursor falls on the member file, and then typing the E or Q commands: E extracts without un-squeezing, and Q extracts and un-squeezes in one step. You can use either command with a drive letter and user area number to send the extracted copy to another disk and/or user area:

```
2. NSWP205 .DQC   2k :E                          (Extract only.)
2. NSWP205 .DQC   2k :Extract to: : ⊃           (To current drive.)
Extracting...
NSWP205 .DQC to AO:NSWP205 .DQC
2. NSWP205 .DQC   2k :Q              (Extract and un-squeeze.)
2. NSWP205 .DQC   2k :Unsqueeze to:B: ⊃          (To drive B.)
```

160 Bove & Rhodes

You can also specify a new filename for the extracted copy.
Here's an example:

```
2. NSWP205 .DQC   2k :Q
2. NSWP205 .DQC   2k :Unsqueeze to: B:NSWEEP.DOC ⏎
```

You can use the V command to view a member file, and P to print
one. These commands come in handy when you want to view a
squeezed information file or print a squeezed ".DOC" file without
actually extracting them from a library.

Running Programs Stored In Libraries

The LRUN command was designed by Gary P. Novosielski
(with help from Ron Fowler) for running programs that are stored
within libraries.

Small ".COM" files usually waste disk space, because many
floppy disk systems allocate 2K for a file even if it is much smaller,
and some hard disk systems allocate up to 8K for each file even if it
is much smaller.

You can save disk space by combining many small ".COM"
files into one library file. For example, you might combine all of
your small utility files into one library called UTILITY.LBR on
your disk.

You can then run any ".COM" file in this library using the
LRUN command:

```
A>LRUN -UTILITY FINDBAD ⏎
```

This command runs the program FINDBAD.COM, which is
stored in the library UTILITY.LBR.

The dash (-) in front of the library name tells LRUN it is a
library name, not a filename. If you use a dash without a library
name, LRUN assumes the name of the library is
COMMAND.LBR. If you specify a drive with the library name
(e.g., -B:UTILITY), LRUN searches that drive only for the library;
otherwise, LRUN searches the current drive for the library, and if

it is not found there, LRUN automatically searches drive A, user area 0.

Here are more examples of LRUN:

```
A)LRUN - ED SAMPLE.TXT ⊃
```

This command searches the library COMMAND.LBR for the program ED.COM, and if it finds it, it runs the program with the parameter SAMPLE.TXT (ED requires such a parameter).

```
A)LRUN -C:SPECIAL LU -O COMMAND -A A:*.COM
```

This command searches the library SPECIAL.LBR on drive C for the LU.COM program. If it is found, LU.COM is executed with the parameter list -O COMMAND -A A:*.COM. These LU commands are described later in this chapter.

LU300 (Library Utility vers. 3.00)

The LU300 program, written by Gary P. Novosielski, lets you organize many similar files into one library file, extract files from a library file, display the member files in a library file and reorganize a library file. The program works with CP/M version 2.0 or a newer version (most CP/M systems in use are version 2.2 or CP/M Plus (3.0)).

LU (version 3.00, or LU300) has two cousins: LTYPE, which displays the contents of member files stored in a library file, and LRUN (version 2.0, or LRUN20), which runs programs that are stored within libraries.

You can start LU by typing its name, and then type LU commands to perform operations; or you can type all of the LU commands to execute, with the parameters you need with them, on the same command line with LU. You can also send LU commands to LU from a disk file.

Why Make Library Files?

One important reason is the ease with which you can transfer packages of software from one system to another using Xmodem. You can transfer one library file and effectively transfer many files at once. Filename conflicts of individual files (such as the many instances of READ.ME in packages) would not occur on the receiving disk. Since Xmodem also has a way of downloading an individual member file from a library file, you can have the best situation: library files and easy extraction.

But there are other reasons. A library file usually takes up less space than the sum of its individual member files. Floppy disk systems allocate disk space in blocks of 2K or more bytes per allocation block, and hard disk systems may allocate up to 8K per block. As a file grows, another block is allocated on disk for it. If the file doesn't use the entire 2K (or up to 8K on hard disk systems), the rest remains as dead space on the disk, not used by any other file.

Files organized in a library file use only as much as they need, because space is allocated for the library file as it grows, not for the member files. A member file cannot grow once it is inside a library file, but you can delete a file from a library and add a new version of the file, or add new files, and not waste disk space. The member files in a library use only the number of sectors they actually need, although the library file itself may have a partially-wasted block at the end.

The library file also saves directory entries. There is a limit on the number of directory entries you can have in one directory, which can limit the number of files you have, especially if most of them are small. The library file consolidates many files under one set of directory entries for the library file.

Although the library file needs to reserve space for its own member information at the beginning of the file, the net effect is usually a saving of total disk space. You get the best results when you combine many small files into one library. Library files are also useful as file archives, where they can act as "labels" for entire "shelves" of files.

There are also reasons for *not* using library files. Member files in a library file are not available to programs like word processors or text editors. Although you can run a ".COM" file that resides in a library file, you have to extract text files, data files and anything else used with your programs.

Library files can actually waste disk space if you delete a member file. The library can't re-use the space left by a deleted file unless you use the -R command to reorganize the library.

Perhaps the strongest reason against using library files is the fact that you cannot rebuild a library file if it is somehow "trashed" on the disk (if one bad sector occurs in the library file). The only solution is to rely on backup copies of the library file.

Extracting Using LU

The easiest way to use the program is to type LU followed by Return, then use LU commands. When you start LU it displays the following:

```
A>LU300 ⤺

Library Utility        Ver:3.00 83-08-16
Copyright (c) 1983 by Gary P. Novosielski
-? 0/A:>
```

The LU prompt -? 0/A:> in the above example changes as you type LU commands. Here's the general meaning of it:

-?   This prompt shows the current LU command in effect (the question mark signifies no command in effect). If you type the -E command, the prompt changes to -E. All LU commands start with a dash.

0/A:>   This part of the LU prompt tells you the current user area (zero) and disk drive (A:).

The first thing to do is determine which drive and user area to use to receive the extractions. You must first make sure the disk you choose has enough space to store the extracted copies. To store the extractions on another disk or in another user area, start your LU session with the -U command.

You can type the command using a lower case letter (-u), but don't forget the dash. If you don't type the dash, LU thinks you are opening a new library file to start adding new members; it calls the new library LIBRARY.LBR. If this happens, answer 0 to the number of entries, and LU will stop. You can then re-start LU.

Here is the -U command changing the current user area to one and the drive to B:

```
-? 0/A:)-u 1/b: ↵
-U 1/B:)
```

The extractions will now be stored on drive B.

The second thing you must do is *open the library* using the -O command. Type the -O command and the name of the library (LU assumes the library file has the extension ".LBR"; if you use another extension for the library file, specify it):

```
-U 1/B:)-o 0/a:mdm740 ↵
Old library: MDM740.LBR has 12 entries, 3 free.
-O 1/B:)
```

Note that although we are "logged into" drive B, user area 1, we can still open a library file that resides in any user area or drive — MDM740.LBR is in user area 0, drive A, so we prefix the name with 0/a: (lower case letters work as well as UPPER case).

Now look at the file members in the library by typing the -L command:

```
-O 1/B:)-1 ↵
Library: MDM740.LBR
Name              Index      Size      CRC
DIRECTORY                    3
M7FNK.COM          3        24        D211
M7FNK.DQC         27        14        67B0
M7LIB.COM         41        15        F500
```

M7LIB.DQC	56	14	EA1E
M7NM-6.AQM	70	34	E1AF
MDM740.COM	104	146	E7B1
MDM740.DQC	250	203	25FB
MDM740.IQF	453	57	DA9A
Active sectors		510	
Unused		2	
Total		512	

Active entries: 9, Deleted: 0, Free: 3, Total: 12.

-? 1/B:⟩

After displaying the list of file members, the prompt changes to a question mark, showing no command in effect.

Scanning this display you can tell how much space you will need to store the extracted copies of the files you want. To extract a file, type the -E command with the name of the file:

```
-? 1/B:⟩-e mdm740.dqc ⟲
Extracting: MDM740.DQC
-E 1/B:⟩
```

When you type an LU command such as -E, it stays in effect until you type another one. Therefore, with the prompt showing the -E command in effect, you can go ahead and type the name of another member file to extract:

```
-E 1/B:⟩m7fnk.dqc ⟲
Extracting: M7FNK.DQC
-E 1/B:⟩
```

LU performs a "cyclic redundancy check" (CRC) to see if the extraction you get is exactly the same file (has exactly the same characters) as the one stored in the library. The CRC check is useful for checking members of libraries which were created on bulletin board systems or other systems and which were transmitted by phone (possibly several times) before you receive them. If the CRC check does not show an exact duplicate, you get this message:

    CRC error. M7FNK.DQC file questionable.

Whenever you add a new member to a library using LU300, a CRC value is calculated for that member and stored in the member's directory entry. When you extract the member file, LU performs the calculation again and compares values. If the value is not the same, it may be due to a glitch in the library file caused by an error in transmission.

However, the error message may also be due to the fact that other library utilities do not use CRC checking. ".LBR" files created by older versions of LU (e.g., LU111) and by NULU have no CRC value, and when LU300 extracts each member, it displays the above error message even though the extracted file is proper. You know this is the case when the CRC value is 0000 — it means the ".LBR" file was created by an older version of LU or by NULU.

You can extract as many files as you wish, or use other LU commands which we summarize in this chapter. All LU commands are a dash and a single character. If you use a dash and a single character as the name of a member file in a library (e.g., -Z as a filename, with no extension), always specify it as -Z. (with a period).

LU Commands

Before you can use LU commands on a library, you must first open a library file with the the -O command, and type its name. The command remains in effect until you type another command; therefore, if you type another filename, the -O will still be in effect and it will close the first library file and open the new one.

Here's a summary of the LU commands:

-A   Add new member files to the library. Any subsequent filenames you type should be names of existing files to be included in the open library file. You can add several files by typing their filenames one by one, or using a filename match with the wildcard ? and * symbols.

-B   Set the buffer size (version 3.00 only), to be used only when you start up LU. The -B command reads the next number you type as the size (in sectors) to allocate for a disk input/output I/O buffer. Usually a 64-sector buffer is used by LU, and this is plenty for normal libraries. However, a larger buffer will increase the speed of adding, extracting and reorganizing, but the increase varies widely with different computers. Also, a large buffer decreases the number of directory entries LU can process.

-C   Close the open library. You don't usually need this command, since any open library is automatically closed when you end your LU session or open another file with the -O command. It is provided for when you want to change disks. You must close the library before changing a disk. After changing the disk, use the -U command.

-D   Delete member files from the open library. It does not free up the space occupied by the files — you have to use the -R command to reorganize the open library.

-E   Extract files from the library by making copies as regular CP/M files by the same name used in the library. If a CP/M file exists by the same name, it is deleted unless it is protected by the read-only attribute. The original copy in the library is not disturbed. You can type a filename match or several individual filenames.

-L   List the member files in the library. Each member filename is displayed with the "index" (starting record within the library), the file size in 1K increments, and the internally-calculated CRC (cyclic redundancy check) value. Also displayed is the number of active entries (members) in the library, the number deleted, the number free for future additions, and the total number allowed in the library.

-N   Rename a member. You provide the new name first (with extension if any), followed by an equal sign and the old name (and extension if any): `newname.ext=oldname.ext`.

-O   Open a library. With `-O` in effect, the next filename you type is treated as the name of a library file to be opened for use. If there is already an open library, it is first closed, and the new one opened. You can open a library on another disk and in another user area by specifying the user number u and the drive d with the filename, like this: `u/d:filename.ext`.

-R   Reorganize the open library. This command reclaims the space left after you've deleted files from the library. It also lets you change the maximum number of directory entries for the library, so that you can add more files. It does this by copying all the active members to a new library, leaving behind and deleting the inactive members occupying space on the disk.

       The new library is organized in the current user area and drive (you can change the current user/drive with the -U command). You must have room on the disk to fit an entire library as big as the existing library. If you want to decrease the size of a library, specify a maximum of 1; LU will automatically set the maximum to the number of active members, leaving no free entries.

-U   Use new default user area/drive. Use this command to change the current user area and/or drive. Express this parameter in the form u/d:, where u is a user area number (0 through 15) and d is an existing drive on the system.

       When you change a drive with -U, any open library is first closed and the disk system is reset. You can therefore change disks and then type -U to "log in" the new disk. Use -O to open a library (which can be on any drive or user area), and have all results occur in the user/drive set with the -U command.

-X   Exit the LU program. This command also closes the open library.

You can put LU commands and corresponding parameters on the LU command line to execute as a "batch operation." For example, you could use this LU command to extract M7FNK.DQC and M7LIB.DQC from the MDM740.LBR library:

```
A>LU300 -U 1/B: -O O/A:MDM740 -E M7FNK.DQC M7LIB.DQC ⊃
```

This command changes the destination user area and drive to 1/B:, then opens the library MDM740.LBR (user area 0, drive A), then extracts M7FNK.DQC and M7LIB.DQC from the library and stores the copies in user area 1 on drive B.

Safety Net

We cannot overemphasize the importance of keeping backup copies of library files. Unlike a normal CP/M file whose directory entry and entire contents can be reconstructed using various "disk surgery" utilities like UNERA (Chapter 7) or DU (Chapter 8), if something happens to damage a library file's directory, it is nearly impossible to reconstruct the entire library file or retrieve its members.

To minimize the risk of damaging the library file's directory entry, LU reads the library file's directory entry into memory and makes changes only to the memory version until you close the library (or until LU closes the library).

For example, let's say you opened a very large library with lots of members, then accidentally typed the -D *.* command, which deletes every member of the library file. Your heart may sink as you watch the names of precious library member files go by with the message DELETED, but the deletions have not yet occurred on disk. After the operation, stop LU by typing a Control-C. This cancels the LU program without updating the disk version of the library file; therefore, the library file should remain intact.

NULU or LU?

NULU's virtue over its competition is that it offers a choice for un-squeezing when extracting member files. LU300 extracts files but knows nothing about un-squeezing squeezed files; LSWEEP13 un-squeezes squeezed files when it extracts them, whether you want to or not (un-squeezing a file requires more disk space than the amount occupied by the squeezed file).

NULU also offers more choices than LU300 or LSWEEP13. You can view and print the contents of member files without extracting them, and NULU will un-squeeze squeezed files before displaying or printing them. You can make bigger libraries with up to 800 member files in each library. Member files are kept in sorted order, and libraries can be reorganized very quickly.

NULU's command set is very similar to LU, with some additional commands and enhancements to existing commands. The only LU function not covered by NULU is the maintaining of CRC numbers for each member file. NULU changes any LU-set CRC numbers to zero; LU regards a NULU-modified library to be like one created by an earlier version of LU that did not use CRC numbers.

Another difference is that filename matches (also called ambiguous filenames) can be abbreviated in certain ways: *.* (specifying all files) can be typed as **, *.TXT (specifying all ".TXT" files) can be typed as *TXT, and if you type a drive or user area (or both) without a filename match, it assumes you meant *.* (all files).

The syntax is liberal for typing drive letters and user area numbers. You can type A15:*.* or 15A:** or 15/A:** to specify all files in user area 15 of drive A. To specify all files on the current drive, you need only type the colon by itself.

As with LU, NULU can be typed on a CP/M command line with numerous NULU commands on the same line (up to 128 characters). Also like LU, all NULU commands are preceded by a dash (-) and are displayed in the prompt.

Here's the NULU command menu, which is displayed whenever you type the -M command:

```
-A Add members          -B Brief toggle
```

-C Close the library	-D Delete members
-E Extract members	-F Filesweep mode
-G Get filespec	-K Krunch the library
-L List members	-M Menu
-N Rename members	-O Open a library
-P Print members	-Q Unsqueeze members
-R Replace members	-T Replace/Add members
-U Drive/User change	-V View members
-X Exit NULU	-Y Disk directory
-(Redirect input	-) Redirect output

Should you get NULU instead of LU300 and LSWEEP? Overall NULU has a better mix of functions, but as of this writing, NULU is still very new (version 1.0) and not yet thoroughly tested. We used NULU and found no problems with it; however, new programs usually need to be tested for months before they are considered foolproof. LU300 (LU version 3.0) is the most reliable of the three, since LSWEEP13 (version 1.3) is also a new program. We recommend that you use LU300 to manage libraries, and USQ to un-squeeze files, until NULU is thoroughly tested.

LU For IBM PC & MS-DOS

A version of the LU utility program is available for the IBM PC and MS-DOS computers. This version of LU manipulates ".LBR" files in the same manner as the CP/M version, but the commands are different. The PC/MS-DOS version of LU can handle both CP/M and PC/MS-DOS library files.

For a quick summary of the LU commands, type LU by itself on a command line, followed by Return. To actually perform LU operations, you must put LU commands on the same command line.

For example, the following command displays all member files within the library file UTILITY.LBR:

```
A)LU T UTILITY.LBR ⊃
```

All LU commands are a single letter (dash is not used). Only one command can be entered at a time. The commands are:

A   Unpack all files from the library. This is the same as using the E (extract) command to extract all the member files by typing the command followed by all the filenames. The A command is much easier to use if you want all of the member files.

L or
T   Display the filenames of all member files in the library file. Each filename is shown with the size of the file in bytes and its starting record number within the library file.

E   Extract a member file from the library. You type the names of the file(s) to be extracted after typing the library name. Each file is extracted and copied to a disk file of the same name.

U   Update a library file. You use this command to create new libraries. Enter filename(s) after the library filename. Each file is added to the library. Any file of the same name already in the library is replaced by the new one.

      If the library file does not exist (you are creating a new one), you are asked for the number of new slots for the library. "Slots" means the maximum number of files that the library file can hold. The number you enter is rounded up to the next highest multiple of four; this is just a peculiarity of the library file structure.

D   Delete a member file. This command marks the member file within the library as "deleted". The library file does not change in size, nor does LU remove the data contained by the file. You must reorganize the library file to reclaim the space.

R   Reorganize the library and reclaim the space from deleted files, or existing files that were updated. The library file generally becomes smaller. You should use this command after using the D or U command.

There are a few known "peculiarities" (read "bugs") in the PC/MS-DOS version of LU. One is that if you specify a filename that has no extension as FILE. (with a period but no extension), LU can't find the file; if you specify it without the period (FILE), LU will find it. Another is that all files are rounded up in size to the nearest 128 bytes. This usually doesn't matter for most files, but some files (like spreadsheets) will not work properly unless the size is exactly correct (not rounded up to the nearest 128-byte boundary). You can't put such files into PC/MS-DOS libraries using LU.

Enhancing or Modifying LU and NULU

The LU programs for CP/M and MS-DOS are written in the C language and compiled with the BDS C Compiler. Source files are available, and a more detailed explanation of library files can be found in a ".DOC" file accompanying LU300.

NULU can also be modified to change many of its operations following the instructions provided in the NULU.DOC file. All changes are made using the DDT utility supplied with CP/M.

CHAPTER 7:
SYSTEM UTILITIES

by Bob Wolff

In the hit parade of public domain software, system utilities are in the forefront. This makes sense because system utility programs perform file and disk "housekeeping" chores which are common to nearly every computer application.

The most common system utility programs are ones that make it easier to see filenames and file sizes in a directory display. Others help manage files, find bad disk sectors, perform delicate disk surgery and other general system maintenance operations.

Whether you're using floppy disks to manage a small business, to write books, or to do scientific research, you need good system utilities to display filenames, find bad disk sectors, un-do an accidental file deletion, or copy a selection of files. If you're using a hard disk, you may want to move files from one user area to another. File manipulation utilities like DISK, MAKE and NSWEEP, as well as various directory utilities, are useful no matter what tasks your computer performs for your business, profession or hobby.

CP/M Disk and File Errors

From windblown phone lines to stepped-on floppy disks, calamities have a way of striking your personal computer just when you need it. Your precious files seem at the mercy of not only the capricious catastrophies like power failures, but also the insidious "intermittent" disk error that can never be reproduced except when you least expect or want it — during a crisis or deadline crunch (Murphy's Law applies here).

The real world spawns not only catastrophies and mysteries but energetic problem-solvers. The public domain is loaded with utilities to handle disk errors and recover lost files. Here are a few of them.

Checking a File's Accuracy

CRCK is one CP/M utility that is recommended for anyone who transfers files over the phone and is concerned with file accuracy. The Modem7/Xmodem protocol is only 99% accurate — it is possible for an error to creep in somehow, perhaps in the sending or receiving computer, or in the phone line, and not be detected.

CRCK.COM is a utility that performs a "CRC check" on a file to see if the file is identical to another file. CRCK.COM is very useful for checking a backup copy's accuracy. In each user area, a file named CRCKLIST.CRC or THISUSER.CRC lists each file's special CRC number. After receiving a copy of a file, and after receiving the CRCK.COM program itself, run the CRCK program on the copy you have to see if it generates the same CRC number shown in the CRCK list for the original file (use the command TYPE *.CRC to see the CRCK list).

For example, assume you want to receive the file SAMPLE.OBJ from a bulletin board system. First get a copy of CRCK.COM. When you have a copy of CRCK.COM on your home disk, go back to the RCPM system and TYPE the CRCK list file to see the special CRC number for SAMPLE.OBJ. Remember this number (it will be a hexadecimal number, which uses digits 0 through 9 and A through F).

Set Xmodem and your Modem7 program to receive the SAMPLE.OBJ file. After receiving the file, type the following CRCK command on your home system after leaving Modem7's terminal mode:

```
A>CRCK SAMPLE.OBJ ⏎
```

If the special CRC number for your version is the same as the number for the bulletin board version, the files are identical; if not, an error occurred and the files are not identical.

CRCK occupies a small amount of disk space, and most users put it on the disk they use for communicating with bulletin board systems.

Finding Bad Disk Sectors

Veteran computer users will tell you how they once lost a very important document or data base or program or whatever to the inexplicable BDOS ERR ON d: BAD SECTOR. Now they swear by the FindBad utility, which lets them use disks that have bad sectors.

FindBad finds bad sectors on your disk that are not currently used by files, and isolates them from future use. The idea is to use FindBad right after formatting a new disk, to see if there are any bad sectors. After using the disk for a while, use FindBad periodically to check for bad sectors.

With FindBad you can continue to use a disk that has a few bad sectors. The bad sectors are assigned to a file called [UNUSED.BAD. *Do not* delete this file, because that puts the bad sectors back into circulation!

Recovering Erased Files

The nimblest fingers cannot keep you from making occasional mistakes, and don't they always occur when you're trying to beat that deadline? One of the most common mistakes is to ERA a file accidentally.

Ah, but they can be brought back from the dead! The UNERA utility performs this miracle.

(If you have a disk editing utility like DU, described in Chapter 8, you can "un-erase" files without getting UNERA.)

First, let us examine how CP/M stores files and maintains the disk directory. Each file is stored on disk with its filename, file size and disk positioning information in an area of the disk called the *directory*. A file will have more than one *directory entry* (filename, size and positioning information) when it reaches a certain size depending on the system. Nevertheless, at least one entry is required for each file.

The directory entry starts with a number corresponding to the user area in which the file is stored on that disk. That number is usually zero (user area zero) or any number between one and fifteen (01 to 0F in hexadecimal numbers).

When a CP/M file is erased with ERA (or from a program like WordStar or NSWEEP), all that actually happens is that this starting number of the directory entry is changed to E5 (hexadecimal). This small action on the part of CP/M frees the disk sectors formerly used by that file, so that new files can use the sectors.

If no files have yet been copied to the disk, or created, or expanded, those sectors would not yet be used, so the data in them would still be intact. If you can change the starting E5 back to 00 or to a user area number between 01 and 0F (fifteen), you can restore the file.

UNERA, written by Gene Cotton, changes the starting E5 to 00, meaning the file is active again (and in user area 0). If no other file was created or copied or expanded to use those sectors, the file is just as it was before you erased it. If you erased several files at once, you can un-erase them one at a time and recover them.

To use UNERA, type its name along with the name of the file you erased:

```
A)UNERA SPECIAL.TXT ⊃
```

If files were created or expanded or copied to the disk before you had a chance to recover the file, the file might be recovered with some sections overwritten but others intact. In any case, examine the recovered file carefully.

UNERA is the simplest "file un-erasing" program to use. You can also "un-erase" files using the DU program described in Chapter 8.

UNERA was improved by Irv Hoff and Paul Traina. Version 1.4 restores the file to the current user area, not to user area zero as with previous versions.

Overcoming CP/M Limitations

Many public domain utilities are created simply to overcome some of CP/M's annoying limitations.

For example, user areas in CP/M are sometimes so annoying that people don't use them. For example, to move a file from one user area to another you have to copy the file to the other user area, thereby having a copy of the file in both user areas. If disk space is limited, it is quite a chore to copy the file to another disk (disk B) first before erasing it from disk A and copying it from disk B to another user area in disk A. The MAKE utility solves this problem.

Another example is the REN command in CP/M version 2.2. Unlike the RENAME utility in CP/M Plus and PC/MS-DOS, REN can only rename one file at a time. The public domain RENAME utility for CP/M 2.2 solves this problem.

Another example is the PIP utility. You can't change the destination disk while PIP is running, and expect to be able to copy a file to the new destination disk. You have to first exit PIP, then type Control-C to "log in" the new disk, then re-start PIP to continue your copying operation. RPIP solves this problem.

Make: User Areas

The MAKE.COM program "makes" a file appear in another user area on the same disk without leaving a copy of the file in the current user area. This utility is very useful if you have to move files from one user area to another on the same disk.

MAKE does this by changing the starting number of the filename entry as described in the section on UNERA. Every filename entry starts with a user area number in hexadecimal notation, or the value E5 (hexadecimal) representing an erased file. MAKE finds the file you specify and changes this byte to whatever user area you specify. MAKE does this no matter what user area you are currently in.

For example, to change the file SAMPLE.TXT from whatever user area it was to user area 5, you would go to the user area where MAKE.COM resides, and type this command:

A>MAKE SAMPLE.TXT 5 ⤶

Be careful if you use MAKE with wildcards to specify several files at once. MAKE dutifully changes all files matching your wildcards to the user area you specify. If you make a mistake and change a lot of files to the wrong user area, it may take some time to use MAKE to change each individual file.

Renaming Files

The RENAME utility renames one or more files on the same disk in one operation. Specify filenames using the * and/or ? wildcards. If you specify the /I "switch" at the end of the command line, RENAME asks you to confirm the renaming of each file.

Here's an example that renames files with the extension ".TXT" to have the extension ".J18":

A>RENAME *.J18 *.TXT ⤶

To rename a lot of files with similar filenames, but not all the files, use the /I (interrogate) "switch", and RENAME asks you to type a Y to confirm the files to be renamed:

A>RENAME *.J18 *.TXT /I ⤶

You can also use the /S "switch" to include system files (files that do not appear in normal DIR displays) in the selection to rename.

The NSWEEP utility, described later, can also rename several files at once, along with a host of other functions. However, the RENAME utility is a smaller program performing a single task. You may need one or the other, or both, depending on your applications.

RPIP: Reset Drives With PIP

RPIP.COM retains all the functions of PIP.COM with one added function: the ability to reset all active disk drives while remaining in RPIP.

For example, assume you have two sets of files to copy to several backup disks. You could run PIP and type the following PIP commands in one single PIP operation:

```
A)PIP ⊃
*B:=*.TXT ⊃
*B:=*.DOC ⊃
*
```

At this point you want to copy to another backup disk in drive B. You replace the disk in drive B, press Return to leave PIP, then type Control-C to reset the drive. Finally you repeat the PIP operation for the second backup disk.

RPIP makes this process much easier. Type RPIP in place of PIP above, and the two PIP commands to copy the files. Then replace the disk in drive B and type this RPIP command:

```
*R ⊃
*
```

This command resets all active drives in your system. You can now continue to type PIP commands without leaving the RPIP program.

Rename RPIP.COM to PIP.COM and you'll notice no difference, except now you can use the R command to reset the drives.

Another RPIP command is Q to "quickly repeat" the last PIP command you typed. For example, typing Q ⊃ after the R ⊃ command shown above would repeat the B:=*.DOC ⊃ command. The combination of the R and Q commands with all of PIP's features make RPIP the most useful copying utility.

Directory Utilities

In both CP/M and MS-DOS (PC-DOS) you have the built-in DIR command to display a directory of files on disk. DIR is inadequate in many respects because it does not sort filenames into alphabetical order, and the CP/M version does not display the sizes of the files and the space available on disk.

In CP/M 2.2 systems, there is no way to improve the operation of DIR. The alternative is to get a public domain directory utility like XDIR.COM or SD.COM. Note that directory utilities should not be called DIR.COM, because when you type its name to run it, you get the built-in DIR instead (unless your system is modified, like bulletin board systems, to run the DIR.COM utility instead of the built-in DIR).

CP/M Plus offers a DIR.COM utility that sorts and displays filenames in alphabetical order, with sizes and disk space. DIR.COM displays the directories of any single user area and drive or all user areas and drives.

The ZCPR2 system, a public domain "overlay" for CP/M systems that provides better built-in commands, provides a DIR command with all these functions. With a ZCPR2-enhanced CP/M system or CP/M Plus, you may not need any of the directory utilities described here, although you may still want one.

In MS-DOS and PC-DOS you can improve a simple DIR operation by using a "filter" called SORT to alphabetize the file listing before displaying it on the screen. For example, you can get a sorted list by entering:

```
A>DIR | SORT
```

The vertical bar (|), called a *filter*, feeds the file display from DIR to the SORT program before displaying it.

DIR with SORT can take a long time to display the filenames — up to 30 seconds or longer, which is much too long for most users. Luckily, early users of computers came up with solutions to this problem. Several programs in the public domain make the task of keeping track of files easier and less time consuming.

LF (PC/MS-DOS)

The LF.COM program displays filenames in alphabetical order, and goes one step further to separate files into groups by their filename extensions. All files with no extension are grouped together and listed alphabetically, then files with the ".COM" extension are grouped and alphabetized, then other extensions. This method makes it easier to find a file within a class of files. For example, it's easier to find a BASIC program in a set of alphabetized ".BAS" files.

LF.COM can list files on a floppy or a hard disk. You can get a list of files for the drive you're currently logged onto, or another drive. LF.COM does *not* allow the use of a path (available in PC-DOS/MS-DOS 2.0) when specifying the drive. It displays only the list for the current directory on the drive specified.

Below are two examples of LF.COM. The first shows a list for the current default drive; the other is a list for another drive:

```
B>LF ⏎
.BAS files:  artill    bigtype   diskmodf  grafge    gsdump
             mempeek   pallette  rescmd    rescmdck  timing
.COM files:  cd        ddate     fk        lf        sd
             systat    vdel      wait
.DOC files:  colour    cpcpro    fk        grafge    gumup1
             rescmd    squish    systat
.EXE files:  sdir      squish
.SRC files:  squish


B>LF E: ⏎
.BAK files:  class     driverc   tpac02    tpac03
.BAS files:  color14   kathy2    nlq       set-prt   setclock
.BAT files:  class     colorscr  copytpac  driverc   slides
             spf       ssdriver  tpac02    tpac03    where
.COM files:  assign    astclock  backup    basica    bind
             chkdsk    command   comp      convert   debug
             diskcopy  edlin     format    graphics  mode
             print     recover   restore   setclock  superdrv
.DAT files:  clparmfl
.EXE files:  gwbasic   sort      tapeback
```

SD (PC/MS-DOS)

The SD.COM program displays a list of all filenames on a floppy or hard disk. You can get a list for the default drive or another drive. You can also specify specific groups of files to be listed using wildcards (* and ?).

The SD.COM list is very different from LF.COM and later examples. It shows the files alphabetically, then tells you how many files are in the list, how much space they take up, and how much space is left. This information is critical when backing up files from floppies or a hard disk.

Below are two examples of lists produced with SD.COM. The first shows a list from the default drive. To get the same type of listing for another drive, type the drive letter and colon after the command (e.g., for drive E, type SD E: ⊃). The second list specifies a drive and a group of files (using wildcards) to be displayed.

```
B>SD ⊃
ARTILL   BAS  8k : BIGTYPE BAS  2k : CD       COM  1k : COLOUR   DOC  9k
CPCPRO   DOC 13k : DDATE   COM  1k : DISKMODF BAS  4k : FK       COM  3k
FK       DOC  9k : GRAFGE  BAS  9k : GRAFGE   DOC  2k : GSDUMP   BAS  1k
         .
         .
         .

B: Total of 137k in 33 files with 43k space remaining.


B>SD E:S*.* ⊃
SD       COM  2k : SET-PRT BAS  1k : SETCLOCK BAS  4k : SETCLOCK COM  1k
SLIDES   BAT  1k : SORT    EXE  2k : SPF      BAT  1k : SSDRIVER BAT  1k
         .
         .
         .

E: Total of 36k in 14 files with 234k space remaining.
```

SD.COM has several parameters. They are "single parameters," meaning they cannot be combined for mutual effect. Parameters are added to the basic form by entering a slash (/) followed by the parameter.

After initial testing, I got only the /X, /S and /D parameters to work. While this is less than half of them, these represent the most common uses.

/X sorts by the file extension. This means the last three characters are put in alphabetical order. This type of file listing was useful to me in writing this book, because I used ".UG" as the extension for half a dozen different files. To check them out, SD /X ⌐ put them all together.

/S sorts by the size of the file. This means the files are ordered from smallest to largest. Again, this has helped me see trends in document development as I've developed more polished versions of this chapter.

/D sorts by the date the file was lasted changed. PC/MS-DOS stamps a date and time on each file when the file is created or changed. Sorted dates make it easier for me to determine the latest version of a document when too many similar names exist.

XDIR (PC/MS-DOS)

The XDIR.COM program for PC/MS-DOS displays an "extended directory" for the default drive or a specified drive. It is *not* alphabetized. What makes XDIR unique is that it shows you the attributes of all files on the floppy or hard drive. These attributes are:

R   Read-only file. You can read the file, but you can't write to it (change it or erase it).

S   System file. System files like IBMIO.COM and IBMDOS.COM do not appear in a normal directory listing.

H   Hidden file. Such files do not appear in normal directory listings.

A   Not Archived. This attribute means the file has not been copied since the *last* formal copying procedure using the special backup copying program.

Unlike the standard DIR command, XDIR.COM does not list subdirectories (under PC-DOS/MS-DOS 2.0). Also, you cannot specify a path when requesting a directory.

Here's an example of XDIR:

```
B>XDIR A: ⊃
Directory of A:
IBMBIO   COM   4608   3-08-83   12:00   RHSA
IBMDOS   COM  17152   3-08-83   12:00   RHSA
COMMAND  COM  17664   3-08-83   12:00      A
ANSI     SYS   1664   3-08-83   12:00      A
FORMAT   COM   6016   3-08-83   12:00      A
CHKDSK   COM   6400   3-08-83   12:00      A
   .
   .
   .
        41 File(s)
```

WHEREIS (PC/MS-DOS)

The WHEREIS.COM program was originally published in the January 1984 issue of *Softalk (IBM)*. It was written by John Socha.

WHEREIS.COM looks for the specified file(s) in all subdirectories on the current drive. If more than one copy exists on the drive (in different directories), the program shows you the directories these files are stored in.

To use this program type:

```
WHEREIS filename.ext ⊃
```

You may search for a single file, or use wildcards to specify a group of files. The example below shows the display of WHEREIS.COM:

```
H>B:WHEREIS *.CBL ⊃
\MISC\SOURCE\EXT00000.CBL
```

```
\MISC\SOURCE\MSC100PS.CBL
\MISC\SOURCE\PRODO100.CBL
\PAY\SOURCE\PAF200PR.CBL
\PAY\SOURCE\PME100PS.CBL
\GL\SOURCE\GSC020PB.CBL
\GL\SOURCE\GDS100PS.CBL
```

.

.

.

SDIR22 (PC/MS-DOS)

The SDIR22.COM program has become the most used of all my public domain utility programs on my IBM PC and MS-DOS computers. It provides most of the options in the individual programs above in a single program. It can do the following:

/A   Display hidden files.

/E   Display without erasing the screen.

/P   Pause the display when the screen is full.

/X   Sort alphabetically by filename extension.

/S   Sort numerically by file size.

/D   Sort by the date/time the file was created.

/N   Do not sort; keep in original order.

You can view a list of the files on a floppy or hard disk in several ways. In addition, /A, /E and /P can be combined with other options to produce unique results.

To get a directory listing type:

```
SDIR22 filename.ext ⏎
```

Wildcards can also be used to specify a group of files. The following example shows a regular SDIR22 display.

```
B>SDIR22 ↵
Capital PC Software Exchange /AEPXSDN/ 2.2DRIVE B:  Date 09/15/84  Time 16:01
FILESPEC.EXT  BYTES-    -LAST CHANGE- FILESPEC.EXT    BYTES-    -LAST CHANGE-
*FREE SPACE*  43520                   SDIR22  .ASM    23429   04/17/84 18:09
BSLASH  .KEY     86   11/10/83 17:38  SDIR22  .COM     1312   04/17/84 18:24
DEFCOPY .BAT    604   02/14/84 08:08  VDISK   .ASM     8724   04/03/84 11:12
DEFKEY  .COM   4421   05/01/84 01:21  VDISK   .COM      672   04/03/84 12:46
      .
      .
      .
```

D.COM (CP/M)

D.COM replaces DIR and STAT in CP/M systems for displaying directories on multiple disks and user areas, sorting the file names, and displaying file attributes. D.COM uses only 4K of space and works on a floppy or hard disk.

D.COM quickly displays a directory of files — either on the current drive and user number, or the same user number of another drive. D.COM sorts the file names by number, by symbol, and then by letter in alphabetical order (ASCII sequence — see Appendix A). STAT also does this, but STAT produces a single column of files, a waste of both screen space and paper if printed. D.COM lists the sorted file names and file sizes, but does it in columns — column 1 contains sorted file names, which are continued in column 2, 3 and 4. It does not list file names across the page, which are hard to read, but sorted in up to 4 columns.

Also, D.COM handles lists of file names longer than 23 lines (one screen) far better than DIR or STAT. It stops after 23 lines, then prompts you on the 24th line to press the spacebar to see the next 22 lines. No more having to use ControlS to stop a scrolling list! In fact, the 23rd line moves to line 1 of the screen when the next group of file names are listed. This feature is helpful when a long list scrolls on the screen.

When a list is longer than 23 lines, the columns are still sorted. Each screen is independent. The columns on screen 1 are sorted, as are columns on each subsequent screen. This is very useful when you are searching for a file, because you don't have to remember the last file name in a column from the previous screen. This is just one of several exceptional features of D.COM.

D.COM has four parameters which separately or in combination expand the information provided about the files:

U   Include all DIR attribute files in all user numbers (user areas) with the file count and total space used.

V   Show the user number (UN) and attributes (AT) of each file, in addition to the file name and size.

SYS   Include files with SYS attribute in the file count and total space used.

F   Show only the file's name and extension.

To add these parameters to the D command line, first type a dollar sign ($), then one or more parameters. Thus, if you type D $UV ↵, D.COM sees the $ and attempts to interpret the letters following it. While the dollar sign ($) should have a space before it, U and V should not have a space between them; if they did, D.COM would ignore the V or any other parameter after it.

Here is the D.COM command by itself:

C)D ↵

Name	Ext	Bytes	Name	Ext	Bytes	Name	Ext	Bytes
ANAGRAM	COM	2K	! COVRPAGE11		2K	! SHOWDEMO430		6K
ATFP	11	40K	! DICTSORTCOM		2K	! SORTDICTCOM		8K
AWARD		2K	! DOCN308		6K	! SPELL	COM	4K
.								
.								
.								

25 File(s), occupying 272K of 390K total capacity
19 directory entries and OK bytes remain on C:

All displays appear in this form unless you choose the V or F parameters. The display includes all files which have the DIR attribute on the current user number and drive. You can choose another drive by entering d: (where d is an existing drive letter between A and P):

A)D d: ⊃

Any file with the SYS attribute, which hides a file under CP/M, is not listed or included in the file count and total space occupied by the listed files.

Note that the file names are sorted in ASCII sequence. For example, BETA405 appears before BETARPT.502 because numbers ("405") appear before letters ("RPT") in the sequence of ASCII codes (see Appendix A for an ASCII chart). The sorted file names also appear sorted *in columns*, rather than across the page. This is the more common method of presenting sorted information.

Common to all directory displays are summary lines which appear after the list of file names. These lines tell you:

1.   The number of files listed.
2.   The space they occupy on the disk in comparison to the total disk capacity.
3.   The remaining directory entries or file names which may be added to the disk's directory.
4.   The space remaining on the disk.

The example display above shows 0K left on the disk. Since the files listed occupy only 272K of the possible 390K, you can infer that files are stored in other user areas or have the SYS attribute. The V and SYS parameters list the other files residing on the disk.

D.COM with the U parameter shows files in all user areas:

A)D $U ⊃

The result looks the same as the previous example, with files sorted in ASCII order into columns. In this example the display includes only files with the DIR attribute.

D.COM with the V parameter shows the files on the current user and drive. However, it also includes the user number (UN) where the file is stored as well as its attribute (AT):

```
C)D $V ⤸
Name    Ext  Bytes  UN At   Name      Ext Bytes  UN At    Name      Ext ...
ANAGRAM COM    2K    1   !   COVRPAGE11     2K   1 R  !  SHOWDEMO430 ...
ATFP    11    40K   1 W  !   DICTSORTCOM    2K   1    !  SORTDICTCOM ...
  .
  .
  .
```

25 File(s), occupying 272K of 390K total capacity
19 directory entries and OK bytes remain on C:

The user area number and attribute information is very useful. For example, the attribute on COVRPAGE.11 is R, meaning it is "read-only" (not to be changed or deleted). Knowing what attributes are used is important because certain files should not be changed or erased.

As in the previous display, the filenames are sorted in columns and summary information about all files is included. Again, only files with the DIR attribute are listed.

You can combine the actions of U and V:

```
A)D $UV ⤸
```

The resulting display includes user area numbers *and* attributes for each file. The U and V parameters make D.COM search all user numbers on the current drive for the file(s) you want. For example, to search for all files with the ".TXT" extension, you type:

```
A)D *.TXT $UV ⤸
```

You can have D.COM search other drives by giving the drive letter before the file name. For example, if files with the extension ".TXT" weren't found on the current drive, drive C could be searched by typing:

```
A>D C:*.TXT $UV ⊃
```

To display system files with the regular files, use D.COM with
the SYS parameter:

```
A>D $SYS ⊃
```

The display now includes system files — files with the SYS file
attribute, which are hidden from normal viewing. Like the previous display, this example displays files sorted in alphabetical order, with file sizes and summary information.

If you use all three parameters you get a display that includes
everything:

```
A>D $UVSYS ⊃
```

This is a "full house." It shows files from all user areas (U parameter) with attributes displayed (V parameter). Also, the SYS parameter includes files with the SYS attribute, indicated by an S in
the AT column. This example accounts for all files on the disk —
390K of 390K.

Like the previous displays, this form displays files sorted in alphabetical order, with file sizes and summary information.

For a concise directory like the one produced by DIR, but with
sorted columns and summary information, use this form:

```
A>D $F ⊃
```

Using the F (just file names) parameter results in a file listing
similar to the CP/M command DIR — just the file name and extension displays. D.COM with this parameter does have advan-
tages over CP/M's DIR alone. The files are sorted in columns
while DIR just lists them as they appear in the disk's directory.
Also, it summarizes the files listed while DIR does not.

You can combine other parameters with F, such as SYS to display
SYS-attribute files, or U to display files from all user areas:

```
A>D $UFSYS ⊃
```

Note that some parameters override others. If you use the V parameter with F (specifying V first), the F overrides the request from V to show user numbers and attributes, and you end up with an F display.

This illustrates that some combinations of parameters are illogical to D.COM. In this case, V indicated one form of display, then F told it to use another form of display. If you experiment with different combinations of parameters, D.COM does not get confused — it chooses the "logical operation" (whatever it was programmed to choose), rather than simply "crashing." This is one indication D.COM is a well-designed program.

XDIR (CP/M)

XDIR is a super CP/M directory utility in the public domain that is supplied with the Osborne 1 and other computers. XDIR can display an alphabetically-sorted directory of files in all disks and user areas and even store the information in a disk file.

To use the simplest form of this command, type XDIR by itself followed by Return. To see a specific set of files, use the ? and/or * wildcards to match several files, as you would with DIR. For example:

```
A>XDIR *.COM ↵
```

This displays files with the ".COM" extension. You can also specify a different disk drive:

```
A>XDIR B:*.COM ↵
```

XDIR has many parameters you can specify on the command line after the filename. Precede all parameters with a dollar sign ($):

S   Include system files in the listing.

F   Copy the XDIR listing to a disk file named XDIR.DIR in the drive/user area you're running XDIR from. If XDIR.DIR already exists, the new XDIR listing is added to the end of the existing listing in XDIR.DIR. You can use this feature to produce a catalog of all your disks.

Un   Show the directory for user area n.

A   Show the directory of all user areas starting at the current user area (usually area 0) or area n specified in a Un command.

R   Reset the disk drive (as a Control-C) before performing the XDIR. This is handy if you want to perform multiple XDIR commands from within a SUBMIT file.

N   "No pause" — turn *off* the "screen pausing" XDIR does normally so that you can read the directory before it scrolls off the screen.

P   Print the listing while simultaneously displaying it.

D   Search all active disk drives starting with the current drive or one specified with the filename.

To use these parameters, you must include at least a drive letter or a filename or filematch with the XDIR command, and follow it with one dollar sign ($) and the parameters, as shown in this example:

```
A>XDIR *.TXT $FAPND
```

This command displays all ".TXT" files on all active drives in all user areas, without pausing the display, and it copies the display into the file XDIR.DIR while also printing it.

Communications Utilities (PC/MS-DOS)

Communicating between two computers has become one of the

most popular areas addressed by public domain software writers.
The need for communications is apparently not obvious to new
computer users, and most manufacturers of computers neglect to
provide software to handle it.

Public domain utilities fill this gap — utilities like HOST.BAS
to transfer text between two IBM PCs; 1RD to make phone calls
using a modem to transfer files between computers; HC to convert
files to and from hexadecimal format for easy file transfer; FIL-
TER to filter out unwanted characters from the received file; and
others to aid in effective communications and file transfer.

HOST.BAS

HOST.BAS is a straightforward BASIC program designed to
transfer text (ASCII) files between IBM Personal Computers running the program. It can be used, for example, to access another
computer over the telephone to send or receive a file. It has password security, and automatically disconnects if three incorrect
passwords have been given.

HOST.BAS requires a Hayes Smartmodem, 64K bytes of
RAM, one disk drive, and an 80-column color monitor. It was written by William Bailey.

Commands available to the user from HOST.BAS's main menu
are:

A   List files on drive A.
B   List files on drive B.
G   Sign-off ("goodbye").
M   Send a message.
R   Receive a file.
T   Transmit a file.
?   Summary of commands.

In addition to the main commands, the person sending the file
has 4 additional commands. These are:

ALT-E — Turn on/off screen echo.

Control-PrtSc — Turn on/off printing.

ALT-M — Send a message to a remote location or to the Smartmodem.

ALT-X — Exit to BASIC.

After a file has started to transfer over the telephone lines, it can be aborted or stopped by typing X. Also, if no file or direct communication is sent over the telephone link for more than 5 minutes, HOST.BAS automatically disconnects the telephone.

1RD (1 Ringy-Dingy)

A common way of offering non-commercial software to potential users is through "User-Supported Software" or Freeware® (Headlands Press). You may copy and use the program as long as it is not used or copied for commercial use or profit. The authors ask for a donation if you find the program useful.

1RD is a user-supported program (an abbreviation for "1 Ringy Dingy" — remember Lily Tomlin and her "Ernestine the Operator" character on the TV show *Laugh-In*?) It is a general purpose modem program for communicating with other personal computers running PC-DOS or MS-DOS or with "timesharing" computers (like The Source or CompuServe).

1RD.COM was written by Jim Button (POB 5786, Bellevue, WA, 98006). While it has simple commands, it also has capabilities that surpass many expensive commercial communications packages.

To run 1RD.COM, your IBM PC or PC-compatible must have 64K RAM with PC-DOS (MS-DOS) version 1.0 or 1.1, or 96K RAM with version 2.0 or newer versions. Your IBM PC or PC-compatible must also have one disk drive, an RS-232 serial port, a modem, and an 80-column monitor.

1RD.COM will communicate at up to 9600 baud, assuming your computer's serial port and modem can communicate at this speed. Many serial ports can operate at this speed, but few commercially available modems do. Most modems operate at 300 or 1200 baud, with a few available that operate at 4800 baud. Another limiting factor is the age of the telephone system in your community. If it has not yet been fully modernized with digital switching equipment, you may be restricted to 300 baud in order to accurately transfer files.

The program can transfer text or non-text files. Text files can be transferred dynamically, meaning you can choose which records in the file should be transferred *while the file is being transferred*. Each item in the file is shown before transferring, and you indicate whether it should be sent or not. This is a highly unique feature!

Non-text files may also be transferred with 1RD.COM. These files are usually compiled programs with the ".COM", ".EXE" or ".BIN" file extension. They can be transferred to any computer running a communications program that supports the Modem7/XMODEM protocol.

You can use any type of modem, whether auto-dial or not. 1RD supports more than just the popular Hayes Smartmodem (and Hayes-compatible modems). Many other auto-dial modems are supported.

After a file is transferred between computers, the user often wants to keep it. Many programs don't let you do that. 1RD.COM is better than these programs, because you can save any incoming information. More, you can filter out unwanted characters often put in the file by the program sending the information.

1RD lets you change the communications parameters dynamically, that is, while the file is being transferred. For example, you may receive a message saying the receiving computer cannot keep up with you, so you may slow your transmission speed. Also, if you log on to a bulletin board system and find out your parity, speed or number of data bits is wrong, 1RD lets you change these parameters without hanging up and calling again. This is a very useful feature.

Like many commercial communication programs, 1RD.COM lets you save an automatic "log-on" sequence for another computer. For example, information utilities like The Source and CompuServe require passwords and access commands. The program lets you save the telephone number for the computer (assuming you have an auto-dial modem), the password(s) to access the computer, and the access commands to get the information desired (like stock quotes).

Here's a summary of function key commands for 1RD:

F1   Receive File. This opens a disk file to save all incoming data.
F2   End Receive. This closes the "receive" file.
F3   Echo. This turns on or off the display of incoming information to the screen ("echoing").
F4   Parameters. Change the communications parameters.
F5   Delay. Change speed of outbound characters.
F6   CHDir. Under DOS 2.0, this changes the current directory.
F7   Send File. This sends an entire file.
F8   Peek. This turns on or off the "peek" function that shows you the next record to be sent.
F9   Send Record. Same as key F7, but only 1 record is sent each time F9 is pressed. You can switch between F7 and F9 as needed.
F10 Stop Send. Close the "send" file.
ALT-R — Re-transmit a record.
ALT-B — Send a "Break character".

1RD can also carry out commands from within a file. Any file you are sending may have these additional commands. A file to be transmitted could, for example, have nothing in it to send — just commands to be carried out. Each command must be preceded by a backslash and be in all capital letters. 1RD file commands are:

\CHDIR — Change the current directory. Type the command like this: \CHDIR NEWNAME.

\COLOR fg, bg — Set the foreground and background colors using the numbers in the BASIC manual.

\COM — Reset the communications parameters. Codes as used in BASIC: \COM1.0300,S,7,1.

\DELAY — Set delay counters for file transmissions.

\FILTER — Set filters for incoming data. Type as shown:
      \FILTER from,to,from,to ...
You can type up to 20 filters using ASCII decimal codes. Example: \FILTER 10,0,12,13.

\PEEK — Turn "peek" on or off. "Peek" lets you see your records before transmitting them. Type \PEEK ON or \PEEK OFF.

\RECYCLE — Branch to the top of the file being transmitted.

\REM — A comment. All text following this command is displayed on the screen.

\TOFILE — Transfer to a new file to be transmitted. Example: \TOFILE B:SOURCE.LOG.

HC: Hex Converter

This is not a program to ward off curses, unless you are cursing about a glitch in your file caused by a communications error.

Compiled programs do not always transfer properly between computers running communication software. This is because many computers communicate using seven data bits per byte, while machine format programs have eight-bit bytes in the file. Because the receiving computer expects seven-bit bytes, files that have eight-bit bytes are jumbled during transfer and are unusable.

HC.COM converts eight-bit machine format files into "hexadecimal format" files. Each byte of the file is converted to two bytes, so the communication program only sends 4 bits of important information. Thus, the seven-bit limitation no longer restricts the transfer of machine format files.

After converting and transferring the file, it cannot be used until it is converted back into a machine format file. HC.COM can convert a hexadecimal file back to its original form. During the conversions it is important not to lose part of the file. This is done using a "checksum", which is the total of all bytes. The checksum is calculated while the file is being converted to hexadecimal. It is checked when the file is converted back to machine format.

To start HC.COM, type a command with these elements as needed (the *italic* elements are optional):

HC *d:path* infile *d:path outfile*

If the file to be converted (infile) doesn't have the ".HEX" extension, HC.COM converts the infile to a hexadecimal file. The new file has the same name, but with a ".HEX" extension. If the infile has a ".HEX" extension, it is converted back to a machine format file.

You may specify the name of the new file with the *outfile* element on the command line. If you don't, HC uses the infile name with the appropriate extension. Also, you can use the full path capabilities of PC-DOS/MS-DOS 2.0. HC.COM should not be used with PC-DOS/MS-DOS 1.0 or 1.1.

HC.COM was written by Marty Smith (310 Cinnamon Oak Lane, Houston, TX, 77079). It can be used with the IBM PC and many PC-compatible computers.

DISKPGM1.BAS

DISKPGM1.BAS was written by Richard Schinnell of the Capital PC Users Group, Washington, D.C. It requires BASICA to run.

This program is simple, but very useful. It displays an alphabetic listing of all text (ASCII) files on the current drive, *and* the time it takes to transfer each file at 300 baud. This is especially important when you're transferring files at long-distance rates.

To start this program, type:

BASICA DISKPGM1.BAS ⊃

After the program starts up, answer the questions about what name you want to print for the disk, and which disk drive to check. It then displays the information.

FILTER.BAS

After transferring files from a remote computer, you may have extra characters that make the file difficult to read. Often these characters are "control characters" — non-printing characters which help the sending computer control its operations. FILTER.BAS can eliminate these and some non-control characters from a file.

To remove unwanted control characters, type:

```
BASICA FILTER.BAS ↵
```

The program asks for the name of the file to be filtered and the name of the new "destination" file, then asks you to confirm the names before proceeding with the filter operation.

CHECKOUT.BAS

Transferring files over telephone lines requires many different components to work together. Often the computer's serial port your modem is connected to isn't set to the right speed. Or maybe the "handshake" protocol between the computers is not set correctly. These problems or others can make the whole transfer a waste of time. CHECKOUT.BAS checks these components and changes the baud rate or serial handshaking protocol quickly.

Figure 7-1 shows the CHECKOUT menu. To use CHECKOUT you need PC-DOS (MS-DOS) version 1.10 and BASICA, and at least 64K RAM.

MOD100IN.BAS

One of the most popular "lap portable" computers for writers is the Radio Shack Model 100. Its built-in programs make writing and communicating over telephone lines easy. However, it is difficult to prepare formatted text for printing with the Model 100. Ken Cooper, Ph.D., created this simple program to let you transfer

CHECKOUT
Version: 821210

By Hamilton Company
Tel (415) 493-2664

NOTE: Requires DOS Rev 1.10 & Basica

SPACE To test ports   Q Quit Program

TEST MENU

Key	Description		
1	Parallel Port	LPT1:	
2	Parallel Port	LPT2:	
3	Parallel Port	LPT3:	
A	Serial Port	COM1:	
B	Serial Port	COM2:	
C	CRT Display	SCRN:	
D	Dial Smart Modem		(COM1:Time Check)
I	Impulse Dial Modem		(COM1:Time Check)
M	Change Printed Message		(Times: 1) (Col:40)
R	Change Baud Rate		(300)
S	Change Serial Handshake		(,N,8,1,RS)
Q	Quit Program		

Figure 7-1. *The CHECKOUT program tests your computer components used in data communications.*

your text to an IBM Personal Computer or PC-compatible.

MOD100IN.BAS can transfer up to 32,000 bytes of text (the maximum RAM in the Model 100). You must have a "null modem" cable to connect the serial ports of the Model 100 computer and the other personal computer. This type of cable can be purchased at most computer stores or Radio Shack.

To minimize the reworking of the text after transfer the author suggests putting two Returns at the end of each paragraph. This is because the program deletes one of them during the transfer. Also, you should not compose a paragraph longer than 220 characters. This corresponds to a typical double-spaced typed page. Few people write paragraphs this long.

To start transferring your text, follow these steps:

1.　Connect the null modem cable to the serial ports of each computer.

2.　Set up TELCOM, the Model 100 communications program, to communicate at 300 baud with even parity, seven data bits, and one stop bit.

3.　Start BASICA and type LOAD ''MOD100IN.BAS'' ↵. *Do not* run the program yet.

4.　Follow the instruction on uploading files in the TELCOM manual. When you reach the prompt message LENGTH =, type 120. *Do not* press Return yet.

5.　Type RUN on the PC, then press Return on the Model 100. The computers appear to be inactive for up to several minutes. Transfer is slow at 300 baud.

6.　After the transfer is complete, the program asks for the name of the file to save the text in. Be sure the disk is not full or write-protected — if it is, you'll have to transfer the text again.

Other Helpful PC-DOS/MS-DOS Programs

Whenever you work with a computer, and as you begin to use it in more sophisticated ways, additional tasks need to be performed. If you are an experienced programmer, you can use many of these unique features of your computer and files. But most users are not and do not want to learn all the little details of their computer.

So how do you do the basic tasks to control your computer system? The following programs should help you do various tasks, and do them quicker and more easily.

SYSTAT

This program is written to be used with PC-DOS/MS-DOS 1.1. The example below was done with PC-DOS 2.1, and showed the same information.

SYSTAT.COM shows you the capacity of each disk drive and how much space is free. Also, if you put a short text file with the extension ".NAM" on the disk, its filename will be displayed and its contents will be shown as a comment. The comment may be up to 40 characters. This is a handy way to keep track of floppy disks and the type of information stored on each.

Here's an example:

```
B)SYSTAT ⊃
MS-DOS Systat version 1.1      16 November 1984  3.43 pm

Drive   Name                 Capacity      Free Comments

A:      none                     354K      109K
B:      none                     156K       37K
C:      none                    7976K      276K
D:      none                    4984K      880K
E:      none                    2986K      132K
F:      none                    3984K      856K
G:      none                    4848K      664K
H:      none                    7976K      632K
I:      none                    3984K      996K


System memory:   512K      Available memory: 469K
```

MOVE

This command renames files across directories. By renaming the file you actually copy it from one directory into another directory. This is essentially copying a file between directories, but without the extra step needed to erase the file from the old directory.

This program works only with PC-DOS/MS-DOS 2.0. Version 1.1 does not support directories, and thus, the command is useless under that version.

To rename a file across directories, enter the following command:

```
MOVE \path\nameold.ext \path\namenew.ext ↵
```

The name of the file may be the same or different. This command does the same thing as the following three commands:

```
COPY \path\nameold.ext \path\namenew.ext ↵
CD \path ↵                        (where nameold.ext is located)
DEL nameold.ext ↵
```

If \path is the same, MOVE.COM acts like the normal Rename command.

ST (Super Typer)

The Super Typer program is a replacement for the TYPE command in PC-DOS/MS-DOS. It has three enhancements over the regular TYPE command:

1. Text is easier to read because the text is "paged" rather than scrolled on the screen.

2. Text can be reviewed again after it has scrolled off the screen by pressing the PageUp and PageDown keys.

3. WordStar "control characters" are converted to normal characters to avoid strange display reactions.

To use ST.COM, you type ST followed by Return, after which you'll be prompted for the text file to display, or you type:

```
ST filename.ext ⊃
```

Each page (screen of text) can be numbered if desired. Do this by pressing the + (plus) key to turn this feature on or off. This may be useful when a large file is being reviewed, because it makes it easier to keep your place. Also, to page up or down through the text, just press PageUp or PageDown on your numeric keypad. (Make sure the number lock is off.)

ST.COM was written by Charles T. Franklin (Apt. 510, 1850 K Street, Washington, D.C., 20006). It is a user-supported program, meaning the author requests a donation if you like the program. In this case, the author requests $5.00.

VDEL (Verify Delete)

Of all the programs needed as built in commands in any operating system, this is one of the most critical. How often have you told the operating system to delete a group of files, then realized one or more of them should not have been erased? Bummer.

VDEL.COM gives you the extra chance to say "Yes" or "No" to each file about to be deleted. You can determine what files in a larger group should be erased, one at a time. This program should make life easier for many users.

To selectively erase files, type:

```
VDEL *.BAS ⊃
```

Each file with the extension ".BAS" is displayed with a question mark. Type a Y to delete the file, or N to *not* delete the file.

File Handling Utilities (CP/M): DISK and NSWEEP

Dealing with CP/M computer files, whether they are text or

program files, is unexciting drudgery. It is hard to keep track of tens or hundreds of files on a hard disk, and determine which files have what attributes, and which disks are formatted and which aren't, and what text files have inside them, and when to erase files or make back up copies, and how much space is left on your hard disk or floppy disk, and so on.

At least six CP/M command are necessary to perform these tasks, not to mention disciplined work habits. You have to learn dozens of command variations, including some you might use only occasionally.

DISK76.COM (DISK version 7.6) and NSWP205.COM (NSWEEP version 2.05) are two public domain utility programs that perform almost every file manipulation commonly done. Although you might expect that DISK and NSWEEP are rival programs (they share many of the same operations), each has something special to offer. If they were commercial programs they *would* be rivals; since they are free public domain programs, both are worth having.

Between the two programs 19 different options are offered. These options replace eight CP/M commands — PIP, ERA, DIR, USER, TYPE, Control-P, REN and STAT. They present these operations in menus and they use prompts. And more, they offer features which make dealing with files easier and less painful.

DISK and NSWEEP features can be grouped into six categories: cursor movement, tagging files, copying files, deleting files, text files, and everything else. These categories mimic much of the work we do with and to files.

The options for DISK and NSWEEP are presented in Table 7-1. Compare each option in the table and as we go through them. Think about which program is best for your work (or if you want both).

Figure 7-2 shows the initial screen information for both DISK and NSWEEP. The primary difference between them is that DISK displays a menu immediately while NSWEEP does not. NSWEEP's menu displays after you enter a question mark. (You don't have to press Return after entering the letter for a menu option in either NSWEEP or DISK.)

DISK displays its menu and tells you how much space (in bytes)

DISK		NSWEEP	
		A	Retag files
B	Backs up	B	Back one file
C	Copy file	C	Copy file
D	Delete file	D	Delete file
		E	Erase T/U files
F	File size	F	Find files
J	Jump 22 files		
L	Log-in	L	Log new disk/user
M	Mass copy	M	Mass file copy
P	Print text	P	Print file
		Q	Squeeze/Unsqueeze tagged files
R	Rename file	R	Rename file(s)
S	Stat drive	S	Check remaining space
T	Tag file	T	Tag file for transfer
U	Untag file	U	Untag file
V	View text file	V	View file
W	Write punch	W	Wildcard Tag of files
X	Exit to CP/M	X	Exit to CP/M
		Y	Set file status
		?	Display this help
space	Advance cursor	sp, cr	Forward one file

Table 1. *The options for DISK and NSWEEP.*

is free on the current drive. If you change to another drive, DISK displays the same information for the new drive.

DISK then displays the first file in the current user area and drive in alphabetical (ASCII) order. It shows the current drive letter and user area number unless you are in user area 0 of the drive (it leaves out the user area number).

NSWEEP displays much the same information, but numbers each file and shows you how many files are in the current user area and drive. It also shows how much space they occupy on the disk.

```
       DISK 7.6 – File Manipulation Program – 07/14/83

C – Copy file      │D – Delete file │F – File Size   │J – Jump 22 files
L – Log-in         │M – Mass copy   │P – Print text  │R – Rename file
S – Stat drive     │T – Tag file    │U – Untag file  │V – View text file
W – Write punch    │X – Exit to CP/M
                                    │ (space) advances cursor – B backs up
    29K bytes free on drive C:


  C: BAUDM     .COM :
```

```
             NSWEEP   –   Version 2.05    04/11/1984
                      (c) Dave Rand, 1983, 1984
                          Edmonton, Alberta


      Drive A0:    363K in   34 files.    27K free.
          1. C0: BAUDM    .COM  2K :
```

Figure 7-2. *The start-up screens for DISK and NSWEEP.*

Unlike DISK, NSWEEP does not suppress the "0" when files are displayed for user 0. Also unlike DISK, NSWEEP also tells you the size of the file without asking.

When first starting up NSWEEP, if you enter a question mark to bring up the menu, you get the display shown in figure 7-3: the program name and version, followed by the menu. NSWEEP also shows the number of files, the space they occupy and total free space. However, before showing the first file name, NSWEEP tells you the total size of tagged files. We describe tagged files later.

DISK and NSWEEP offer several ways to move the cursor through the sorted list of files. Both programs make it easy to move forward or backward through the list. For example, if a list has 45 files in it and you want to see one beginning with the letter 'T', mov-

```
        NSWEEP  -   Version 2.05    04/11/1984
               (c) Dave Rand, 1983, 1984
                    Edmonton, Alberta

A - Retag files        ¦ Q - Squeeze/Unsqueeze tagged files
B - Back one file      ¦ R - Rename file(s)
C - Copy file          ¦ S - Check remaining space
D - Delete file        ¦ T - Tag file for transfer
E - Erase T/U files    ¦ U - Untag file
F - Find file          ¦ V - View file
L - Log new disk/user  ¦ W - Wildcard tag of files
M - Mass file copy     ¦ Y - Set file status.
P - Print file         ¦ ? - Display this help
X - Exit to CP/M        ¦ cr, sp - Forward one file
    363K in   34 files.  27K free.
     Tagged files =   OK (   OK).

              1. CO: BAUDM   .COM  2K :
```

Figure 7-3. *The menu display for NSWEEP.*

ing backward through the list is faster.

Both DISK and NSWEEP move forward through the list of files by pressing the spacebar. NSWEEP also advances to the next file when you press Return. DISK advances like NSWEEP when you press Return, but its menu doesn't say so.

As mentioned above, both programs let you move backward through the list of files. Just press B (no Return needed) and you move back one file.

DISK offers a convenient method called "jump" to move rapidly through a list of files. Pressing J displays the next 22 files. If you don't have 22 files left in the list, it starts the list over again. This command is handy when you're browsing through a list trying to remember the name of a file.

NSWEEP has a similar option called "find" which moves you

rapidly through the list. Pressing F prompts you for the file name you want to locate. You may use wildcards or just the first few letters of the file name if you want. When you know all or part of the file name, this is a quick way to move to a file.

Which is better is a toss up. We find both useful in different situations.

Tagging Files

DISK and NSWEEP let you tag or mark files for group copying or some other task. You may untag a file also. Tagging is a quick way to identify what files you want to copy.

Both programs use T to tag and U to untag files. When you tag a file using either program, the program tells you the size of the file. Both programs also accumulate file sizes as you tag each file. In addition, NSWEEP gives you a second size indicating an accumulation of the true size before CP/M rounding. Both programs place an asterisk (*) next to the file name to indicate it is tagged. The asterisk appears when you review the list.

Similar information is shown when you press U to untag a file. The accumulated size is reduced by the file size and the tag (indicated by the asterisk) is removed.

The tagging and untagging of files is useful for backing up several related files. You don't have to enter PIP or parameters repeatedly. Just tag the files, use the Mass Copy operation (explained below), then untag them. If you're finished with DISK or NSWEEP, you can untag the files by just leaving the program.

NSWEEP in comparison offers a fast way to tag files called the "Wildcard Tag," shown as option W. NSWEEP asks you what you want to tag, and allows you to use the CP/M wildcards for file matching — question mark (?) and asterisk (*). NSWEEP shows all matches as they are tagged. This feature dramatically speeds up the process when copying or deleting files with similar file names or extensions.

As mentioned above, after a file has been tagged, it appears in the list with an asterisk next to its file name. Once tagged, DISK and NSWEEP lets you Mass Copy these files to another user number and/or drive. NSWEEP also lets you erase or squeeze/unsqueeze tagged files (see below).

NSWEEP handles tagged files differently after a task like copying or squeezing is performed. It changes the asterisk to a pound sign (#), indicating the files have been used. You may retag these files by using the A option. These features are highly desirable in the late hours or during busy days when you have trouble remembering what happened 30 seconds before.

Copying Files

DISK and NSWEEP both offer options to copy one or more files. Copy (C) in both programs transfers the current file in the list to the drive and user number desired. However, you may *not* transfer a file to the same drive and user (see NSWEEP exception below). Both programs ask what drive and user number you want the file copied to.

DISK reminds you what file it is copying and tells you the transfer is CRC Verified. CRC stands for Cyclic Redundancy Check. It is a method of checking for accurate transfer of files. NSWEEP does not say anything about CRC checking, but nonetheless it may do this common checking method as it copies.

In addition, DISK warns you when a file with the same name exists on the disk you're copying to. This is very useful after many hours of work. A careless slip of a finger in NSWEEP could wipe it all out.

DISK and NSWEEP differ in another significant way: NSWEEP lets you change the name of the file during transfer, and if you do change the name, you can copy it to the same user number and drive. If you need to keep separate versions of documents or programs, this feature is particularly useful.

Both programs let you copy all tagged files. The files can be "mass-copied" to another user number, or another user number and drive. When "mass copying," *neither DISK nor NSWEEP check the receiving disk to determine if a file with the same name exists*. This is a weakness in both programs.

NSWEEP offers a unique option not offered by CP/M or by

DISK. The Squeeze/Unsqueeze option compresses files so that they take up less space. It doesn't change the original file, but creates a new one with a similar file name and extension.

Squeezing is useful when backing up word processing and source programs to archive disks. The reduced space a compressed file uses saves many dollars in disks. The ability to squeeze and unsqueeze makes NSWEEP a useful substitute for SQ and USQ (Chapter 5).

Deleting Files

Both programs offer an easy method to delete files. After choosing D to delete a file, answer Y (yes) to delete the current file, or N (no) if you change your mind. The only difference in the way the programs delete files is DISK shows your options — (Y/N).

NSWEEP offers the option to erase a group of files. You may erase all tagged or all untagged files. With the prompt (Y/N/A) option, you can selectively delete tagged or untagged files with a Y (yes answer). The A answer lets you abort this option.

Be careful with both types of deleting, because unless you have a program to "undelete" a file or an accurate backup copy, you'll never see the file again.

Viewing/Printing Text Files

DISK and NSWEEP offer two ways to look at text files created by most common word processors or editors. They are View and Print. As the names indicate, View (V) displays the text on the screen so you can view it, and Print (P) sends it to your printer.

The View (V) option has two minor differences in the way they work in DISK and NSWEEP. With DISK you use the space bar to advance the text one line, while with NSWEEP you use the letter L. The other difference is that DISK says to press any other key to display the next 22 lines of text. NSWEEP says to press Return, but any key other than L does the same thing.

In brief, in either program press Control-X to stop viewing the text, or any key to see the next 22 lines. Press the spacebar in DISK or L in NSWEEP to see the next line of text.

The Print (P) option in both programs work the same. They send the text to your printer. If you have two printers connected to your computer, you'll first have to tell CP/M which printer to use. DISK and NSWEEP just tell CP/M to print the text; CP/M has to know where.

Other Options

Both DISK and NSWEEP let you change between user areas and/or drives with the L option. L makes it very easy to search your hard disk for files and do several task involving different user numbers and drives. The programs would be dramatically less beneficial without this option.

Renaming files is similar in both programs. You simply choose R, then enter the new name. NSWEEP has an added feature — it lets you rename files using wildcards. For example, all the files that make up this chapter have the ".CH7" extension. I may want to rename them as I develop new versions. You can probably think of several uses yourself.

DISK has an option which tells you the size of the current file. When determining which files will fit on a back up disk, the file's size is critical. NSWEEP provides this information automatically.

Both programs have an option to determine how much space is left on a disk, whether a floppy or hard disk. This is also important when making back up copies.

DISK or NSWEEP: which is better? The question is like being asked whether you like vanilla or chocolate ice cream, when you actually prefer fudge ripple. I've been using DISK for a long time — it does things very well but has a few quirks. NSWEEP is newer, has more features and does wildcard filename tagging faster.

Do I prefer one over the other? I want both, and more! While I'm not a programmer, there are many who are and who enjoy creating innovative utility programs. And if the history of public domain programs is any indication, someone will create a good cross between them. Then I'll have fudge ripple.

CHAPTER 8:
THE DISK UTILITY (DU)

by Kelly Smith

Disk Utility, known as DU or DUU (original version by Ward Christensen), is a comprehensive utility that allows a user to examine and modify *any portion* of a floppy disk or hard disk. DU is available for CP/M-80 systems (version 2.0 or greater). For a similar utility for PC/MS-DOS computers, try the Norton Utilities (commercial product), or the free programs DISKRTN.EXE (PC-SIG disk #38) or DISKMODF (PC-SIG disk #28).

The Disk Utility lets you "perform surgery" on a disk to recover erased files, isolate bad sectors from use, and make "data transplants." DU is an invaluable tool for recovering disks with "crashed" directories, or for modifying CP/M "run time" parameters, or for recovering accidentally-erased files, or even for making a backup copy of your disk's directory and preserving it in a safer place on your disk. The possibilities are virtually endless.

How does DU have such flexibility in applications? DU lets you change memory locations directly on the disk. There is no other program we know about that can directly change any memory location on a disk. Such a direct method may seem logical to an assembly language programmer, but for users who are unfamiliar with *bytes* (memory locations holding single characters) and hexadecimal numbers, DU can not only be hard to learn, but dangerous!

You must know what you are doing, or follow the directions of one who knows. To use DU you must know how to add and subtract in hexadecimal notation, and you need to know about the CP/M file structure. Newer versions may provide extra help for newcomers. For information about the CP/M file structure, see *User's Guide to CP/M Systems* by Bove & Rhodes (Baen Books, Jerry Pournelle Series).

A word of caution: it is possible to DU a disk to death! That is, casual modification of portions of the CP/M-80 operating system data tracks is usually destructive to the proper operation of your system disk. Use particular care when writing your modifications back to disk!

Newcomers and non-programmers: just because we say it's dangerous and hard to use, *don't* consider DU to be for hackers only. It can be an invaluable aid at a time when you most need some aid — for example, when the directory of a very important disk refuses to function correctly.

DU is free and available from most user groups (and there's usually a DU hacker lurking in the group). Versions of DU can be found in CP/MUG vol. 78, SIG/M vol. 152, or in a FOG utilities disk. The "universal version" (version 7.0 or newer) should work with any floppy or hard disk.

Installation

Versions 7.0 and later of DU are designed to be installed with a minimum of trouble. In fact, in almost all cases, no changes are necessary to get DU up and running. For those who want to customize DU, and for those who have non-standard CP/M systems, the 8080 source code is available with the program in the public domain library.

The only requirement is that you must be running a CP/M-80 system, version 2.0 or 2.2 (some versions work also with CP/M version 1.4). This is because DU uses the disk parameter block incorporated in the 2.0 and newer releases of Digital Research's CP/M-80 to determine the characteristics of the disk environment.

The only parameter you might want to change (not required), is the CPU clock speed flag at address 103H (when DU is loaded into system memory). Leave this byte alone (keep it zero) if your system has a 2 MHz (megahertz) clock. Change it to 0FFH if your system has a 4 MHz clock (refer to your Digital Research DDT documentation, or *User's Guide to CP/M Systems* by Bove & Rhodes (Baen Books — Jerry Pournelle Series) if you are unfamiliar with modification of program files, and patching techniques). This modification is needed only to use the Z (sleep) command — a command that lets you place a pause in a stream of commands to, for example, pause every 24 lines to read long displays. An alternative to modifying the program: use larger than usual numbers with the Z command when running DU with a computer system clock rate of 4MHz or greater.

Usage

The simple way to run DU is to type the program name from CP/M:

```
A>DU ⊃
```

Once DU is running, it will display a colon (:) as the DU command level prompt. DU expects single-letter commands followed by Return. To specify several commands at once, place them on one line and separate them with semicolons (;). You can also repeat the execution of a given command or string of commands a given number of times, or indefinitely (until you type a Control-C, shown from now on as ^C).

If you want to perform a few operations in "expert mode," you can put DU commands on the CP/M command line with DU. For example, you can type:

```
A>DU G0;D;G2;=OK<D><A><1A>;D ⊃
```

That's a complex example, but it shows that you can type many commands at once, and execute them without further ado. Here's an example with an explanation:

```
A>DU M;X ⊃
```

This command runs DU and executes DU's M command. The M command displays a disk *map* — a display of the disk's group allocations. Figure 8-1 shows a disk map of a CompuPro 8/16

```
0004-0005  00 COPY    .COM 00 : 0006-000D  00 WS      .COM 00
000E-0010  00 DDT     .COM 00 : 0011-0018  00 FMTMEM  .COM 00
0019-001A  00 FORMAT  .COM 00 : 001B-001B  00 CONV    .COM 00
001C-001C  00 CRCK    .COM 00 : 001D-001D  00 CROSSREF.COM 00
001E-001E  00 D       .COM 00 : 001F-0021  00 DU      .TXT 00
0022-0025  00 PIP     .COM 00 : 0026-0026  00 XDIR    .COM 00
0027-0027  00 FILE-XT2.COM 00 : 0028-002E  00 RMAC    .COM 00
002F-0033  00 LINK    .COM 00 : 0034-0034  00 EXEC    .COM 00
0035-0035  00 SYSGEN  .COM 00 : 0036-0036  00 FMAP    .COM 00
```

. The disk "map" shown here is edited for brevity.

.

.

.

.

← Group Allocation Number

← User Number

← Filename

← Filetype

← Extent Number

```
020F-020F  00 PBIOS   .ASM 03 : 0210-0216  01 ALIENS  .COM 00
0217-0218  00 PBIOS   .ASM 03 : 0219-0219  00 MOVCPM  .COM 00
021A-021A  00 MNTR    .DOC 00 : 021B-021C  00 PRNT    .DOC 00
021D-0220  00 REQ'D-SW.DOC 00 : 0221-0228  00 SW-DEF  .TXT 00
0229-0230  00 SW-DEF  .TXT 01 : 0231-0238  00 SW-DEF  .TXT 02
0239-023E  00 MOVCPM  .COM 00 : 023F-0241  00 FORMAT  .ASM 00
0242-0242  00 FORMAT  .ASM 01 : 0243-0247     ++FREE++
0248-024B  00 PBIOS   .ASM 04 : 024C-0253  00 SETATR  .ASM 00
0254-0254  00 PBIOS   .ASM 04 : 0255-0257     ++FREE++

G=0000:00, T=4, S=1, PS=0
```

Figure 8-1. *This is a partial disk map for a CompuPro 8/16 system disk, showing the group allocation number, filename, extension ("filetype"), extent number and user number for each file.*

System disk.

You must type the X command to leave DU (if you type a Control-C (^C) accidentally or on purpose, you will not "drop out" of DU).

Summary of Functions

All DU commands end with Return. If you type a question mark (?) and press Return (↵), DU displays a summary of the DU commands. The commands act on disk *sectors* which are grouped together into *groups*.

Positioning

The only way to know where you are is to understand the indicators in this terse display:

    G=009C:04, T=43, S=5, PS=4

G stands for group allocation and sector block number, T for physical track on the disk, S for logical sector number, and PS for physical sector number. To best illustrate what the display means, type the following command:

    :+;/ ↵

        — Advance to the next sector and repeat until you type a Control-C.

The group, track, logical sector, and physical sector assignments are displayed incrementally for your entire disk as shown in figure 8-2 (type Control-C to quit). "Sector blocks" are always 128 bytes each.

You move through the disk with Group (Gnn), Track (Tnn), and Sector (Snn) movement commands:

Gnn   By allocation group. Example:
      : G0 ↺
      G=0000:00, T=2, S=1, PS=1

Tnn   By track. Example:
      : T8 ↺
      G=0018:00, T=8, S=1, PS=1

Snn   By sector. Example:
      : S6 ↺
      G=0018:05, T=8, S=6, PS=6

+nn   Move ahead nn sectors. Example:
      : +2 ↺
      G=0018:07, T=8, S=8, PS=8

-nn   Move back nn sectors. Example:
      : -1 ↺
      G=0018:06, T=8, S=7, PS=7

Input/Output

The following commands let you read data from or write data directly to the disk, or to and from the buffer:

R   Read a sector.
W   Write a sector.
(Save the current sector in a temporary buffer.
)   Recall the previously saved sector.

Displaying Disk Sectors

G   Show current group, track, sector.
M   Map the entire disk (file group allocations). Another version:
Mnn   Map starting at group nn.

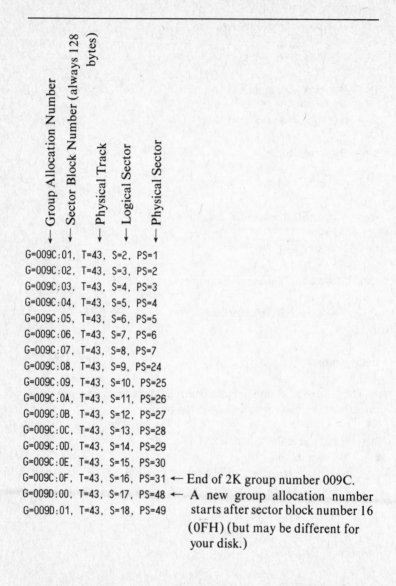

G=009C:01, T=43, S=2, PS=1
G=009C:02, T=43, S=3, PS=2
G=009C:03, T=43, S=4, PS=3
G=009C:04, T=43, S=5, PS=4
G=009C:05, T=43, S=6, PS=5
G=009C:06, T=43, S=7, PS=6
G=009C:07, T=43, S=8, PS=7
G=009C:08, T=43, S=9, PS=24
G=009C:09, T=43, S=10, PS=25
G=009C:0A, T=43, S=11, PS=26
G=009C:0B, T=43, S=12, PS=27
G=009C:0C, T=43, S=13, PS=28
G=009C:0D, T=43, S=14, PS=29
G=009C:0E, T=43, S=15, PS=30
G=009C:0F, T=43, S=16, PS=31 ← End of 2K group number 009C.
G=009D:00, T=43, S=17, PS=48 ← A new group allocation number
G=009D:01, T=43, S=18, PS=49   starts after sector block number 16
                                  (0FH) (but may be different for
                                  your disk.)

Figure 8-2. *Continuous incremental display of all group allocation, physical track, logical sector and physical sector assignments.*

D   Display the current sector (display in hexadecimal and ASCII).

A   Display the current sector in ASCII.

H   Display the current sector in hexadecimal.

Vnn   View nn sectors (as if you were using the CP/M TYPE command).

Show disk parameters. Example:

```
:# ⊃
Disk Information:
Tracks:            154
Sec/trk:            64
Grpsize:            16          (sectors per group)
Tot grps:          599
Dir entries:       256
Sys tracks:          4
```

Changing Disks and Data

CHnn,val

     Change data in hexadecimal.

CAnn,val

     Change data in ASCII (hexadecimal numbers enclosed within ‹ and › symbols).

N   Insert new disk.

Unn   Change user directory number to nn.

Searching For Data

Fname

     Find a file in the directory.

F   Find next occurrence (extent) of same name.

=aaaa

     Scan for aaaa (ASCII characters) from current sector on.

Miscellaneous

Znn   "Sleep" for nn tenths of a second to allow data viewing before it scrolls off.

Ld   Log in disk d (drive letter A, B, etc.).

P   Turn on/off printer output (echo console output).

Q   Use before any command to make execution "quiet" (no console output).

X   Exit to CP/M.

/nn   Repeat previous command nn times (until you type ^C if you omit the nn).

Quick Reference

Arguments in *italics* are optional; for numeric values, n or *n* is decimal, x or *x* is hexadecimal.

+*n*   Move forward *n* sectors.

-*n*   Move back *n* sectors.

\#   Display disk parameters for the current drive.

=aaa   Search for the ASCII characters aaa from current sector. Upper and lower case letters are different. Use ⟨xx⟩ for hexadecimal number xx. For example, to find "IN 0" use:
=⟨DB⟩⟨0⟩ ↩
To find "(tab)H,0(CR)(LF)" use:
=⟨9⟩H,0⟨D⟩⟨A⟩ ↩

⟨   Save current sector in the buffer.

⟩   Restore saved sector.

?   Display help message.

A*ff,tt*

ASCII display "dump" of current sector, or from addresses *ff* to *tt*.

CHaddr,byte,byte...

Change address to byte (hexadecimal number).

CAaddr,char...

Change address to char (ASCII character, ⟨xx⟩ allowed for hexadecimal numbers).

CHff-tt,byte

    Change addresses from ff through tt to hexadecimal byte

    Example:

    CH0-7F,E5 ⊃

CAff-tt,char

    Change addresses from ff through tt to ASCII char

    Example:

    CA0-7F,A ⊃

D*ff,tt*

    Display addresses in hexadecimal and ASCII.

Fname.ext

    Find a file by its name.

Gnn   CP/M Allocation Group nn.

H*ff,tt*

    Display in hexadecimal.

L   Log in disk in current drive.

Ld   Log in disk in drive d

M*nn*   Map from group *nn* or entire disk.

N   New disk.

P   Printer echo on/off switch.

Q   Quiet mode (no console output).

R   Read current sector from disk.

Snn   Move to sector nn.

Tnn   Move to track nn.

Unn   Set User nn for Find command (CP/M 2.2 only).

V*nn*   View *nn* sectors (display in ASCII).

W   Write the current sector to disk.

X   Exit DU program, return to CP/M.

Y   Yank current sector into sequential memory.

Z*nn*   Sleep *nn* tenths of a second.

/*nn*   Repeat *nn* times (decimal).

Cancel a function with C or Control-C (^C). Suspend output with S or Control-S. Separate DU commands on a multiple command line with a semicolon (;).

For example, the first command moves you to group 0; the second command moves in, displays, pauses for 2 seconds, and repeats the entire command until you type a Control-C.

```
:g0 ⏎
:+;d;z#20;/ ⏎
```

All numbers are in hexadecimal unless you precede them with #.

Command Summary

\#   Display information about the disk (sectors per track, number of tracks, etc.).

\+   Move forward one sector (if below track 2, this moves you to next numerical; if 2 or greater, this moves you based on CP/M's normal sector scrambling algorithm — + gets you to the next logical sector of the file.

\-   Move backward one logical sector. You can include a decimal number with +or - to move forward or backward by several sectors. For example, +15 ⏎ moves you forward by 15 logical sectors.

/nn   Repeat the entire command an optional *nn* times, or forever (until you type a Control-c). The number for nn can be from 2 to 65535.

⟨   Save the current sector in a save buffer, and reset the buffer pointer used by ⟨⟨ and ⟩⟩ commands.

⟨⟨   Save the current sector and increment the memory pointer so that the next ⟨⟨ command saves to the next buffer. Use the ⟨ command to reset, or the ⟩⟩ command to retrieve buffers sequentially, in order to move several sectors from one place on disk to another, or to another disk, or to memory (at 2000H where DDT can be used to access them).

=string

Search for ASCII-character string, starting at the current sector. You can use ⟨xx⟩ to represent a hexadecimal number

xxH in the search string. In fact, DU ignores "bit number 7"
(the "eighth bit," or parity bit) and treats all characters as
ASCII unless you use ⟨xx⟩. Since ; is a command delimiter,
you have to use ⟨3B⟩ to search for a semicolon. Since ⟨ is a special character, use ⟨⟨ to represent a single ⟨ in string. Also
note that the special symbol @ contains the displacement at
which the match occurred. You can use it in a C command, as
in:

```
:=LIX;CA
,LXI;W⊃
```

— this searches for the string LIX, changes it to LXI, and
writes the sector back to disk.

⟩   Get the saved buffer. The ⟨ and ⟩ commands can be used to
move a sector to another place.

⟩⟩   Restore the "oldest" unrestored sector saved by the ⟨⟨ command. This command may be placed in the middle of an infi-
nite repeat / command, since it will stop operating when
there are no more sectors in the buffer.

?   Display the command summary.

A   Display ("dump") the current sector, ASCII characters only.

CHaddr,val,val,val...
Change to hexadecimal val in current sector starting at the
addr.

CAaddr,string...
Change to ASCII string in current sector starting at the addr.
Use ⟨xx⟩ for hexadecimal number xxH in string. Use the W
command to write changes to disk. The C command "echoes"
for verification when you overlay existing data.

`CHff-tt.byte`
or
`CAff-tt.char`

Change a range of addresses, from address `ff` to `tt` (e.g., 05-E5), to either a hexadecimal `byte` or an ASCII `char`.

D   Display ("dump") the current sector in hexadecimal and ASCII.

`Fname.ext`

Display the directory entry for the file named. You are subsequently moved to the file's directory sector.

F   Find the next occurrence of name in the directory (the next extent).

`Gnn`   Move to group `nn`. `and read`.

G   Show your current position.

H   Display ("dump") the current sector in hexadecimal only.

L   "Log-in" the current disk again. You may replace a disk with a new one, and use `L` to log-in the new disk.

`Ld`   "Log-in" disk `d` (as in `LB` ⊃ for drive B).

M   Display a map of the group allocations for files on the entire disk.

`Mnn`   Show which file is allocated to group `nn`.

N   Reset CP/M through its BDOS module. This may make it possible under some implementations of CP/M to change the disk format (i.e., disk density, one-sided to two-sided disks, etc).

P   Turn on or off the printer "echo" of console input and output.

Q   "Quiet" mode. Preceding any command, this command suppresses console output.

R   Reads the current sector (currently positioned to) into memory. R (read) is implicit in the G, +, and - commands, but *not* in the S and T commands.

Snn   Move to sector nn and read.

Tnn   Move ("seek") to track nn (no read).

Un   "Log-in" user n for the next F command. This command displays the ? error if you are not using CP/M-80 version 2.0 or a newer version.

V   View the current sector (assumes ASCII data and displays like the CP/M TYPE command).

Vnn   View nn sectors.

W   Write the current sector back to disk. Note: this command should not be used after using an F command, since F uses CP/M to find the file in the directory.

X   Exit DU, return to CP/M.

Z*nn*   Sleep — cause the program to pause, to let you look at a display before it scrolls past. Z is one second. Znn sets the pause to nn tenths of a second on a 2 MHz 8080 CPU.

DU Commands in Action
Erasing a Disk Directory

The following commands will erase all files on drive B by changing the B: disk directory to E5H ("H" stands for hexadecimal):

:LB ⊃   ("Log-in" the B drive.)

   :GO ⊃   (Move to start of directory.)

   :CHO-7F,E5 ⊃   (Fill with E5H.)

   :< ⊃   (Save the sector.)

   :);W;+;/16 ⊃
        (Restore, write, move to next and repeat 16 times.)

This example could be shortened to:

   :LB;GO;CHO-7F,E5;< ⊃
   :);W;+;/16 ⊃

Display Commands

You can add to a display command (D, A and H) an optional starting and ending address:

   :D0,7F ⊃   (This is the same as D ⊃.)

   :D3,5 ⊃

   :A20,3F ⊃

Logging In a Disk

Some problems may occur when "logging in" (setting as the current disk) a mixed-density disk (e.g., track 00 is single density, and the directory tracks are double density, as in IBM System 34 disks).

One solution is to first "log-in" a disk that you know will work, and that is also of the same density as the disk that you want to examine and alter. Then put in the new disk *without* performing a "log-in." However, if you do this, you are opening yourself up to possible problems related to the buffering of physical sectors in the

BIOS.

Another technique (not guaranteed) is to seek to the unused inner tracks of the first disk, then do the read, *and then* change disks. If anything is written, you will not have destroyed anything — assuming the disk is not completely full.

Another possible solution, assuming the second disk does not contain a CP/M system, would be to seek to track 1, do the read operation there, and then change disks to the new one.

Sector Buffers

You can store up to 255 sectors in a buffer with the ⟨⟨ command; use ⟩⟩ for every ⟨⟨ to make the buffer contents available for writing. To reset (throw away the contents of) the buffer, use one ⟨ command.

The M command (directory map) also uses an area of memory for a buffer. To minimize problems, the map buffer is placed at the end of the currently highest used ⟨⟨ buffer.

In small systems, where many buffers have been saved using ⟨⟨, the M command might report that it ran out of memory. By executing the ⟨ or ⟩⟩ command a sufficient number of times for it to tell you there are no more sectors in the buffer, you can make room available in memory at a lower address, and M can again be used for "mapping" the directory.

Interpreting CP/M Directory Data

The following explains the format of a CP/M single-density disk directory entry, as shown by DU using either the F (find file) command or using D to display ("dump") the directory sectors, which are located in groups 0 and 1 on a single-density disk.

Figure 8-3 shows the result of the command   FSID.COM ⊃ (find the SID.COM file).

A file *extent* indicates to CP/M the number of 16 thousand (actually 16K) consecutive bytes contained within a file. Extents are numbered from 0 to 31. One extent may contain one, two, four,

```
40   00534944  20202020  20434F4D  0000003A   *.SID    COM...:*
50   33343536  3738393A  00000000  00000000   *3456789:........*
```

First line

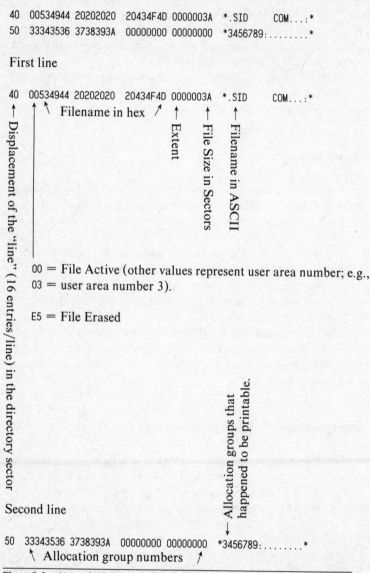

Figure 8-3. *Using the find command to find the file SID.COM on a single-density disk.*

```
:FSID.COM↩                              (Find SID.COM on the disk.)

00  00534944 20202020 20434F4D 0000003A  *.SID    COM...:*
10  38003900 3A003B00 00000000 00000000  *8.9.:.;.........*
G=0000:00, T=2, S=1, PS=0
```

Figure 8-4. *Using the find command on a double-density disk.*

---

eight or sixteen blocks. A *block* is the basic unit of disk space allocation, and may be 1K, 2K, 4K, 8K or 16K consecutive bytes.

These blocks are assigned *group numbers* (a "group" is a set of
disk sectors). Group numbers are allocated dynamically to accommodate the required disk space used by a given file (group 0 is *always* the start of the directory group).

More than one filename might appear in the directory for one
file, depending on the number of extents required to accommodate
the file's size. (See figure 8-1 for an example of this —
PBIOS.ASM has two entries in the directory for one file.)

Figure 8-4 shows an example of finding SID.COM running on a
double-density disk system.

The major difference between single and double density is that
the groups now occupy 2 bytes. This convention follows the Intel
and CP/M convention of putting 16 bit values with the high byte
first: "38 00", "39 00", etc. means groups 0038, 0039, etc.

Note also that in double-density disks, each group represents
2K, not 1K, so there are half as many groups for the same file.

Be *very careful* when patching a double-density disk directory. I
once made the mistake of typing the following command:

```
:CH10,38,39,3A,3B...↩
```

When I tried to read this file, DU tried to access group 3938,
causing angry exclamations from the disk stepper as it attempted
to go south to Peoria for the data.

DU Examples

The following DU examples show typical operations with DU: recovering an accidentally-erased file, making an auto-start disk that automatically starts a program when you boot the system from that disk, and performing a bad sector test. These examples show that with some work on your part, you can make DU take the place of the UNERA and FINDBAD utilities and still perform operations that cannot be performed with any other utility.

Recovery of an Erased File

Suppose you have just added the final touches to your latest and greatest program or text file. Being of usual slothful weekend mind and spirit, you (of course) forgot to make a backup copy after having invested thousands of hours into it. You proudly examine the directory of your disk:

```
A)DIR B: ↵

B:BIZ-INIT BAS :BIZ-CALC BAS :BIZ-CHRT BAS
B:BIZ-WIZ  BAS :BIZ-WIZ  TXT
```

Everything is there, but the telephone rings and it's a friend who wants to download via modem the latest version of FOOBAR to you to try. So, in the hurry to get your system ready and create space on a "scratch" disk for FOOBAR, you type this very easy-to-use command to clear the space:

```
A)ERA B:*.* ↵
```

— Get rid of whatever junk is there.

```
ALL (Y/N)?Y ↵
```

— Sure, can't remember what's there, can't be important.

A⟩DIR B: ⮐   — and just to be sure...

NO FILE

        — Yep! No files left... but...

Oh No! You left the wrong disk in the drive! That wasn't a
scratch disk, that was... #$%@&*!!
Now what do you do? DU to the rescue!

A0⟩DU ⮐

DISK UTILITY ver 7.7
Universal Version

Type ? for help
Type X to exit

:LB ⮐

        — "Log-in" disk B (— a forest reclamation project!).

:G0;D ⮐

        — Go to Group 0, which is always the *directory group*,
and "dump" it:

```
G=00:00, T=2, S=1, PS=1
00 E542495A 2D494E49 54424153 0000001C *eBIZ-INITBAS....*
10 02030405 00000000 00000000 00000000 *...............*
20 E542495A 2D43414C 43424153 00000050 *eBIZ-CALCBAS...P*
30 06070809 0A0B0C0D 0E0F0000 00000000 *...............*
40 E542495A 2D434852 54424153 00000019 *eBIZ-CHRTBAS....*
50 10111213 00000000 00000000 00000000 *...............*
60 E542495A 2D57495A 20545854 00000029 *eBIZ-WIZ TXT...)*
70 14151617 18190000 00000000 00000000 *...............*
```

Your files should appear, but with e's in front of each filename.

Look also at the next directory sector:

```
:+;D ⊃
```

> – Move +1 sector and "dump" it also:

```
G=00:01, T=2, S=2, PS=7
00 E542495A 2D57495A 20424153 00000080 *eBIZ-WIZ BAS....*
10 1A1B1C1D 1E1F2021 22232425 26272829 *...... ! '#$%&'()*
20 E542495A 2D57495A 20424153 0100006B *eBIZ-WIZ BAS...k*
30 2A2B2C2D 2E2F3031 32333435 36370000 **+,-./01234567..*
40 E5E5E5E5 E5E5E5E5 E5E5E5E5 E5E5E5E5 *eeeeeeeeeeeeeeee*
50 E5E5E5E5 E5E5E5E5 E5E5E5E5 E5E5E5E5 *eeeeeeeeeeeeeeee*
60 E5E5E5E5 E5E5E5E5 E5E5E5E5 E5E5E5E5 *eeeeeeeeeeeeeeee*
70 E5E5E5E5 E5E5E5E5 E5E5E5E5 E5E5E5E5 *eeeeeeeeeeeeeeee*
```

When you are searching a disk with more files, you may need to move forward and "dump" several sectors to see all the filenames.

Here's how to move back one sector and start fixing the directory to recover those erased files:

```
:⁻ ⊃
```

> — Move back one sector.

```
G=00:00, T=2, S=1, PS=1
```

```
:CH0,0;CH20,0;CH40,0;CH60,0 ⊃
```

— Change these locations in the sector (all E5's) to zeros. DU displays the previous values of these disk locations:

```
E5E5E5E5
```

The E5's (erased file flags) evaporate before your very eyes! But you should "dump" to make sure:

```
:D ⊃
```

```
00 0042495A 2D494E49 54424153 0000001C *.BIZ-INITBAS....*
10 02030405 00000000 00000000 00000000 *...............*
20 0042495A 2D43414C 43424153 00000050 *.BIZ-CALCBAS...P*
30 06070809 0A0B0C0D 0E0F0000 00000000 *...............*
40 0042495A 2D434852 54424153 00000019 *.BIZ-CHRTBAS....*
50 10111213 00000000 00000000 00000000 *...............*
60 0042495A 2D57495A 20545854 00000029 *.BIZ-WIZ TXT...)*
70 14151617 18190000 00000000 00000000 *...............*
```

The display shows the filenames starting with 00's this time,
which is the proper way for active files to be represented in the directory. However, this change has not yet occurred on disk but only
in DU's memory. To save the change you must use W to write this
directory sector back to the disk:

   :W ↵

Now you can move to the next directory sector and "dump" it:

   :+ ↵

G=00:01, T=2, S=2, PS=7
:D ↵

```
00 E542495A 2D57495A 20424153 00000080 *eBIZ-WIZ BAS....*
10 1A1B1C1D 1E1F2021 22232425 26272829 *...... !''#$%&'()*
20 E542495A 2D57495A 20424153 0100006B *eBIZ-WIZ BAS...k*
30 2A2B2C2D 2E2F3031 32333435 36370000 **+,-./01234567..*
40 E5E5E5E5 E5E5E5E5 E5E5E5E5 E5E5E5E5 *eeeeeeeeeeeeeeee*
50 E5E5E5E5 E5E5E5E5 E5E5E5E5 E5E5E5E5 *eeeeeeeeeeeeeeee*
60 E5E5E5E5 E5E5E5E5 E5E5E5E5 E5E5E5E5 *eeeeeeeeeeeeeeee*
70 E5E5E5E5 E5E5E5E5 E5E5E5E5 E5E5E5E5 *eeeeeeeeeeeeeeee*
```

To change the two directory entries, type this command:

   :CH0,0;CH20,0 ↵

   E5E5

The locations in this sector are changed to zero from E5 with this command. To be sure, "dump" the sector:

```
:D ⏎
```

```
00 0042495A 2D57495A 20424153 00000080 *.BIZ-WIZ BAS....*
10 1A1B1C1D 1E1F2021 22232425 26272829 *...... !''#$%&'()*
20 0042495A 2D57495A 20424153 0100006B *.BIZ-WIZ BAS...k*
30 2A2B2C2D 2E2F3031 32333435 36370000 **+,-./01234567..*
40 E5E5E5E5 E5E5E5E5 E5E5E5E5 E5E5E5E5 *eeeeeeeeeeeeeeee*
50 E5E5E5E5 E5E5E5E5 E5E5E5E5 E5E5E5E5 *eeeeeeeeeeeeeeee*
60 E5E5E5E5 E5E5E5E5 E5E5E5E5 E5E5E5E5 *eeeeeeeeeeeeeeee*
70 E5E5E5E5 E5E5E5E5 E5E5E5E5 E5E5E5E5 *eeeeeeeeeeeeeeee*
```

Now write the sector to disk (don't forget this step!):

```
:W ⏎
```

With all of the filenames changed and all the changed sectors in the directory written to disk, you can exit DU by typing this:

```
:X ⏎
```

Now check the directory of the disk:

```
A>DIR B: ⏎

B:BIZ-INIT BAS :BIZ-CALC BAS :BIZ-CHRT BAS :BIZ-WIZ  TXT
B:BIZ-WIZ  BAS

A>
```

As if by magic, the erased files appear once again! (It's all done with mirrors.)

Modifying a Disk For Program Autoload

By modifying a portion of the CP/M operating system, you can force it to automatically load and execute a command file every time CP/M starts up from a cold start or reset.

This feature can be particularly useful if you want to set up some fancy printer initialization, modify serial port baud rates or data format parameters, or start a menu program after every cold start or reset.

To enter an "autoload" filename to a CP/M disk (some of the data in this example is representative of my disk only), follow these steps. First move to track 2, sector 1, and dump:

```
:T2;S1;D ⊃

T=2, S=1, PS=0
T=2, S=1, PS=0
00 C35CDDC3 58DD7F00 20202020 20202020 *C              *
10 20202020 20202020 434F5059 52494748 *        COPYRIGH*
20 54202843 29203139 37392C20 44494749 *T (C) 1979, DIGI*
30 54414C20 52455345 41524348 20200000 *TAL RESEARCH  ..*
40 00000000 00000000 00000000 00000000 *................*
50 00000000 00000000 00000000 00000000 *................*
60 00000000 00000000 00000000 00000000 *................*
70 00000000 00000000 00000000 00000000 *................*
```

Now use the CA command (change using ASCII characters) to change addresses 08 through 0D to the ASCII characters "SIGNON" and address 0E to the hexadecimal value 0H:

```
:CA8,SIGNON(0) ⊃
```

The CP/M command to start the program is now inserted in the proper place on the disk; however, CP/M does not yet know about the command. To tell CP/M that the command should be used on auto-start, you have to place a hexadecimal value in address 07H (immediately before the inserted CP/M command) equal to the number of characters in the CP/M command. SIGNON has six characters; therefore, the value is 6H.

Now use the CH command (change using hexadecimal values) to change address 07 to the value 6H:

```
:CH7,6 ⊃
00
```

DU displays 00 to show you what address 07H had previously contained. Now dump the disk sector for display:

```
:D ⊃

00 C35CDDC3 58DD7F06 5349474E 4F4E0020 *C       SIGNON. *
10 20202020 20202020 434F5059 52494748 *        COPYRIGH*
20 54202843 29203139 37392C20 44494749 *T (C) 1979, DIGI*
30 54414C20 52455345 41524348 20200000 *TAL RESEARCH  ..*
40 00000000 00000000 00000000 00000000 *................*
50 00000000 00000000 00000000 00000000 *................*
60 00000000 00000000 00000000 00000000 *................*
70 00000000 00000000 00000000 00000000 *................*
```

The display should show the command SIGNON occupying addresses 08H through 0DH. If everything is correct (that is, the CP/M command you are using is in the place where SIGNON is shown, and the preceding byte holds the length of this CP/M command, and the CP/M command is followed by a byte holding 00), you should write the sector to disk to save it:

```
:W ⊃
```

Now you can leave DU and return to CP/M:

```
:X ⊃
```

You can now reset or "cold start" this CP/M system disk, and it will automatically start the SIGNON program prior to doing anything else. Of course, you should substitute your own program name for SIGNON in the above example.

Many users like to start a SUBMIT file of commands this way; in this case you would use the CP/M command SUBMIT STARTUP (if the name of the ".SUB" file is STARTUP.SUB) in place of SIGNON. Therefore you would put SUBMIT STARTUP (including the space be-

tween the words) in locations 08H through 15H, with 00 in location
16H and E (for 0EH) in location 07H (the length of the command,
including the space).

A "Poor Man's Disk Test"

DU can also function as a "Poor Man's disk test" that can perform simple sequential write/read/seek functions with user-speci-
fied data patterns.

The following is a four-sector non-destructive read-only/seek
test. Any subsequent errors would be trapped by the CP/M BDOS
and stop the test with whatever error message was appropriate
(e.g., BDOS Err on B: BAD SECTOR). You can incorporate this idea in a
larger routine to test many sectors in a track, or all sectors on all
tracks.

First move to a track and sector (we chose track 20, sector 1):

```
:T20;S1⤸
G=0040:00, T=20, S=1, PS=0
```

Now read forward four sectors, read backward four sectors, and
repeat (until you type a Control-C).

```
:+;+;+;+;-;-;-;-;/⤸
G=0040:01, T=20, S=2, PS=1
G=0040:02, T=20, S=3, PS=2
G=0040:03, T=20, S=4, PS=3
G=0040:04, T=20, S=5, PS=4
G=0040:03, T=20, S=4, PS=3
G=0040:02, T=20, S=3, PS=2
G=0040:01, T=20, S=2, PS=1
G=0040:00, T=20, S=1, PS=0
G=0040:01, T=20, S=2, PS=1
G=0040:02, T=20, S=3, PS=2
```

Days or weeks later...

```
G=0040:03, T=20, S=4, PS=3
G=0040:02, T=20, S=3, PS=2
G=0040:01, T=20, S=2, PS=1
G=0040:00, T=20, S=1, PS=0
G=0040:01,
```

Ah... the routine is finally interrupted with Control-C from the keyboard.

By using your imagination, you can come up with a variety of useful applications for DU. Remember, however, that DU can permanently change bytes on the disk, and if you change the wrong bytes, you can make an entire disk unusable. With that in mind, forge ahead!

CHAPTER 9:
DAN'S INFORMATION MANAGEMENT SYSTEM

by Dan Dugan

DIMS (Dan's Information Management System) is a complete data base management system in the public domain that has been described as an inexpensive (free!) alternative to dBASE II for many data management applications. The system is a set of BASIC programs (Microsoft BASIC-80) chained together and designed so that it can be used by anyone with no prior BASIC experience.

DIMS has been known to be useful in managing mailing lists with thousands of names. You can find it in the SIG/M library, disk volume #61. It was written by Dan Dugan who is (among other things) a sound designer for the performing arts, a computer programmer, and a freelance writer. In this chapter he describes how to install and use DIMS version 1.03.

Features and Limitations

DIMS is a set of BASIC programs that chain together automatically to create a versatile list-managing system. It has been proven under pressure to be suitable for medium-scale mailing-list operations (hundreds to thousands of names), inventories, indexes, ledgers and other applications. It must be installed by a person who knows Microsoft BASIC-80; once it is installed it can be used successfully by almost anybody.

Records in a DIMS data base file can be either 128 bytes (characters) long with up to 15 data fields, or 256 bytes (characters) long with up to 30 data fields. Within each record the data fields can be random in length. An indicator appears to show how much space is left when length limits are being approached.

New records are added to the end of the data base file. You can delete records, but record numbers stay the same until you use the "renumber" command. When you are updating records, DIMS shows the old data field by field, and you have the choice of keeping or replacing the data in each field.

All data files are automatically kept in duplicate on two different disks. When a record is updated it is automatically updated on both disks. Therefore it is difficult to lose a DIMS file. The files can be scanned with the CP/M "type" command. Except for temporary files kept during operations like sorting, there are no index files.

You can search data files rapidly for a literal substring anywhere in the record, or more slowly for up to 10 selection keys in specific fields and up to 10 rejection keys in fields. A subset of records so selected may be written out to another DIMS file, or written to a standard BASIC sequential data file for use by other programs.

You can add a standard BASIC sequential data file from any source onto a DIMS file. A quite flexible multi-key sorting command is included which can sort a whole file or a range of records within it. The sort output may be overlaid on the original file or sent to a new file.

File size is limited only by disk space. The DIMS "sort" command is limited by the memory space used by its key array, which depends on the size of the desired keys and the number of records. Where there are thousands of records or long keys an external sorting utility may be needed — I use SuperSort® from MicroPro International (San Rafael, CA).

Complete screen and printer form design is provided for. You can display scrolling forms or stationary (one record per screen) forms. You can design more than one form for a file and you can switch between them with a two-word command. At any time any data fields can be hidden from view.

Most operations include self-explanatory dialogue. In the file editor DEDIT.BAS several screens of help text may be displayed with the command help.

Installation

DIMS is written in Microsoft BASIC-80 and must be modified to run properly with your display screen and printer. You can edit the program files, which are in ASCII text format (".ASC" files), using any text editing or word processing program as long as you refrain from using special control characters or printing characters. For example, I use WordStar® (from MicroPro) in its non-document mode.

The version of Microsoft BASIC-80® (MBASIC®, Microsoft Inc.) plays an important role. This chapter cannot possibly explain BASIC programming; it is therefore assumed you already know how to program in Microsoft BASIC-80 (see Chapter 2 for a description and for references to other books on MBASIC).

There are two critical differences between Microsoft BASIC-80 version 4.5 and 5.x (x represents versions starting with 5.0). One is that the CLEAR statement has changed syntax. This statement is used once, in the main menu program DIMS. If you are installing with version 4.5, use CLEAR 1000 which sets string space. If you are using version 5.x, use CLEAR,,1000 which sets *stack* space. In 5.x string space is used dynamically, but the stack space is determined from an algorithm which will result in DIMS crashing with an Out of Memory error, which will be puzzling because FRE(X) will still show plenty of memory.

The second difference is that BASIC-80 version 5.x has the command INKEY$ which allows checking the keyboard without stopping. If you need to install DIMS on version 4.5, you will have to either give up the z scrolling control command, or write code that looks at your hardware ports. For example, in place of X$=INKEY$ (version 5.x) use X=INP(KEYBD.DATA.PORT) (version 4.5).

The program files are supplied as ASCII text files with the ".ASC" extension (saved in this manner by MBASIC). You must first use MBASIC's LOAD command to load each ".ASC" file, and then use the SAVE command to save each file as a ".BAS" file, before running DIMS. This is explained in Chapter 2.

Memory Requirement

DIMS fits snugly in a 64K CP/M system that has at least 59K of internal memory available for running programs. I run it in a Morrow hard disk system on my S-100 computer with 62K available. CP/M computers usually leave from 59K to 62K available for loading a program like DIMS.

A smaller system may not have room for the entire file editor program called DEDIT, which is big. The program STRIP.BAS is provided for removing comments from DEDIT. With comments removed, DEDIT will fit in a system with 54K available.

If your system is smaller and you're adept at MBASIC, you could shrink DEDIT by taking out all the code relating to the format command and replacing all the complicated positioning code with simple listing in the default format. If you strip the comments keep your development version with the comments in, and then strip it for running, so you'll have the comments to guide you in making modifications.

Terminal Display

DIMS uses the clear-screen and cursor positioning functions of your terminal display. Since all terminals are different, *all the DIMS programs must be modified to suit your terminal display characteristics.*

In the Microsoft BASIC-80 code you will see (TERM DEP) in comments at each place where customization is necessary. Use your text editing program to search for these spots. DEDIT uses the most functions and therefore requires the most work. The supplied transient programs don't use cursor positioning but they do use screen clear and keyboard testing.

Whether or not you edit the ".ASC" files, *all the program segments must be loaded and saved again* using the MBASIC interpreter. This is because DIMS uses CHAIN and the programs, which are stored and edited in ASCII format, will at first appear to work properly but will crash soon after with misleading error messages (e.g., the message WRONG FILE MODE).

When writing BASIC-80 code, typing a Line Feed produces a new line in the listing which is not counted as a line by BASIC. The combination of these and tabs makes it possible to get a lot of clarifying white space into the code with very little cost in terms of characters. However, if you edit a program.ASC file with WordStar (in non-document mode), you will see extra lines inserted and signs of confusion in the right hand column. This is because BASIC-80 has put in a Line Feed code followed by a Return code, which is the opposite of the usual sequence (Return then Line Feed) in the file. WordStar can't edit this sequence. Leave those effects alone when using WordStar and all will be well.

Special problems can arise if you use an upper-case only terminal. If you must use one, copy all the program *and data* files with PIP using the [u] option. Then use a text editor to find all occurrences of CHR$(in the programs and change those numbers which represent lower-case characters (in the range 97 to 122) to upper-case codes by subtracting 32 from the number.

Printer

The DIMS system as delivered is designed for a Diablo 1610 or 1620 printer, and uses many of its special control sequences such as setting vertical and horizontal pitch for listing in a pre-recorded form, and high speed absolute tabbing. To use DIMS with other printers, you must rewrite this BASIC code. Diablo control sequences start with Escape, which is CHR$(27). DIMS will allow you to create a format specification which uses reverse scrolling on the printer, but don't do it unless you have a bi-directional forms tractor.

Supplied Files

DIMS is supplied as program segments in separate files. In addition, several MBASIC tools are provided, and a complete manual in the DINSTALL.DOC file.

Group 0: Development

Keep these files on your "DIMS Development" set of disks. They are not needed for working with files under DIMS.

READ-ME.103   Release letter
DINSTALL.DOC   Installation and Operation Manual
STRIP.BAS   BASIC-80 utility for making DEDIT smaller.
FORMFORM.DWS   Source file to be copied when designing screen/printer formats with the aid of WordStar.
FIELDFOR.DWS   Source file to be appended to copies of FORMFORM.DWS.

Group 1: Main Programs

The following BASIC-80 programs are provided in ASCII text format to make them easier to transmit, scan, and edit during installation. *They must be merged into memory using the MBASIC interpreter and then stored with the SAVE command in ".BAS" files in order to run them.*

DIMS.ASC   Opening menu program.
DEDIT.ASC   The file editor program.

Group 2: Transient Programs

All of the following except DCREATE chain from and return to the file editor, DEDIT:

DCFORM.ASC   Command for creating a screen/printer format for a file.
DCHESHIR.ASC   Command for printing labels four-across

	on wide paper for a Cheshire automatic label application machine. This file can also be used as a stand-alone program to print from a comma-delimited data file.
DCREATE.ASC	Program to create a new file format (chains from DIMS main menu program).
DDOC.ASC	Command that displays or writes to a text file of notes associated with a data file.
DGET.ASC	Command which gets a sequential file and adds it to a DIMS file.
DHELP.ASC	Command which displays screens describing file editor commands. The screens are stored in the file DHELP.DOC.
DLABELS.ASC	Command for printing "one-up" mailing labels.
DLETTERS.ASC	Command for printing form letters with file data inserted.
DNADIN.ASC	Command for inputting a NAD-like data file to a DIMS "standard" form mailing list file.
DPUT.ASC	Command which puts a set of records out to a sequential file.
DSORT.ASC	Command for sorting files.
DSTAT.ASC	Command for calculating descriptive statistics for data in a numeric field.

Group 3: Main Data Files

LONGADDR.D	Example data file for long form address lists.
STANDADD.D	Example data file for standard form address lists.
SHORTADD.D	Example data file for short form address lists.
ARTICLES.D	Example data file for magazine articles.
MEMBERS.D	Example data file for neighborhood association.

Group 4: Backup Data Files

LONGADDR.DD   Example backup data file.
(etc.).DD

Group 5: Auxiliary Files

SHORT.DFO   Example format control file.
SHORT1.DFO   Example format control file.
STANDADD.DFO   Example format control file.
MEMBERS.DFO   Example format control file — used for
                    printer listing.
MEMBERS.DOC   Example of a notes file read and written via
                    doc command when editing MEMBERS
                    file.
DHELP.DOC   Screen texts used by help command.

Putting Files on Working Disks

I recommend that besides the distribution master, you keep a set of disks called "Dims Development" which consist of all the release files in compressed form, the demonstration files, and small samples of the data files you create for yourself. Use this set of disks to create and test formats and to create and test your own transient utilities.

You can then keep sets of working disks, which will be changed in pairs, with just the DIMS components you need and plenty of space for data files. With three disk drives available, I use drive A for the everyday program library and drives B and C for data. I change the disks in drives B and C for different sets of files (see below).

After each program segment is checked over and modified for your terminal, save it using MBASIC SAVE command to the file filename.BAS You can then erase the corresponding ".ASC" file of the same name. Depending on how many drives you have, you must copy the files provided on the distribution disk to disks on the appropriate drives of your system. Then change the initial value of the variable NDRIVES near the beginning of DIMS.BAS to the number of drives you are using.

If you are using a hard disk, "comment out" (make into comments) the two RESET statements near the top of DIMS.BAS. They are necessary for changing floppies, which is only allowed at the no-file menu.

Two-drive System

Programs are split between drives A: and B:, attempting to make balanced space for data (.D) and backup (.DD) files:

Drive A:

MBASIC.COM
DIMS.BAS
DEDIT.BAS
LONGADDR.D
STANDADD.D
SHORTADD.D
ARTICLES.D
MEMBERS.D

Drive B:

DCFORM.BAS
DCHESHIR.BAS
DCREATE.BAS
DDOC.BAS
DGET.BAS
DHELP.BAS
DLABELS.BAS
DLETTERS.BAS
DNADIN.BAS
DPUT.BAS
DSORT.BAS
DSTAT.BAS
SHORT.DFO
SHORT1.DFO
MEMBERS.DFO
STANDADD.DFO
MEMBERS.DOC
DHELP.DOC
LONGADDR.DD
STANDADD.DD
SHORTADD.DD
ARTICLES.DD
MEMBERS.DD

Small-capacity Two-drive System

Computers with small-capacity disk drives (such as the early Osborne 1 computers) can operate with the minimum number of files needed to build a data base (shown below). To give the maximum possible space for data, MBASIC.COM is stored on drive B: The system is started from drive A: by typing B:MBASIC DIMS ⤸. On an Osborne 1, you can add 400 data records.

Drive A: Drive B:

DIMS.BAS   MBASIC.COM
DEDIT.BAS   STANDADD.DD
STANDADD.D

Three-drive System

The program library is kept together on drive A:, and drives B: and C: are saved for large data files. A data file can be as big as the whole user disk space, and still have 100% backup on the other disk.

Drive A: Drive B: Drive C:

MBASIC.COM   LONGADDR.D   LONGADDR.DD
DIMS.BAS   STANDADD.D   STANDADD.DD
DEDIT.BAS   SHORTADD.D   SHORTADD.DD
DCFORM.BAS   ARTICLES.D   ARTICLES.DD
DCHESHIR.BAS   MEMBERS.D   MEMBERS.DD
DCREATE .BAS
DDOC.BAS
DGET.BAS
DHELP.BAS
DLABELS.BAS
DLETTERS.BAS
DNADIN.BAS

DPUT.BAS
DSORT.BAS
DSTAT.BAS
SHORT.DFO
SHORT1.DFO
STANDADD.DFO
MEMBERS.DFO
DHELP.DOC
MEMBERS.DOC

Four-drive System

Auxiliary files (".DOC", ".DFO" and temporary ".$$$") are kept on the fourth drive.

Drive A:	Drive B:	Drive C:	Drive D:
MBASIC.COM	LONGADDR.D	LONGADDR.DD	SHORT.DFO
DIMS.BAS	STANDADD.D	STANDADD.DD	SHORT1.DFO
DEDIT.BAS	SHORTADD.D	SHORTADD.DD	STANDADD.DFO
DCFORM.BAS	ARTICLES.D	ARTICLES.DD	MEMBERS.DFO
DCHESHIR.BAS	MEMBERS.D	MEMBERS.DD	MEMBERS.DOC
DCREATE.BAS			DHELP.DOC
DDOC.BAS			
DGET.BAS			
DHELP.BAS			
DLABELS.BAS			
DLETTERS.BAS			
DNADIN.BAS			
DPUT.BAS			
DSORT.BAS			
DSTAT.BAS			

Main Menu

After the files have been put on the appropriate drives and have
been modified for your terminal and drive configuration, and then
saved using the MBASIC interpreter in the standard ".BAS" compressed format (".ASC" files won't CHAIN), you can start the
system by running DIMS.

You should get the no-file menu with a directory of the provided
test data files displayed. If you then press Return, you will get
menu choice 1, Open a file. Enter the name of one of the existing
files, just the main part of the name, skipping the extension. It may
be in either lower or UPPER case letters.

DEDIT should load and display the last record in the file. (If
you get the message BAD FILE MODE IN 6250, it means that DEDIT
hasn't been saved as a ".BAS" file in normal compressed format;
that is, using the MBASIC SAVE command.) Type help ⊃ for a
series of screens explaining the available commands. At the pause
prompt Ready⟩, if you type h ⊃ a menu of pause options will appear.

When you are editing a file the only safe exit is to type the command done ⊃ (or don ⊃). This will return you to the main menu.
Other choices available from the no-file menu include a RESET
which is intended to show the new directory when data disks have
been changed. If DIMS has been properly installed (two RESET
statements enabled), no harm will come if you skip this step and
open a file. There is also a command for changing the number of
disks in the system for the current session. This is for emergency
use. It is necessary to first use PIP to move the files around to the
appropriate drives if you intend to do this.

The no-file menu includes DCREATE, the sub-program that
sets up a new file from scratch. It asks for the name, and choice of
size. 128-byte records are just right for mailing lists and most
things; the 256-byte record size is available for records that need
more space.

You are also asked to give the default four-character name for
each field, and whether it is an alphabetic or numeric field. You
can just press Return for alphabetic. *Everywhere in DIMS dia-
logues, if you just press Return (⊃), you get the first choice in the
menu or options.* Enter stop ⊃ when all fields have been defined,

and after approval the new file will be opened.

If you want to make a new file with the same field scheme as an existing one, there's an easier way. Just open the file and copy one record (copy 1⊃), giving the new file name. Then type done⊃ to close the old file, open the new file and type change⊃ to put new data in the copied record. Then you can start adding records.

File Editing Commands

DEDIT has two prompts: Edit FILENAME: and Ready⟩. Edit FILENAME: is the command level, and accepts a command line. Ready⟩ is the "pause prompt" between records in a sequence being run through in response to a command line.

The pause prompt Ready⟩ takes single-key instant commands such as z (scroll), Escape key, or space bar. Pressing the space bar will show the next record. Pressing z will start continuous scrolling until you press the space bar to stop it. The Escape key will always quit the sequence and give you the Edit FILENAME: prompt. At the pause prompt Ready⟩, you can display a list of the options by typing h.

The Edit FILENAME: prompt takes a somewhat free-form command line. This line can only have valid command words. The sequence can be pretty loose, but after a final command anything else (up to the Return key) will be ignored, *except* for range-of-records words and numbers like from 10 to 20.

If there's a record number or a pair of record numbers anywhere in the command line, the command will be done on the specified range of records. The words from, to, all, end, next, or last may be used when talking about record numbers. A period (.) instead of a number means "use the most recently displayed record." All the built-in commands may be shortened to three letters.

For example, all the following are valid commands:

```
add
delete from 10 to 20
delete 10 20
print to 75
```

```
print select labels
change 57
cha .                              (Change last record shown.)
10 20
list from 10 to 20                     (Same result as 10 20.)
select copy delete             (Moves records to another file.)
```

Final Commands

These commands are normally the last word in the command sentence. Any following words except record numbers will be ignored by DIMS.

add   Append records to the end of the file, prompting field by field. In this mode the following commands take effect:
stop — alone in any field quits adding.
\ — (backslash) at end of any field skips back 1 field.
; — alone in the field copies data from last record shown.

done   Close the file and return to the no-file menu.

goto filename
      Close the file and open any named file on the same disks.

fields
      Allow "hiding" fields you don't want to show. You may "un-hide" them with the same command. This command controls the output of the put command.

format 0
      Install the default display and print formats.

format formname
      Install a format definition (named by formname) for screen and printer.

formats
> Display the available format definition files.

backup
> Make a completely new backup file from main file. This command is rarely needed since a backup file is maintained automatically by DIMS.

renumber
> Renumber all records sequentially from the top in both main and backup files, closing up holes from deleted records.

Miscellaneous Commands

The following commands may be given freely anywhere in the command line:

change n
> Display record number n or range of records, field by field. You can enter new data for each field or keep the old data by pressing Return. To erase a field enter just one space, then Return. A backslash (\) backs you up to previous field. If you include more than one record in a change command, you are given the option to select fields to change, which speeds up the process when you're adding something quickly to an existing file.

delete n
> Display record or records and ask approval to erase.

list n
> Display records (assumed if you give no other final command).

find word
> Find records containing the exact string word. A phrase can be

found if you use underlines instead of spaces (e.g., this_phrase).

select
> Find records containing up to 10 different words or phrases. You can use regular spaces in phrases, but no upper/lower case conversion is done. If you hit Return when asked what field to look in the word will be searched for in all fields. You also can specify up to 10 words or phrases that will cause the record to be skipped. Design your coding system to work with this.

print Send to the printer rather than the screen, using the current format.

copy Copy data records and add them on to the end of another DIMS file. You are asked for the filename. You may create a new file this way or add to an existing one, but the field definitions must be the same. New records have no automatic backup.

and Permitted for clarity in command lines, but ignored by DIMS.

page Set the page number to use for the first page of the printout (valid for this command line only).

margin
> Set the printer margin if you don't want the margin that comes with the form you're using (for this command line only).

flag Combined with add or change to a range of records, this command asks you for a string to be added automatically to any (one) field in the record.

programs
> Show a directory of available "transient commands," i.e. various batch processes that can work on the file.

Transient Commands

Transient commands are sub-programs which do a batch of work and then return you to DEDIT. Where appropriate, they will take a range of records and selection criteria from the command line. Example:

```
print select labels 100 to 150
```

The most commonly used transient commands are described here:

cform   Process for creating format definition files.

doc   A "notepad" where you can read or write notes associated with the data file. The ".DOC" file can be edited later with a text editor. Useful for documenting on the spot codes you invent for your file.

labels

Print a batch of mailing labels (for example, print labels) with blank fields closed up. This works only with three standard address file formats. It's not hard to modify if necessary. After the labels are aligned, press the space bar to print one at a time (to make sure they print properly). Then type a Z to cause continuous printing. Press a space again to pause, or ESC to abort.

letters

Print a text file with data from a DIMS file inserted. A personal salutation line or other data lines may be included if you want. DLETTERS.BAS must be modified for each job. If you have MailMerge it's easier to use put to make a sequential data file which is a subset of the DIMS data file and use MailMerge with that.

sort   Sort the records into a new sequence in the whole file or just a range of the file. You are asked questions about the operation. Alphabetic keys may be truncated and/or blank-filled to a specified length. The command sorts alphabetically unless all fields specified for keys are numeric. The sorted product may replace the old file or make a new file. You may be limited by memory space to sort only small files.

stat Compute descriptive statistics for a selected numeric field. To count records in a particular subset, use select stat and specify the zip field for calculations.

put Make an output file in standard MBASIC sequential form for further processing with other programs. You may select a range of records in the invoking command line, and selection specifications. Hidden fields (see fields) are skipped.

get Add data from a conventional MBASIC sequential data file to the end of the DIMS file from which it is called, adding records to the end. Allows skipping and re-ordering of fields.

File Styles

If you're opening up a new mailing list file, it's convenient to use one of three established sets of field names. Look at the example files provided: LONGADDR, STANDADD, SHORTADD and MEMBERS. The transient command labels has code built-in to deal with any of these three forms. The long form is used for government or academic work where titles and organizations abound. The standard form is for general purposes. The short form is for short files that won't need to be sorted into last name order.

To make a special-purpose mailing list such as an organization which would want membership status or other special fields, imitate one of the three standard field layouts for everything up to the zip code, then design the layout beyond that point to suit the application. This way the labels program will work with the file. For example, study MEMBERS.DOC, which explains the fields of MEMBERS.D.

The ZIP field is of the numeric type so it will reject un-sortable mistakes (like using the letter "l" for the numeral "1"). Put European and Canadian postal codes after the province in the C-ST field, and leave the ZIP field blank.

Designing Codes For Record Selections

If you design your code fields with compatibility in mind, the limited selection/rejection logic in DIMS can do quite a good job of pulling out the selection of records you are looking for.

One technique that works well is to use codes made up of one lower-case letter and one digit, such as a0, a1, b0, c8, etc. Any number of codes can be jumbled in any order in a single code field. This makes it easy to add codes to the scheme as it develops - you can use the doc command to note their meaning when you think them up. If this form of coding is strictly adhered to, find will pull a subset of a single code very rapidly, since this combination of letter and digit doesn't occur anywhere else in the fields.

For example:

```
print find a2 labels ⊃
```

This finds all records containing the code a2 and prints labels for them.

Creating Screen and Printer Formats

You can create *formats*, which are defined ways of naming and displaying the data on the screen and on the printer. Open the example data file SHORTADD and try the sample formats SHORT and SHORT1 with it. You can see the names of the formats (".DFO" files) available by typing the command formats ⊃. A format is usually designed for use with a particular file, though if the fields are compatible there's no reason why a whole family of files couldn't use the same one. A format specification includes both the screen and the printer images.

You can design either scrolling or screen-oriented forms. The

designers of commercial data-entry programs (e.g. DataStar®
from MicroPro, dBASE II® from Ashton-Tate) seem to prefer
screen-oriented displays, where the screen shows you just one file
record at a time displayed in a designed form. You can design such
fixed-position formats for DIMS. I prefer scrolling data entry because you can orient yourself to what you just did. I haven't used
fixed-position format designs and consequently I must warn you
that though provided for in DIMS this mode hasn't been fully tested and there may be bugs.

Using cform to Create a Format Control File

There are two ways of creating the format specification file,
which will have the extension ".DFO." The first is to use the command cform in DEDIT.

The cform transient command lets you print out a long paper
form on which you fill out your design for the screen and printer
form. You can make screen and/or page headings up to three lines
long. These lines will only be printed if they are not blank. Field
names (prompts) may be omitted, the default 4-character field
name may be used, or a custom name may be printed anywhere.

In positioning names and data fields, if the line is specified the
item will always be printed at that line. If the line is 0 it will be
printed wherever the cursor or printhead was left at the end of the
previous field. Similarly, if a column is specified the data will be
printed there, and if column 0 is given it will print at the column
where it was left by the previous operation. This allows, for example, printing:

```
Firstname Lastname
```

You print this by defining the field name prompt for Lastname as
a single space, at line 0 and column 0.

Take care when entering the data from the filled-out form, because cform doesn't let you back up. If you make an error you must
start over. Enter all the specifications and test it on your data file.

When you're debugging a format design, you can take a short

cut by using a text editor program on the ".DFO" file that cform creates from the specification entry dialogue. Compare the numbers on the paper form with the file image to figure out where in the format control file you are. The file is read as a sequential file when it is used by DIMS, so take great care to preserve the exact number of lines and items per line.

Using WordStar to Create a Format Control File

If you have WordStar, the method is easier. You can edit a text file that has prompts included as non-printing comments to fill in all the desired specifications. The file is then printed to disk to create the control file.

Start WordStar. Type n to begin a "non-document" file, and name the new file with a new name. I suggest using the extension ".DWS" for this type of file.

At the top of the blank new file, type Control-KR, and give the name FORMFORM.DWS ↵. The FORMFORM.DWS file contains complete prompts and instructions for creating the format control file. Append as many copies of the file FIELDFOR.DWS as you need for the data fields, using Control-KR.

Now simulate printing of the file using the WordStar P option (from the no-file menu), selecting a disk file to receive the printout rather than the printer. The filename you use for the file to receive the printout must have the extension ".DFO".

You then edit the ".DFO" file to remove extra blank lines from the end. Then it may be tried out while editing the DIMS file. Give the command form name (where name.DFO is your format control file). After corrections are noted, work on the ".DWS" source file again and "print" it to the ".DFO" file again.

Crash Recovery

DIMS records every record that you enter or update immediately in two places: the main and backup data files. Hopefully your system will be set up so that these are on different disks, so that you are protected even if a disk or directory fails to work.

When a disk is bad and you "crash" with one of CP/M's cryptic BDOS ERR messages, you still have all your data except the last record you were entering. If you were in the process of adding records, all the newly-added records will be in the file but the number of records will not have been updated in the DIMS file header record. If you remember what the highest record number was, skip to step 2.

Step 1: Use CP/M's STAT utility to look at the data file. Note the number of records shown in the left-hand column. If your file is 128-byte records, the number of data records (the number you want) is that number minus one. If the file is double-size records, the number of data records is the number of CP/M records divided by two, then minus one.

Step 2: Re-start DIMS. Open the file. Note that DIMS still thinks that the file has the number of records that it had when you did the last done. Type Control-C. Enter N=986 (use your own number). Enter C=1. Enter cont then Return, and see if the file appears to be normal now. Do a done.

If a crash occurs while the sort command is writing its output over the backup file, the backup file is invalid. Use the BACKUP command to restore it. Should the main or backup file be lost, PIP can be used to copy the valid file, and then use the CP/M REN command to rename the file. The main and backup data files should be identical.

Interface, Modification, and File Compatibility

DIMS files are comprised of ASCII text in fixed-length random access blocks, and all records are either 128 bytes in length or 256 bytes in length, depending on which was chosen when the file was created.

This has nothing to do with your disks being double or single density. MBASIC and CP/M pack the records on the disk with no carriage returns between them and no Control-Z at the end.

Within each record the fields are jammed sequentially with the delimiter character tilde (˜, ASCII 126 decimal or 07E hexadecimal) between the fields and the left-over space filled with blanks. This character may not be used in data, but commas and quotes may be entered freely. Here is an example of what a file record looks like on the disk:

Header record (the last item is the number of records in the file):

```
LNAM.a~FNAM.a~N2  .a~ADDR.
a~C-ST.a~ZIP .n~PHON.a~CODE.a~NOTE.a~stop0~ 1~
```

Data record 1:

```
Dugan~Dan~Dan Dugan Sound Design~290 Napoleon Street.
Studio E~San Francisco. CA~94124~(415) 821-9776~~DIMS~
```

You can display the file with the CP/M TYPE command, or examine and edit it with ED or WordStar version 1 (version 3 will crash) in the non-document mode. Christensens's DU.COM utility (Chapter 8) may be used to repair a crashed file. SuperSort does not accept DIMS files directly because it insists on comma-delimited or fixed-length field files.

The DIMS transient programs DPUT and DGET provide a convenient means for interfacing to other programs. DPUT outputs a standard MBASIC sequential file of comma-delimited records. It can be invoked in a command line with range and selection commands to output a subset file, like select put. DGET does the exact reverse, loading a standard sequential file into a DIMS file, and allows stuffing the fields in any combination or order.

Quotes and commas may be used freely in DIMS data fields. To make files compatible with other programs, DPUT automatically puts quotes around fields containing commas. It encodes existing quotes in the file into the tilde character "~" (CHR$(126)). DGET drops the surrounding quotes and converts ~ back to ".

You can re-design a DIMS file by using the PUT command to output the data to a temporary file, using DCREATE (main menu) to create a new DIMS file with the desired field names, and using the GET command to stuff the data back in the re-designed order.

History of DIMS

When I got started in personal computing with an S-100 microcomputer at the end of 1977, there was no generalized data base management program available. I studied a full-fledged system written in BASIC called RISS which is published as a book — *RISS: A Relational Database Management System For Microcomputers* by Meldman *et al* (Van Nostrand Reinhold Co. 1978). It was too complex for me to understand. I spun my wheels for a year until I saw an ad for Scelbi Publications' PIMS — Personal Information Management System. This was a complete functioning data base manager for cassette-based computers like the Radio Shack TRS-80 or Commodore PET. I bought it for $10, typed it in and got it to work.

I learned later that this program was first published as "A People's Data Base System" by Madan Gupta and Brent Lander in 1977. Then Scelbi published PIMS by Gupta in 1979.

With PIMS I had a working framework which I converted to disk random-access files. After that the program immediately went to work for me and my clients, and just grew and grew as the pressure of doing real work determined. I rented machine time to the San Francisco Charter Revision Commission for their mailing lists, and made many improvements to the program as that project grew. The system of chaining the transient programs developed when the program got too big to be all in memory at the same time. I have not changed the variable names, storage format or default listing format from PIMS.

I've put my large personal address lists onto DIMS, and a successful system for storing technical magazine article citations. A book, *The Hearts of Space Guide To Cosmic, Transcendent and Innerspace Music* started out as a DIMS data file, was transformed (by a purpose-built transient) to WordStar when the data was complete, then sent to the typesetter on a CP/M disk. I also have parts lists for my products and the membership list for my neighborhood association.

All this activity made me want more real-time availability of my data bases, and in 1981 I used all my available credit to install a Morrow M26 hard disk. DIMS runs with a satisfying speed increase on the hard disk. During '81-82 pre-release versions were running on two systems in my lab and on five other CP/M systems belonging to friends.

DIMS version 1.0 was released to the public domain by Dan Dugan Sound Design on March 20, 1982, my 39th birthday. In April '82 Jim Ayers made the whole system available on the bulletin board of Computer Systems of Marin. The program was subsequently released as SIG/M disk #61.

The most recent growth in DIMS has been stimulated by a mailing list I am keeping for a client which has grown to 21,000 names. Currently the update cycle is working like this:

1. Names are entered and edited in DIMS.

2. To print labels, I use PUT to write the data to a sequential file, then use SuperSort to sort that file by zip codes, and print labels with DCHESHIR.BAS reading the sorted sequential file.

3. The zip-sorted file is re-sorted to alphabetical by SuperSort. The original DIMS file is archived to a floppy disk and the hard disk file is erased.

4. An alpha-sorted new DIMS file is made using GET from the sorted sequential file. The sequential file is then erased and a listing of the DIMS file is printed as a guide for corrections and editing during the next cycle.

This work required writing DCHESHIR.BAS, bullet-proofing DGET.BAS, and designing a much better default printer listing format. These improvements and some general improvements/fixes comprise DIMS version 1.03, released in January, 1983.

DIMS received a rave review from Chris Terry in *Microsystems* magazine (May 1983). He said "If you can't afford dBASE II, get DIMS." I am using dBASE II also, and prefer it for my financial records. I still prefer DIMS for mailing lists.

APPENDIX A: ASCII CHART

LEGEND:

Character code in decimal
EBCDIC equivalent hexadecimal code

↑ means CONTROL

Example box:
	04_
0	64 / 7C @

HEX	00_		01_		02_		03_	
0	0 / 00	NUL	16 / 10	DLE ↑P	32 / 40	SPACE	48 / F0	0
1	1 / 01	SOH ↑A	17 / 11	DC1 ↑Q	33 / 5A	!	49 / F1	1
2	2 / 02	STX ↑B	18 / 12	DC2 ↑R	34 / 7F	" (QUOTE)	50 / F2	2
3	3 / 03	ETX ↑C	19 / 13	DC3 ↑S	35 / 7B	#	51 / F3	3
4	4 / 37	EOT ↑D	20 / 3C	DC4 ↑T	36 / 5B	$	52 / F4	4
5	5 / 2D	ENQ ↑E	21 / 3D	NAK ↑U	37 / 6C	%	53 / F5	5
6	6 / 2E	ACK ↑F	22 / 32	SYN ↑V	38 / 50	&	54 / F6	6
7	7 / 2F	BEL ↑G	23 / 26	ETB ↑W	39 / 7D	' (APOS)	55 / F7	7
8	8 / 16	BS (BACK-SPACE)	24 / 18	CAN ↑X	40 / 4D	(	56 / F8	8
9	9 / 05	HT (TAB)	25 / 19	EM ↑Y	41 / 5D	)	57 / F9	9
A	10 / 15	NL (NEW LINE)	26 / 3F	SUB ↑Z	42 / 5C	*	58 / 7A	: (COLON)
B	11 / 0B	VT (VERT. TAB)	27 / 27	ESC (ESCAPE)	43 / 4E	+	59 / 5E	; (SEMI)
C	12 / 06	FF (FORM FEED)	28 / 1C	FS ↑\	44 / 6B	, (COMMA)	60 / 4C	<
D	13 / 0D	RT (RETURN)	29 / 1D	CS ↑]	45 / 60	-	61 / 7E	=
E	14 / 0E	SO ↑N	30 / 1E	RS ↑↑	46 / 4B	. (PERIOD)	62 / 6E	>
F	15 / 0F	SI ↑O	31 / 1F	US ↑←	47 / 61	/	63 / 6F	?

The ASCII chart is the programmer's equivalent to the chemist's periodic table of the elements. The American Standard Code for Information Interchange (ASCII) has a unique code number reserved for each UPPER and lower case letter, each digit, each punctuation symbol, and each Control-key function. The codes are used mostly in communications, data transfer, and printing. The code numbers are in hexadecimal (base 16) and decimal (base 10).

To find the hexadecimal value of a character (including symbol, digit, or unprintable code), find the character on the chart, and combine the first two digits at the top of the character's column with the third digit in the far left column on the same row. For example, the letter "F" is 046 in hexadecimal, and a question mark (?) is 03F in hexadecimal (F in hex is 15 in decimal).

HEX	04_		05_		06_		07_	
0	64 / 7C	@	80 / D7	P	96 / 79	(GRAVE)	112 / 97	p
1	65 / C1	A	81 / D8	Q	97 / 81	a	113 / 98	q
2	66 / C2	B	82 / D9	R	98 / 82	b	114 / 99	r
3	67 / C3	C	83 / E2	S	99 / 83	c	115 / A2	s
4	68 / C4	D	84 / E3	T	100 / 84	d	116 / A3	t
5	69 / 65	E	85 / E4	U	101 / 85	e	117 / A4	u
6	70 / C6	F	86 / E5	V	102 / 86	f	118 / A5	v
7	71 / C7	G	87 / E6	W	103 / 87	g	119 / A6	w
8	72 / C8	H	88 / E7	X	104 / 88	h	120 / A7	x
9	73 / C9	I	89 / E8	Y	105 / 89	i	121 / A8	y
A	74 / D1	J	90 / E9	Z	106 / 91	j	122 / A9	z
B	75 / D2	K	91 / 8D	[	107 / 92	k	123 / C0	{
C	76 / D3	L	92 / EO	\	108 / 93	l	124 / 4F	|
D	77 / D4	M	93 / 9D	]	109 / 94	m	125 / D0	}
E	78 / D5	N	94 / 5F	↑ or ^	110 / 95	n	126 / A1	~ (TILDE)
F	79 / D6	O	95 / 6D	← or —	111 / 96	o	127 / 07	DEL (RUBOUT)

Control Codes

Some ASCII codes control the printing of text or the transmission of data. Here are brief explanations of some of these codes in the order they appear in the ASCII table, with the corresponding Control-key commands that invoke the codes:

ASCII code	Control-key	Meaning
NUL		null value (not zero)
SOH	Control-A	start of heading
STX	Control-B	start of text
ETX	Control-C	end of text
EOT	Control-D	end of transmission
ENQ	Control-E	enquiry
ACK	Control-F	acknowledge
BEL	Control-G	bell
BS	Control-H	backspace
HT	Control-I	horizontal tab
LF	Control-J	line feed
VT	Control-K	vertical tab
FF	Control-L	form feed
CR	Control-M	carriage return
SO	Control-N	shift out
SI	Control-O	shift in
DLE	Control-P	data link escape
DC1	Control-Q	device control, XON (scroll)
DC2	Control-R	device control, tape
DC3	Control-S	device control, XOFF (no scroll)
DC4	Control-T	device control, tape
NAK	Control-U	negative acknowledge
SYN	Control-V	synchronous idle
ETB	Control-W	end of transmission
CAN	Control-X	cancel
EM	Control-Y	end of medium
SUB	Control-Z	substitute
ESC	Control-[	escape
FS	Control-\	file separator
GS	Control-]	group separator
RS	Control-^	record separator
US	Control-_	unit separator

APPENDIX B:
BBS-RCP/M PHONE LIST

This appendix lists the FOG and PRACSA bulletin board and remote CP/M (RCP/M) software exchange systems. FOG is the First Osborne Group, whose libraries are summarized in Appendix D. PRACSA is the Public Remote Access Computer Standards Association. All of these systems use the the Xmodem/Modem7 (Christensen) protocol (the XMODEM program), for file transfers. These systems are available to the general public for the exchange of public domain software. All are 300/1200 baud except where noted.

A larger list of RCP/M systems, which is updated *monthly* and contains hundreds of phone numbers, is available on the bulletin boards listed below, stored in a file named RCPMxx.LST (sometimes squeezed and called RCPMxx.LQT).

FOG and PRACSA Bulletin Boards

FOG #1 415-755-2030 FOG office
FOG #2 604-596-0314 Vancouver, B.C
FOG #3 415-992-8542 Daly City, CA
FOG #4 415-591-6259 Belmont, CA
FOG #5 415-424-1482 Palo Alto, CA
FOG #6 415-755-8315 FOG office (upload only)
FOG #10 717-657-8699 Harrisburg, PA
FOG #11 415-285-2687 San Francisco, CA KAY*FOG
FOG #12 415-851-7732 Woodside, CA (300)
FOG #13 405-848-5317 Oklahoma City, OK
FOG #14 217-344-4032 Urbana, IL
FOG #17 602-268-4474 Phoenix, AZ
FOG #18 707-557-4403 Vallejo, CA
FOG #19 818-362-3690 Sylmar, CA
FOG #20 813-788-6515 Zephyrills, FL
FOG #21 0908-615274 Blakelands,England

FOG #22 817-662-2487 Waco, TX (300)
FOG #24 502-241-4109 Louisville, KY (300)
FOG #25 319-326-3904 Davenport, IA

PRACSA Member Systems:

PICONET #1 415:965-4097 Mountain View, CA
POTPOURRI 408:378-7474 Campbell, CA
SERVU 408:238-9621 San Jose, CA
MARIN COUNTY RBBS 415:383-0473 Mill Valley, CA
SJ HUG 408:262-5150 San Jose, CA (300) 7pm-12pm

COMPUSERVE

CP-MIG . . . . on MicroNet $
Type R CP-MIG ⊃ or GO PCS-47. Dave Kozinn, Tom Jorgenson, Charlie Strom arranging to have MN carry much new CPMUG and SIG/M software, plus a newsletter and a CP/M-oriented CBBS. COMPUSERVE users have full access to CP-MIG. (Fees required to join CompuServe.)

NOTE:

Call-back systems are those where a computer and real people share the same telephone line. To contact the people, just dial and let the phone ring until you get an answer. To contact the computer: (1) dial, (2) let the phone ring once, (3) hang up just before the 2nd ring, and (4) re-dial.

APPENDIX C:
CATALOGS AND USER
GROUPS

SIG/M and NYACC Libraries

Catalogs for the SIG/M volumes (over 200) are available from the New York Amateur Computer Club: NYACC, P.O. Box 106, Church St. Station, New York, NY 10008. NYACC Hot-Line (answering service): (212) 864-4595.

SIG/M (Special Interest Group/Micros), which is part of the Amateur Computer Group of New Jersey (ACGNJ), makes available the entire SIG/M library on eight-inch disks ($6 per disk, $14 overseas), and a pamphlet describing the volumes and listing the catalog contents (catalogs available from NYACC). For information, please enclose a self-addressed stamped envelope: SIG/M User's Group of ACG-NJ, P.O. Box 97, Iselin, NJ 08830. BBS (by modem): (201) 272-1874, (215) 398-3937, (215) 398-1634; voice line: (201) 272-1793.

Volume 0 of the SIG/M volumes contains the huge file SIG/M.CAT, which is a complete listing of the SIG/M volumes and program names, and the file REGIONS.SIG, which is a listing of the SIG/M distribution points worldwide. The disk also contains a listing of CP/MUG volumes.

Regional distributors can offer various disk formats, and their charges differ — you must check with them first. The ACGNJ has local New Jersey user groups set up to maintain specific computer disk formats.

CP/M User's Group (CP/MUG)

CP/MUG offers eight-inch disks, single-density, for $13 each. North Star, Apple, Kaypro, and others are $18 each. CP/M User's Group, 1651 Third Ave., NY, NY 10028.

First Osborne Group (FOG)

FOG is headquartered in Daly City, CA, but regional FOG
affiliates have public domain software disks available. You must
join FOG ($24 per year) to order disks for $5 a disk. FOG can
supply a variety of disk formats including Osborne, Kaypro II,
Morrow and Zorba. A typeset catalog is available to members for
$5.

First Osborne Group (FOG), P.O. Box 3474, Daly City, CA
94015-0474. Voice phone: (415) 755-4140.

For modem calls, see the very beginning of the BBS list in
Appendix B.

PC Software Interest Group (PC-SIG)

The PC Software Interest Group (PC-SIG) makes available
IBM PC software on PC disks for $6 each plus $4 ($10 foreign) for
shipping and handling and 6.5% sales tax for CA residents:

PC-SIG, 1556 Halford Ave., Suite 130, Santa Clara, CA
95051.

PC-Blue

The PC-Blue public domain library is maintained by the New
York Amateur Computer Club (NYACC), which also offers a
catalog for $10 ($15 overseas). You do not have to be a member to
order disks for $6 per disk sent UPS ($9 overseas).

New York Amateur Computer Club, P.O. Box 106, Church
Street Station, New York, NY 10008.

Capital PC User Group

The Capital PC User Group is one of the most well-organized
groups for IBM PC software. PC disks are $8 (including
shipping/handling) available to members only; membership is $25
($40 international).

Capital PC User Group, P.O. Box 3189, Gaithersburg, MD
20878. By modem: (301) 949-8848 (password IBMPC).

APPENDIX D:
PUBLIC DOMAIN DIGEST

This appendix lists volumes of CP/M public domain software from the CP/M User's Group (CP/MUG), the Pascal/Z User Group, the Special Interest Group/Microcomputers (SIG/M), and the First Osborne Group (FOG). It also lists volumes IBM PC (MS-DOS) software from PC-SIG. For addresses and ordering information, see Appendix C.

CP/MUG, SIG/M and Pascal/Z Cross Reference

There is some duplication among the CP/MUG, SIG/M and Pascal/Z public domain libraries.
CP/MUG volumes 1-33, 35-54 and 78-91 are unique to CP/MUG (CP/MUG vol. 34 is replaced by SIG/M vol. 53). CP/MUG volumes 55-77 are duplicated in SIG/M volumes.
SIG/M Volumes 0, 12, 26, 30-61, 65-68, 70, 73-79, 83-84, 86-93, 96, 98-130, 135-147, and 149-157 are unique to SIG/M. SIG/M Volumes 1-2, 4-11 and 13-25 are duplicated in CP/MUG volumes (SIG/M vol. 3 is replaced by SIG/M vol. 11, a.k.a. CP/MUG vol. 57). SIG/M Volumes 19-25, 27-28, 62-64, 69, 71-72, 80-82, 85, 94-95, 97, 131-134 and 148 are duplicated in Pascal/Z volumes.
Pascal/Z Volumes 1-27 are partially duplicated in the CP/MUG and fully duplicated in the SIG/M volumes. Pascal/Z last entry is Vol. 27.
FOG public domain libraries are organized by type of computer and type of program. Although there is much duplication, there is no one-to-one correspondence between volumes. The FOG library contains mostly machine-specific versions of the popular public domain programs.

Disk Summaries

You may find the following volumes most useful. Summary catalogs of disk contents are contained on these volumes:
SIG/M #0 — summary catalog of SIG/M files, distribution points and newsletters.
SIG/M #12 — cross reference index of CP/MUG vols. 1-47 and SIG/M vols. 1-11.
SIG/M #15 a.k.a. CP/MUG #67 — compiled and published by NYACC, ".DOC", ABSTRACT, READ.ME and other documentation files of CP/MUG volumes 1-42 and SIG/M volumes 1-3.
SIG/M #29 — addendum #1 to SIG/M #15.
SIG/M #30 — addendum #2 to SIG/M #15.
SIG/M #55 — addendum #3 to SIG/M #15 (covers up to SIG/M vol. 53).

Popular Programs

The abbreviations used are as follows: **c** is CP/MUG, **s** is SIG/M, **p** is Pascal/Z User's Group, **f** is FOG, and **pc** is PC-SIG.

Application Software

General Ledger program c9.
CBASIC2 programs c37.
MUSIC programs c39 (require hardware).
Osborne CBASIC2 Accounting programs c43-45 (buy Osborne/McGraw Hill books for documentation and other info).
BusinessMaster II (volumes 1-5) c86-90.
FELIX Graphics Animation System c35.

BYE Programs

PMMIBYE3 original c40, replaced by PMMIBYE5 c46.
BYE79 c85.

CATALOG Programs

Catalog.doc orig. c25, duplicated c40.
CAT.ASM c25.
CAT.COM c40.
CAT2.ASM c70 (CP/M 2.x).

Disk Copying Programs

COPYDSK c16.
SCOPY c19.
XFER (system file copy) c19.
MOVE6/12 c61.
SDCOPY c78.
SWAPCOPY c78.
COPY c1.
CDOSCOPY (for CDOS-Cromemco DOS) c49.
COPYFIL15 c63.

Disk Utility (DU)

DU c40, c46, update c58.
DU-10/26 c63.
DU (Z80) c73.

DU-V75 c68.
DUU (1.4 & 2.1) c78.
DUV86 s152.

Editors

EDIT c16, c29 (Intel-like editor), update to EDITM.
EDITM c81 (update to EDIT).

FindBad Programs

FINDBD37 c58 & s4.
FINDBD38 c63 & s9.
FINDBD42 c68 & s16.
FINDBAD c76 and s24 and p6 (locate bad sectors under CP/M 2.x).

Languages

BASIC-E compiler c5.
CP/M BASIC-E v.1.4 (PLM) c29-30.
Lawrence Livermore BASIC orig. c2, replaced by c10.
Disk Tiny BASIC orig. c2, duplicated on c11.
Disk Proc. Tech. BASIC/5 c11.
Xitan disk BASIC c54 (some programs also run under MBASIC).
Denver Tiny BASIC c17 (no CP/M I/O).
Tarbell BASIC c31-32.
BDS-C sampler c48 (Adventure programs c53).
8086 Small C (C86) s149.
Z8000 Forth s150.
FIG Forth 1.1 c65 a.k.a. s13.
Forth83 s154.
Pascal Pascal Compiler (Bob van Valzah) c50.
PILOT c7, c12.
SAM76 orig. c34, replaced by update s53.

Library Utility (LU)

LU, s119 and others.
s129 has instructions.
UNIX-LU s149.

Macroassemblers

MACASM c16.
Z80ASM c16.
XREF c36 (cross references .ASM files).

MODEM Programs (Including Modem7)

MODEM c6, c25 includes ".DOC" file.

MODEM4 c40, updated to MODEM926 c61 and s7.
MODEM7 c47.
MODEM741 c79.
MODEM765 c84.
MBOOT3.ASM c62 (compact version of MODEM for Receive only).
APLMODEM c68 (Apple II w/DC Hayes Micromodem II).
CHAT15 c70.
PLINK c46.
LINK original c19, updated to PLINK925 c61, PLINK1018 c62.
SMODEM37 c79.
MODEM7-Z s149 (MODEM7 for Zenith 100).
XMODEM s149 (XMODEM in Fortran for VAX).
XMODEM32 c61.
XMODEM38 c62.
XMODEM41 c69.
XMODEM50 c84.

Utilities

CRCK3 orig. c46, c58, upgraded to CRCK10/6 c63.
COMPARE c6, c40.
DIRS9/8 c47.
DIRSIO/1 c58 (sorted DIR with SYS & MP/M options).
DIRS1015 c63.
DUMP programs c5, c14, c24, c71.
FIND program (find ASCII string in 1 or more files) c36.
LINES program (count lines in an ASCII file) c36.
SDIR22 (PC-SIG vol. 34).
SPEED c50 (for CP/M 1.4 & 2.2).
SUPERSUB c81 (super SUBMIT program).
SQ c85 (1.6).
SUPERSUB c81 (super SUBMIT program).
SWEEP40 s152.
USQ c85 (1.9), s152 & s154 have wildcard version.
TYPE programs: TYPE1 s152 (wildcard TYPE, unsqueezes too).
WASH programs: NSWP s152 (big and little versions of WASH).
XDIR c4, c24, c58, c69 update.
ZCOMPAR c76 (Pascal file compare).

CP/MUG:

#1. Various CP/M utility programs, including Ward Christensen disassembler, A to B disk copying utility, Intel Maze program.

#2 STARTREK.DOC, original release of Lawrence Livermore BASIC (replaced by #10) and Disk Tiny BASIC (copied on #11) plus Tiny BASIC STARTREK (copied on #11).

#3 Various BASIC-E programs, including STARTREK, ANIMAL, CRAPS, LANDER, and WUMPUS games.

#4 ACTOR, ML80 and FORTRAN-80 code, including ML80 version of XDIR, ACTOR interpreter and programs, Fortran MAZE program.

#5 BASIC-E compilers & interpreters, BASIC-E programs, Microsoft BASIC programs and CP/M source files, including BDOS.PLM, LOAD.PLM and Z-PIP.PLM.

#6 Chicago Area Computer Hobbiest Exchange (CACHE) assembly language programs, including early versions of COMPARE.ASM and MODEM.ASM, plus a mailing list program (updated CP/MUG #28).

#7 PILOT (Programmed Inquiry, Learning and Teaching), for Intel MDS. See #12 for CP/M patched version.

#8 Various CP/M utility programs, including DDTPATCH to correct assembler errors in DDT, MAKEFCB.LIB routine to create File Control Blocks, and XREF to create cross reference table from Intel asssembler source.

#9 General Ledger program (requires MITS 12K disk BASIC ver. 4.0) by Bud Shamburger from Interface Age 9/77.

#10 Lawrence Livermore BASIC for CP/M (replaces CP/MUG #2).

#11 Disk Tiny BASIC and disk Processor Technology BASIC/5.

#12 PILOT interpreters patched for CP/M (8080 and Z80).

#13 BASIC-E/CBASIC and Microsoft BASIC programs, summarized in ZOSO.2 file of reviewer remarks.

#14 Various CP/M utilities, including MOVE and PUT, also original DUMP program (revised #24).

#15 Utilities and non-BASIC games, including OTHELLO in Fortran and other assembly language games.

#16 Assemblers (Z80ASM, MACASM), other utilities (EDIT-Intel like editor, updated to MEDIT CPM/UG #81, COPYDSK-disk copy utility) and FOCAL language interpreter.

#17 Utilities (DISASM-revision of Intel disassembler), Denver Tiny BASIC and assembly language games.

#18 Yale and Intel Maths routines, MILMON80 (stand-alone monitor, editor, assembler), and CASUAL language.

#19 Various utilities, including COPY, SCOPY, XFER (disk and file copy programs), LINK & LINK73 (remote computer control for DC Hayes and standard modems), and RM80

resident PROM monitor.

#20 BASIC-E/CBASIC games (including STARTREK, LUNAR1 and BLACKJAC), and pictures (including PINUP, SNOOPY and TWEETY).

#21 Microsoft BASIC programs and pictures including Startrek, Lunar Lander, Blackjack, BANNER and SNOOPY.

#22 Monstrous STARTREK games for 8K BASIC, including BIGTREK trimmed down version for TDL disk BASIC with 64K RAM. See #27 for MEGATREK (Microsoft BASIC ver. 4.5 with 63K CP/M), derived from BIGTREK.

#23 STOIC (Stack Oriented Interactive Compiler) is a FORTH-like compiler, editor, assembler, debugger, loader and stand-alone operating system (with floating point package) for 8080 machines and does not require a resident FDOS, such as CP/M or ISIS (Intel). See CP/MUG #25 for CP/M STOIC files.

#24 CP/M utilities (Updated DUMP from #14, XDIR directory program, updated in CP/MUG #58 & #69), MACRO Libraries for MAC, and RATFOR preprocessor to translate RATFOR/Fortran.

#25 Various assembler utilities, more STOIC, MODEM, and CAT disk cataloging programs (CP/MUG #70 has updates for CP/M 2.x).

#26 Microsoft BASIC/Fortran IV games and utility programs, including Fortran Othello (from #15) and CHASE (from #21).

#27 Games (MEGATREK, FOOTBALL, NIM, and more), Snoopy picture, and DISSAMBR (disassembler), all in Microsoft BASIC.

#28 BASIC-E utilities and games, a data base system and ALGOL-like language (ALGOLM compiler by Mark S. Moranville), plus updates to Mailing list program (CP/MUG #6).

#29 Assembly language games and utilities, CP/M BASIC-E version 1.4 compiler (requires #30). Utilities include UNLOAD (requires MAC to convert .COM file to .HEX) and NCOMPARE.LIB (correction to DRI distributed version).

#30 CP/M BASIC-E version 1.4 compiler (PLM source) with floating point (requires #29).

#31 Tarbell BASIC (assembly language source) and manual (requires #32).

#32 Tarbell BASIC (TBASIC) with instructions (requires #31).

#33 Search and Rescue programs from R: A. Gregoire (see SAR.DOC for descriptions) for CBASIC and Microsoft BASIC.

#34 SAM76 language first released. This volume is replaced by SIG/M #53 (updated release of SAM76).

#35 FELIX graphics animation system with assembler, interpreter and utilities (see FELIX.DOC and FELIXVI.CAT for details).

#36 Assemblers (LINKASM is ASM with file linking feature, MAC6 is TDL macro assembler), editor (TED), text processors (POW and TOP), MBMBOT (memory bank boot and manager), and misc. utilities (FIND, LINES, XREF).

#37 CBASIC2 programs for CRAPS, accounting, parts list, and arithmetic teaching programs. Also PASSWORD.BAS to change BASIC keywords to protect your programs.

#38 CP/M speed up utilities and BIOS auto-relocation utility programs for Tarbell, Delta, Digital Micro Systems, Discus 2D, Micropolis disk controllers. Includes SPEED.COM CCP replacement.

#39 MUSIC programs to play 3 part harmony through 8080 interrupt enable, 4 part harmony through 8 bit DAC. See MUSIC.DOC for how to add hardware, etc. Includes tune constructing program and sample scores.

#40 Disk cataloguing system, various utilities, including DU (disk utility, updated CP/MUG #58 & #63, Z80 version #73), file compare programs (COMPARE, CK-FIX, CV, and D), and modem programs, MODEM4 for PMMI/Hayes/serial (updated to MODEM926 CP/MUG #61), PMMIBYE3 (updated to PMMIBYE5 CP/MUG #46).

#41 Ham radio programs (mailing list and Morse code receiver for BASIC-E, Morse code teaching program in assembly language, etc), Cromemco Z80 Fortran Chess program, VDM Pong program (revised from buggy version CP/MUG #6) and Fortran least squares curve fitting program. Also, TTY Baudot/ASCII conversion programs.

#42 Disassemblers RESOURCE and DIS, bidirectional Diablo printer driver (BIDI), clock routines, MNEMONIC memory test, and more.

#43 Osborne/McGraw Hill CBASIC2 Accounts payable/Accounts receivable software. Requires book from publisher to run. CP/MUG #44 and #45 are companions to this volume.

#44 Osborne/McGraw Hill CBASIC2 General ledger software. Requires book from publisher to run. Also contained are Pat Cunningham programs BUDGET1, LEDGER1 and ROBO math game.

#45 Osborne/McGraw Hill CBASIC2 Payroll with Cost accounting software. Requires book from publisher to run.

#46 CP/M utilities include CPMLABEL (CBASIC2 program to make CPMUG disk labels), CRCK3 (full 16 bit CRC a file, also on CP/MUG #58, updated CP/MUG #63 to CRCK10.6), DU-8/12 (disk dump/patch supports many controllers), DU-V61 (single density version DU from CP/MUG #40), PLINK823 (send/rcv to memory via modem) and PMMIBYE5 (update of PMMIBYE3 CP/MUG #40), TDL mnemonic disassembler RETDL based on RESOURCE (CP/MUG #42).

#47 CP/M utility disk includes many modem programs (MODEM7, DIAL6/23, CYBER and FLIP3 (answer/originate mode -BYE.COM). See ABSTRACT.047 for abstracts and reviews.

#48 BDS-C sampler disk, compiled by Leor Zolman of BD Software (see VOLUME48.DOC for Leor's comments). Most files in .COM form (except RALLY) do not require BDS-C, though are Heath/Zenith H19/H89 only. Interesting games, good programming examples in C, plus BDS-C user manual.

#49 Fortran/RATFOR (Rational Fortran) programs for Z80 only, Cromemco CDOS only (check ABSTRACT.049 for details), plus CDOS routines for CP/M.

#50 Bob Van Valzah's Pascal Pascal compiler (PPC) and programs, SPEED for CP/M 1.4, SPEED2 for 2.2, Keith Petersen's CRCK program and misc. programs for printing via UNIX (see ABSTRACT.050 for details).

#51 STAGE2 Macroprocessor programming language by Dick Curtiss is a general purpose text-replacement processor, described in ABSTRACT.051. Keith Petersen's CRCK CRC (cyclic redundancy check) file validation program is also included (from CP/MUG # 50).

#52 COPYFAST ver. 3.5 by Chuck Weingart and BATCH/VARBATCH by Daniel Ross.

#53 BDS-C Users Group original 350 point ADVENTURE by Crowther/Woods (MIT/Stanford), converted to BDS-C by Jay R. Jagger and updated for ver. 1.43 by L. C. Calahan.

#54 Xitan Disk BASIC games and CAI programs (contributed by William P. Ruf, reviewed and abstracted by Jim Kennedy). Though written or modified for Xitan Disk BASIC, many run under MBASIC as is or with slight modification.

#55 Original 350 point ADVENTURE in 8080 code, run time implemented for CP/M.

#56 Original 350 point ADVENTURE Fortran source code, implemented for CP/M.

#57 Super ADVENTURE (expanded 550 point version) senses the type of processor (Z80 or 8080) and uses Z80 instruction set if available. Replaces SIG/M #3.

#58 Miscellaneous CP/M disk utilities include DU-8/12 (update of CP/MUG #40, updated again CP/MUG #63 to DU-10/26), DIRSIO/1 (sorted DIR w/SYS and MP/M options, updated CP/MUG # 63 to DIRS1015), 3740UTIL (copy CP/M to and from IBM 3740 format), FINDBD37 (INTERFACE program update locks out bad blocks, updated again CP/MUG #63), and XDIR6/28 (sorted directory with sizes).

#59 8080/8085 CPU test, memory test, and ICOM disk controller diagnostics with .DOC (documentation) files. Also CP/M-NET.MSG proposal to network user groups.

#60 Interprocessor Tools/Utilities 6502 simulator for Z80, 6502 version ZAPPLE MONITOR.

#61 Bulletin board related system software and file transfer utilities, including DCHBYE55 (remote console for DC Hayes modem, updated to DCHBYE57 on CP/MUG #62), FLIP-8/8 (switches remote console to originate), MODEM926 (updates MODEM4 from CP/MUG #40), PLINK925 (updates LINK from CP/MUG #19), and XMODEM32 (for DC Hayes remote CP/M to CP/M file transfers, updated CP/MUG #62 to XMODEM38). XFER5-8 and XFER8-5 transfer files between 5'' and 8''. MOVE6/12 is a single drive copy program, and CP/M utilities include TEXCLEAN (clears bit 7 of a text file).

#62 Pascal related programs and communications utilities include CHAT13 (2 way communication with remote caller), DCHBYE57, MODEM5A (auto dial and re-dial capability for DC Hayes and PMMI modem boards), PLINK1018 (upgrade of PLINK925 on CP/MUG #19 & LINK on CP/MUG #61), RBBS22 (RBBS update for CP/MUG #61), MBOOT3 (compacted version of MODEM for receive only) and XMODEM38 (updates XMODEM32 CP/MUG #61).

#63 CP/M Utilities include CPYFIL15 (copy files larger than 512K through PIP utility), CRCK10/6 (upgrade of CRCK3 from CP/MUG #58), DU-10/26 (upgrade of DU-8/12), FINDBD38 (upgrade of FINDBD37), and DIRS1015 (upgrade of DIRSIO/1).

#64 Microsoft BASIC games, RESOURCE disassembler (renamed REZ, and modified for 8080, Z80 TDL and Zilog op codes), North Star BASIC patch for CP/M, and CDOS simulator.

#65 MITS to CP/M file conversion system, HELP file system, FIG-Forth version 1.1 and system support programs including SD (updated super directory display) and LOOPBAK1 (PMMI loop back test).

#66 HELP file system on Major SYSTEMS D level software.

#67 Documentation catalog of CP/MUG #1-42 and SIG/M #1-3, as compiled and published by the NYACC.

#68 Miscellaneous CP/M utilities and communications utilities include BYE67 (PMMI remote console program), DU-V75 (disk utility system), FINDBD42, APLMODEM (Apple II CP/M with DC Hayes Micromodem 2 file transfer program), and COMBINE (merges multiple files).

#69 Miscellaneous CP/M utilities include TAG2 (set/reset display "no copy" flag), WHICH/1 (returns size and version of CP/M), XMODEM41, MOVPATCH (modifies MOVCPM for remote access), and XDIR.

#70 More CP/M utilities include CHAT15 (chat with local RCP/M SYSOP), CAT2 master cataloguing system for CP/M 2.x, various real time clock patches.

#71 Miscellaneous Pascal/Z programs from Pascal/Z User Group #1. AUTOBOOT, ZMNEMONS, COMPARE (compare source code files — UCSD Pascal), and DUMP (expanded from CP/MUG #14 & #24) programs, and many demo programs.

#72 PCE System Monitor programs from Pascal/Z User Group #2.

#73 More Pascal/Z utilities from Pascal/Z User Group #3. Includes DU (updated from CP/MUG #40, for Z80 code) and WUMPUS game (note updated Wumpus CAVEs in SIG/M #28).

#74 Pascal/Z utilities, demos and programs from Pascal/Z User Group #4.

#75 MBASIC disassembler (DISASMB), date and miscellaneous routines from Pascal/Z User Group #5. Also, HANOI game and CONFER conference scheduling programs.

#76 Popular miscellaneous Pascal/Z utilities from Pascal/Z User Group #6. Includes FINDBAD (for CP/M 2.x), NAD4 (name/address data entry), OTHELLO (UCSD version), QSORT and QQSORT (Pascal quick sort program), ZCOMPAR (Pascal file compare utility), and RECIPE program.

#77 Pascal/Z User Group #7 database seed system by Dr. Bowles, multi-track system BIOS, fixed length disk sort program and print format program.

#78 Utility disk contains DUU (Disk Utility Universal works with 1.4 and 2.2 CP/M), SDCOPY and SWAPCOPY (single-disk file copy programs), UN (unprotects MBASIC programs), / (for quick SUBMIT from command line), and more.

#79 MODEM programs for PMMI, Smartmodem, and Serial I/O. Require DRI MAC macro assembler to configure. MODEM7, MODEM741, MODEM7X (bug report), SMODEM37 and related files. See CP/MUG #84 for updates.

#80 Cromemco Structured BASIC programs by David E. Trachtenbarg for spelling, statistics, mail list, Startrek and miscellaneous.

#81 CP/M utility disk contains POW2 text processing program, SUPERSUB SUBMIT replacemnet, EDITM (updates EDIT CP/MUG #16) Intel-like editor, AUTOLOAD (auto start up program) and BACKUP hard disk backup utility.

#82 North Star BIOS by Steve Bogolub.

#83 Extensions for commercial languages. MuMath/MuSimp enhancements by G. A. Edgar, CBASIC complex math routines by E. R. Le Clear, and CP/M functions for Fortran-80 by W. R. Brandoni.

#84 MODEM7 documentation, MODEM76.LIB (macro library for MODEM765), MODEM765, XMODEM47 (XMODEM documentation), XMODEM50, XMODEM51 (bug fix for XMODEM), and SEQIO22.LIB (macro library for XMODEM50).

#85 BYE79 remote user i/o program, SD-44 super directory program, SQ-16 squeezer program and USQ-19 unsqueezer program.

#86 BusinessMaster II general business CBASIC2 software package by Bud Aaron, Suite M, 1207 Elm Ave., Carlsbad, CA 92008. Disk 1: documentation.

#87 BusinessMaster II CBASIC2 software by Bud Aaron. Disk 2: initialization, startup, modify and maintain modules, inventory/fixed asset accounts and mailing list. Requires common programs from CP/MUG #88.

#88 BusinessMaster II Disk 3: sample data files, payroll programs and common programs needed by CP/MUG #87, #88 & #89.

#89 BusinessMaster II Disk 4: purchase order/payables, order entry/receivables. Requires ALL, FORMAT, and CONTROL common programs from CP/MUG #88.

#90 BusinessMaster II Disk 5: general ledger, includes copies of ALL, FORMAT and CONTROL programs (from CP/MUG #88).

#91 Spectrum analysis programs and ASM and Fortran print formatting program.

Pascal/Z

#1 Miscellaneous Pascal/Z programs. See CP/MUG #71 or SIG/M #19.

#2 PCE System Monitor. See CP/MUG #72 or SIG/M #20.

#3 Miscellaneous Pascal/Z Utilities. See CP/MUG #73 or SIG/M #21.

#4 Miscellaneous Pascal/Z Utilities. See CP/MUG #74 or SIG/M #22.

#5 Miscellaneous Pascal/Z Utilities and MBASIC Disassembler. See CP/MUG #75 or SIG/M #23.

#6 Miscellaneous Pascal/Z Utilities. See CP/MUG #76 or SIG/M #24.

#7 Database seed system, multi-track BIOS. See CP/MUG #77 or SIG/M #25.

#8 Advanced Terminal System Monitor, submitted by Dan Steele. See SIG/M #27.

#9 Miscellaneous Utility programs. See SIG/M #28.

#10 Disk Test, formatting program, and Pretty Print. See SIG/M #62.

#11 NAD program, Fast Copy. See SIG/M #63.

#12 NAD, BASIC Equivalents, XREF. See SIG/M #64.

#13 Term Install, Game, Tree, 3D Graphics. See SIG/M #69.

#14 Lisp in Pascal, Statistical Analysis, Bit Manipulation. See SIG/M #71.

#15 Miscellaneous Utilities. See SIG/M #72.

#16 Speed Tests, NAD modification, Text Editor, Games. See SIG/M #80.

#17 Pretty Print, Text Processor, Cross Reference. See SIG/M #81.

#18 Complete JRT Pascal. See SIG/M #82.

#19 Binary Tree, Large Letters, Text Formatting Program, SUPERSUB. See SIG/M #85.

#20 Printer Setup, Dictionary and Index program. See SIG/M #94.

#21 Z80 Assembler, EPROM, TDL Disassembler. See SIG/M #95.

#22 Float Point, Combine, Pascal cross reference and Annotates. See SIG/M #97.

#23 Library of procedures and functions. See SIG/M #131.

#24 Miscellaneous programs. See SIG/M #132.

#25 Metric conversion, Floating Point, Cattle feed system. See SIG/M #133.

#26 Games and Miscellaneous programs. See SIG/M #134.

#27 Pascal LISP, Cryptography, Formatting. See SIG/M #148.

SIG/M

#0 Information Catalog, summarizes SIG/M volumes, lists SIG/M distribution points, and published SIG/M newsletters.

#1 (CP/MUG #55) Original 350 point ADVENTURE in 8080 code, run time implemented for CP/M.

#2 (CP/MUG #56) Original 350 point ADVENTURE Fortran source code, implemented for CP/M.

#3 has been replaced by SIG/M #11 (CP/MUG #57). Expanded ADVENTURE.

#4 (CP/MUG #58) Miscellaneous CP/M disk utilities include DU-8/12 (update of CP/MUG #40, updated again CP/MUG #63 to DU-10/26), DIRSIO/1 (sorted DIR w/SYS and MP/M options, updated CP/MUG #63 to DIRS1015), 3740UTIL (copy CP/M to and from IBM 3740 format, see SIG/M #39 for update), FINDBD37 (INTERFACE program update locks out bad blocks, updated again CP/MUG #63), and XDIR6/28 (sorted directory with sizes).

#5 (CP/MUG #59) 8080/8085 CPU test, memory test, and ICOM disk controller diagnostics with .DOC (documentation) files. Also CP/M-NET.MSG proposal to network user groups.

#6 (CP/MUG #60) 6502 simulator for Z80, 6502 version ZAPPLE MONITOR.

#7 (CP/MUG #61) Bulletin board related system software and file transfer utilities, including DCHBYE55 (remote console for DC Hayes modem, updated to DCHBYE57 on CP/MUG #62), FLIP-8/8 (switches remote console to originate), MODEM926 (updates MODEM4 from CP/MUG #40), PLINK925 (updates LINK from CP/MUG #19), and XMODEM32 (for DC Hayes remote CP/M to CP/M file transfers, updated CP/MUG #62 to XMODEM38). XFER5-8 and XFER8-5 transfer files between 5'' and 8'', MOVE6/12 is a single drive copy program, and CP/M utilities include TEXCLEAN (clears bit 7 of a text file).

#8 (CP/MUG #62) Pascal related programs and communications utilities include CHAT13 (2 way communication with remote caller), DCHBYE57, MODEM5A (auto dial and re-dial capability for DC Hayes and PMMI modem boards), PLINK1018 (upgrade of PLINK925 on

CP/MUG #19 & LINK on CP/MUG #61), RBBS22 (RBBS update for CP/MUG #61), MBOOT3 (compacted version of MODEM for receive only) and XMODEM38 (updates XMODEM32 CP/MUG #61).

#9 (CP/MUG #63) CP/M Utilities include CPYFIL15 (copy files larger than 512K through PIP utility), CRCK10/6 (upgrade of CRCK3 from CP/MUG #58), DU-10/26 (upgrade of DU-8/12), FINDBD38 (upgrade of FINDBD37), and DIRS1015 (upgrade of DIRSIO/1).

#10 (CP/MUG #64) Microsoft BASIC games, RESOURCE disassembler (renamed REZ, and modified for 8080, Z80 TDL and Zilog op codes), North Star BASIC patch for CP/M, and CDOS simulator.

#11 (CP/MUG #57) Super ADVENTURE (expanded 550 point version) senses the type of processor (Z80 or 8080) and uses Z80 instruction set if available. Replaces SIG/M #3.

#12 Cross reference index of CP/MUG #1-47 and SIG/M #1-11. See SIG/M #51 and #52 for updates and cross reference. See also SIG/M #15, #29, #30 and #55.

#13 (CP/MUG #65) MITS to CP/M file conversion system, HELP file system, FIG-Forth version 1.1 and system support programs including SD (updated super directory display) and LOOPBAK1 (PMMI loop back test).

#14 (CP/MUG #66) HELP file system on systems level software (Help for CP/M, ASM, MAC, MBASIC, CBASIC2, CBASIC, BASIC-E, MACRO-80 (M80), ALGOL-M, BDS-C, Microsoft Fortran, Pascal/MT).

#15 (CP/MUG #67) Documentation catalog of CP/MUG #1-42 and SIG/M #1-3, as compiled and published by the NYACC. Addendums are SIG/M #29, #30 and #55. See also SIG/M #12, #51 and #52 for cross references.

#16 (CP/MUG #68) Miscellaneous CP/M utilities and communications utilities include BYE67 (PMMI remote console program), DU-V75 (disk utility system), FINDBD42, APLMODEM (Apple II CP/M with DC Hayes Micromodem 2 file transfer program), and COMBINE (merges multiple files).

#17 (CP/MUG #69) Miscellaneous CP/M utilities include TAG2 (set/reset display ''no copy'' flag), WHICH/1 (returns size and version of CP/M), XMODEM41, MOVPATCH (modifies MOVCPM for remote access), and XDIR.

#18 (CP/MUG #70) More CP/M utilities include CHAT15 (chat with local RCP/M SYSOP), CAT2 master cataloguing system for CP/M 2.x, various real time clock patches.

#19 (CP/MUG #71) Miscellaneous Pascal/Z programs from Pascal/Z User Group #1. AUTOBOOT, ZMNEMONS, COMPARE (compare source code files — UCSD Pascal), and

DUMP (expanded from CP/MUG #14 & #24) programs, and many demo programs.

#20 (CP/MUG #72) PCE System Monitor programs from Pascal/Z User Group #2.

#21 (CP/MUG #73) More Pascal/Z utilities from Pascal/Z User Group #3. Includes DU (updated from CP/MUG #40, for Z80 code) and WUMPUS game (note updated Wumpus CAVEs in SIG/M #28).

#22 (CP/MUG #74) Pascal/Z utilities, demos and programs from Pascal/Z User Group #4.

#23 (CP/MUG #75) MBASIC disassembler (DISASMB), date and miscellaneous routines from Pascal/Z User Group #5. Also, HANOI game and CONFER conference scheduling programs.

#24 (CP/MUG #76) Popular miscellaneous Pascal/Z utilities from Pascal/Z User Group #6. Includes FINDBAD (for CP/M 2.x), NAD4 (name/address data entry), OTHELLO (UCSD version), QSORT and QQSORT (Pascal quick sort program), ZCOMPAR (Pascal file compare utility), and RECIPE program.

#25 (CP/MUG #77) Pascal/Z User Group #7 database seed system by Dr. Bowles, multi-track system BIOS, fixed length disk sort program and print format program.

#26 Games, simple mail label system (XMAIL), electrical engineering package, ham notebook, front panel emulator (SYSMON), Verafloppy II double density BIOS. CHEAT is the unofficial ADVENTURE cheat sheet, VEGAS is a super slot machine. EL-E is an EE design system, QSO is a CBASIC ham notebook.

#27 Advanced Terminal System Monitor is a series of confidence tests by Dan Steele, from Pascal/Z #8.

#28 Library for Pascal/Z, Life program, Wumpus CAVE updates, NAD Accounts receivable system, Doctor billing programs, home remote control programs, compiled by Charlie Foster, from Pascal/Z #9.

#29 Documentation addendum #1 of SIG/M and CP/MUG catalogs. See SIG/M #15 (CP/MUG #67) for original catalog, published by NYACC. Addendum #2 is SIG/M #30, Addendum #3 is SIG/M #55. See also SIG/M #12, #51 and #52.

#30 Documentation addendum #2 of SIG/M and CP/MUG catalogs. See SIG/M #15 (CP/MUG #67) for original catalog, published by NYACC. Addendum #1 is SIG/M #29, Addendum #3 is SIG/M #55. See also SIG/M #12, #51 and #52.

#31-38 Yale catalog of bright stars (8 disks). Compiled by Dr. Wayne Warren, National Space Science Data Center, Code 601, Goddard Space Center, Greenbelt, MD 20771. Converted by John Borders c/o NSWSES ERA, PO Box 43-111, Port Hueneme, CA 93043.

#39 Updated IBM 3740 Disk Utility (from original SIG/M #4 or CP/MUG #58), and Language Analyzer.

#40 Miscellaneous system support utilities include ISIS/CPM (PROM resident ISIS (Intel) system emulator), MDS (MDS FDC emulator), MENU-V2 (menu driver), HOST (file load between CP/M and Z8000), COMP2 (text compression routine), XFERTIME (RCPM file transfer time program), PAUSWAIT (pause option for SUBMIT), CHARFREQ (character frequency analysis BASIC program), and VMAP (MBASIC variable mapper).

#41 Cromemco CDOS-CP/M system support, with updated BIOS, disk cataloging and disk copy programs, including XEROX (fast copy for single sided disks: 40 seconds single density, 70 seconds double density).

#42 SD Sales Hard Disk support (VersaFloppy 2/XComp/Seagate) Pertec and CP/M file utilities, WordMaster customization notes, plus BYE for CDOS.

#43 8080 TINCMP compiler and PIDGIN programming system (DESCRIP.DOC gives details), and CP/M-86 BIOS (CBIOS, GOCPM86 and ERQ) source files plus SD (CP/M-86 directory sort program).

#44 Updated CP/M utilities include CHAT16, DU-V77, FMAP4, and SD-41. WASH-16 and UNERA include .DOC and .HLP files. PIPPATCH is a patch for PIP. FLAGS allows file attribute editing, CPM2HELI and HELI2CPM are Helios CP/M utilities.

#45-47 Dungeon (3 disks) in PDP-11 original code.

#48 Communication utilities (MODEM73 update, XMODEM46, and SENDOUT3 (PMMI utility)), and CP/M utilities SQ, USQ, UNSPOOL (DESPOOL look-alike), and CARRY12 (pause prior to load .COM files).

#49 Accounts Payable/Receivable system and Master DataBase System.

#50 DTC hard disk BIOS support, Voice synthesis system and U (select drive and user area with one command).

#51 1981 Information catalog (pub. 1/82), updates SIG/M #12 with summaries of SIG/M and CP/MUG volumes, 1980-81 SIG/M newsletters.

#52 SIG/M and CP/MUG cross reference to public domain software volumes. SIG/M #29, #30 and #52 are contained in the NYACC "Catalog of Public Domain Software, Book 2". UN, a program to unprotect MBASIC programs is also on SIG/M #52.

#53 Updated SAM76 with corrections. Originally submitted to CP/MUG order #34. Order "SAM76 The First Language Manual" from SAM76 Inc., Box 257 RR1, Pennington, NJ 08534 for detailed documentation. VOLSAM.DOC is a lengthy description of SAM76, and IDUMP is a hex/ASCII interpreted file dump program (since SAM76 files begin with CONTROL-Z, CP/M refuses to TYPE them).

#54 Z80 Command Processor (CCP)Replacement (ZCPR, updated SIG/M #66, #77, #98, #124 and #125), I/O-CAP (capture CONIN and CONOUT onto disk), 2.2 BIOS for Thinker Toys (TTCBIOS).

#55 Documentation addendum #3 of SIG/M and CP/MUG catalogs. See SIG/M #15 (CP/MUG #67) for original catalog, published by NYACC. Addendum #1 is SIG/M #29, Addendum #2 is SIG/M #30. See also SIG/M #12, #51 and #52.

#56-58 Musicraft Software System (3 disks).

#59 PISTOL (Portably-Implemented Stack Oriented Language) by Ernest Bergmann, is a language in the footsteps of FORTH and STOIC. This original release has been updated to PISTOL version 2.0 on SIG/M #114.

#60 CP/M utilities include FLIP4 (updated originate/answerback FLIP), RBBS22 (updated RBBS system files), SD-42 (updated super directory), SQ-15, USQ-15, and FLS-11 (updated file squeeze and un-squeeze programs), and MLIST50 (multiple file list directory program).

#61 DIMS (Dan's Information Management System) by Dan Dugan Sound Design, released 5/82. See chapter 9 for details.

#62 Extracts from Pascal/Z User Group #10 (duplicate SIG/M and CP/MUG files omitted). Pretty Print program, text formatting program and DTST (disk test diagnostic).

#63 Extracts from Pascal/Z User Group #11 (duplicate SIG/M and CP/MUG files omitted). NAD3 (name and address program), COPYFST3 (fast copy program), FILEDUMP (file dump utility), FINDHI (search for high order bit) and other Pascal programs.

#64 Pascal/Z User Group #12 Pascal utilities, NAD extensions, random number generator, scientific calculator, XREF (cross reference) and LCASE, UCASE, STR, SPACE, INPUT, and other BASIC equivalents.

#65 Updated Bulletin Board and CP/M utility programs include BYE78, MODEM76, ENTAB (replace spaces with tabs), SUBGEN12 (".SUB" file generator) and FILECOPY (single drive file copy).

#66 More Bulletin Board and CP/M utility programs. Apple modem support programs (APBYE, APMBOOT and APMODM22), MODEM3 (PMM103 modem support), SD-44 (update from SIG/M #60), and ZCPR-14 (customized CCP, updated SIG/M #77).

#67 SMODEM36 (updated MODEM7 for Hayes SmartModem), NEWBAUD2 (changes BAUD rate w/o redialing), and miscellaneous utility programs REZ7/31 (update RESOURCE), FINDBD54 (update FINDBAD), I8085 (8085 Macro library), SMFORTH1 (minimal FORTH), SUB (extended SUBMIT), and WHODERE2 (record disk I/O onto LST:).

#68 DYNATRCE (8080 emulator/trace program), ED/ASM (editor/assembler), ICOPY1 (ISIS II to CP/M conversion, updated to double density SIG/M #73), MFT46A (single drive file transfer), PLINK65 (PLINK update), USERID1 (BBS support program), ZESOURCE (updated RESOURCE disassembler), UNSPOL33 (updated DESPOOL look-alike), TURNKEY programs for CP/M turnkey commands (see SIG/M #75 for Apple versions).

#69 Pascal/Z User Group #13 contains ANIMALS (AI learning game), prime number generator, 3D computer graphics, terminal installation program, MILEAGE (MPG averaging program) and TREE2 (binary tree structure, updated SIG/M #71 and #85).

#70 NorthStar BASIC programs (ELIZA, BOMBER, MICKEY, DRUNK and others) FORTH 1.1 for CP/M, and XREF141 (cross reference for ".ASM/.PRN").

#71 Pascal/Z User Group #14 contains LISP written in Pascal, TREE4 (demo binary tree program, see SIG/M #69 and #85 for more), and other Pascal programs to compute age, do bit manipulation for Pascal/Z, a RANDOMIZE function, a statistical analysis package and PROFILE (program optimization analysis).

#72 Pascal/Z User Group #15 includes DCMODEM (modem program for DC Hayes), ACOUSTIC (acoustic version of DCMODEM), CCP and CP/M notes, a checkbook program, a calendar program, a dumb terminal program, XREFPRN (direct to CP/M list device), UTILITY (upper to lower case), / (extended SUBMIT), NOTATE (notates .ASM files) and FMAP (updated cataloguing program) and other utility programs.

#73 Contributed by Software Tools of Australia, DD6 (enhanced DDUMP), DAISYDRIV (BIOS for DIABLO 1610/1620), DLABEL (prints disk labels), MACRO3 (Bill Bolton macro library programs), ICOPY (ISIS to CP/M including double density), DIABLO (bidirectional driver) and PAGE-10 (displays files, full screen), PUT (move a file from user to user), and WIDIR (ISIS directory, wide display) and more.

#74 More from Software Tools of Australia, including BACKUP (disk backup program), COPY and COPY21 (disk copy programs), Godbout clock programs, COMPARE (binary file compare), DDTTOMAC (converts DDT Disassembly to .ASM), FIXDIR (cleans illegal file names from directory), USART and other interface programs for HITE and BSTAM, and MBASIC and CBASIC programs.

#75 Software Tools from Australia include games, graphics, FFT (Fourier Transform program), FM (modified FMAP for all user areas), TURNKEY (auto-load patch for Apple CP/M), and BDS-C supplemental libraries.

#76 Software Tools of Australia has contributed ED (a screen based editor in C), FAST (updated FAST program to speed up CP/M 2.2), SDIR (MBASIC directory sort program), WCT3 (updated file word count now shows columns of printing), UNERA (updated recover erased files program now allows wildcards; e.g. **UNERA * . ***) and more.

#77 ZCPR revisions 1.0 and 1.6 replace the CP/M CCP. See SIG/M #124 and #125 for ZCPR2.

#78 Software Tools of Australia BENCHMK (several benchmark tests in BASIC, Fortran, C, Pascal), DECR (strips carriage returns), L2NEW (enhanced L2 BDS-C linker), MXREF (MBASIC cross reference utility), SURVIVAL (CBASIC2 game), TALK1 (interrupt driven modem program for Zilog SIOs) and other utility programs.

#79 PL/I-80 User's Group Library contains an inventory and point-of-sale system, file utilities (copy, erase with query, parsing routines with and without wildcards) and other utility programs (PL/I-80 interface for direct MP/M calls, hex memory dump routines, CHAIN chains two PL/I programs).

#80 Pascal/Z User Group #16 contains two player duel game and 1982 calendar programs (pinup and Snoopy), SIGHTRED (formulae for spherical triangle calculations for celestial navigation), SORT (update to NAD-3 from SIG/M #63 and #64), TED simple text editor, a random number generator, and speed tests in various languages.

#81 Pascal/Z User Group #17 has XREF (cross reference), and Pretty Print utility set for IDS Paper Tiger. See DISK.DOC for details.

#82 Pascal/Z User Group #18 contains CONVERTM (Microsoft Utility), and complete JRT Pascal system.

#83 Software Tools of Australia (#12) consists of ICE (In Context Editor) and TTYPE (comprehensive touch typing tutor in MBASIC and compiled BASIC), both set for ADM-31 or terminal with direct cursor addressing.

#84 Software Tools of Australia updates for communications programs with international operation options (BYE72G, CHAT19, FLIP4, MBOOT3-A, XSTAM+, ENTRBBS, EXITRBBS, MINIRBBS, and RBBSUTIL), and updates for FIND

(FIND+), HELP (HELP14), and TAG (TAG3).

#85 Pascal/Z User Group #19 includes RUNOFF (text formatting program patterned after DEC PDP-11 text formatter), SIGNS (prints a string of 7 letters in large type), TREE5 (updated binary tree with disk storage, deletion and relinking), REMOVECC (removes or changes high order bits or control characters), TRIMCOLS (trims right column or trailing blanks, SUPERSUB (updated SUBMIT), XSUB (executes external programs via SUBMIT), and PAUSE (stops program, prints note on console, and awaits input).

#86 TRS-80 Model I CP/M programs for use with Omikron Mapper systems, includes DU, MODEM7, WASH, XTYPE, FINDBAD, ZCPR-10 and more.

#87 THE FED™ Econometric Model by Decision Sciences and Software, Irvine, CA, and miscellaneous programs from Software Tools of Australia. THEFED is a CBASIC version of the model used by the St. Louis Federal Reserve District to test alternate money supply policies. Miscellaneous .HLP files for bulletin board systems include MESSAGES, MODEM, QUICK, RATFOR, SOFTWARE, THIS-SYS, and HELP. TYP+ types files with wildcards, DISPLAY+ types files without. BDSCAT is a squeezed (.AQL) BDS-C catalog.

#88-90 SYSLIB (SYStem LIBrary), an integrated library of assembly language utility subroutines for Microsoft M80 assembler by Richard Conn, 12/82. 3 disks: documentation, HLP and REL files, and library files.

#91 XLATE2 translates Intel 8080 source code to Zilog Z80 code, DUTIL is revised and extended DU, and DASM, based on RESOURCE, disassembles Zilog Z80 or TDL mnemonics.

#92 68000 Cross-assembler (A68K), RBBS31 (bulletin board program), and Little Ada compiler for Polymorphic system.

#93 MODEM updates include MODEM798, TRSMODEM, various MODEM configure programs (MCOSB798, Osborne 1, MCQXS798, Epson QX-10, and MCNFG798, general), and phone number file programs to change modem phone library.

#94 Pascal/Z User Group #20 has printer menu files to control print features for Epson MX and Okidata 82/83 printers, a menu file to run major CP/M commands including SUBMIT, PIP, STAT, SYSGEN and FORMAT, INDEXER automatic document indexer, and TERMS (creates dictionary of words and/or phrases. DIRSCAN scans a directory and MEMAVAIL displays available memory.

#95 Pascal/Z User Group #21 contains EPROM (help for PROM burners), REZ7/31 (updated TDL disassembler), and CROWE (Micro-C Users Group CROWE Z80 assembler).

#96 CP/M-86 utility programs include CRCK-51 checksum

program, FINDBAD disk checker, SD super directory, ERQ file erase with query, XDIR detailed directory display and more.

#97 Pascal/Z User Group #22 contains CROSS (indents, cross references and annotates Pascal programs), MATHPACK floating point package, CCT (updates COMBINE; joins many small files into one large file), and PURGE (erases all files on H19, except .COM, or .PAS, or other types you select).

#98-107 ZCPR2 (ten disks) is a CP/M CCP replacement for Z80 systems. SYSLIB version 2.3 is an integrated library of assembly language utility subroutines by Richard Conn. See SIG/M #122 for ZCPR2 8080 upgrade, SIG/M #124 and #125 for other upgrades.

#108 Upgrades for ZCPR2 and SYSLIB. Released 3/83. ZCPR2 is a CP/M CCP replacement for Z80 systems. See SIG/M #122 for ZCPR2 8080 upgrade, SIG/M #124 and #125 for other upgrades.

#109 The Secretary word processing program, includes NSSEC (NorthStar version).

#110 dBASE II™ and SuperCalc™ programs. ACGNJ modular data base demonstration program; other dBASE files read directories, print labels, display memory, poke memory, and print DBASE fields and structure. SuperCalc files are: ARCS-DEP (calculates depreciation) and RULE-78 (Rule-78 calculation). Updated utilities are SAP27 (sorts and packs), and SWEEP37 (updated SWEEP (WASH) program).

#111 Hard disk utilities for backup to floppy disks.

#112 SIGNON/RBBS programs from Toronto RCP/M system. SIGNON.SEE explains.

#113 KERMIT (from Columbia University Center for Computing Activities) for Z80/8080 CP/M and IBM PC-DOS modem communications with main frame host systems.

#114 PISTOL 2.0 (replaces SIG/M #59), released 4/83.

#115 UNSPOOL updated spooler, RCPM-36.LST revised bulletin board system list, CPMDEC (processes CP/M format 8 inch single density disks on DEC PDP-11 under RT-11 and TSX-Plus operating systems), utility programs to compare binary nad ASCII files, a MUMATH fix, Canadian Mortgage payment calculation program, Canadian tax SuperCalc matrix, and more utility programs.

#116 Programs from Toronto RCP/M include FORTH for the Apple II, unofficial ZCPR2 upgrades, and Okidata 84 specific print program.

#117 Programs from Toronto RCP/M include MACRO toolkit and MODEM overlays for KayPro, H-19, DC Hayes modem, and slow dialing feature for MODEM705. REDEF al-lows simple redefinition of key input, and CATXRF11 updates CAT.

#118 XLISP: an experimental object oriented language by David Betz, released 6/83.

#119 Library filing and utility system, and BYE11 library file. Use the Library utility system to extract the portions of .LBR files you need. Since most program modules are compacted into single .LBR (library) files, you will find many uses for this utility. First read the .DOC files for help. Quick summary of how to extract files: type LU to start the program, O at the prompt to open a file: Type the name of the .LBR file, type E *.* to extract all files (be sure you have room on your disk, or extract only some of the files at one time), type C to close the file, and type C to exit.

#120 MODEM901 merges MODEM796 and MDM707 in library form (you need SIG/M # #119 to extract portions). ABBA is a music composing program for H-89 or any GI AY38910 program sound chip board.

#121 MODEM updates for MDM7xx, Smartmodem, and SD-48A super directory program update.

#122 ZCPR2 modification for the 8080; requires SIG/M #98-108 for ".DOC" files and other implementation programs.

#123 16 bit math for 6805, 8048 and Z80, SORTUSER (sorts bulletin board users), XMODEM74 update and other .LBR files.

#124-125 ZCPR2 and SYSLIB upgrades (2 disks).

#126 ROFF4, V1.50 Text Formatter by Ernest Bergmann.

#127 COMM7 (full feature communication program uses Christensen protocol for file transfers), DISK7 (disk file program, copies, renames, logs, deletes and classifies disk files), and SAP update by Frank Gaude.

#128 Bulletin Board Software upgrades (from Software Tools of Australia), and XMODEM for UNIX and VAX/VMS 11-750 and 780.

#129 JRT Pascal User Group #1, dBASE II order and inventory program runs on both CP/M and CP/M 86. LU is provided for extracting the .LBR files on this disk. See SIG/M #119 for full documentation.

#130 SIGNON system of programs for RCP/M use by Dick Lieber of CACHE (Chicago Area Computer Hobbyist Exchange). SYSOP configuration and utility programs are included.

#131 Pascal/Z User Group #23, library of procedures and functions.

#132 Pascal/Z User Group #24. Miscellaneous routines include Epson printer program, dump program with many options, ROTATE game, student grade keeping, TRACER (to trace execution of Z80 programs), and file delete and directory listing programs.

#133 Pascal/Z User Group #25. METRICS metric conversion program, cattle feed system and extended precision floating point.

#134 Pascal/Z User Group #26. Debugged ANIMAL guessing game, checkbook program, collection of macros, and number conversion routines.

#135 Software Tools of Australia miscellaneous programs and CP/M utilities include RELOC (moves a program to top of TPA and runs it), Epson printer program, multiple file transfer program, EXTCOM1 (exit from CP/M to Communications program (8251 UART)), a loader for machine language programs, and a graphics driver for C. Itoh 8010.

#136 Big Board utilities, MODEM patches, documentation for 8080 LISP interpreter and more from Software Tools of Australia.

#137-138 MICROPAS 1.0, Building Energy Design Analysis from the California Energy Commission. 2 disks.

#139 MODEM712 and updates, and UN (for BASIC-80) and UN-PROT (fix for Apple UN) recover erased files programs.

#140 68000 and Motorola 6800 cross assemblers, faster BDS-C for 8085, macro library of Motorola MC6805 opcodes, Z80 disk diagnostic and more from Software Tools of Australia.

#141 KayPro, Osborne and Big Board programs for communications and programming tips from Software Tools of Australia.

#142 MBASIC games for Osborne and KayPro include ADVENTURE, SPACEWAR, and a PACMAN game for cursor addressable terminals, from Software Tools of Australia.

#143 Packet radio and printer (Epson MX-80 and Okidata) utilities, WordStar indexing utility and more from Software Tools of Australia.

#144 Miscellaneous programs from Software Tools of Australia include wildcard rename program, update to SQUEEZE (wildcard and other features), text transfer programs for UCSD Pascal disk to CP/M, and more.

#145 VFILER, a screen oriented file manipulation utility by Richard Conn, released 10/83.

#146 CP/M-86 translations of CP/M-80 favorites by Harry Van Tassell.

#147 More CP/M-86 programs, TimeEPROMer board (adjustable for other clock boards) and Apple dumb terminal, plus UNERA12 (corrects bug in CP/M-80 version of UNERASE).

#148 Pascal/Z User Group #27, updated LISP in Pascal, illustration of public key cryptography, updated student program, calendar and user friendly erase programs, random numbers library file, and a formatting program for 80 and 132 column printers.

#149 CP/M-86 Small C, XMODEM in Fortran for the VAX, MODEM7 for Zenith 100, and UNIX-LU (similar to LU, but written in C).

#150 Citadel (bulletin board system in C), and Z8000 FORTH.

#151 68000 FORTH, DEC Rainbow utilities, MODEM for DEC Rainbow.

#152 Disk drive tester for 1793 controller, apple CAT II modem, DU-V86 (updated DU), NSWP and SWEEP40 (big and little versions of WASH update SIG/M #44 and #110). Plus wildcard versions of un-squeeze and TYPE1 (wildcard TYPE, un-squeezes too) and more.

#153 XLISP for CP/M-86, by David Betz as released on SIG/M #118. Modified for CP/M-86 by Harry Van Tassell. REGIONS.SIG is a list of regional distributors of SIG/M software.

#154 FORTH-83 with CP/M interface, editor and multitasking.

#155 dBASE II programs and information includes Atlanta Data Base Users Society #1. Letter mailing and member data records system, banking system, periodical tracking data base, and updates to SIG/M #129.

#156 Miscellaneous Z80 and 8080 programs include updated FIND40, LU301, SQ-17, and MODEM and XMODEM for TRS-80 Models 2,12 and 16.

#157 CP/M-86 relocatable utility routines (RASM86), Z80-EMUL(runs 8080 on 8086, but buggy), MODEM86 (for CP/M-86), MODEMGB (for Godbout 8/16 with Interfacer 3, PMMI), SCRUB (8086 program to clean up WordStar files), LTYPE14 (types squeezed and un-squeezed ".LBR" files, and ATARIBUS (how to attach an ATARI to your CP/M computer), plus more.

FOG: Applications

-FOG/APP.001 and -FOG/APP.002 The Osborne/McGraw-Hill General Ledger system modified for the Osborne 1.

-FOG/APP.003 The BUDGET1/LEDGER1/ANNTOT1 general ledger system, and RJ, for inserting special printer micro-justification control codes to perform right justification of text files.

-FOG/APP.004 LABELS program to print mailing labels using an Epson printer; SUNRISE which provides various solar data for specified locations and dates; MPLABELS and ROLLLIST to produce mailing labels on any printer using MergePrint (MailMerge); 2NDMTG, AMORT, and LOANPMT are SuperCalc templates for loan payment.

-FOG/APP.005 MBASIC application programs: AMORT, AMORTIZR, MCOMP1, MORTCOM, and PROPERTY pertain to loans. DEPRE and DEPREC calculate depreciation. RETURN and SINKFUND determine cash flow. EXPOTIME and FSTOP are for camera hobbyists. DATES determines years for a given day/date combination. MONTHS displays a calendar. CURVFIT fits a polynomial through a set of data points. SIMEQU solves a set of simultaneous linear equations. STANDEV provides statistics regarding a set of data. PERT2 is a project management aid explained in *BYTE* (May 1982, p.465). WSPATCH patches WordStar for blinking cursor and for automatic re-definition of the arrow keys between WordStar and CP/M. The changes are incompatible with those made by WSFAST found on - FOG/APP.006.

-FOG/APP.006 TEACH is a program to teach Morse code. INDEX produces an index for a WordStar text file, which must be marked with special control characters. SORT is an MBASIC program to sort data input at run time. WSFAST is a corrected version of Thom Hogan's article on p.45 of the June/July 1982 issue of *The Portable Companion*.

-FOG/APP.007 The Electronic Card File (ECF) system is a menu driven database system written in MBASIC.

-FOG/APP.008 The general matrix calculator MCALC and the eigenvalue problem solver EIGEN.

-FOG/APP.009 DATABASE is used in conjunction with WordStar's MergePrint (MailMerge) option to enter data about business contacts into a file. RATIOS calculates financial ratios from balance sheet information. CAL2 is a CBASIC program that keeps track of an appointment calendar. AMPRESP, CONNHORN, RFUTIL, SAMP, and STRPLINE are electrical engineering related MBASIC programs.

-FOG/APP.010 MPG1.CAL is a SuperCalc spreadsheet to calculate cost of fuel given mi/gal and $/gal. EDITOR is a line oriented editor like ED that lets you edit an MBASIC program while remaining in MBASIC. STCKEXMP and STOCKS help manage a portfolio of stocks. NFLSTATS is used to initialize each team's Power Rating as published in "Pro Football Annual" during the summer. Then NFLUPDAT updates this rating following weekend games. NFLFYL is used to store the data. TRAVS is a CBASIC solution for the "traveling salesman" optimization problem — find the path of least cost thru all of a set of objectives.

-FOG/APP.011 The CBASIC checkbook management system CHKBOOK.DOC (CMENU, CBOOK, CDAILY, and C-UP-DATE). LOOKUP searches a text file for all lines of data containing a keyword. FINANCE is an MBASIC program for calculating loans, deposits, and compound interest. MEASURE performs conversions between common units. NEWGENEA is an MBASIC program for genealogists. MAGE recovers all or part of a WordStar file left in memory.

-FOG/APP.012 RPN, a programmers calculator, OWS (used to eliminate the side-to-side jitter during vertical scrolling in WordStar), and SuperCalc spreadsheets relating to a dealership.

-FOG/APP.013 PERT project management system (enhanced version of PERT1 and PERT2).

-FOG/APP.014 dBASE II command files: general menu, managing a membership list. Also, CHARGES provides a screen representation of electrical fields, and DRAW lets you compose charts on the screen. KPLOT displays a bar chart or point plot of numeric data. SCDESIGN lets you design screen displays.

FOG/APP.015 SuperCalc spreadsheet templates: ANOVA-RM performs analysis of variance with repeated measures, LIN-REG performs linear regression, TAXBASE prepares form 1040 for 1982 income, 1040AB82 also prepares 1040 and schedules A and B for 1982.

FOG/APP.016 SuperCalc templates: AMORT60 calculates a 60 month loan amortization. GEMLOAN and GEM2 are for Growing Equity Mortgages.

FOG/APP.017 DIRECTORY and DSORT: system for extracting file names from a disk directory and maintaining a database of the names. TEACH2 is a revision of TEACH.

FOG/APP.018 EAC is an Extended Arithmetic Calculator based upon an article in *Dr. Dobb's Journal* (March 1977). WSPATCH2 combines several useful WordStar modifications into one complete and easy to use procedure.

FOG/APP.019 THE LETTER, a correspondence management system for use with WordStar. DALSPACH is another version of WSPATCH designed for the Prowriter (C. Itoh 8510, NEC 8023, TEC) printer.

FOG/APP.020 SuperCalc templates for IRS tax return forms 1040, A, B, D, E, G, and 2106. Also, WSMODS is a version of WSFAST containing double-density and other corrections described in *The Portable Companion* (April/May 1983, p. 107). ENVELOPE.MRG is a format for printing envelopes using WordStar's MergePrint (MailMerge) option. W2.MRG is for printing employee's W2 forms.

FOG/APP.021 and .022 SuperCalc templates for federal income tax return forms 1040, A, B, C, D, E, G, and 4562.

FOG/APP.023 and .024 Spelling checker system, create your own dictionary.

FOG/APP.025 thru .027 Stock Base system, written in CBASIC, used to track the performance of a stock portfolio.

FOG/APP.028 The complete PC-FILE database management system. Also CHECK.CAL, a checkbook template for SuperCalc.

FOG/APP.029 Complete PC-FILE documentation; MBASIC programs to work with the Radio Shack CGP-115 plotter. Assembled version of WordStar patch file WSPATCH2 for Okidata 92 printer, and WSPTCHDD (version of WSPATCH for double-density Osborne 1's).

FOG/APP.030 SuperCalc templates: AMORTAB2 for loan amortization, ELNA for stock portfolio analysis. Also a dBASE II mail list system.

FOG/APP.031 BYMAIL, a dBASE II mail list system. CPA is a critical path analysis programmed in MBASIC. Various SuperCalc templates.

FOG/APP.032 Apex Toolworks Inc. General Mailing List System (dBASE II command files).

FOG/APP.033 Osborne/McGraw-Hill General Ledger System documentation (system found in FOG/APP.001 and 002). SuperCalc templates: NETWORTH does personal net worth analysis, SMBUS for small business general ledger application.

FOG/APP.034 dBASE II command files: UGRAPH displays point or bar graphs, SQRT calculates square root, rest is a membership and mailing list system.

FOG/APP.035 3DGRAPH displays a 3D bar graph using input data. 1040ES, CALCTAX, and SCHEDG are SuperCalc templates to aid income tax calculations (1983). SCTOVC and VCTOSC converts a SuperCalc spreadsheet into a VisiCalc spreadsheet or vice versa. LABELPRT is a dBASE II command file for printing mailing labels.

FOG/APP.036 PAINT2 is similar to SCDESIGN (draw displays); ARCHIVE.HLP describes the ARCHIVE system for packing several small files into one file.

FOG/APP.037 Rest of the ARCHIVE system. Also BINOM2, a CBASIC program for binomial and cumulative binomial statistical calculations, and WSPATCH3, a revision of WSPATCH2 for modifying WordStar.

FOG/APP.038 CHEX is a dBASE II application to manage one or more checkbooks. DBSQUASH compacts dBASE II command (CMD) files.

FOG/APP.039 VMAP2 (revised version of VMAP) cross references an MBASIC program. BCSQUASH compacts BASIC programs. MULTREG performs linear multiple regression.

FOG/APP.040 Corrections to the Stock Base portfolio management system found on FOG/APP.025 thru 027. STKBASE.FIX describes changes. Also, ELECTRON provides assistance with radio fundamentals and theory, and LISTINGS lets you enter data regarding a real estate listing. TAXTMPL4 and 7 are two of the federal income tax SuperCalc templates updated for 1983.

FOG/APP.041 Update of the TAXTMPL federal income tax SuperCalc templates from FOG/APP.022.

FOG/APP.042 - 044 Osborne/McGraw-Hill Accounts Payable (A/P) system, with General Ledger (G/L) system modified for compatibility with A/P.

FOG/APP.045 READINV, READVEND, SUBS1, WRITEINV, and WRITEVND.BAS complete the Osborne/McGraw-Hill Accounts Payable initiated on FOG/APP.042 thru 044. Also, ENVELOP enables your keyboard/printer combination to be used as a normal typewriter. FFT performs fast fourier transform calculations. FINANAL is a SuperCalc template for various financial analyses. EMF is a multi-purpose dBASE II invoice, inventory, and purchase order processing application for a small publishing business.

FOG/APP.046 LOAN is an amortization program; STAT calculates mean, variance, and standard deviation statistics (MBASIC programs). PORTLBL is a dBASE II command file for printing mailing labels. Also, the rest of the EMF system.

FOG/APP.047 CHECKS is a dBASE II checkbook management application. NEWNAMES maintains a file of names and addresses. BALANCE is a SuperCalc checkbook statement reconciliation template. COMMSN compares Merrill-Lynch vs Schwab stock broker commissions. FINANCE performs a variety of financial calculations. STOCGRPH will display a table of weekly prices of a security.

FOG/APP.048 AMORTAB3 is an update of the loan amortization template AMORTAB2 found on FOG/APP.030. ENSOFT2 converts a standard text file containing "hard" spaces and carriage returns into a WordStar compatible file with "soft" spaces and carriage returns. UNSOFT converts a WordStar Document mode file into a standard ASCII text file. SPELLTST helps a teacher set up a spelling test or other computerized lesson. TYPEFAST is a typing tutor.

FOG/APP.049 FTNOTE12 organizes footnotes for a WordStar text file. ROFF formats and prints a text file, adding headers, footers, margins, etc. TAX83 is a SuperCalc Version 1.06 template for 1983 IRS Form 1040 and Schedules A, B, and W.

FOG: Games

-FOG/GAM.001 ADVENTURE and PACMAN.

-FOG/GAM.002 CHESS (from CP/MUG vol. 41) and Three-D Tic-Tac-Toe (from CP/MUG vol. 29).

-FOG/GAM.003 MBASIC games: BACCARAT, ELIZA, STARTREK, CASTLE, BACCRRT (CP/MUG vol. 26), and E-SKETCH.

-FOG/GAM.004 MBASIC games: CIA, QUEST, STARLANE, YAHTZEE, CIVILW, DSPACE, FIGHTER, GRANPRIX, LIFE, and STARLAN4.

-FOG/GAM.005 MBASIC games: MONOPOLY, BLACKJCK, OTHELLO (CP/MUG vol. 26), HANGMN, MASTERMD, ROULETTE (from CP/MUG vol. 27).

-FOG/GAM.006 CBASIC games: ROBO and CRAPS (from CP/MUG vol. 37).

-FOG/GAM.007 MBASIC games: AWARI, DCHARGE, GAMMON, HANOI (an interesting display of graphics), NUCREAC, HEXAPAWN, BIO-FF (CP/MUG vol. 5), CHECKERS (from CP/MUG vol 13), CRAZY-8 (from CP/MUG vol. 26), MENU, BUBBLE, DESIGN, ETCH, and SEARCH.

-FOG/GAM.008 - 011 Various MBASIC games.

-FOG/GAM.012 MBASIC programs: ALIEN, PRITPICT, and SKET. Also KONG, MONSTER, ANDY-500, ELIZA, LANDER1, and TREKINS.

-FOG/GAM.013 Support files for the Adventure game AD.COM found on — FOG/GAM.014.

FOG/GAM.014 AD.COM, an enhanced Adventure game supported by files found on FOG/GAM.013. ALIENS is a graphics game. BOUNCE displays an interesting graphics pattern. PACMANOS is another version of the popular game distinct from PACMAN found on FOG/GAM.001. WORDPUZL is a word puzzle game written in small-c.

FOG/GAM.015 PPONG is a Polish Pong game. STARTREK is another version of the familiar MBASIC game. OZDOT is a connect-the-dots game. In BREAKOUT the objective is to break out a wall by bouncing a ball off paddles directed by the 9 and 3 keys on the keypad. The objective in OTHELLO is to surround your opponents pieces, eliminating his and filling the board with yours.

FOG/GAM.016 DUCK is a graphics shooting gallery game. ESCAPE is a tank battle game using screen graphics. PINGPONG, also with graphics, is a pong game. SLOTS simulates a slot machine customized for the Osborne 1 (another ver-

sion on FOG/GAM.011). TYPERACE is a typing tutor and horserace game. FASTLIFE is a faster version of the LIFE games found on FOG/GAM.004 and 010. LIFEASC is a compiled CBASIC version of the LIFE game.

FOG/GAM.017 CRAPS is a graphics version of the dice game on FOG/GAM.006 and 009. SMURF is a modified version of MONSTER found on FOG/GAM.012. BACCRRT is a baccarat game (modified version of the same program on FOG/GAM.003). CROSSPUZ prepares a word search puzzle using words you supply. BATTLSHP requires sinking ships hidden in a square matrix by targeting one square after another. CAPITALS tests knowledge of state capitals. DARTS requires hitting a target on the screen. MATH is an arithmetic drill. NUMBERSQ is similar to the game of moving tiles within a square matrix containing one missing tile until all tiles are in sequence. PIGLATIN will translate input phrases into pig latin. VOCAB helps you create a series of flashcards for testing purposes. BRIDGE is a bridge card game played against yourself.

FOG: Languages

-FOG/LNG.001 Z80 Assembler (see CP/MUG #16) and sample programs, also the Z80.LIB library of macros for use with Digital Research's MAC assembler to produce Z80 code.

-FOG/LNG.002 - .004 C Compiler.

-FOG/LNG.005 - .006 A version of Algol called ALGOLM (see CP/MUG vol. 28).

-FOG/LNG.007 The ML80 system (see CP/MUG vol. 4 and vol. 36). M80 is a general macro processor, and L80 is a structured assembly language for the 8080.

-FOG/LNG.008 and .009 The JRT Pascal system.

FOG/LNG.010 M80.HLP and MAC.HLP provide information about the Microsoft M80 and Digital Research MAC macro-assemblers. MACREF appends a program cross-reference to the ".PRN" file generated by MAC. XMAC.ASM is for cross-assembling. EM2 is an 8080 emulator. STDLIB20 is an update of the small-c standard library of input/output routines. JRTFIX.SUB is a SUBMIT file designed to patch the JRT Pascal run-time environment EXEC.COM to correct an error which occurs when multiplying a real number by zero.

FOG/LNG.011 - 013 The MVP-FORTH system. MVPFORTH.DOC describes the system. AUTOST.COM is an assembled version of MVP-FORTH with the utility and editor "screens" loaded.

FOG/LNG.014 - 016 The manual for JRT Pascal version 3.0. Version 2.0 of the JRT Pascal system is on FOG/LNG.008

and 009. The differences between the two versions are described in the manual.

FOG/LNG.017 A library of routines enabling Microsoft FORTRAN programs to make CP/M BDOS function calls.

FOG: Utilities

-FOG.001 MODEM714, another version of MODEM7, with OSMODN for the Osborne. CRCK4 and CK-FIX permit verification of file transfer activities. UMPIRE provides hardware diagnostics for the Osborne. WASH (version 1.0) is a versatile file maintenance utility.

-FOG/UTL.002 CAT cataloguing utility and related programs CROSSREF, FMAP, and UCAT. Also NEWCAT, DISPLAY, LIST for printing files, LOGIN to reset each active disk drive, LOOK for searching RAM for a specific byte pattern, and SHOW.

-FOG/UTL.003 Squeeze/un-squeeze utilities SQ, USQ, and TYPESQ. Also, COMBINE, LINES, and LIST from CP/MUG vol. 36, and D from CP/MUG vol. 40.

-FOG/UTL.004 Updated squeeze/un-squeeze utilities SQ-15, USQ-15, TYPESQ14, and FLS-11, also COMPARE from CP/MUG vol 40. SUPERSUB is a super SUBMIT utility. SUPRSUB2 is an update of SUPERSUB.

-FOG/UTL.005 FINDBAD locates and locks out bad sectors on a disk. SORT sorts a file into ASCII order, line by line. HELP is used with ".HLP" files to display information. SUPERDIR is a super DIR utility. WASH is an updated version of the file manipulation utility found on -FOG/UTL.001. SWEEP14 is a super WASH utility.

-FOG/UTL.006 DUU (Disk Utility, see Chapter 8) performs byte-level disk "surgery". DUMP is from CP/MUG vol. 24.

-FOG/UTL.007 RESOURCE performs detailed disassembly of a ".COM" file (from CP/MUG vol. 42). REZ80 is a version of RESOURCE which can use TDL Z80 mnemonics. ZDT is a version of DDT which can use the same mnemonics. TRANSLAT converts 8080 assembler code to Z80 code. DISASSEM is an MBASIC program to disassemble a ".COM" file.

-FOG/UTL.008 BMAP7/11 (from CP/MUG vol. 47) provides a bit map representation of the allocation of information on your disk. TYPER permits typing directly to your printer (LST: device). XREF cross-references labels used in assembly language programs. TED is a text editor program.

-FOG/UTL.009 Utilities for manipulating the Osborne 1 auto-start (AUTOST) feature: AUTOMOD enables entry of a command line up to 36 characters which will be executed upon

cold start, SETAUTO lets you change the command executed upon cold start. FUNCTION displays function key settings. MAKE re-defines the user area number for specified files, and RPIP is an extension to PIP (see Chapter 7). UNERA recovers files erased with ERA.

-FOG/UTL.010 CV (from CP/MUG vol. 40) lets you simultaneously view and and compare two separate files. OTERM emulates terminals. UNSPOL30 permits printing an ASCII file as a background activity while simultaneously performing other functions.

-FOG/UTL.011 DIF2 helps you identify differences between two files. OZCPR replaces your Console Command Processor (CCP) and adds several new built-in functions to CP/M.

-FOG/UTL.012 OTERM303 is an update of OTERM (above). NCAT32 is an update of NEWCAT and XCAT36 is an update of CROSSREF -FOG/UTL.002).

-FOG/UTL.013 CTERM and PLNK0124, two terminal emulator programs for communicating with a modem. SWEEP36 is an update of SWEEP14 found on-FOG/UTL.005.

-FOG/UTL.014 Several utilities for setting special print modes on matrix printers. Also, SQ-16, USQ-19, and TYPE17, which are updated versions of the squeeze/un-squeeze utilities. SAP sorts and packs disk directories. OREMOTE lets you attach a remote console (terminal or computer) through the serial/modem port in parallel with the CP/M console (keyboard and screen).

-FOG/UTL.015 OSPATCH1 patches the Osborne 1 COPY.COM utility for more reliable disk formatting and copying. LISTT prints a file on the CP/M list device with a versatile selection of options. OPLINK is an update of PLINK. EX12 lets you enter a series of CP/M commands and related line input to be executed sequentially.

-FOG/UTL.016 MENU displays a list of ".COM" command files on your disk. CPYFIL15 copies files from one disk to another. XAMN is a general disk examination utility similar to DUU. SYNONYM creates a ".COM" file having a name of your choice which, when executed, will cause another ".COM" file to run. FILEFIND searches all disks and user numbers to locate a specified file. PBH prints a banner heading and/or the text of a file on your list device.

-FOG/UTL.017 The library utility LU (see Chapter 6), which lets you pack many small files into one larger library file. SAFRAM allows you to protect an area of high memory from being overwritten. FMAP displays information about your disk directory. VMAP is an MBASIC program which will prepare a cross-reference of variables used in another MBASIC program. XCOPY copies files from one disk to another using a single drive.

-FOG/UTL.018 OTERM4.COM, a terminal emulator and modem program for Osborne 1.

FOG/UTL.019 ALLOC displays a bit map showing use of a disk. FCB displays the first 256 bytes of RAM where the default File Control Block (FCB) is located. MEMMAP displays a map indicating available memory (64K on the Osborne 1). SECTRAN displays the logical to physical disk sector translation table. DUPUSR21 lets you access a file from more than one user area. MOVUSER2 moves a file from one user area to another. DU-V77 is a general disk utility permitting access to any track, sector, or byte on a disk (see Chapter 8). SCRAMBL21 scrambles a file, making it unreadable until it is unscrambled.

FOG/UTL.020 DDTF adds search capability to DDT. DIRCHK displays information for verification of a disk directory. FAST speeds up the MPI disk drives on the Osborne 1. FILTER11 removes all control characters from a text file. FIND-20 is an update of FIND on FOG/UTL.002. RENAME can rename several files at once. STRIP deletes comment lines from an assembly language source file. ZDASM14 disassembles Z80 code.

FOG/UTL.021 BACK2DDT lets you exit from and return to DDT. MENU permits definition of menu screens along with command lines. SETIO may be used instead of STAT to set the IOBYTE, which relates physical devices to the logical input/output devices. SMODEM4 is a version of Modem7 for the Hayes Stack Smartmodem.

FOG/UTL.022 LCAT displays a text file contained within a library file. OSBMDM76 is another version of MODEM7 for the Osborne 1. PASSWORD assigns a password for runtime access to a ".COM" file. RECOVER restores from memory an MBASIC program lost due to a NEW command or a sudden drop out of MBASIC.

FOG/UTL.023 APPEND concatenates one text file onto the end of another. AUTOMODD is a double-density compatible version of AUTOMOD found on FOG/UTL.009, to set up a command line to be executed upon each cold and/or warm start. CAT2 is part of the CATALOG system found on FOG/UTL.002. FNDBD541 is an update of FINDBAD found on FOG/UTL.005. LISTCAT prints a catalog of your disk library maintained by CATALOG system found on FOG/UTL.002 and .012.

FOG/UTL.024 NZCPR is a New version of ZCPR, the Console Command Processor (CCP) replacement found on FOG/UTL.011.

FOG/UTL.025 RAMDSK defines a pseudo disk drive D contained in 20K bytes of RAM (memory), which will operate more efficiently than a regular floppy disk.

FOG/UTL.026 - 030 The UTOOLS system of utilities written in BDS C.

FOG/UTL.031 MODEM712 (version of Modem7) for the Osborne 1. This version supports special features of the Hayes Smartmodem, including autodial. NSWEEP is a new version of SWEEP (see Chapter 7). USQNEW is a new version of USQ (see Chapter 5).

FOG/UTL.032 The program "/" lets you type several CP/M commands on one line. DELBR unpacks the files from a ".LBR" file created by LU (see Chapter 6). HOSTCM is a smart terminal interface to the HOSTCM mainframe communication program to upload files to an IBM running VM/CMS.

FOG/UTL.033 DUMP copies text from your Osborne 1 screen to a file. GRAPH prints graphics characters from the screen to an Epson with Graftrax. I/O-CAP captures all console I/O into a 2K buffer. KERMIT is a smart terminal communications program.

FOG/UTL.034 DSKLABL1 is an update of DSCLABEL and DIRLABEL found on FOG/UTL.009 and 013, which prints on an Epson printer a label listing for files on a disk and other information. MLOAD is a substitute for the CP/M utility LOAD, which makes a ".COM" file from a ".HEX" file. UNLOAD converts a binary ".COM" file into a ".HEX" file.

FOG/UTL.035 CHEK10 calculates the cyclic redundancy check (CRC) parameter for a set of files. COPYFILE copies files from one disk to another. PROPOR prepares a WordStar Document mode file to be printed using proportional type style on an NEC 8023A or C. Itoh Prowriter matrix printer. ZCPR2 is the latest in the series of ZCPR customized console command processor (CCP) substitutes.

FOG/UTL.036 FILE is an updated version of FILEFIND found on FOG/UTL.016. It will search all drives and users to find files satisfying a command line specification. PRINTSQ may be used to print a squeezed file without first un-squeezing it. UNERA15 is an update of UNERA found on FOG/UTL.009. IDUMP displays a file in hexadecimal and ASCII formats. Q displays memory in hexadecimal and ASCII. MB-SAVE recovers an MBASIC program which was not saved, and WS-SAVE recovers a WordStar file lost by not saving to disk. QWIKKEY lets you define of up to 16 additional special function keys using any key on the keyboard.

FOG/UTL.037 AUTOBOOT executes a series of CP/M commands built into AUTOBOOT via DATA statements. It is similar to running the CP/M utility SUBMIT, but as a subroutine to your own MBASIC programs. EX14 is an update of EX12 found on FOG/UTL.015 — a replacement for SUBMIT. DISK72 is a generalized file maintenance utility similar to SWEEP and NSWEEP (see Chapter 7).

FOG/UTL.038 PRINT is an MBASIC program that sets up an Epson printer in a variety of print modes. SETSTAR sets up print control options on a Gemini-10x/15x printer. WORDS counts the number of words in one or more text files.

FOG/UTL.039 CHUSER modifies the CP/M user area number for specified files. HEXDUMP displays 128 bytes of memory from any specified starting address. FILTER performs housekeeping functions on text files. STARTER creates a customized version of AUTOST.COM.

FOG/UTL.040 MSA15 is a ".COM" file disassembler, producing 8080 mnemonics. FLAGS lets you set or reset flags for a file on the disk. MAKEAUTO builds an AUTOST.COM file. STATUS displays the status of various CP/M system parameters. OSDISK76 is a generalized file maintenance utility similar to NSWEEP. PCPIP permits a double-density Osborne to read and write an IBM PC PC-DOS or MS-DOS formatted disk.

FOG/UTL.041 CHGCHAR changes each occurrence of a specified character in a file to another character. DIRBANER prints a 4" x 1 7/16" label identifying up to 64 files contained in a disk directory. LSWEEP13 lets you view and/or extract files which are members of an ".LBR" library created by LU (see Chapter 6). SAP38 is an update of the disk directory sort and pack program found on FOG/UTL.014.

FOG/UTL.042 EDFILE is a full-screen DDT. FUNCTDD is a revision of FUNCTN2 found on FOG/UTL.009. NSWP205 is an update of the NSWEEP generalized file maintenance utility (see Chapter 7). TABSET replaces blank spaces in a file with appropriate TAB characters.

FOG/UTL.043 CCHECK will check a C language source file for balanced punctuation and violations of other rules. CCREF cross-references all words used in a file with the exception of C language keywords and operators. PCPIP2 is an update of PCPIP found on FOG/UTL.040 to permit a double-density Osborne 1 to read and write PC-DOS or MS-DOS formatted disks.

FOG/UTL.044 DU2V18 is an update of the general disk examination utility DU-V77 found on FOG/UTL.019 (see Chapter 8). DIAL works with an auto-dial modem to repeatedly dial a single number or a series of numbers until establishing connection.

FOG/UTL.045 - 047 The latest versions of Modem7 (start of the MDM7 series), including ODMDM730 for the Osborne 1 Comm-Pac or CTS Knights modem, and OSMDM740 for other modems (such as the Hayes Smartmodem).

FOG/UTL.048 Documentation for MDM740 and OSMDM740, versions of Modem7.

FOG/UTL.049 HELP18A is an updated version of HELP found on FOG/UTL.005. LUX helps you work with ".LBR" files created by LU.

FOG/UTL.050 LU300 is an update of the Library Utility LU (see Chapter 6), which packs several files into a single ".LBR" library file.

FOG/UTL.051 MCAT43 is the latest version of the CAT disk library catalog utility found on FOG/UTL.002 and 012 and on FOG/LIB.001 and FOG/LIB.CAT. FIND40 is the latest version of FIND found on FOG/UTL.002 and 020.

FOG: Miscellaneous

-FOG/MIS.001 EPSON4 demonstrates operation of the Epson printer. ZLOVE provides an artistic display. SINEWAVE provides an interesting visual display. BANNER will print oversize letters on your printer. BUNNY prints out the familiar Playboy monogram. CALENDAR displays a full calendar.

-FOG/MIS.002 Information files: WSMODS.DOC describes how to modify WordStar for printers. RUBIK.CUB gives information regarding solution of the famous puzzle. CPM.DOC contains instructions on using CP/M.

-FOG/MIS.003 Various demonstration files for use with WordStar and MailMerge.

-FOG/MIS.004 Information files: EPSONWS.DOC describes modifying WordStar for Epson printers. INFO.CPM describes MODEM7, software tricks, DDT, MBASIC, SYSGEN, autoload, stack management, and quick loading of ".COM" files. NOTES.VAN describes BDOS functions. WSTIPS.TXT describes ways to modify WordStar.

-FOG/MIS.005 MBASIC programs: BIORYTHM prints a chart based on your birth date; COMPAT determines whether two people are compatible; EASTER calculates the date of Easter for any given year; GRAPHNUM displays the full range of Osborne graphics; POETRY prints verse; OZIPS converts ZIP codes to states; YKW presents an interesting graphical display. BBSLIST.001 is a list of computerized bulletin board services around the nation. CPMFTH and FTHCPM convert between CP/M text and FORTH screen files.

-FOG/MIS.006 Demonstration of the Fancy Font software from SoftCraft, for use with an Epson printer with Graftrax. OSCREEN.BAS groups together Osborne 1 screen controls for use in BASIC programs. OSBDSCIO.C and OSMDIO.C contain C language routines related to Osborne 1 input/output.

-FOG/MIS.007 HINTS3, OSHINTS, OSPATCH, and OSTRICKS contain useful information about Osborne 1 computers. WS-MNEM.MSG and WSLABELS both describe the patch labels for WordStar. SCANNER.TXT has information for those who use radios which scan police, fire, ambulance, etc., frequencies. RCPMLIST.24 is a list of remote CP/M systems. BASCOM53.DOC describes version 5.3 of Microsoft's BASIC compiler. MICROSFT.SAV describes Microsoft's FORTRAN and M80 packages.

FOG/MIS.008 Picture (".PIC") files CINDY, DRAGON, KIRK, MONA, RAQUEL, and SHIP. EXPERT.DOC is a humorous description of a computer hacker.

290 *Bove & Rhodes*

FOG/MIS.009 The *FOGHORN*, Vol. 1, Numbers 1 through 3. BLOCK generates block letters on your printer. DISKID.DOC describes how to label a disk. NLART is a newsletter article describing Micromodem, the Hayes Stack Smartmodem, MYCHESS, and miscellaneous information for novices. PUBLIC.ABS is an abstract of the CACHE public domain disk library.

FOG/MIS.010 The *FOGHORN*, Vol. 1, Numbers. 4 and 5. DIRCUR provides an interesting screen display. CALENDR prints a calendar on your printer. WEEKDAY provides the day of the week for any date. NUDE83.CAL and SNOOPY83.CAL are also calendars. UNDOCCPM.DOC describes an undocumented "feature" of CP/M which may be of interest to assembly language programmers.

FOG/MIS.011 The *FOGHORN*, Vol. 1, Numbers. 6 and 7. CCPBUG.FIX describes patches to the CP/M CCP module to make use of user areas. ZSID.FIX describes patches to ZSID to make the DUMP display similar to DDT and SID.

FOG/MIS.012 The *FOGHORN*, Vol. 1, No. 8, parts 1 and 2. LIBRARY.CTL suggests procedures for controlling your own disk library. MDMPRTCL.DOC by Ward Christensen documents his Modem7 communication protocol. MOVCPM.FIX describes patches to MOVCPM.COM. SPELSTAR.FIX recommends a correction to MicroPro's SpellStar program.

FOG/MIS.013 Index for dBASE II and Osborne 1 user's guides. BDS-C.HLP describes the BDS implementation of the C programming language. CPMCHAIN.DOC explains how to chain one CP/M program to another.

FOG/MIS.014 INDEXSC.TXT and INDEXWS.TXT provide an index to SuperCalc and WordStar documentation. LABELS.DOC is one approach for labeling Osborne 1's function keys. READMEFI.RST describes SCPATCHS.TXT and WSPATCHS.TXT, which provide information on patching SuperCalc and WordStar for certain printers.

FOG/MIS.015 AUTOST.OSZ is a text file containing information about auto-start. CONFIG.TXT describes interfacing an Okidata 82/83 to the Osborne 1. MODEM.SET identifies patch locations for modifying versions of Modem7 to interface with any particular computer.

FOG/MIS.016 RCPMDATA.17A describes etiquette when using a remote CP/M (RCP/M) system. SILVER2.DOC is a tutorial describing use of the CP/M utilities PIP and STAT. MBASIC-P.DOC describes how to POKE an address in MBASIC, so that a file saved with the protect attribute can be converted to unprotected mode. WORDSTAR.DOC identifies patch locations in WordStar and recommends modifications for Epson printers. Similarly, WS-EPSON.DOC describes patches for use of WordStar with an Epson. WYLBUR.DOC describes use of OTERM4 found on FOG/UTL.018 with a mainframe Wylbur system.

FOG/MIS.017 AREACODE displays the geographical region represented by a given telephone area code. DBASE2.TIP describes use of the dBASE II CALL statement, which is not fully documented in dBASE II manuals. DBHINTS.DOC provides additional information about dBASE II. Also dBASE II command files: ASCIIDEC converts an ASCII string to a string of decimal equivalents of each character, separated by commas. DBDIR illustrates use of CALL to execute an assembly language routine previously loaded into memory. FORM prints a form describing the structure of a specified database file. POKE1 demonstrates use of POKE and PEEK. SHOWMEM uses PEEK to display specified areas of memory.

FOG/MIS.018 BARCODE generates Universal Product Code A barcode using an Epson with Graftrax. PLOT displays converted TRS-80 block graphics plots on an Osborne 1 screen. UNPROTEC.DOC describes a procedure for unprotecting a protected MBASIC file. CBASIC.HLP describes use of CBASIC. MBASIC.HLP describes use of MBASIC. WS.HLP describes use of WordStar. XMODEM.HLP describes use of the XMODEM program. ZCPR2TEZ.DOC describes the CCP replacement ZCPR2 found on FOG/UTL.035.

FOG/MIS.019 CITOH.MOD describes WordStar modifications for a C. Itoh 8510 (or NEC 8023) matrix printer. Also parts of the SPOCK picture.

FOG/MIS.020 Remaining parts of the SPOCK picture.

FOG/MIS.021 ARTICLES is a database that includes information from *The Portable Companion*, Aug/Sept. 82 through Oct. 83, and *FOGHORN*, May 83 through Sept. 83, organized by program, category, volume, date, and miscellaneous information. LIMITS provides a test of Boeing 727 limits for use as a pilot training aid. BIO prepares a biorythm chart.

FOG/MIS.022 CALENDAR is a SuperCalc template that generates a calendar for any year from 1900 thru 1999. SUBJECT files list contents of the FOG Disk Library, by subject, through July, 1983.

FOG: For Hackers

-FOG/HAK.001 The personal finance system by Software Design Engineering, and the Osborne/McGraw-Hill Accounts Receivable/Payable system.

-FOG/HAK.004 DUMP24X, ROM, JRNL, PASSWORD, RESIZE, POW and macro library ".LIB" files.

-FOG/HAK.005 Macro ".LIB" files, MOONLOC and HAM programs.

-FOG/HAK.006 The Tarbell data base programs DBSETUP, DBENTRY, and DBQUERY. Also STRTRK/2, an MBASIC Star Trek program. ADE is an absolute disk editor from CP/MUG vol. 19). DDTPATCH (from CP/MUG vol. 8) is a patch for DDT. UCOPY is a universal disk copy program. DIRS9/8 is a sorted directory program. PROM is for programming PROMs (from CP/MUG vol. 47).

FOG/HAK.007 Floating-point arithmetic routines from CP/MUG vol. 29: FPCONV, FPDATA, FPINT, FPPKG, and TRAN.SQC. MAKSUB is an example of how one ".COM" command file can chain to another. MEGATREK is an extra large version of STARTREK. MLIST3 and VLIST11 send files to the printer.

FOG/HAK.008 MBOOT3OS is an Osborne version of MBOOT, a "starter" program to retrieve the source code of Modem7 (now obsoleted by the availability of so many versions of Modem7). MODEM781 is one of the more "recent" versions of Modem7. It uses MODEM780.LIB and MAC for assembly. MCAL780 lets you change the telephone directory.

FOG/HAK.009 RECV and SEND permit transferring files between two computers. SMODEM39 is a source file for a Hayes Smartmodem version of Modem7. An Osborne-compatible SMODEM4 is on FOG/UTL.021.

FOG/HAK.010 COPYFAST (from CP/MUG vol. 47) copies files quickly from one disk to another. DIAL6/23 and FLIP3 (also from CP/MUG vol. 47), automatically dial the phone and change the baud rate (PMMI modem only). PMMIBYE3 (from CP/MUG vol. 40) is a PMMI version of the BYE program used by remote bulletin board systems (RBBS). RBBS30 is a BASIC language RBBS control program. It uses MENURBBS and NEWCOM files.

FOG/HAK.011 FINDBAD.MAC is a source file for the bad sector lockout program found on FOG/UTL.005. KID permits definition of keyboard macros (programmable function keys) using any key. MOVUSER1 re-defines the user area number associated with a file. NCAT32 and XCAT36 are assembly language source files for the catalog programs found on FOG/UTL.012. UNERA13 is an assembly language source file for the erased file recovery program found on FOG/UTL.009.

FOG/HAK.012 COMAND and DISKDEF are library files used by certain programs written in macro assembly language MAC. SEQIO22 is an update of the library file found on FOG/HAK.004. FAST2 and PACKUP2 are disk I/O buffering routines. MEMLNK20 simulates a disk in RAM. MORSE, PRACTICE, and RANDTEXT all relate to morse code drill (from CP/MUG vol. 41; see also TEACH2 on FOG/APP.017).

FOG/HAK.013 and 014 The FINANCE system and the BUSINESS system.

FOG/HAK.015 PDQFILE is an MBASIC inventory file system described in *BYTE* magazine (11/81, p. 236). Also the MUSIC system (from CP/MUG vol. 39).

FOG/HAK.016 BBSCON2 is similar to BYE, which is often used by remote CP/M (RCP/M) systems. ODBS is an MBASIC Osborne data base system. SPELL-OS is an Osborne version of the poor man's spelling checker. SPELL-ED is designed to work with SPELL-OS. YAM is an Osborne 1 version of Yet Another Modem program.

FOG/HAK.017 ENCRYPT and DECRYPT are public key encryption/decryption programs based on an article in *BYTE* magazine (10/83). QUME3 describes the QD driver for WordStar and a Qume Sprint 3 printer. DISKMON is a disk monitor similar to DU found on FOG/UTL.006 and 019.

FOG/HAK.018 FUNDTRND is a mutual fund trend analysis application. OSBYEZ2H is an assembly language version of the RCP/M program BYE for the Osborne 1 with ZCPR and a Hayes Smartmodem. WSPTCHDD is another version of the WSPATCH program found on FOG/APP.005, converted for the double-density Osborne 1.

FOG/HAK.019 CPMDEC is a FORTRAN program for use on a DEC PDP computer running RSX. It will transfer a text file using the Modem7 protocol. GB is a teachers gradebook record keeping program. Also, YAM (Yet Another Modem program) documentation.

PC-SIG (IBM PC)

Note: Many programs have updated versions available from PC-SIG. Return your old version on disk to PC-SIG with a 7x10 self-addressed stamped disk envelope.

#1 Set of games (yahtzee, blackjack and others) with menu selection and DOS 1.0 or 1.1 disk copy programs. The random pattern and number game programs require a color adapter.

#2 Print spooler programs to allow other uses of computer during printing, and other very popular system and BASIC utility programs. Version 1.1 is available.

#3 RatBAS language (adapted from *PC* magazine 10/82 article) generates ASCII files from structured BASIC programs. The ASCII file can be read by the BASIC interpreter or compiler.

#4 Menu driven and buggy DBMS, buggy CHESS and ELIZA. Other BASIC games and MODEM7 (see also #34 to add XMODEM protocol to PC-Talk 2.0, #54 for XMODEM program and .DOC, and #81 for Ward Christensen version of MODEM.ASM (ver. 3.0) for the IBM PC).

#5 Very popular version 9.1 PC-FILE user supported software by Jim Button is a data base manager (with a limit of 4000 records per database) suited for mailing list and other data file applications. Suggested donation of $35 should be mailed to Jim Button, PO Box 5786, Bellevue, WA 98006 if you find the program useful. Update version 3.0 available from PC-SIG. PC-FILE III is also available for a $45 suggested donation to Jim Button. PC-File III (for DOS 1.1 and 2.x) allows 9999 records per data base and requires a 96K minimum memory (128K recommended, speed improvements noticeable through 160K). PC-FILE III (190K) is written in Microsoft BASIC.

#6   ELECTRONIC DISK (RAM disk program) creates high speed disk from extra memory, plus system utility programs for printing, port and device testing and BASIC programs. Graphics programs require color adapter.

#7   EXPLIST prints BASIC programs in easy to read format, and LF (alpha-sort directory list program) and BIHEX (converts binary fiels to ASCII hex and back).

#8   CROSSREF program prints cross reference listing of variables used in BASIC programs. MONITOR is BASIC subroutines for formatted screen displays.

#9   SQUISH compacts BASIC programs so they take up less space on disk. WASH is a disk maintenance program. CRCK4 is a file checksum program. See ACATALOG.BAS for a catalog of the 31 programs (including lots of function key programs) on this disk.

#10   CHASM is a popular CHeap ASseMbler. Version 2.01 is written in BASIC and requires either BASIC or BASICA. Includes example assembly language program to clear the screen. CHASM is user supported, and a newer copyrighted compiled (8086) version is available for a $30 requested donation from David Whitman, 136 Wellington Terrace, Landsdale, PA 19446. The BASIC version of CHASM is on disk #15 from the Capital PC User Group, PO Box 3189, Gaithersburg, MD 20878, Phone (301) 978-1530. Capital PC disk 15 (Assembler II) and disk 13 (Assembler I) contain many assembly language programs you can assemble with CHASM. A revised version is available from PC-SIG.

#11   SPEEDUP speeds up disk operations, other disk utilities and several games. Graphics demo programs require color adapter. MENU contains six programs from dealer demo drive A (system) disk, not on PC-DOS system disk. Use the AUTOEXEC.BAT on this disk to call up the MENU program and others on the DOS disk, plus games, sound effects and other demo programs on PC-SIG #12.

#12   DEMO3 is for use with MENU on disk 11. Color adapter required for all pictures and programs except FENCE game, LIFE demo and music and siren sound effects.

#13   STARTREK with sound effects and instructions, IBMSONG (80 screen BASIC IBM rally song with lyrics and bouncing ball), and PDRAW drawing program (requires color adapter) make this disk popular.

#14   BASMENU automatic menu for BASIC programs, METEOR game, VisiCalc tax, home budget and other templates, FINANCE package of financial programs, bar graph mono display program, sound effects and more popular programs.

#15   All programs require color adapter. PCMAN game is untested and uses joysticks, PATHMAN game uses keypad. COLORDEM is an excellent animated color demo in BASIC.

#16   PC-TALK version 2.0 (does not support the XMODEM protocol — add it with XOFF, PC-SIG #34). Modem program published by Freeware™ (user supported software), send $35 for the latest version, PC-TALK III (includes XMODEM support, 1200 baud auto-dial modem support and more) with SASE to Headlands Press, PO Box 862, Tiburon, CA 94920. PC-TALK III requires a communications card and modem to run, and minimum of 64K RAM (128K for compiled version). Games on this disk are BREAKOUT, CHESS1, CRAPS, MASTMIND, and two Startreks; STARTREK (a revised version of STARTREK on PC-SIG #13) and SUPRTREK.

#17   Games include another version of Startrek, Pac-Man (80-column version), Survival, 2 versions of Breakout and more, with a MENU program for this disk. METEOR is adapted from PC-SIG #14, FENCE is adapted from PC-SIG #12.

#18   IQ Builder Series popular entertaining educational programs (reading, spelling, math and language skills) and games.

#19   RV-EDIT is a full screen editor, ARCHIE is a game, basic tutorial and fun teaching program.

#20   DRAW requires a color adapter to draw pictures on a color screen. Version 1.1 is newest available from PC-SIG. BASMENU automatic menu for BASIC programs updates BASMENU on #14. B-SIMPLE and other popular BASIC utilities, and popular games like YAHTZEE (with color monitor options), Christmas songs, and EDIT utility for RV-EDIT on PC-SIG #19.

#21   PCMAN game stores and displays 10 highest scores, has joystick option. PCHEERS song (Christmas), and PACGIRLA game.

#22   CHECKDIR (CHKDIR version 1.1 from PC-SIG) disk catalog utility program, PC-MAP is a PC-FILE (see PC-SIG #5) utility program, BMENU creates menus for BASIC programs (requires BASICA or Disk BASIC), and LDIR (List DIRectory) is a BASIC program.

#23   League Secretary Bowling programs, STARWARS and MOUNTAIN games, TAXRETRN VisiCalc tax template, DRAW2 update to PDRAW requires color adapter.

#24   GAMES disk 3, updated to version 1.1, contains the favorite color graphics version of PACKMAN (requires color adapter), plus other games (including another version of

Startrek), and songs you can choose from a menu.

#25 FINANCE version 1.1 is 25 popular financial programs.

#26 Index utility for creating book indexes and Pascal source code and compiled programs. Source code requires 128K RAM to compile.

#27 ZOOSORT (requires color adapter) is a graphical demonstration of bubble sort that is educational with great graphics, though buggy. Also three games (color Startrek requires color adapter), a cycle sound demo program and disk and printer utilities.

#28 DISKMODF (version 1.1 is newest) is a disk sector modifier utility used to recover files from disks. SQUISH is an updated version of the PC-SIG #9 BASIC program that compresses BASIC programs, removes REM statements and more. Other games, disk, and other utilities (some require color adapter) include an alternate color character set generator, and FK (function key handler for DOS 1.0 and 1.1.

#29 BASIC financial programs to calculate compound interest, accrued bond interest, future value of an investment, incomes averages for taxes, lease versus buying values, mean, variance and standard deviation, net present value of an investment, value of a treasury bill and more. BUDGET is a recursive personal budget model, and CRITICAL is a critical path method scheduler.

#30 Pascal demos, described in IOSTUFF.DOC.

#31 MVP-FORTH is the Mountain View Press public domain version of the FORTH (version 1.1 is newest) language. This popular version is compatible with the book *Starting Forth* by Leo Brody.

#32 MVP-FORTH screens (for use with PC-SIG #31). Directory is on screen 11. Since this disk is not a DOS disk, no files, directory or file allocation table will be found, giving disk copy errors (DOS 2.0) when you copy this disk.

#33 Utilities include DIR (version 1.1 is newest), a very colorful disk cataloguing program, and other DOS 2.0 utilities. HANG hangs up, and DIAL dials for Hayes Smartmodems, HOST is a communications program that allows remote access, SOUND generates different sounds, GRAFTRAX does a screen dump using PrtSc key to Epson/NEC/C.Itoh printers. BUZOFF and COMPRS are Epson printer utilities you can execute from WordStar.

#34 SDIR22 (version 1.1 is newest) is a sorted directory program for DOS 2.0 (also works with DOS 2.1). PC3SC adds split screen capability to PC-TALK III, VDISK and VDISK2 use spare memory as a RAMdisk, XOFF adds XMODEM protocol to PC-TALK 2.0 (see PC-SIG #54 for more XMODEM), DEFKEY is a keyboard reassignment program (for DOS 1.1 and 2.0), including 2 keyboard configuration files. DEFCOPY copies a distribution disk, and VOLSER writes DOS 2.0 volume labels on disks.

#35 Games in BASIC, none require color. CHESS, LANDER, dice games, story creation games, math games, number games, logic, golf, and space games and more. Non-games are BANKER checking account maintenance program with expense categories, ADDRESS address and phone number program, and LOAN loan amortization program. BARGRAPH creates bargraphs.

#36 Pascal utility programs (described in CONTENTS.TXT), to print multiple files, print in pretty format, create batch compile files, BIOS video interrrupt routine, program to read disk directory, and more.

#37 More games in BASIC. WILLTELL music program, ATTACK (destroy the Apple computer manufacturing plant) and SPINOUT (high resolution version of BREAKOUT) games both require color adapter. Other games include mazes, arcade games, adventure and guessing games. MENU (menu program) and other non-games CHR (displays complete character set on screen), EQNSOLVE (linear equation solver), INVEN (48K inventory program), PERMUTE (displays all possible permutations for a set of characters) and ROMCHAR (displays dot matrix characters from ROM patterns).

#38 DRAW is a drawing program that is a favorite for medium and high resolution drawing. Other programs include printer spoolers for color and monochrome display cards, color/monochrome display setting programs, and utility programs for use with WordStar to set up dot matrix and letter quality printers. FILTER strips control characters from downloaded files. DISKRTN examines and modifies a disk directory.

#39 JETSET is a flight simulator (in BASIC) that has been judged too slow and boring by some users.

#40 Stock Market Analysis Program with example data files for securities, judged by users to be useful and popular. Data can be manually entered, then analyzed.

#41 Kermit communication system (see PC-SIG #42 for documentation). Written in assembly language.

#42 Kermit communication system documentation files (193K and 101K, fill a double sided disk).

#43 Exidy word processor demo.

#44 More games in BASIC. LINES (draws patterns of lines on screen) and USALIST (draws map of USA on color display) both require color adapter. BLKFRI3 (Black Friday on the stock market), Startrek (45K version), and KING (run a kingdom) are three favorite games, printer pictures include ENTEP (draws the

Starship Enterprise) and BANNER (produces large letters).

#45 Many educational games (SYNONYMS, SHOP, MINIMATH, MEMBRAIN, GREEKRTS, CLOUD-9, CLIMATES, and ANTONYMS) and other enjoyable games. BIO prints biorythms and SNOOPY prints SNOOPY; both require a printer.

#46 Utilities disk (version 1.2 fixes bugs, available from PC-SIG) contains some DOS (2.0 only) alternate keyboards (DVO-RAK and QWERTY), XOFF file download program, WS-ASCII (WordStar to ASCII conversion program), CAT (sorts directory) and two programs that some users have found to be buggy (CLOCK and HIDEFILE).

#47 CASTLE game includes instructions, PLOT (requires color adapter) creates plots on color display, and XMAS plays a Christmas song. Utility programs (in BASIC) include KILLNULL (removes nulls from sequential files), SORT-BLK (sorts fixed length record files), DISRTN (undeletes and recovers lost first sectors on disk), and programs to set and read a Hayes stack chronograph. GDUMP1 and GDUMP1 are graphics dump programs, MAILLIST (mailing list program), FINPAK (package of 20 financial programs), and ELECTRIC (computes energy use).

#48 RUNOFF is a simple text formatter, FORTH.BAS is Dr. Dobbs implementation of the FORTH language in BASIC. Print utility programs and various calculation programs.

#49 FINISH is a text formatter written in BASIC. XREFMOD is supposed to produce a cross-reference of variables used in a BASIC program, but is buggy. PRINTSET and CALEPSON are Epson printer utilities, DAYLOG is a calendar program. Joystick programs, games, calculation and various utility programs are included.

#50 ROFF is a Runoff program, written in C. REBOOT is a program to reboot the operating system, SDIR is a routine to list sorted directories. MUSICBOX is a music editor, TABLET is a color graphics editor; both require a color adapter. DEPREC calculates depreciation based on the Economic Recovery Act of 1981. COLOR and MONO switch color/monochrome displays, ASCFILTR removes control characters from downloaded files, ADDCRS adds carriage returns to downloaded files, and TICCLOCK is a digital screen clock.

#51 Hyperdrive RAM disk program (320K and 512K memory versions), date determining program, Hebrew character generation program, two games, a digital clock program, globe drawing program, and INTERUPT (macro assembly language interrupt routine).

#52 Various utility programs, include FREE4 and FREE5 (updates to FREE1 and FREE3 RAM disk programs on PC-SIG #6), HEX (converts binary files to and from hex format for downloading), FILTER (removes control and non-ASCII characters from disk files), printer patches and more.

#53 Various sounds (written in BASIC), WordStar screen/printer control modification hints, patch to install various WordStar printers, and other routines.

#54 XMODEM (modem communication program), Sony Profeel monitor modification notes, and 64K and 96K versions of IBM ASYNC COM PROGRAM modifications.

#55 Games include roulette, golf, card games, horserace, jet pilot control. POKER (single user) and LANDER require color adapter for color graphics. Four songs and BIO (biorythms) complete the volume.

#56 Keyboard utilities, IPCO animated Christmas card (requires color adapter), decision maker, filing system for names, addresses and phone numbers, stellar parameter computer, and other programs include MINI-WP (mini word processor).

#57-58 Text processing tools (2 disks).

#59 PEPSON print formatter for Epson printers, FASTPRT Speedup utility for the PrtSc function on PC or XT, and QUICKREF creates keyboard reference templates. Supplied templates include BASIC, Easywriter, Volkswriter, Temple of Apshai, and a blank template file.

#60 UTIL (program for manipulating text files, with 8 demos) and MAKE (converts Easywriter (1.1) files to DOS files), both updated to version 1.1. BAS-REF produces cross-reference list of variables in a BASIC program.

#61 PRINTGR prints medium and high resolution graphics, various IPCO programs complete the volume. BANNER (prints large letters on printer)and STATCAPS (graphic program to name the states and capitals, requires BASICA and color adapter) are most popular. Other IPCO selections include programs to reset top of memory, print ASCII files in italic on Epson MX-80 printer, and pick point spreads between the 29 teams of the NFL.

#62 MAILIST2 is a mailing list program with search and alphabetic sort, WB-UPTLE modifies PC-iALK 2.0 to allow file transmission while using host computer editor. INVENTRY keeps list of possessions on computer (includes data file). HEBREW loads Hebrew character set, CASHACC is a simple cash accounting system, and CHARS2 displays ASCII character set with octal, hex or decimal values. LINREGRS calculates multiple linear regression coefficients.

#63 BASIC scientific subroutines converted from the book *BASIC Scientific Subroutines, Vol. II*, by F. R. Ruckdeschel (BYTE/McGraw-Hill, 1981).

#64-65 DESKTOP (2 disks) requires Lotus 1-2-3 version 1A.

#66 GINACO utility programs, good variety and popular

routines. Color graphics programs require color adapter.

#67 NONLIN performs non-linear least squares fit, UN unprotects BASIC programs, four more modifications to PC-TALK 2.0, a label maker, plotting program, growth rate projection program, Epson printer routine, APPLECOM (simple communication program), and two IPCO programs.

#68 WORDFLEX word processor and AUTOEXEC automatic start file. Users judge the latest version of WORDFLEX (version 2) an excellent word processor, with great documentation.

#69 DESIGNER (requires BASICA) is a favorite animated graphics utility.

#70 DISKCAT (disk cataloguing program) works with DOS 1.1, needs organizing, PAGE (version 1.1) sends formfeed to printer, VPRINT redirects printer output to a file, DIRMANIP is a directory manipulation program, and Epson print format routines complete the disk.

#71 Another version of Startrek, plus more IPCO games.

#72 ELIZA (simulates psychoanalyst) and IPCO games.

#73 IPCO BASIC calculation programs and 3D graphics programs. 3D is not popular, hard to get to work, and requires color adapter.

#74 Pascal utilities demo (from Software Labs), updated to version 1.1. README describes utilities. Distributed on double-sided disk.

#75 Forms manager system demo, distributed on double-sided disk.

#76 History educational programs. Good presentation and screens make this program popular. Includes utility to create new lessons.

#77 1RD (1-Ringy-Dingy or PC-Dial™) is a user supported modem communications package from Jim Button. Order direct from Jim Button, PO Box 5786, Bellevue, WA 98006, for a suggested contribution of $25. PC-DIAL requires 64K RAM (DOS 1.0 or 1.1; 96K with DOS 2.x), one disk drive, an RS-232 port and 80-column display. It supports XON/XOFF and XMODEM protocols, and lets you store log-on procedures.

#78 PC-WRITE (updated to version 2.2) is a powerful text processor by Bob Wallace. Color is well used, but not required. Send $10 to Quicksoft, 219 First N. #224, Seattle, WA 98109, or phone (206) 282-0452. $75 contribution is requested to register you as a user to receive these benefits: $25 commission for registering a new user, a printed manual, latest updates, telephone support, copy of the assembly language and Pascal source code. PC-WRITE Requires 64K RAM minimum (allows 6 pages to be edited); 128K or more recommended (allows 31 pages to be edited at one time); DOS 1.0, 1.1 and 2.x

are supported, a single disk drive is required.

#79 QuadRAM drive programs, MX-80 printer setup utility, games (some require color adapter), mail list program, disk drive test program and more.

#80 DOS 2.0 utilities include ALTER (change file attributes), BIGANSI (redefine 40 keys), and SD20 (sorted directory). Music, games, ET4 (EDLIN alternative); BASIC text file line editor), CISEXE (communications program supporting CompuServe protocol), and more utility programs include MOVE (move files across directories without copying).

#81 MODEM is the IBM PC version of Ward Christensen's MODEM.ASM (version 3.0). HOST2 upgrades HOST on PC-SIG #33. Various sort routines, UNWS (strips high order bits from WordStar files), SCNMAP (creates screen layout form on Epson printer with Script), and MAGDALEN (Bach music).

#82 Batch file utilities, with tutorials in batch file. See README for directions.

#83 FRED is a free editor similar to IBM's Personal Editor. FRED has been user voted "handy, effective and easy to use." Games and pictures (some require color adapter), and utility programs (COM2ASM adds labels to DEBUG's UNASSEMBLE, aids modification of ASM code).

#84 DOWDIF converts Dow Jones data to DIF format for VisiCalc and 1-2-3 use, CHMOD (C86 program to change file attribute byte), UPVC (hints on how to unprotect VisiCalc), and a file print routine written in C86, plus a graphics draw utility and menu selected multiple file delete program; both require color adapter. Other programs include file utilities for DOS 1.1 and 2.0.

#85 VisiCalc templates distributed on double-sided disk.

#86 SCREEN text editor has many features and is distributed on double-sided disk. MMOUSE is a batch file to copy Microsoft Mouse software onto disk.

#87 Programmer's calculator (version 1.2).

#88 EPISTAT is a user supported set of statistical analysis programs (written in BASICA) by Tracy Gustafson, M.D., 1705 Gattis School Rd., Round Rock, TX 78664. Requires color graphics and 64K RAM (96K recommended), includes graph program to display data samples on high resolution display, and is suitable for sample size of 28 or less, with less than 1000 observations per sample. Send $25 contribution. Latest version is 3.0.

#89 MAIL (mailmerge program), MINICALC (11 column x 22 row spreadsheet), PC-LIB (disk file library program), other utility programs for blanking color and monochrome displays, spooling and printing, and adding/changing disk volume labels.

#90 Genealogy package, on double-sided disk (updated to version 2.0).

#91 Games include new versions of ADVENTURE and CHESS (both disliked). Utility programs are BASCOM (patches for IBM BASIC compiler) and DKSPAT (DISKCOPY and DISKCOMP patches for large memory (over 320K) systems). GLOBE (rotating globe) requires color adapter.

#92 MUSIC (music scoring system), VCCOM (hints on how to load VisiCalc as a .COM file), NMACNV (file naming suggestions for public domain software), hints on using St. Louis and other BBSs, games and pictures.

#93 ASMGEN (judged a useful tool by users) generates IBM Macro Assembler source code from executable file, DETAB expands tabs in text files, IPCO games and puzzles, VW128FIX modifies Volkswriter to bypass title page, and loan analysis and morse code programs.

#94 Ladybug (latest version 1.2) is an educational user-supported LOGO for kids. The language, documentation and several procedures (for sound and graphics) are included on double-sided disk. Send $35 contribution to David Smith, 44 Ole Musket Lane, Danbury, CT 06810. Requires 128K RAM, color adapter, and one disk drive (two drives are preferred).

#95 Math Tutor is popular with kids.

#96 Introduction to THE SOURCE, disk 1. CHAT and ED instructions, help with electronic mail, public bulletin boards, and MailGrams, list of IBM users. How to make money publishing on THE SOURCE.

#97 Introduction to THE SOURCE, disk 2. Airline guide, travel service, discount electronic shopping service, wine guidance and other services explained. Catalog of PUBLIC functions available to THE SOURCE users. St. Louis BBS instructions and sample session.

#98 SOURCE and CompuServe access numbers (TYMNET, TELENET, UNINET, SOURCENET and COMPUSERVENET as of 11/83).

#99 BBS and SIG access for IBM PC users. CompuServe's IBM SIG (includes list of IBM SIG members), list of public BBSs from THE SOURCE, and St. Louis BBS list of other BBSs.

#100 Jukebox music playing program with tunes included. ALIEN and other adventure games, plus 3D Tic Tac Toe (requires color adapter).

#101 The Portsworth (investment portfolio) package.

#102 dBASE II Ad agency accounting package.

#103 CompuServe services sampler (business, professional, travel and public bulletin board), and three St. Louis public BBS sample sessions (topics include TRS-80 and sex boards).

#104 CompuServe educational and home services sampler and index to services as of 12/83.

#105 PC Professor BASIC tutorial is easy, educational and enjoyed by beginners. AUTOEXEC batch file included for automatic program startups.

#106 DISKAT 4 (revision 2.0) is latest version of DISKCAT (disk cataloguing) system.

#107 FOS home finance management, financial analysis programs, a VisiCalc template for 1982 Federal income tax preparation, music, a program to blank the PC screen unless a key is pressed every three minutes, and notes on how a PC user group was started.

#108 Various APL functions (more on PC-SIG #109 and #110), DOS 2.0 bug descriptions, patch to configure Epson printers, disk format determining program, and BATMENU (menu prompts for batch files).

#109 BBS utilities (more on PC-SIG #110 and #111) to dump hex files to display, set CTRL-ESC as breakpoint to trace program execution, and UTIL (favorite set of screen/file/directory and more utilities). 1-2-3 1040 worksheet, and schedules A, B, C and W, dBASE II program to validate dates, APL functions, program to display 8088 registers in real time.

#110 BBS utilities (more on PC-SIG #109 and #111) include WHEREIS (names all subdirs for specified file), UPPER (converts lower to upper case), SIZER (sets ERRORLEVEL and checks file size), TABLET (interactive graphics editor), DOSCOLOR (set DOS 2.0 colors), PRINTER (printer setup program with menu of choices), HC (fast hex-binary file converter) and SCRN (routines for display windowing, callable from BASIC programs).

#111 BBS utilities (see PC-SIG #109 and #110 for more) include ENTAB and DETAB (convert blanks to tabs, tabs to blanks), FIXTEXT (DOS to WordStar conversion, better than UNWS (PC-SIG #53 and #81)), GETMEM (reserve memory), fixes for DOS SHELL and COMP commands, and other utility programs.

#112 Computer Security Package (latest version is 1.2) encodes and decodes files. Distribution restricted to U.S. (not for export) and shipped on double sided disk.

#113 Datamorphics Screen programs, COMPARE program, and DEFKEY (reassigns function keys, DOS 2.0) are all user supported programs.

#114 Assembly language tutorial, PCT3AN (adds Vidtex, VT52, VT100 and ANSI cursor control to PC-TALK III), BASIC compiler patches, TERM (adds auto dial and log on to IBM Async. Comm. 2.0), Lotus 1-2-3 macro for straight line/exponential curves and more.

#115 SQUEEZE and UNSQUEEZ (file compression/uncompress programs), FREE.DOC (catalog of User Supported software), 1-2-3 numeric keypad, and routine to print wave forms on graphics printer (8087 required) are included on this utility disk, along with 4 pinup pictures for your printer.

#116-117 microGOURMET (2 disks) is written in dBASE II, comes in both floppy and hard disk versions. See READ.ME for description of programs. #117 includes manual and UNWS (converts WordStar files to DOS) program.

#118 QSYS DOS menu and security package, version 2.0.

#119 ABC Database (updated to version 1.1). Includes utility to transport dBASE II files to ABC, and distribution is on double sided disk.

#120 PC-CHESS can be played by 2 players, or 1 player vs. computer.

#121-123 Letus A-B-C (3 disks). Requires PC-FILE. Distributed on double sided disk. #121 and #122 refer to 1982 issues of *Softalk, PC, PC Age,* and *BYTE.* #123 refers to 1983 issues of *PC World, PC* (Jul-Dec), *PC Tech Journal* and *BYTE*

#124 Extended Batch Language, by Seaware (version 2.0; see PC-SIG #139 for version 2.00d).

#125 HOST-III Public Bulletin Board package, receives and initiates telephone calls. Distributed on double-sided disk.

#126 dBASE II mailing label manager, form letter generator, state and zipcode checker and backup routines.

#127 PC-MUSICIAN (latest version is 1.1), includes song files.

#128 dBASE II programs, program to generate dBASE II screens, games (BASIC), 3-D graphics demo (requires color), GEMINI (do graphics dump to Gemini printer, DOS 2.0), and KBDOFIX (159 character keyboard buffer).

#129 PC-DIAL modem communications package. See PC-SIG #77 for earlier version (1RD) and author information. This package is user supported.

#130-132 Pascal tools (3 disks). Distributed on double-sided disks. See README1 for user notes.

#133 Ultra-Utilities (U-FILE, U-FORMAT and U-ZAP) distrib-

uted on double-sided disk. Version 4.0 is latest.

#134 XLISP (LISP interpreter), and turtles written in XLISP, MENUMAKR (creates menus callable from BASIC programs), C program checker (finds mismatched parentheses), DOS I/O redirection bugs explained, 8087 assembler macros, and more.

#135 Where to find an APL character generator chip for IBM APL, program to fix BASIC compiler bugs, procedures for DOS file access from Pascal, comm. I/O driver for Lattice C, tips on using PC-DOS, 1-2-3 desktop worksheet with several built-in functions, LAR (see PC-SIG #142 for more) program to combine files into libraries (save disk space), and more.

#136 PCPG (PC Picture Graphics) by E. Ying is a graphics drawing package (requires graphics board) includes 10 demos.

#137 EDIT (31K compiled program) is a C screen editor.

#138 Bly programs (color card support for 100 line virtual screen in DOS, breakout game, printer setup program, DOS type command replacement, program entry utility program), DOS 2.0 version of Lattice C routines, patch to Norton utilities 2.0 (adds TEAC 42 track drive support), and more BBS utilities.

#139 BAT200D (see PC-SIG #124 for earlier version) and applications for use, more DOS 2.0 Lattice C functions, DIR201 (an easy to use disk catalog program), fast un-squeeze program (NUSQ), color graphics (160x100 16-color secret PC graphics mode revealed) routines and demos, dBASE II utility, and BBS utilities.

#140 LU (library maintenance and more), EJLUTIL (use LU to open and retrieve this library of useful routines), file squeeze and un-squeeze programs, multi-file copy/delete from full-screen menu programs, 8087 macros, 1-2-3 worksheet for flow charting, and BBS utilities.

#141 123PREP (converts text files to 1-2-3 loadable form), W20 (WASH program for multiple file list/copy/delete/view activity), and more BBS utilities.

#142 Utility macros and subroutines for IBM assembler, Xenix-like routines for DOS 2.0 functions in C, transcendental functions in C, LISP interpreter in Pascal, and LDIR (lists TofC of library files made by LAR and LU), plus more BBS utilities.

#143 dBASE II program to copy fields from one file to another, home projects data base manager, file compare utility (useful for binary files of different length), and more BBS utilities.

#144 FABULA (disk 1 of 2) batch files for various directory sort programs, TALK450 adds 450 baud rate (Hayes Smartmodem 300 is capable of 450 baud transfers) to PC-TALK III, SQIBM and USQIBM (squeeze and un-squeeze files), and SCROLLK and SCRNSAVE.

#145 FABULA (disk 2 of 2) disk file utilities and more, including MAKEDATA (checksummed data files for .COM and .EXE files) and more.

#146 EasyRite/LabelFile from GINACO word processing and label/file programs. User supported by GINACO, 10708 Santa Fe Drive, Sun City AZ 85351.

#147 SDB is a Simple Data base System (written in C).

#148 XLISP (written in C) with sample files (some not yet converted to PC).

#149 C Utilities include LUMP and UNLUMP (lump files together and split them apart), C program checker and cross reference utilities and Unix-like GREP command to find strings in files.

#150 IBM BBS by Gene Plantz, distributed on double-sided disk.

#151 Finance Manager (FM) version 2.0 from Genesis Software, distributed on double-sided disk.

#152 Capital PC User Group RBBS to set up on your IBM PC.

#153 Norland Software Hangman (version 4.1) has large vocabulary of words, music, quotations and riddles, and includes AUTOEXEC program for automatic Hangman startup.

#154 Snoopy and Schroeder (Charles Schultz characters), Pink Panther, Darth Vader, Starship Enterprise, Challenger space shuttle, McDonnell-Douglas F-4E Phantom II, clown, Santa Claus (with reindeer), and nine nude females are collected in this volume of printer art.

#155 Budget program, task planning program, and lease/buy auto loan analysis programs.

#156 IBM Users Group Newsletter #1 (published by IBM Boca Raton).

#157 IBM Users Group Newsletter #2 (published by IBM Boca Raton).

#158 IBM Users Group Newsletter #3 (published by IBM Boca Raton).

#159 PC Firing Line/PC Underground disk magazine #1. Book and software reviews, news, and programs.

#160 PC Firing Line/PC Underground disk magazine #2 (part 1). Book and software reviews, news, and programs.

#161 PC Firing Line/PC Underground disk magazine #2 (part 2). Book and software reviews, news, and programs.

#162 RASCAL (IBM (MS) BASIC preprocessor) and programming utilities.

#163 Dscreen (dBASE II screen generator) and text filtering/processing utilities.

#164 TeleWare Personal Finance manager (version 2.3) checking, savings, investment, tax and budget package.

#165 Personal General Ledger program, requires Lotus 1-2-3. Distributed on double-sided disk.

#166 IBM macro assembler five part tutorial and utilities.

#167 BASIC and BASICA programming aids.

#168 Music, spelling bee, and other educational programs (some require color adapter) and classroom attendance system.

#169 EASYMAIL, MAILLIST1 and MAILLIST (mailing label programs), and MEMBERS (membership system based on EASYMAIL).

#170 FreeCalc (spreadsheet program version 1.0), PC-PAD (text oriented spreadsheet program version 1.3) and MINICALC (small spreadsheet) program. Distributed on double-sided disk, require DOS 2.0 or greater.

#171 POS inventory package and miscellaneous financial programs to compute investment values and loans (BUSIN lets you select from 20 item menu).

#172 Steve's Disk (double-sided) contains many Pascal routines, file and disk utilities and more.

#173 PCMAN (monochrome PacMan game) and ESP (Extra Sensory Perception tests).

#174 Nothing but 12 games (Frogger and Star Wars require color adapter), distributed on double-sided disk.

#175 Simulation and board games, music class management package, and MEDLEY (name that tune, requires DOS 2.0).

#176 Space Invaders and graphics demos by various artists.

#177 Arcade games (some require color) and PENCIL (use joystick to draw on color monitor) program.

#178 Star Trek, Chess and more games require color monitor.

#179 Pizza recipe program and MA (Micro Accounting check register system).

#180 Math (26) and Statistics (18) routines with menu selection programs, and TRADENET and DATANET samplers.

#181 Keyboard utility programs.

#182 AutoFile (small indexed file system), EasyFile (simple file manager), and time and date utilities.

#183 DOS patches and utilities, diagnostics, etc.

#184 Disk utilities include how to unprotect Lotus 1-2-3 and 1-2-3 (1A), BASIC compiler, EasyWriter, Flight Simulator, Memory Shift, PFS File, VisiCalc, Word and Zork.

#185 Sorted directory programs and more disk utility programs.

#186 CRT and Epson printer (format, spooler, etc.) utilities.

#187 Data communications utilities.

#188 MINITEL file transfer communications system (version 1.0) for the IBM PC.

#189 TECH PRINT (version 2.01) improved printing for WordStar with Epson FX printer.

#190 Text editors (for full screen data entry, writing quick memos, PC-FILE form generator, RV-EDIT (full screen editor ver. 1.2) by Bob Vollmer, and more) and utility programs.

#191 DVED screen editor, Easel (drawing system, requires color graphics and light pen), and Easygraf (drawing package, requires color graphics), and more drawing programs, distributed on double-sided disk.

#192 Cnter for Disease Control health risk appraisal program, IBM PC version on double-sided disk.

#193 FREEWILL contains text and forms for do-it-yourself will preparation.

#194 ROFF (modified from PC-SIG #50), FOGFIND (checks clarity of text files), and C and Pascal routines.

#195 GRAPH2 (plot line and figure x-y plots), SKETCH (joystick drawing program) and more. Distributed on double-sided disk.

#196 Prepare and show slides on graphics display, and file utility programs include DIRCOMP (compares two directories, lists duplicated files) and more.

#197 Graphic or monochrome display version of super Star Trek game, and IBMMINI (supports several file transfer protocols) communications package.

#198 CASTLE (text, pictures, animation combined in Adventure game), best RAM disk program (many config. parameters supported), and L4 (full-screen list program with 4-way scroll and search).

INDEX